The empathy and tenderness that Tremblay has for his characters are evident on every page. —*Le Devoir*

Few men write about women with his empathetic immediacy and emotional acuity. The way they talk to each other, the various masks and voices they adopt according to the needs of the moment, their deep reserves of humour and compassion – the Desrosiers sisters, and indeed the young Nana, are so alive on the page that you all but hear them speaking. —*Montreal Gazette*

One of the most poignant novel cycles in contemporary Québec literature, shedding new light on a gallery of characters increasingly inseparable from our collective imagination. —Voir.ca

Tremblay ... sets the groundwork for understanding that the world and the people in it are Janus-like. Good and bad, French and English, country and city, moral and immoral, brave and scared, everything is all rolled up into this thing called life. —*Globe and Mail*

It would be unforgivable not to highlight the mastery with which the author depicts the social context of the time and, in particular, the injustice experienced daily by the working class and, more generally, by women. It is undoubtedly one of Tremblay's great strengths to be able to re-enact whole societies and families, portrayals in which the personal and the intimate forcefully unite with great social movements. —fugues.com

FOR MORE ABOUT THE
DESROSIERS DIASPORA SERIES
PLEASE SEE PAGE 319

ALSO BY MICHEL TREMBLAY

All published by Talonbooks

THE DESROSIERS DIASPORA
BOOK VI

TWISTS OF FATE

If by Chance & Destination Paradise

MICHEL TREMBLAY

Translated by Linda Gaboriau

 TALONBOOKS

Talonbooks
9259 Shaughnessy Street, Vancouver, British Columbia, Canada V6P 6R4
talonbooks.com

Talonbooks is located on xʷməθkʷəy̓əm, Sḵwx̱wú7mesh, Stó:lō, and səl̓ilwətaʔł Lands.

First printing: 2022

Typeset in Caslon
Printed and bound in Canada on 100% post-consumer recycled paper

Cover design by andrea bennett and Typesmith. Interior design by Typesmith
Cover illustration by Brad Collins
Inside cover image via Flickr / Rawpixel: *Wild Tulip* by William Morris (CC BY 4.0)

Talonbooks acknowledges the financial support of the Canada Council for the Arts, the Government of Canada through the Canada Book Fund, and the Province of British Columbia through the British Columbia Arts Council and the Book Publishing Tax Credit.

This work was originally published in French in two parts, *If by Chance* as *Au hasard la chance* in 2012 and *Destination Paradise* as *Les clefs du Paradise* in 2013, by Leméac Éditeur, Montréal, Québec, and Actes Sud, Arles, France. We acknowledge the financial support of the Government of Canada through the National Translation Program for Book Publishing, an initiative of the *Roadmap for Canada's Official Languages 2013–2018: Education, Immigration, Communities*, for our translation activities.

LIBRARY AND ARCHIVES CANADA CATALOGUING IN PUBLICATION

Title: Twists of fate : If by chance, & Destination paradise / Michel Tremblay ; translated by Linda Gaboriau.
Other titles: Novels. Selections. English | If by chance | Destination paradise
Names: Tremblay, Michel, 1942- author. | Gaboriau, Linda, translator. | Container of (expression): Tremblay, Michel, 1942- Au hasard la chance. English. | Container of (expression): Tremblay, Michel, 1942- Clefs du Paradise. English.
Description: Series statement: The Desrosiers diaspora ; book VI | Translation of two titles: Au hasard la chance, and Les clefs du Paradise.
Identifiers: Canadiana 20210360526 | ISBN 9781772013580 (softcover)
Subjects: LCGFT: Novels.
Classification: LCC PS8539.R47 A2 2022 | DDC C843/.54—dc23

THE ART OF THE CHRONICLE

IF BY CHANCE

DESTINATION PARADISE

ABOUT THE DESROSIERS DIASPORA SERIES

THE ART OF THE CHRONICLE

When *The Fat Woman Next Door Is Pregnant* was published in 1978, Michel Tremblay was unaware that he was embarking on the immense project that would become the Chronicles of the Plateau-Mont-Royal. The cycle – which would later amount to six volumes published over the next two decades and become a staple of francophone literature – was immediately adopted by thousands of readers. Anthologized in 2000 in Éditions Leméac's prestigious Thesaurus series (and individually published in English by Talonbooks in the 1980s and 1990s), the six volumes of Tremblay's Chronicles (*The Fat Woman Next Door Is Pregnant, Thérèse and Pierrette and the Little Hanging Angel, The Duchess and the Commoner, News from Édouard, The First Quarter of the Moon,* and *A Thing of Beauty*) have continued to gain new aficionados in both French and English.

Himself an avid reader of chronicles and literary sagas of all kinds – Balzac's La Comédie humaine, Zola's Les Rougon-Macquart, Proust's *In Search of Lost Time*, Sartre's The Roads to Freedom, Asimov's Foundation series, Herbert's Dune novels, Simmons's Hyperion Cantos, and, more recently, Follett's Century Trilogy – Michel Tremblay had already staged several hundred characters, both real and fictional, in his theatrical works when he began the writing of the Chronicles of the Plateau-Mont-Royal. Many of these characters at one point left the theatrical stage and moved into novel territory, a passage that allows readers to trace their evolution. And so the Chronicles, set between 1942 and 1963 and taking up more than a thousand pages, are the sum of several entwined stories forming a coherent narrative whole. Contemporary writers capable of creating a family tree of characters of such magnitude are rare. In fifty years of writing, Tremblay has given life to more than three thousand characters; they circulate in an oeuvre that celebrates their deeds, their youth and old age, their joys and sorrows, their freedom and *mal de vivre* – that indefinable virus always so impermeable to happiness.

Twenty years after the publication of the last book of the Chronicles, the nine volumes of the second of Michel Tremblay's great sagas, The Desrosiers Diaspora, have also been anthologized in a fourteen-hundred-page Thesaurus edition by Leméac, and are in the process of being translated into English by Talonbooks (*Crossing the Continent*, 2011; *Crossing the City*, 2014; *A Crossing of Hearts*, 2017; *Rite of Passage*, 2019; *The Grand Melee*, 2021; *Twists of Fate*, 2022; *A Great Consolation* forthcoming 2023). The Diaspora follows the lives of hundreds of Felliniesque new characters – pragmatists, dreamers, poor souls, frolickers, inconsolable or unrepentant, but always bolstered by the natural resilience of ordinary people – who mingle with the old ones by getting off trains, checking into hotels, walking up and down avenues, visiting shops, entering train stations, boarding trams, exiting kitchens, setting foot in clubs. They end up piecing together the great puzzle of a clan scattered across North America, from Sainte-Maria-de-Saskatchewan to Providence, Rhode Island, to Regina, Winnipeg, Ottawa, Montréal, and Duhamel, in the Laurentians. The Desrosiers move a lot, eager to believe that happiness is (always) elsewhere – but they all have a lump in their throats and a weight on their hearts.

Rhéauna, nicknamed Nana – the "fat woman next door" who will give birth to Jean-Marc, the author's alter ego – is undeniably the central figure of Michel Tremblay's fictional universe. But the story of the artist's origins, his childhood and love stories, the household of his youth and the women who helped him grow through the joys and sorrows of his destiny – his great-grandmother, Joséphine, and his grandmother, Maria, his great-aunts Tititte and Teena, his heroic cousin Ti-Lou, a.k.a. the She-Wolf of Ottawa – all remained to be written. Starting with *Crossing the Continent*, the first volume of the Desrosiers Diaspora, Tremblay has listened to the gentle stream of maternal memories and begun to narrate, sometimes by way of invention, the incredible adventures of the Desrosiers family. He has started to unearth the treasures of his own family's maternal side. This grand story, unfolding from one novel to the next, takes on fantastical accents, to re-enact the real and the marvellous, the comic and the tragic, the faded romances and the impossible ones, to weave the personal and collective memories.

The art of the chronicle consists of staging real or fictional characters, all the while evoking authentic social and historical facts, and respecting the chronology of their unfolding. However the art of the chronicler is to blend the true and the false, the intimate and the social, the near and the far, the grand design and the modest story, all with their different lineages and their chance occurrences, so as to snatch a little more meaning from flowing, tranquil, impetuous life.

The art of the chronicle, of course – but the art of the chronicler, especially.

—PIERRE FILION, June 2017
translated by Charles Simard

These are works of fiction. The names of some characters are real, but everything else is made up.

—M.T.

IF BY CHANCE

For Jacqueline Rousseau and Pierre Perrault, who were there when I finished writing this novel

Promises never made,
promises never broken.

—JAPANESE PROVERB

We can't tear a single page out of our lives,
but we can burn the entire book.

—GEORGE SAND
Mauprat (1837)

Ti-Lou Decides to Retire

OTTAWA, 1925

The news of Dr. McKenny's death came as a shock to Ti-Lou. Who would take care of her now, who would worry about the state of her diabetes, scold her when she confessed to another binge on Cherry Delights provided, sadistically or not, by her clients who knew her weakness and wanted to please her? Who would beg her to follow a diet, her only alternative if she wanted to live a long and still-prosperous life? Threaten her with the prospect of diabetic comas, dangerous surges of blood sugar, and brandish the spectre of amputation, the only thing that terrified her enough to make her promise anything, no more desserts, salads for lunch, long walks along the Rideau Canal, even in the winter? And prescribe her medicine? Who would carefully examine the state of her toes every month, saying: "No cause for alarm yet, but they're still too swollen. If they begin to turn blue, come see me immediately…" or recommend once again those sugar-free candies she'd tried once just to please him and that tasted, in her words, like soft tar? "My cat won't get near them and he's the one who tests my food! He's too fat, too, maybe he has diabetes like me, who knows, but he's my dear companion and we're not about to change. Keep your tar sweets for diabetics who aren't as fussy as me. And for their cats."

The old man had sighed.

"You've never had a cat, Madame Ti-Lou."

"That doesn't matter. If I'd had one, he would've hated them."

With Dr. McKenny gone, she found herself on her own with her boxes of chocolate-covered cherries and the irresistible desire to nap in the middle of the afternoon when she'd eaten too many. With no hope of easing her conscience by making her elderly doctor laugh with her risqué stories about some of her clients, more specifically his political enemies whom he enjoyed seeing undressed and mocked with wit and relevance. And cruelty. She'd tell him: "You have to practise professional secrecy, but not me! Listen to this …" And the following half-hour was filled with tales featuring all sorts of louts who behaved like pigs with her and she loved denouncing them to Dr. McKenny, knowing he would be discreet. This always amused him and brought her some relief. He was so entertained he'd forget to nag her and she'd lay it on thick so he'd forget his threats. Threats she actually needed. An ironic situation that gave her the illusion of buying time. "I made it through today, I'll make it through tomorrow." Twenty-four hours stolen from destiny.

Occasionally, at a reception, they would find themselves in the presence of one of Ti-Lou's clients and they would have to practise great self-control not to burst out laughing in his face. That Montréal prelate, for example, met at a charity ball for Ottawa's Girl Guides and Boy Scouts, who always sweated profusely in the pulpit during his famous retreats for which he was paid handsome fees, fuming and chastising sinners in the name of the holy sacraments – his eyes bulging like billiard balls and literally foaming at the mouth when he spoke of young men's lust – while they were both aware of his ridiculous sexual deviations and his silly preferences bordering on pathetic while he considered himself a great Don Juan. Ti-Lou would report: "The minute he takes off his scarlet robes, believe me, there's nothing sexy about him! He just wants me to tell him how well-endowed he is, when he isn't, and what a great lover he is, when he's like an awkward teenager who's never seen a naked woman. I hope his pope in Rome isn't such a fool." After a little bow to the cardinal, she'd turn back to the doctor: "He expects me to kiss his ring in public, but that's not what he wants me to fuss over when we're alone in my *sweet* at the Château Laurier!" When they couldn't prevent themselves from laughing, they'd take refuge behind a potted fern or dive into the buffet.

In recent months Ti-Lou had noticed the dark circles under the elderly doctor's eyes. And the slight tremor of his hands, too. He'd claimed he was overworked, but she hadn't believed him. When her questions became too insistent, he'd answer that they were there to discuss her diabetes and not to chat about his little problems. At what turned out to be her last appointment in his office, she saw he was all skin and bones. And when she asked after his health, he'd ignored the question and promptly resumed his chiding and warning: she had gained weight again, her blood sugar had shot up and her blood pressure was too high, he could see that she was short of breath, she shouldn't wait until it was too late to act. She'd replied that he'd been repeating the same thing for years and he'd reminded her that was his duty and said he regretted not having been stricter with her in the past.

"You've been wrapping me around your little finger for twenty-five years, Madame Ti-Lou, you make me laugh, you avoid the issue when I attempt to be serious, you enter my office flitting about like a drunken butterfly and you waltz out the door, but in the meantime, your health is failing and you're doing nothing about it. You might not be alarmed, but I am."

She had removed the hatpin and placed the enormous bonnet on his desk, hiding her medical file beneath a lacey flight of silk swallows.

"You know very well that I come to see you more for the monthly examination required by my profession than to talk about my diabetes, doctor ... and for the pleasure of chatting with you. I bet you don't chat with many of your patients."

"No, that's true. But that's not why you're here."

"I'm here for that as well. You enjoy our chats and so do I. After we've had a good laugh, you stick your head between my legs, not for the same reasons as other men, then I go home ..."

He didn't laugh that time. Didn't even smile. He simply lowered his head.

That was when she realized that he was truly sick. No witty reply, no mention of the dangers ahead for her, blindness, gangrene – the ugliest, most terrifying words she knew. If he was no longer attempting to frighten her, it meant that he had abdicated. And if he had abdicated…

And when she lifted her skirts and lowered her bloomers – she still wore bloomers – so he could position his head between her thighs, he hadn't quipped, "And now, my lovely lady, let's examine your livelihood." It was the first time. She almost cried.

She heard of his death by accident. And that was what precipitated her departure from Ottawa.

After a long walk around the neighbourhood one April afternoon, she was walking by Madame Carlyle's shop in the lobby of the Château Laurier, when she remembered that she had run out of toothpaste. The brand of dubious quality that Madame Carlyle sold in a tiny format tasted awful and burned the tongue, but Ti-Lou was expecting a client at the cocktail hour and didn't have time to run to the closest pharmacy to purchase the brand she preferred: Ipana. A woman in her position had to silently endure the atrocious breath of some of her clients while always smelling of cool mint or cinnamon herself, but that was part of the job description.

Madame Carlyle made her usual face when she saw Ti-Lou enter her den overflowing with curios as useless as they were overpriced: Union Jacks, dolls dressed in Mountie uniforms, good luck charms made from the so-called skin of seals or baby bears, candies, chocolates (ah! Cherry Delights!), and paper flowers for men who were too cheap – and they were numerous – to buy fresh bouquets. The two women had never tried to conceal their antipathy for each other and didn't even attempt to be polite, limiting their exchanges to dry, short sentences. Ti-Lou was convinced that Mrs. Carlyle was jealous of her extravagant lifestyle, and the owner of the shop, after all these years, remained shocked that a fallen woman could live in a luxury suite, surrounded and admired by the (masculine) elite of the nation's capital (proof of her unadulterated jealousy).

Jeannine Carlyle, née Théberge, was a Québécoise from Hull who had married an anglophone with a promising future, hoping to escape the poverty and overcrowded living quarters of her family. She soon regretted her decision. The promising future never came to pass, her husband died young of cirrhosis of the liver without leaving her a penny, and she slaved for years to save the nest egg needed to purchase the rights to the tiny shop in Ottawa's fanciest hotel. Her customers, aside from travellers passing through, were largely made up of the most influential citizens in the national capital, imposing, powerful men who haunted the floor the government of Canada reserved at the Château Laurier for international meetings and gatherings. Ministers whose photos appeared constantly on the front page of newspapers often came into the shop and she treated them with near indecent obsequiousness, without reserving the same welcome for their staff whom she referred to as "small fry," wrinkling her nose. She had become one of the most snobbish women in Ottawa, imagining she was part of this elite although her contact with them was limited to the sale of paper flowers, souvenirs, and candies. And condoms, which she called "prophylactics" because it sounded classier. When someone asked for condoms, she made a point of pronouncing the only four-syllable word she knew as she passed the small package under the counter since only pharmacies were authorized to sell them. When her customer was a priest pretending that it was "for a young man in danger" or some such nonsense, she felt like scratching his eyes out.

She knew what carryings-on took place on the "international" floor of the Château Laurier, the privileges reserved for important foreign visitors: the many bottles of champagne and the gargantuan meals, the Cuban cigars the size of chair spindles, the "legitimate" women allowed only until eleven in the evening.

And Ti-Lou. The She-Wolf of Ottawa. The devourer of men. The one they all requested, even those who arrived from distant shores, because her reputation reached far and wide. The woman who needed only to loll on silk and velvet and spread her legs to be showered with gold and compliments. While eating those damn Cherry Delights Jeannine Carlyle herself supplied to her clients from the case she kept behind the counter because they were so in demand.

Madame Carlisle not only hated everything Ti-Lou represented but also what her disgraceful occupation brought her. Money, always cash never declared, and notoriety – even abroad! The French bought Cherry Delights for Petit-Loup, the Asians for T'lou, the Anglo-Saxons for Tee-Lou.

She was delighted to see that the She-Wolf had been gaining weight in recent years and could hardly wait for the day when the hussy, clearly overweight, would be rejected by the very same men who had desired her. Maybe she would be banned from the Château Laurier as undesirable, who knows. Every box of Cherry Delights she sold was like a consolation, a balm on the open wound she'd been enduring for so long, a cure for her unhealthy jealousy towards the woman she never could have been, because, one by one, those chocolate-covered cherries would undoubtedly lead to Ti-Lou's downfall.

After slipping the tiny tube of toothpaste into a little brown bag and taking the change Ti-Lou had handed her, Madame Carlyle – for once – seemed inclined to chat.

"You must have been disappointed to hear the news about Dr. McKenny."

Ti-Lou immediately knew what to expect – she'd sensed it, she'd seen it coming for a while – and she had to brace herself on the counter to avoid collapsing on the floor.

"Did something happen to Dr. McKenny?"

Madame Carlyle dropped the coins into the cash register and closed the drawer sharply.

"It was Madame Chagnon, the head of the chambermaids, who

told me the news. She had an appointment with him the day before yesterday, and when she arrived at his office, there was a notice on his door –"

"Dr. McKenny died!"

"A while ago, apparently. At least a few weeks ago. Haven't you needed to see him recently?"

Usually Ti-Lou would have picked up on that allusion and responded with one of her inimitable retorts that left her interlocutors speechless; this time, however, she was stunned by Madame Carlisle's arrogance and to her dismay, she felt her eyes fill with tears. She couldn't let Madame Carlisle see her cry. She grabbed the little brown bag, turned on her heels, and left the shop without saying goodbye, holding her head high, but clearly distressed.

When she entered her suite, she dropped the keys on the sideboard where for several months, the previous year, she'd placed a bouquet of red camelias on the days when she was unable to entertain. Since virtually no one among her ignorant clientele had read *La dame aux camélias*, the message was not understood. She resumed the habit of allowing the elderly elevator operator to inform her gentlemen visitors that Madame Ti-Lou would be indisposed for several days.

She closed the heavy draperies at the window overlooking Rideau Street.

She stood there, her arms crossed, for a good half-hour. During that moment of reflection, it became apparent that her life would never be the same. At first she didn't understand why Dr. McKenny's death changed everything. She was very sad, of course. She would miss him, his sense of humour, his gentle grey eyes, the scent of expensive soap that followed him around – specially imported from his native Scotland, he claimed – the tactful, non-judgmental way he referred to her profession as if he not only accepted it, but even understood it. But surely a doctor can be replaced, there must be others in Ottawa as tactful and understanding ... And it was thinking of the doctor's kindness, his empathy devoid of all moral judgment, that triggered a moment of frightening lucidity: she suddenly realized that Dr. McKenny was the only person she met – and then only once a month and for reasons that had nothing to do with friendship – outside the Château Laurier. She had no friends. She'd never wanted any, that's true, she had rejected the few relationships that might have become close for fear of hurting or getting hurt herself. She always went out alone, to go to the theatre or the movies, to do her errands, in a town where unaccompanied women were regarded with pity – for the old maids or widows – or with contempt – for women who liked to act independently. And now here she was, alone at an age where any self-respecting floozie would have retired ages ago, still beautiful and desirable, but for how much longer? How long before they start turning their backs on her? Before the telephone announcing that there's a gentleman in the elevator stops ringing? Before the boxes of Cherry Delights become rarer and rarer?

She's aware of the state of her hands, the age spots, the prominent blue veins, she's taken to adopting uncomfortable poses in bed designed to conceal her plumpness, although she's far from sure that they work – lying on her back, holding her stomach in, her arms stretched out – she's noticed the distressing appearance of wrinkles on her neck which she hides with chiffon scarves or knotted hankies, like a gypsy in the movies, the beginning of a double chin, the curse of her father's family, and the tiny soft jowls on either side of her mouth that tremble when she moves her head. The lighting in her bedroom is soft pink now, a sad concession for a woman who always prided herself on greeting her visitors in broad daylight so they could appreciate in advance what they had paid such a high price for.

The She-Wolf isn't what she used to be.

Alone and aging. A walking cliché.

And with no one left in her life to reprimand her when she gets carried away.

Time to leave all that. The city where she had reigned for decades, the rich but despicable clientele – unscrupulous, unfaithful men, ambitious scoundrels, dark unconscionable souls who nevertheless had the power to determine the destiny of a country – this life she had chosen out of spite, a life that had made her rich – a fortune in cash kept in safety deposit boxes all around Ottawa – but, as she'd known in advance, far from happy.

Time to sell her few belongings, her phaeton, and her horses. Start from scratch at over fifty. Leave everything to chance. But where? Dive into the unknown, with her suitcases full of money her only companions. And do what? Travel, keep moving in the hope that old age, the kind of ugly old age that devastates before it kills, will never catch up with her? Or let herself go to pot, right here, in her bed in the Château Laurier, committing gradual suicide with an overdose of champagne and Cherry Delights? The way Tante Bebette's husband killed himself eating his wife's fatty cooking?

She stares across Rideau Street. The train station. Endless possibilities. Departures for everywhere and nowhere. A hotel on rails that would allow her to visit everything, see everything, test everything ... live in a hotel suite constantly on the move. Travel away, without looking back. Contemplate from the window the ever-changing landscape and life unfolding. Toronto. Vancouver. Seattle. San Francisco. Los Angeles. Return to the East. New York with its theatres, puritanical Boston with its rednecks.

No. Too tiring.

Then she thinks of Montréal, of her brief visit there three years ago on the occasion of Rhéauna's wedding. The peace and quiet of the apartments on boulevard Saint-Joseph, dark enough to conceal her own decay, Maria with whom she could try to reconnect. One person, at least one person, who will agree to become ... what ... a friend?

After an understanding doctor, an indulgent cousin?

She lets out the gale of laughter that has made so many men tremble, a thunderbolt that cascades and ends in a kind of primitive snort, a burst of something she can't really call joy that comes from deep inside and becomes a painful gasp.

A friend. As if such a thing were possible.

She braces herself on the window.

Smash the glass with her fist. Fly across the street. Land in a first-class car that smells of new leather and polished wood … right now. And surrender to chance.

She laughs again, her forehead pressed against the windowpane.

Expect nothing, risk everything.

She is weightless.

Several days later, the She-Wolf of Ottawa crossed Rideau Street on foot for the first time in years.

MONTRÉAL, 1925

No one in Ottawa knew that Ti-Lou was leaving. One morning she was seen crossing the big lobby in the Château Laurier a bit earlier than usual. She didn't seem to be in a hurry, and she'd told the elevator operator she was going for a walk, that she needed time to think and she wouldn't be back until late afternoon. He suspected an intimate appointment – those outside the hotel were rare and Madame Ti-Lou had explained one day that they paid well since the customers had to cover her travel as well as the rest. She was only carrying a small overnight case, not surprising for a woman of her trade, so no one thought twice about it.

She bought two huge leather bags in a shop on Elgin Street, made the tour of the banks where she'd rented safety deposit boxes for years, filled the bags with money, took a taxi back to the entrance of the Château Laurier. After making sure that no one was watching – it was too early for the usual stream of senators and travellers and the doorman, for some inexplicable reason, was not at his post – she picked up her bags and walked across Rideau Street, making her way to the train station on the other side of the street. The day before she would have refused to cross the street on foot, she would have ordered her phaeton and demanded that they circle the station to let her off at the entrance. Just for the show of it. Today that all seemed childish to her and she was smiling as she pushed open the ornate bronze door.

The train was waiting, her seat in first class was a window seat, as she'd requested. She took her seat solemnly and, just as the train moved forward, she gobbled what she swore would be her last Cherry Delight, for a while at least. Without a single glance back at the Château Laurier or the Rideau Canal, or at Ottawa streaming by on both sides.

She'd promised herself that, upon arrival in Montréal, she'd rush out of Windsor Station, grab a taxi, and immediately take refuge in her new apartment on boulevard Saint-Joseph that she'd already baptized her lair. She would lie low for at least a week, without speaking to anyone, savouring the peace and quiet, in a true retreat the likes of which she hadn't known since convent school. Silence by choice. Alone she was, alone she would stay. Only leaving the house for what she needed to survive: meat, fish, vegetables, fruit, no sweets, especially no sweets. But lots of tea. She would begin her new life by eliminating the toxins that she'd been accumulating for so long. A purification cure before confronting the unknown. Then ... then time would tell what paths in life would beckon to her. She knew she couldn't take a solitary existence for very long, she had no intention of becoming a mean old lady who terrorizes everyone, and she believed she'd make new friends because in this city, undoubtedly more open-minded, less uptight than Ottawa, no one knew her, and her less-than-flattering reputation would not precede her. She'd let herself be guided by chance. By simple, everyday choices. To go out or not to go out. To get dressed or spend the day in her housecoat. To read romance novels or Tolstoy, or listen to Beniamino Gigli's records, her ear glued to the speaker of the gramophone, accompanying the maudlin tenor sobbing as Pagliaccio or in Turridu's farewell to his mother. A free woman. No telephone. The telephone could come later, if she felt the need. Long, excessively hot baths followed by lavish scented creams and moisturizing oils. For whom? For herself. Herself alone. She would smell good and her skin would be soft for her own personal satisfaction.

When the train came to a stop in Windsor Station in Montréal, she was already standing at the door, wearing her hat and gloves.

Her two suitcases full of dollars, French francs, lira, sterling pounds, pesetas, but no roubles, as roubles became worthless after the Russian Revolution, were placed at her feet, like two enormous, plump cats. Nothing else, because she intended to start afresh, just a few toiletries thrown into her overnight bag, along with clean underwear and her nightgown. Tomorrow morning, she would buy herself a completely new wardrobe. All the clothing she owned had remained in the closets and dresser drawers at the Château Laurier. Except for her jewellery, of course. She had a lot of jewellery, it was her insurance policy against poverty if she ever ran out of money, and the jewels were hidden along with paper money and coins, under the false bottom in one of her suitcases.

As she walked down the metal steps and was about to set foot on the station platform, she had a thought that made her smile. When people at the Château Laurier realized she had disappeared, would they launch a search for her, would they call the police, even worry about her? She hoped not. She hoped the disappearance of a floozie, no matter how popular she'd been, would make no waves and that only her clients would feel a little twinge of regret. And maybe not, even. Another woman would replace her. In her still warm bed. In the suite haunted by her presence and the wafts of her gardenia perfume.

The minute she set foot on the platform, a young porter appeared.

"You got any baggage, Madame?"

She pointed to her two small suitcases and her overnight bag.

"Just these, but you can help me anyway."

"Do you want a taxi?"

"Yes."

"Are you going far?"

"I'll tell the driver."

She followed him into the concourse and suddenly found herself in the middle of a noisy, excited crowd bustling around a bronze angel holding a dead soldier in his arms. Undoubtedly a memorial to the victims of the war of 1914.

She glanced at her watch. Almost tea time. She hadn't eaten since morning.

"Is there a restaurant here?"

The young man pointed towards the exit.

"One just opened right next to the exit. It's expensive but they say it's good. You want to go there?"

"Yes, I'm hungry."

"Okay, but promise you'll hire me to take you to the taxis."

"Fine. Stay close by, I'll wave to you."

He sat down on his wagon, between the two suitcases full of money – if he only knew what was inside – and he lit a cigarette. Before entering the restaurant, Ti-Lou turned to him.

"You won't go running off with my only belongings, will you?"

He tipped his cap, as if to greet her.

"Two little suitcases ... doesn't look like your stuff's very interesting ... If you had six or seven suitcases, like some people, maybe ..."

He flashed her a big smile so she'd understand he was joking.

"Well, just stay where I can see you."

"Sit yourself down by the window, Madame. I'll take my fifteen-minute break while you eat."

"Fifteen minutes! You expect me to eat fast."

"Sorry. I gobble down my food and I figure everyone else does, too."

The restaurant was trying to look Parisian, with wicker tables and chairs, decorated in the latest style, with varnished wood panels and stained glass in pastel shades of blue, pale green, pinks, and yellow depicting parrots, strutting peacocks, and tousled nymphs. Ladies – some wearing gloves – were sipping tea and chatting. Faced with the plates of scones, butter, and marmalade, and the various pastries that adorned the little round tables, Ti-Lou realized how hungry she was. She sat down at a discreet table, in the back, far from the window so the porter wouldn't think she was keeping an eye on him, but she didn't escape notice. She wondered why – the word floozie wasn't printed on her forehead – until she looked more closely at the clothes these women, no longer young but clearly concerned with their appearance, were wearing.

Flappers!

Even the older ones, with stooped backs and trembling hands, who could hardly guide their cups to their lips, were disguised like the movie stars who'd started this cheeky style of dressing that Ti-Lou loathed because it didn't emphasize or flatter feminine curves, on the contrary, it made women look like tomboys: shapeless dresses with short sleeves that hung on the body like rags, the cloche hats that covered the entire head and looked like cannon balls, too many necklaces, so long they almost reached the knees, the excessively red lips and charcoal eyes, the shoes with heels so high they were certainly dangerous. What must she look like in her long travel dress from another age, her huge hat with its veil, and her enormous handbag? Like a bumpkin. Straight off the train from her home village. Probably come to visit a sick relative. A poor cousin brought from the back of beyond, supposedly to help her out, but in fact so she could become an underpaid servant. Hadn't the latest fashion reached her hamlet?

In Ottawa, where the women detested her, she was nevertheless the most fashionable creature in town, admired by the men, a paragon of good taste and *savoir-faire*. But here…

Did she notice smiles concealed behind hands as she made her way to the table she'd chosen? No. Really. No time for paranoia on her first day in Montréal.

From afar she can see the young porter lighting up his second cigarette.

Did he also peg her as fresh from the boondocks? Despite the fortune spent on her new outfit?

She raises her hand, gestures to the waiter, who approaches all smiles. She orders a full tea service, with only sweets, *juste du sucré, pas de sandwiches.*

"Sorry, I don't speak French."

"*Mon Dieu*, there are people like you in this town, too?"

She orders in English, raises her arms, removes the hat pins, and places her hat on the table. Yes, she dares appear bareheaded, in public. Pure provocation. The other women glance at her from beneath their cloche hats. I dare you to do the same, *Mesdames*…

The waiter steps back. Shocked? Probably. But she can sense his admiration nevertheless. She might be gaining a bit of weight, but she's still beautiful, she knows it and knows how to use it. Her hair, a cascade of waves that she's been keeping a rather shocking brick red lately, has always unnerved men and she knows how to show it off.

Several women, more perspicacious than others, Ti-Lou assumes, turn their backs on her, some pointedly, while others casually shift on their chairs as if to pick up their napkin or crane their necks to look for the supposed arrival of a friend.

The scones are warm and moist, the marmalade tickles the tongue perfectly, the cream is fresh and slightly tart and adds a cool, satiny touch. She could easily eat four, or even six of them. The tea is of the same fine quality served in the best restaurants in Ottawa; she requests a refill.

The porter is still waiting for her. Ti-Lou smiles. What would happen if he ran off with her fortune and left her alone with her one and only outdated dress, a hat she'll never wear again and her oversized handbag?

Did she do this on purpose? Risking everything? Just to tempt fate? Just to see? If someone takes off with my fortune, I'm meant to go back to where I came from, otherwise I will have earned my freedom...? Risking decades of hard work for something which, ultimately, seems like a kind of superstitious game? Risking everything to start over again? She shakes her head. No. He looked honest, she trusted him, that's all. She knows men. This one is honest.

The young man pointedly takes his watch out of his vest pocket, indicating that he's beginning to find the wait long. He pretends to take off with her suitcases. He laughs. So does she.

She gestures that she has finished, pays her bill, walks through the restaurant without donning her hat, letting it hang at her side like a little girl tired of wearing her riding hood because of the heat. There are murmurs and clucking and tsking. She's taunting them, they're reacting. A game she knows well and has been practising for years ... But she has retired from all that, the provocation, the jealousy, the revenge, and from now on she'll devote her time to other matters. She feels a twinge of regret. To slip into obscurity and be forgotten after being the centre of attention for her whole life, it probably won't be easy. It will mean a period of adjustment. Possibly a long one. She sighs and turns back before leaving the restaurant. Are these her last victims? Insignificant dowagers waiting for a train, or for a friend arriving from afar. Not a single wife of a minister or a senator. And behind them, her absent father, always the real target of her shameful behaviour, her secret prey, the man to be defeated.

"I had time to smoke four cigarettes! And I didn't light them all in a row!"

She walks ahead of him, hurrying towards the exit.

"When you see your tip, you'll have no regrets."

He takes off his cap and wipes his forehead before lifting her suitcases.

"That's what I was hopin'... Now you're talkin'."

FIRST CHANCE ENCOUNTER

Windsor Hotel

Peel Street and rue De La Gauchetière are jammed with cars. The smell of horse manure no longer fills the air, automobiles must have taken over since Ti-Lou's last visit to Montréal. Taxis are parked outside the station entrance. The porter is about to pick up her suitcases, his whistle has already attracted the attention of a driver. Ti-Lou places her hand on his arm to stop him.

"Wait."

Something is wrong. She's not sure what, but suddenly everything around her is spinning.

"Don't you want a taxi, Madame?"

She stares at the crowd, the traffic, the lights, she feels a strange throbbing as if an enormous heart were pumping all that, the humans and the machines, too much blood coursing through an overweight body. Of course, she thinks about her own body, her sickness, the sugar she just ingurgitated that is raising her blood pressure. An illusion. Undoubtedly just a sugar rush.

But still...

A threat? No. An uneasiness. That's it. A vague but insistent uneasiness. She tries to imagine herself arriving at her new apartment at nightfall – the sun is already setting – the strangeness of an unknown place, a large apartment after living so many years in a hotel suite, all those doors opening onto empty rooms, all those windows on the ground floor overlooking the street, after living for so long in the heights...

She turns to the young porter.

"If I asked you to accompany me to the Windsor Hotel across the street, are you allowed?"

He frowns and scratches his head.

"I think so. I think we've got an agreement with the hotel 'cause customers can't be expected to drag their luggage over there even if it's not that far, and they can't take a taxi, that'd be ridiculous. But you told me you wanted a taxi."

"I've changed my mind."

"But you don't have a reservation."

"I'm not worried about that. They always have suites available."

"You got the money to pay for a suite?"

"For one night. I can afford to pay for a suite for one night."

He takes another look at her. Was she wrong about him? Does she suddenly see a predator concealed beneath his adolescent awkwardness? What if he's guessed what she has in her suitcases, after all ...?

As they cross rue De La Gauchetière heading north, she catches herself shivering. What if she's not ready? For retirement? For freedom? For an anonymous apartment on a boulevard that's beautiful but inhabited by professionals, stuffy people, often uninteresting, maybe even hopelessly boring. Beautiful houses, a lovely median strip, beautiful trees that will soon be budding, and nothing else ... Is she ready for the hopelessly boring, anonymous life of a wealthy lady in retirement? Is she really ready to be anonymous?

At the entrance to the Windsor Hotel, she takes a dollar bill out of her pocketbook and hands it to the young porter who can't believe his eyes.

"You givin' me one whole buck?"

Ti-Lou smiles.

"You deserve it more than you realize, believe me."

She bends over to pick up her suitcases, but the doorman has already come down the steps.

"Madame is waiting for her husband? Or maybe he's already arrived?"

Ti-Lou shrugs and walks ahead of him.

"Madame isn't waiting for anyone. Madame is simply tired. But at least you speak French, that's a good start."

The porter from Windsor Station is walking off, caressing the dollar bill stuffed in his pocket. How many packs of cigarettes or glasses of beer will that buy him?

A woman travelling alone who shows up at the reception desk in a fancy hotel without a reservation is problematic. Ti-Lou knows that, but tonight she's too exhausted to undergo the insidious questioning and the dubious looks, so she promptly places a series of bank notes on the reception desk counter.

"Madame Georges Desrosiers, widow, I've just come in from Ottawa, I don't have a reservation, I'm tired and I want a suite, one of your best, I'll be leaving for Québec City on the first train tomorrow morning, and I'll be paying cash."

A few minutes later, she has entered what the man at the reception called the "Royal Suite," assuming that the price would frighten the strange lady facing him. (A widow, certainly not, given her colourful outfit, unless her widowhood wasn't recent. And her red hair was more the sign of a woman of ill repute than a respectable lady.) To his great surprise, she didn't flinch and simply asked where the elevator was. He handed her the key and pocketed part of the money before putting the rest – the real price of the suite – in the cash register.

As she tosses her hat onto the big bed, Ti-Lou thinks, the suite is royal, all right. Under other circumstances she would have burst out laughing at the pretension of the place: gold everywhere, from the carpet to the ceiling, heavy, cumbersome furniture, a massive canopy bed, truly ugly paintings hung too high on the walls. For a royal prostitute maybe, but not for a king.

It's been ages since she's slept anywhere except the Château Laurier, she's afraid she'll have insomnia. Besides, it's too early for bed. She sits down between her two suitcases and her overnight bag on the gold brocade bedspread. And she starts to laugh because the only activity she could engage in now would be to count her money.

How much does she actually have? As much as she imagines? Less than she dreams?

She stands up and goes to put the suitcases in the closet.

There she is, standing by the door of the Royal Suite, not knowing where to go, left or right, open the door and run away, take a long bath before going to bed, go back down to the lobby in search of candies that could replace the Cherry Delights she already misses ... She should have brought at least one box with her, instead of her absurd decision to do without them as soon as she reached Montréal. She could've begun her withdrawal the following day. At least she would've had one small consolation. And God knows she needs consolation, now, right away ...

Don't panic. Everything will be all right. Get through this first night, take advantage of the comfort of this place, as ridiculous as it is, and quietly head for her new home tomorrow morning, in the bright of day, sunny preferably, and move in ... Move in? She has nothing to move. She has no clothes, the apartment is furnished. She shakes her head and leans against the closet door.

She glances at her watch. In Ottawa, she would be preparing for her first client. No. Don't think about that.

She rushes across the room and opens the draperies at a window overlooking Peel Street.

Directly across from the hotel there's a park. Dominion Square. She remembers that because she once stayed in the Windsor Hotel, a long time ago, in the company of some politician whose name and sexual prowess she has long forgotten. Dominion Square is almost empty. It's suppertime, the downtown restaurants are undoubtedly full, no one would think of taking a walk. A couple, clearly late for an appointment, are crossing the park on the diagonal, a few men are smoking a cigar after an early dinner, a solitary man is walking his dog.

It's too early to go to bed, she doesn't have anything to read, she's not looking forward to the long hours ahead spent twiddling her thumbs or pacing back and forth in the Royal Suite. No bags to unpack. She could take a long bath. For lack of anything better to do. Soak until her skin begins to wrinkle, without using the soap provided by the hotel always too cheap for her delicate skin. Even in the Royal Suite? Maybe not, after all.

She should have jumped into a taxi and gone straight to her new home, she might have found something to do there, a floor to wash, for a woman who has never washed a floor in her entire life, some knick-knacks to dust, more flattering lighting to be organized, anything rather than this inactivity.

A twinge of anxiety tugs at her heart.

Is this anxiety she feels now, this distress, is this what her life will be like from now on? At least, for a while? Wondering what she will do with her day, her evening? Now that her nights will no longer be busy, will she toss and turn in her bed for hours, exhausted by insomnia, overcome by solitude? Is this the freedom she chose so impulsively?

To prevent herself from dwelling on this and sinking into discouragement, she picks up the hat she tossed onto the bed, her handbag, and her gloves, and rushes out of the suite almost at a run.

Keep herself busy by eating. Again. Although she ate so recently.

Stepping out of the elevator on the ground floor, she stops the first bellboy she sees.

"Can you recommend a good restaurant in the neighbourhood?"

The young man looks her up and down, clearly wondering who is this woman in such a hurry to go eat alone in a restaurant.

"There's a fine restaurant here in the hotel, Madame ... a lovely big dining room ..."

"No, no, I want to go out. Maybe on rue Sainte-Catherine?"

"Yes, there are lots. But there's a really good one on the other side of Dominion Square, on Metcalf, at the corner of Dorchester. It's called Two Pounds. It's a steak joint, if you're really hungry."

"Thank you. Very kind of you."

She slips a quarter into his hand and hurries towards the hotel entrance. The doorman tips his cap and greets her.

"Good evening, Madame. Do you need a taxi?"

"No, thank you. But tell me, is the Two Pounds right there at the corner, on the other side of the park?"

"Yes, but if I were you, I'd walk around the outside of the Square."

"Why? Is it dangerous?"

"No, but a beautiful woman like you, all alone in a park…"

She shrugs her shoulders and gives him a sly smile.

"Are you trying to tell me there are floozies who go walking in Dominion Square?"

"No, but there are no women on their own, either… Walk down Peel, then walk along the park on Dorchester and you'll find the Two Pounds on the corner."

Another quarter, another tip of the cap.

But Ti-Lou doesn't follow the doorman's advice. She crosses Peel Street in front of the hotel and takes the walkway that crosses Dominion Square on the diagonal, walking around the monument that's difficult to see in the dark. Another bronze angel with soldiers? Does she really feel like tackling an enormous steak in a noisy restaurant where she'll be the only woman on her own and the target of critical looks and unpleasant comments from the other customers? When she isn't even hungry? No. She decides to take a little walk, long enough for her heart to settle down and her anxiety to pass. She'll walk around the park a couple of times, then go back to the hotel.

The damp evening air feels good. She takes deep breaths through her nose, she knows that will calm her. Indeed, her heart slows down, her nervousness gradually evaporates, and she starts to envisage the night ahead and her arrival at her new apartment the following morning with less anxiety.

She has walked around the square twice, at a brisker pace because light rain has started to fall, when she spots the same man walking his dog she saw from the window of her suite. The hound, a huge animal all nerves and muscle, probably delighted with the odours he's picked up here and there, and especially with the gifts he left all around, at the foot of trees or in the middle of the lawn, wags his tail as he sees her approaching.

Ti-Lou hopes his master will know how to control him, that the beast won't come to sniff her, she hates the familiarity of badly trained animals.

Should she compliment his master nevertheless? It is a magnificent specimen.

She is about to bend over to pet him, perhaps even start a conversation with the man, an insignificant exchange between two people passing each other in a park who have nothing significant to say to each other, just an exchange of more-or-less sincere compliments, but she doesn't have time. The man comes between her and the animal, and she barely has time to detect the movement of a hand passing by her face holding something that glints in the light of the gas street lamps, before she feels a cold sensation in her neck. She lifts her gloved hand, touches her throat, looks down. Liquid. Blood. A lot of blood. She opens her mouth to scream, but nothing comes out, just a flow of red liquid almost black in the dark. She can no longer breathe.

She falls to her knees, reaching out to the dog who starts to bark furiously.

The man leans over her, the way she almost did with his dog just as he was about to attack her.

"Excuse me, Madame, I can't help myself."

Ti-Lou has time to realize that he is very handsome before collapsing on her back, both hands clutching her throat.

To come from so far to such a pitiful end.

The barking is fading, the rain blurring her sight.

She closes her eyes and has one last thought before dying:

"Is this what dying is like? No more than this? Doesn't it hurt more than this?"

The following morning, Montréal newspapers all had the same front-page headline: THE RAZOR MANIAC STRIKES AGAIN!

The articles reported the murder, the night before, of a prostitute from Ottawa who had rented the Royal Suite at the Windsor Hotel, earlier that evening under the name Widow Georges Desrosiers, but whose true identity turned out to be Louise Wilson, alias Louise Desrosiers, known in the nation's capital as Ti-Lou, the She-Wolf of Ottawa. Quite a life.

She was the fifth victim of the man who'd been nicknamed the

Razor Maniac and over the past few months had been attacking women who dared walk alone at night downtown.

The hotel doorman and a bellboy reported that she was heading for a restaurant on the other side of Dominion Square. The bellboy was terribly upset because he was the one who had recommended that restaurant. And the doorman claimed that he had warned the hotel guest, he had even advised her not to cross the park but to walk around it.

In *La Presse*, one clever journalist did his homework – apparently the victim was the daughter of an influential Ottawa citizen, possibly even a senator.

Further investigation would follow …

The search for the murderer was underway.

Nowhere was there any mention of the two suitcases full of cash that Ti-Lou had left in the closet of the Royal Suite at the Hotel Windsor. That was the end of the story.

SECOND CHANCE ENCOUNTER

Paradise

Stepping out of the elevator on the ground floor, she stops the first bellboy she sees.

"Excuse me ... Is Dorchester and Saint-Laurent far from here?"

The young man looks her up and down, clearly wondering, who is this woman in such a hurry to go looking for trouble on the Main so early in the evening.

"Less than five minutes in a taxi, Madame."

"So I can walk there ..."

"Yes, but ..."

She slips a quarter into his hand and hurries towards the hotel entrance.

"There's a nice bar here in the hotel, real elegant ..."

"I'm not going for a drink."

The doorman tips his cap and greets her.

"Good evening, Madame. Do you need a taxi?"

"I'm not sure. I'm going to the corner of Dorchester and Saint-Laurent, I don't think it's very far ..."

"You're better off in a taxi."

"Why? Is it dangerous?"

"Let's just say the way there isn't so safe. If you're looking for a place to have a drink, we have –"

"I know, you have a real elegant bar here. It's not an elegant bar I'm looking for. I'm going to visit my cousin who works at the Paradise Club."

He lifts his cap again and scratches his head.

"The Paradise. Does that place still exist?"

"Why do you ask? Has it closed?"

"Well, I don't know, but the last I heard, business wasn't that great."

"Just call me a taxi. If I see that it's closed, I'll come right back."

After blowing his whistle to call one of the taxis waiting a few yards away, he comes down the steps to join Ti-Lou on the sidewalk.

"Boulevard Saint-Laurent's changing, you know. The Paradise isn't the only place now, there's a few new cabarets. The best is the Coconut Inn, that's where you should go. I haven't been yet but they say it's special. Real stars perform there."

"What's the deal, do they pay you to send customers to the Coconut Inn? You on their payroll? I told you I'm going to visit a relative who works at the Paradise."

She was about to lean over to disappear into the taxi while the doorman held the door open for her. She straightened up.

"You don't believe me? You think I'm an old alcoholic looking for a dive to get drunk."

He lifts his cap one last time.

"I sure didn't think you were old, Madame ..."

She smiles and takes a fifty-cent piece out of her bag.

"At least you're diplomatic."

As she settles on the back seat of the car, she notices the man she saw from her window earlier still walking his dog in Dominion Square. He turns towards her. A handsome man, but as her mother would have said, she wouldn't want to meet him in a dark place ... Something in his brief glance at her gave her the chills.

The dog is barking. As if he were calling her.

The taxi driver seems disappointed by the short distance to their destination and grumbles as he navigates their way through the almost non-existent traffic at this hour. The Paradise Club isn't at all what Ti-Lou expected. It's a dirty, decrepit building, the show-case announcing the singer of the week has been shattered, and the sidewalk is strewn with cigarette butts and dubious stains. She didn't expect a palace, but still ...

After accepting the fare, the driver sticks his head out the window of his car.

"You sure this is where you wanted to go?"

Ti-Lou hesitates briefly before answering.

"In fact, I'm not so sure now … Is there another Paradise on Saint-Laurent?"

"No, this is the only one."

"Well, I'm here."

"Be careful now."

"Is it dangerous?"

"No, but it's become a real dive since customers with money started going somewhere else. Only the ones who can't get into other places keep coming here. You sure you don't want me to drive you back to the hotel?"

"Yes, I'm sure. I'll be fine. I know how to defend myself."

She pushes open the door to the Paradise as the taxi drives off. The smell of stale beer, cheap alcohol, sweat, and sawdust is overpowering. A piano is playing too loudly while a singer butchers a music-hall song no one is listening to. Ti-Lou catches some of the lyrics about a prostitute named Nini peau d'chien. It's a call-and-response song. No response.

The place is almost empty. But it's still early. This must be the singer's first set.

So this is where her cousin Maria works. Maria, the only friend she's had in her whole life, almost her sister since her cousin's parents more or less adopted her back in Saskatchewan more than thirty years ago.

Two waitresses are circulating among the tables waiting for orders that seem few and far between and Ti-Lou has trouble recognizing Maria, she's changed so much since the last time they saw each other at her daughter Rhéauna's wedding.

Ti-Lou sits down at a table in the back to observe her before saying hello. Maria is still a pretty woman, her waitress uniform is neat, her hair well groomed, but there's something in her posture, some hesitation in her walk, a new stoop in her back that suggest a woman less energetic than the dynamo who, just three years earlier, had organized the craziest, wildest wedding her neighbourhood had ever known.

Ti-Lou waits until Maria comes closer before saying, in an overly playful tone of voice:

"You're not going to offer your cousin a little drink?"

It takes Maria a couple of seconds to recognize Ti-Lou, as if a cabaret in Montréal was the last place she expected to see her, when she should have been earning her living in Ottawa.

The cousins' reunion is loud, effusive, all heads are turned towards the two crazy women who are shouting and crying. Maria rushes to the bar to fetch a flute of sparkling wine for Ti-Lou – real champagne is too expensive for the Paradise clientele – and to ask her boss for a half-hour break so she can catch up with her cousin who's come from far away to visit her.

Charlotte, the other waitress, agrees to cover her tables. There are so few customers in the establishment, one waitress would be enough anyway.

What are you doing in Montréal, you have to be kidding, you haven't retired, are you sure you want to live here, won't you get bored in a strange town, where are you going to live, are you going to look for work ... the first fifteen minutes are taken up with Maria's barrage of questions and Ti-Lou's clear and concise answers.

"But why disappear on boulevard Saint-Joseph? You'll die of boredom!"

It's the only question Ti-Lou can't answer because she doesn't know why.

"Peace and quiet, maybe. The trees. I don't know. I don't know. Sometimes I dream of looking out my window, watching the snow fall and nibbling on chocolates, and other times, I wonder how anyone can stand it for month after month. I couldn't do that in Ottawa, I couldn't disappear like you say, too many people know me, I'd never have peace and quiet there ... so I had to leave town. I'm tired, Maria, I'm getting old, and I'd rather leave my profession before it leaves me."

Maria places her hand on her cousin's arm.

"Still, why boulevard Saint-Joseph?"

They both laugh.

Ti-Lou takes a last sip of lukewarm bubbly.

"You look tired, too."

Maria sits up straight, smooths her hair that didn't need it, coughs into her fist.

"Is it that obvious?"

"You look… slower than before. You were so full of energy the last time I saw you."

"The last time you saw me, I was over-excited because my daughter was getting married, that wasn't my natural state. But I think I'm more fed up than tired. I'm getting older, too, Ti-Lou. I've been working here for twelve years, always the same faces, always the same beer, the same drinks. The sawdust on the floor, the spittoons that have to be moved, the customers' dumb jokes. It saved my life when I first arrived in Montréal, but it's killing me now."

"So, leave. Find work somewhere else."

"Where? I'm almost fifty, too. Where do you think I could find work? This is all I know how to do, sell drinks to drunks! No, that's not true. I worked in a cotton mill for years in New England. Can you see me going back to a factory at my age? Anyway, the Coconut Inn's gonna do us in, and I might be out of work soon. And there's no way they'd hire me, even though I'm good at this job."

"You still haven't married your Monsieur Rambert?"

"No, my Monsieur Rambert is still waiting. If he feels like waiting, that's his problem."

"You're so pigheaded!"

"It's more about pride, Ti-Lou. I've managed on my own so far, I'll manage on my own till the end. Monsieur Rambert is a wonderful man, but he'll never be my husband. He knows that, and he accepts it. I'm managing."

"You said it was killing you."

"A manner of speaking. Nothing can kill me."

Several tables have filled up since they began talking. Maria starts to stand up.

"Time to get back to work. You can stay if you want. The singer's pretty bad but it helps pass the time. Anyway, you sure chose a weird way to spend your first evening in Montréal."

"I wanted to see you."

"You could've waited till tomorrow."

"No, Maria. I was panicking and you're the only person I know here."

"So stay. I'll come back to chat every so often. You feel less panicky now?"

"Yes. A bit."

Ti-Lou holds on to the sleeve of Maria's black-and-white striped blouse.

She doesn't want to be left alone, she has to find a question.

"How's Nana doing?"

Maria glances towards the bar where her boss is getting impatient. He gives her a dirty look, points to the clock over the entrance door.

"She's fine. They're not rich but they're managing. Nana had a little boy last year, so she had to stop working. I'll tell you more later on."

"In the meantime, bring me the rest of the bottle, I feel like drinking tonight."

"You know that's not the real stuff, you'll wake up with a godawful headache tomorrow morning."

"I've drunk worse."

"I doubt it."

She walks away, indicating to her boss she's on her way, then changes her mind and goes back to Ti-Lou's table.

"Be careful on your way back to the hotel. Let me know when you're leaving, I'll call you a cab. There's some crazy guy going around downtown killing women these days. Everyone calls him the Razor Maniac. Some call him the barber 'cause he uses a razor as a weapon. We don't want anything to happen to you the night of your arrival! Coming all this way, getting attacked your first night here, that would be stupid."

A table behind her is calling for a waitress. She heads straight for the six drunks sitting there. They greet her with raucous cries and apparently lascivious compliments because Maria delivers a few well-placed slaps. Obviously, regular customers who know how she'll react to their fooling around, and they enjoy provoking her.

They call her Auntie.

Ti-Lou can see her blush.

She waits for her bottle of faux champagne, listening vaguely to the singer.

She feels like drinking. Something that doesn't happen often. She'd like to drown her anxiety, her doubts, let the fumes of alcohol go to her brain and extinguish, one by one, the annoying questions that are haunting her. And convince herself, in that beneficial haze, that she has made the right choice, that she'll be happy tomorrow morning to arrive at her apartment on Saint-Joseph and to settle in, taking her time to buy whatever furniture is missing, changing the ugly curtains in the living room and the kitchen, and, who knows, maybe even repainting. To make it prettier and brighter. To erase the heavy atmosphere of an apartment left empty by a tenant who died, "after a long sickness," as the landlord told her. A diabetic woman come to replace someone who died of cancer. Strange twist of fate.

A long sickness.

She thinks of the sugar circulating in her veins, the poison that is slowly killing her, the threat of a heart attack, and gangrene, and blindness, all possibly lying in wait for her.

No. Don't think about that.

Why not enjoy this moment of peace, despite the noise all around her, instead of worrying about what might happen tomorrow, or in half an hour? The singer is atrocious, she could find it amusing, this cabaret full of human specimens the likes of which she has rarely met in her life, she could find them interesting, observe them, listen to them shout and laugh and burp. Stay in her corner, remaining as discreet as possible so no one comes to bother her. There's little risk of that, actually, she noticed while chatting with Maria that several tables were occupied by women alone, women who wanted to *stay* alone and who made that clear with their defiant look of serious drinkers who certainly hadn't come to fraternize with anyone. Like her.

She closed her eyes for a few seconds. Or a few minutes.

The sound of a bottle being placed on the table.

"Good luck with the headache. Read the label, for a good laugh."
Maria walks off chuckling.

Ti-Lou picks up the bottle. It's "Champale Mouette & Chardon."
She bursts out laughing and fills her flute.

Her first binge on "champale." For better or for worse.

So eager to catch up with her cousin's news, she hadn't noticed
the acidic, metallic taste of this imitation alcohol so rough on the
tongue and the throat. She wonders where it could have been fab-
ricated. Certainly not in France. Maybe here, in the province of
Québec, in a sugar shack during the winter, before the sap rises in
the maples in the spring. An adulterated alcohol distilled in the
same barrels that, a few months later, will contain the maple syrup.

Whatever. It certainly goes to your head. Fast. After downing her
fourth flute in ten minutes, she feels a comforting warmth irradiat-
ing from her brain to her solar plexus. The establishment starts to
spin around her. A rather pleasant sensation. For the time being.
Perhaps she won't think so later on, when she's kneeling on the
bathroom floor in her Hotel Windsor suite, but right now it does
the trick, she feels as if she's floating and there's a certain charm to
being caught inside this novel place for her, the kind of place where
she very well might have landed if she had been less fortunate at the
beginning of her career. Or had less talent. Or talents, rather. Plural.

She laughs and pours herself another glass.

The famous Ti-Lou, the most beautiful floozie in Ottawa, the
most highly paid, slumming it in a dive on the Main in Montréal.
Guzzling champale! Who would have thought?

Her downfall?

No.

She is here by choice.

She can leave this establishment whenever she pleases and never
return. She isn't a prisoner.

One more flute of Mouette & Chardon. She laughs. Do they
also make Veuve Calico?

The bottle is almost empty. She drank in less than half an hour
the equivalent of what she usually drinks in an entire evening. She
closes her eyes and takes a few deep breaths. If she opens her eyes,

she knows everything will start to spin, a slow merry-go-round where she'd never dare mount one of the horses because she has vertigo, so she keeps her eyes closed. Nausea and heartburn will come later. In her suite at the Windsor Hotel. Meanwhile ...

She's reached the point where she thinks the singer has some talent when she hears her name. Spoken by a man.

She opens her eyes. Lit from behind, because he is standing between her table and the stage. Who can it be? She knows that voice and that build ...

He repeats:

"What are you doing here, Madame Ti-Lou?"

She smiles and opens her arms.

"Senator Morin!"

She promptly covers her mouth.

"I'm sorry. I spoke too loud. Perhaps you don't want people to know that you're here. A senator from Ottawa. Actually ... what are *you* doing here?"

He sits down, leans over to her, looks at the bottle of champale.

"That will kill you!"

"You might be right. But in the meantime, the effect is fabulous. Fabulous!"

She realizes she can't control her voice or her gestures and apologizes, trying to lower her voice.

"I've never seen you in such a state, Madame Ti-Lou. Are you sure you're all right?"

"No, I'm not sure, and I'm sure I won't be all right when I get back to my *sweet* at the Windsor."

"Sorry to repeat myself, but what are you doing in a dive like this? I'll give you my answer afterwards."

She tells him the whole story, her decision to retire, her impulsive departure from Ottawa, her panic about facing the dark, empty apartment she's rented, the Windsor Hotel for one night, to ease the transition, a last fling of opulence and luxury before retreating into her den, and finally, her cousin Maria, the only person she really knows in Montréal, who works here at the Paradise Club. And the bottle of Mouette & Chardon. She's talkative because of the champale, but also because he's listening to her so attentively. As if he understood her. She asks him not to tell anyone she's in Montréal, and he promises total discretion.

They laugh, though they are both embarrassed to meet in a place like this when they always ran into each other in Ottawa's high society. And especially in the hallways of the Château Laurier. Senator Morin is the only one of her visitors who understood the meaning of the bouquet of camellias, he respected it and Ti-Lou is grateful to him for that.

Maria, hands on her hips and frowning, comes to stand between them.

"This man bothering you, Ti-Lou? Just say so, okay? The bouncer's paid to deal with guys like this."

Ti-Lou puts her hand on Maria's arm.

"No, no. Everything's fine. Sen– Mr. Morin is an old acquaintance from Ottawa, here in town on business. He's not a problem. Don't worry."

"You sure?"

"Absolutely sure."

As her cousin walks off, Ti-Lou thinks that Senator Morin is more than not a problem. He's the only client, the only one in all those years, for whom she felt some affection. A real gentleman. Not at all vulgar. Always respectful. Never gross with her.

She looks at him.

Good lord.

Is this really him?

Is she so drunk she's confusing him with someone else?

She leans over to him.

"You really are Senator Morin, right? I'm not mistaken?"

"You're not mistaken but I think you've had enough to drink for tonight. It's great to celebrate, but enough is enough."

"Yes, you're right. Enough is enough. I should ... I should get back to the hotel now. They must've put too much alcohol, or too much poison in their faux champagne, this is crazy ..."

She tries to stand up but can't.

"You haven't answered me, Senator. What are you doing here

48

yourself? Have you retired in Montréal? Do you have a cousin who works here, too?"

She laughs, wipes her eyes.

"Omigod, I'm plastered."

He takes the flute out of her hands, places it on the table. She wants to protest but can't.

"You're right. I've had enough. Not sure I'd understand anything you told me ... I havta leave ... havta get back to the hotel ... havta sleep ... Havta think about what I'll do tomorrow once I've cured my hangover ..."

"I'll drive you back."

"No, no. Maria's going to call me a cab."

"It would be safer for me to take you to your hotel."

She straightens up and looks him in the eye.

"I told you I've retired. Don't you go thinkin'..."

She stops short and blushes. He hadn't said anything to make her think he wanted to spend the night with her.

"Excuse me. I'm sorry."

"Don't worry. I have a car."

He offers her his arm. She leans on it to stand up.

"I hope you'll act like a gentleman all the way ... Did I tell you I'm staying at the Windsor Hotel? Yes, I told you. Windsor Hotel, please, driver!"

Her laughter attracts a lot of attention.

Maria comes rushing over, carrying a trayful of glasses of beer.

"You leaving already?"

She gives Senator Morin a suspicious look.

"With him?"

He smiles and bows deeply.

"Senator Pierre-Gilles Morin. I'm one of your cousin's ... friends. Don't worry, she's in good hands."

Ti-Lou kisses her cousin on the cheek and whispers in her ear:

"He's got good hands, all right ..."

As she watches her leave, Maria thinks that Ti-Lou should update her wardrobe. She looks like she's stepped out of a turn-of-the-century bordello.

He drives up to the entrance of the Windsor Hotel and turns off the engine.

The doorman promptly comes down the steps to open the passenger door for her.

"Did you find the Paradise Club, Madame?"

Ti-Lou smiles at him.

"Yes, and an old friend at the same time."

She knows she should say goodbye to Senator Morin, thank him for driving her home, and go up to her room. But the champale has left her exhausted, she feels heavy, numb, and she'd like to spend the night right there, leaning back in the seat, chatting. Or sleeping. Safe and sound. Until the effect of the cheap alcohol wears off. Everything is spinning before her eyes, Peel Street, the hotel, the car, the doorman's red cap swinging back and forth until it settles back on the head of the man leaning over to offer his hand, smiling.

She laughs.

"You almost lost your cap."

The doorman raises his hand to check.

"No."

Senator Morin leans over to speak to the doorman. His head almost touches Ti-Lou's. The haunting smell of gardenias mixed with her personal scent ... so many memories.

"Perhaps I should accompany Madame to her room."

"We can take care of that, Monsieur ..."

"I'm sure, but I know Madame very well ..."

"Besides, you can't park here, it's reserved for taxis."

"Not even for five minutes?"

"Not even for two minutes. They enforce it. By the time you got back, your car would be gone."

"You could tell them I'll be right back."

"They might not believe me."

The senator lifts his hat.

"Congratulations. You defend your guests well."

The doorman lifts his cap.

"Thanks for the compliment. You can't always know who you're dealing with."

"I could park around the corner. There must be somewhere I could park?"

The doorman turns to Ti-Lou, although he's not sure she'll understand what he says. She's clearly too intoxicated to make any decisions.

"It's up to you, Madame."

She swings one foot out of the car and extends her hand.

"I can manage on my own. I've always managed on my own."

She turns back to the man she's seen so often naked, the man she's heard groan, snort, and roar with pleasure and he seems like a stranger in this environment so unfamiliar to both of them. The smell of his Cuban cigars, his irresistible eyes of a cocker spaniel in distress. So many memories.

"Thanks so much, Senator Morin. So kind of you. I always knew you were a real gentleman. But I can manage. I'm not that drunk."

The doorman helps her out of the car.

"But some day you'll have to explain what you were doing at the Paradise tonight, it's really not your kind of establishment."

He passes his business card to her.

"I'll be in Montréal for a few days. If you want my explanation, I'd love to have dinner with you."

She smiles at him the way she always did when he left her suite at the Château Laurier after a night that had delighted them both. Because with him she'd always allowed herself to enjoy the pleasures of what she usually did to earn her living.

"I'll be leaving the hotel tomorrow morning to settle into my apartment. I don't have a phone yet. But maybe I'll find a way to call you in the late afternoon ... maybe."

"So we can have dinner tomorrow night?"

"That's right, maybe we can have dinner tomorrow night."

Backfire. The engine stalled. Then the car took off down the almost deserted Peel Street.

The doorman helps Ti-Lou up the steps with his hand under her elbow.

Suddenly she feels lighter, she's less tired. Perhaps she shouldn't have let Senator Morin leave. She could've invited him in for one last drink. No. She was right. She needs a good night's sleep. She probably will be in no state to take care of a man when she wakes up tomorrow morning.

After he opens the door for her, she gives the doorman a generous tip.

"Do you know what champale is?"

He frowns.

"Champ ... what?"

"Champale. It's like cheap champagne."

"No, but you know, I stick to beer."

She places her hand on his arm.

"Anyway, if anyone ever offers you some, say NO!"

Lead. In her head and everywhere in her body. And a headache, as anticipated. Twice as bad! A knife is probing her brain, she feels as if her eyes might pop out of her head, and she feels her blood throbbing in her ears. She's convinced that if she opens her eyes, daylight will kill her. But she has to take some aspirin. A lot of aspirin. She forgot to leave the tube on her night table when she went to bed. Now she has to cross the room to get to the bathroom. But she can't move. She knows she's lying on her right side, she can feel the wrinkled sheet on her leg and the pillow slip under her ear. She probably didn't move all night. She collapsed on the big bed, passed out more than fell asleep and without moving an inch, fermented in her sleep the cheap alcohol she'd been so happy to guzzle down the night before, knowing full well what to expect. Never again. The intoxication, the light bubbles tickling her brain, the world spinning and dancing around her weren't worth the price she has to pay this morning, something she expected but chose to ignore. Did she think she was stronger than she really is? No, she simply wanted to enjoy the moment at hand and face the consequences the following morning.

She remembers Senator Morin, his kindness, his brown eyes and she lets out a cry of exasperation. She should've drunk less and paid more attention to him.

Okay. Time to act. First move her leg, try to swing it out of the bed, then give herself a push from her elbow, without opening her eyes. Then grope her way to the bathroom where she'll find the aspirin and a hot, then cold, shower for fifteen minutes, maybe more.

Good. Her leg is out of the bed. She realizes she's not nude. She fell asleep fully dressed. Did she even manage to take off her hat before falling into bed? She touches her head. Good, no hat. It must be on the floor somewhere between the living room and the bedroom. Wait a minute, who opened the door to the suite? Was she able to do it herself? And her handbag? Where is her handbag? And the two suitcases full of money?

Now, without realizing it, undoubtedly a reflex, a move repeated so often it's unconscious, she finds herself standing beside the bed. She thinks it's ridiculous to keep her eyes closed, the curtains are drawn and the light, even if it's late, even if it's the middle of the afternoon, will be filtered and won't hurt. She opens one eye. It's late because there's no sunshine coming through the crack in the draperies drawn by the chambermaid who prepared the room for the night. Her windows face east, so if it were morning, there would be some sunlight, a ray of light on the rug. But the sun is already too high.

How long did she sleep? She looks at her watch. Half past noon. She has to vacate the room by one o'clock.

"Let them wait!"

Her voice startles her. Hoarser than usual, almost the cry of a wounded animal.

She staggers to the bathroom, turns on the light – too bright, unbearable – and turns it off. She'll take her shower in the dark.

She finds the aspirin, swallows four wondering if it's enough or too much.

She spends a long time under the shower as planned, hot first, then cold and colder. Slowly but surely she feels her nerves unwind and relax, the burning sensation on her skin feels good. Her hair hangs down on either side of her face and she wonders what she'll look like when she crosses the big lobby in a while, with her hair still wet, wearing her wrinkled clothes, her crushed hat. She, who always brings her gardenia soap with her because she hates the poor quality of the toiletries provided in hotels, forgot this time but she remembers that she's in the Windsor Hotel, one of Montréal's gems, so the toiletries are probably luxurious. She unwraps the small bar of soap and sniffs it. It smells good.

She stays in the shower until the aspirin begins to take effect. At home at the Château Laurier, she would have taken a long bath, with a cool facecloth on her forehead, if necessary, even spending part of the day in the tub, adding hot water as soon as it felt too cool.

The Château Laurier. At home. No. Her new home is waiting for her farther north on the island of Montréal, and soon she will know whether she made a mistake renting it. A phrase comes to mind: for the rest of her days. She braces herself on the little white tiles of the shower stall and starts to sob. The rest of her days: a gaping hole and she has no idea what she'll fill it with. Perhaps it's a hole she'll never manage to fill. An empty, idle existence after such a busy, full life.

When she looks at herself in the big mirror just before leaving the suite, she thinks she was stupid not to have brought at least one change of clothes. Did she really believe she'd go shopping in the streets of Montréal the day after her arrival? She wanted to start anew, fine, a totally fresh start, leaving everything behind, all the signs of her profession, the material reminders and her memories, but she could have been more practical. Especially since she spent the night in the clothes she's wearing. How can she cross the lobby in a wrinkled dress and a tired hat? Then appear in the shops? Holding her head high, that's how. As always. Never showing her distress. Not letting them see – who, them? the customers, the salesgirls, people in general, the whole world? – the least hesitation, the slightest doubt. Plow ahead. Never turn back, ignoring the laughter and sarcastic comments. Make way for Ti-Lou, and nothing affects Ti-Lou.

She's no longer in Ottawa, however, and she has left behind the female desired by the greatest. Here, she is just another client in a chic hotel and her exit will not resemble those, sometimes spectacular, she often staged in the federal capital. For the first time, it's possible that the opinion of other hotel guests will matter to her.

So make it fast. Get the hell out of here and never again set foot in a hotel suite that reminds her of the past, hide, lock herself up, lie low, execute her plan, actually. Before it's too late, while the choice is still hers, because so far no one had the nerve to suggest that the time had come for her to retire.

Before leaving she looks around the suite one last time, pointlessly, since she only has her two suitcases full of money and her little overnight bag, but she spots the business card Senator Morin gave her the night before, left on the bedside table.

She sits down on the unmade bed.

Should she call him right away? She doesn't have a phone in her apartment yet, God knows when she will, and later in the day she'll have no idea where to find one on boulevard Saint-Joseph. He didn't say how long he intended to stay in Montréal. She smiles. Is that just an excuse she's found, simply because she wants to talk to him? After all, ending her first day of exile in pleasant company might not be such a bad idea.

A real weathercock. She just told herself she has to hide, and now ... But she'd have to find a dress, a hairdresser, and, most of all, decide not to drink like the night before, not even real champagne, so she can stay in control.

No. It's too soon, it's impossible, she'll never have time to do all that.

Although it's still early. She could find something in a shop on avenue du Mont-Royal, one of those shapeless dresses so popular these days, a cloche hat that would hide her fatigue, and wear the same shoes because men never notice a woman's shoes ...

She tries to remind herself that she's taken refuge in Montréal to be alone, to no longer subject herself to the presence of men, but the prospect of spending a few hours in the company of Senator Morin whose discretion and sense of humour she's always appreciated makes her forget her headache. A little splurge before disappearing completely, why not?

Playing with fire?

No.

When she explains everything to him – did she already do that the night before? She can't remember; yes, she believes she did – he'll understand. He might even go so far as to drive her home – home! – but that's all. He's a gentleman. A real gentleman.

She turns the business card over in her hand.

Something like a flicker of hope dissolves the lingering haze of her headache.

The apartment on Saint-Joseph is not as dark and as sad as she remembered it. That's a relief, it almost makes her forget the first sign of a migraine.

The living room, especially, a big double room featuring two plaster columns yellowed by generations of cigarette smoke, will make a cozy corner, and, who knows, nicely decorated, a pleasant sitting room should she decide to receive guests. Everything is old, of course, and brown, the colour she hates most, is everywhere, but with a bit of effort – and quite a bit of money – she should be able to turn it into an acceptably frilly space. That's where she should begin her renovations. A pale rug, lace curtains, a pastel colour on the walls should be enough to begin with.

She scolded herself as she unpacked her overnight bag: wanting to leave everything behind and start her life over again is all very well, but she could have at least brought a change of underwear and one or two daytime dresses to see her through, until she goes on her shopping spree. Her usual impulsive behaviour went too far this time. All or nothing. But nothing shouldn't mean nothing at all!

She has a date with a man, and not just any man, at seven o'clock this evening and that means she has to strike out immediately to find something decent to wear. Where should she go? She's heard about avenue du Mont-Royal where her aunt Teena has been selling shoes for years. But what kind of shops will she find there? This is the first time for a very long time that she has looked for clothes that weren't made to measure for her. Mind you, with these shapeless dresses that are the fashion now...

She found everything at L.N. Messier, the department store on Mont-Royal. She dressed herself from head to foot for a pittance and is far from sure that she likes her new look. In the department pompously named "The Elegant Woman's Palace," facing the racks of "new styles," she decided to take the leap and try on one of the sack-like dresses that hang loosely and hide curves. And a cloche hat. And a sequined clutch bag.

She's standing now in front of the long mirror hidden behind the bedroom door of her new apartment – was the previous tenant ashamed to contemplate her reflection? – cursing those designers in New York or in the old country who force women to wear these awful rags. Farewell the tiny waist, the bold cleavage, and the mystery of ruffled skirts. Too much is visible, nothing left to the imagination. Her legs are still lovely, but now anyone can admire them, when she had always reserved them for the highest bidders.

She smooths the skirt scattered with sequins and its four silk tassels. It moves when she walks but loses all personality when she stands still. And this hat that crushes her hair and gives her blinkers like the ones horses wear! Her hats have always been airy, vaporous; this one clamps her head inside a felt tube shaped like a bowling ball.

Will Senator Morin be shocked to find her transformed like this, will he find her less attractive, too ordinary? At least, too much "like other women"?

She checks her watch. Five o'clock. She has two hours to get ready, to do her makeup and her hair, to mitigate, frankly, the lack of mystery of these new clothes with tricks that will distract Senator Morin's gaze from this potato sack that hides her advantages, and draw his attention, she hopes, to her face. Perfume will be important, of course. She's not used to being unsure of herself and it annoys her.

She shrugs. Here she is already thinking like a floozie when she retired less than twenty-four hours ago. She'd promised herself, when she called her ex-client from the suite in the Windsor Hotel, that she'd simply enjoy an evening with an old friend, an inconsequential evening, and she'd make it clear as soon as he arrived that there would be no ...

Who does she think she's kidding? Once a seductress, always a seductress, even retired. She knows she can't prevent herself from being dazzling, she'll use her deep-throated laugh, her graceful arms, her sparkling eyes, it's automatic, her second nature, why fight it?

Dressed like this? Like a flapper from an American movie? Restrain her gestures of a faux grande dame, stifle her devastating laughter, be reserved when she's always exaggerated everything? Then she thinks of Theda Bara in *The Unchastened Woman*, which she recently saw in Ottawa, how she managed to be attractive despite the get-up like the one she's wearing now. That reassures her. A bit. But surely she can't force herself to think of Theda Bara all evening so her behaviour matches her clothes!

She has just placed the empty shopping bags on the bed when the doorbell rings. She's not expecting anyone. As she heads for the door, she thinks she'll probably have to get used to the idea of peddlers, a bothersome breed she never had to deal with, living protected on an upper floor of the Château Laurier.

She recognizes his silhouette through the lace curtain.

Senator Morin, holding his hat in his hand. Two hours in advance. And bringing a bouquet disproportionately big for the occasion.

The minute she opens the door, he bursts out laughing, then gets a hold of himself.

"Are you wearing that outfit for the first time, Madame Ti-Lou? I see at least three tags still attached."

She is mortified. What should she do? Apologize? Try to find the tags, tear them off, and run the risk of tearing her damn new clothes? Pretend nothing's wrong and start chatting with the price of her hat hanging over her ear?

She simply hopes she hasn't blushed too obviously.

But he resumes a serious tone so quickly she realizes something must be wrong, that she's about to learn bad news, that she'll be spending her first evening in her new apartment alone.

"I apologize for showing up so early, but there was no other way to reach you. This or a telegram. A telegram would have been impolite. I have to cancel our supper date. I got a phone call from Ottawa. My wife has fallen ill, I have to leave immediately. I'm so sorry, I was really looking forward to spending the evening with you."

A trace of a smile appears at the corner of his lips.

"Especially since you went to the trouble ..."

He hands her the bouquet.

"I managed to find gardenias. I think the concierge at the Ritz had never heard the word! He thought I said 'gardener' and must've wondered what I was going to do with a gardener."

He looks embarrassed by his attempt at humour and coughs into his fist.

"Believe me, I'm really sorry."

She hides her disappointment with a shrug of her shoulders.

"It doesn't matter, Senator, we'll take a rain check. I'll have lots of time on my hands."

They stand there, awkwardly.

"Would you like to come in for a few minutes? A cup of tea? Or coffee? I think I saw some in the pantry."

He steps back and puts his hat on his head.

"No, thank you. I wish I could, but ... it's a long way to Ottawa. And I don't like driving in the dark."

"I hope it's nothing serious."

"What?"

"Your wife. I hope it's not serious."

"Oh! I don't know. The telegram was vague."

"Does she get sick often?"

What is she doing? Trying to postpone his departure? Let him leave, let him go back to his legitimate spouse, after all, what does she care?

"Yes. It's chronic. But let's not talk about that. You have my card. When you get your phone, call me. At the office, of course. I come to Montréal often, it would be fun to see each other again."

The coy woman rises to the surface. Ti-Lou straightens her shoulders and lifts her chin.

"I called you once, Senator, I'm not about to make a habit of it."

He frowns.

"Of course. Well, I'll come ring your doorbell if I have your permission."

"Fine. If I'm home. We'll see."

She catches his disappointed look. It's not his fault, really, she's being too harsh with him, maybe she's acting a bit too independent. Then, at the word independence, she stands even straighter.

Let him go to hell, after all, she doesn't need him.

He extends his hand.

"I really have to leave. I'm so sorry. Maybe next time."

"Sure. Maybe next time."

His hand is firm and warm. Friendly.

Perhaps, like her, all he wanted was to spend the evening with an old friend, why is she acting so distant with him?

She attempts a warm smile. Unconvincingly.

"Oh well, I'm off."

"Yes, bon voyage, be careful. Did you say you were driving?"

"Yes."

"I thought senators had chauffeurs."

"No, senators don't have chauffeurs. Besides, I was here on personal business."

Let him get going! Let him jump in his car and take off for Ottawa now!

He has turned away. Walked down the three steps. Pushed open the freshly painted wrought iron gate.

She closes the door and watches him get into his car through the lace curtain.

She's back facing the big mirror hanging on the back of her bedroom door (she must find a better place for it, she's not in a convent here!).

There's the little tag hanging over her right ear.

Idiot!

Letting herself believe. Anything. Even for an instant. That she might have continued, "on the side," for instance. Because that's probably what she was thinking, without admitting it to herself. A little extra spending money, rainy day savings, whatever image comes to mind, it seems ridiculous, childish, naive, borderline pathetic. To make an adult decision, a choice that will change her life, and then regress to such childishness, that's so unlike her.

She must have wanted to hang on for a while, before really letting go. And she lost her balance. In front of one of the few decent clients she had ever known. If he tries to see her again, next week, in two months, she'll have to find the courage, dig her nails into the palm of her hand, like Gloria Swanson or Theda Bara in those American melodramas, become a bad actress, her lips parted, her eyes wide open, and refuse any invitation. To prevent herself from dreaming.

Remain alone.

That's the verdict.

And no matter what, don't consider it a punishment. On the contrary. Envisage it all, the peace, the silence, even if it's difficult at first, worse than difficult, unbearable, as a well-earned reward.

She leans forward and looks herself in the eye.

But how can she see solitude as a reward? Because she has known too many people? Intimately? For too long? Because she wanted to be *la dame aux gardénias*? And succeeded? And now she's had enough?

Has she really had enough? No, of course not. If her body hadn't begun to betray her, if her appearance had been immutable, if time hadn't taken its toll, she would've gone on. It's not true that she's tired. She's not tired. She made an intelligent, carefully weighed choice: to abandon her trade before it abandoned her.

That life is over. Get that into your head once and for all. It's finished. Right now you find that terrible, the prospect of what's ahead terrorizes you, but think about the peace and quiet. Peace and quiet. Imagine lying on a chaise longue on your balcony, you who have never known a balcony in your life. A little cigarillo in one hand (that's right, a woman can't give up everything), a Cherry Delight in the other, and a bottle of real champagne floating in the ice bucket. Your eyes, your entire body focussed on the delightful tastes flowing down your throat. Reading perhaps, movies definitely. Long walks for a woman who went everywhere in her phaeton that probably was nothing but an ordinary carriage, actually.

Between these activities ...

Nothing?

Anxiety?

Panic lurking, to be kept at bay through sheer courage and denial? Isn't idleness the mother of madness?

So, no idleness. Ever. Keep busy. Like right now, find something to do, unwrap the packages she brought back from the shops on Mont-Royal, containing the embryo of a new wardrobe, the bare essentials, underwear, "housedresses," slippers, toiletries.

No. She'll never succeed.

She's meant for something else. Another life. She's not meant to end her life like this.

To prevent herself from grabbing her suitcases full of money and running to Windsor Station to catch the first train home to Ottawa, to her suite in the Château Laurier, the sheets with the scent of her beloved gardenia, the arms of smelly, ungrateful men, she places the palm of her right hand on the mirror.

And for several minutes she contemplates the bluish veins, the ugly liver spots, the irreversible signs of aging.

Some things don't lie.

THIRD CHANCE ENCOUNTER

An Unexpected Partner

Stepping out of the elevator on the ground floor, she stops the first bellboy she sees.

"Excuse me, where is the bar?"

The young man looks her up and down, clearly wondering, who is this woman, attractive despite her outdated clothes, in such a hurry to find the bar. On her own.

"You have to go through the rotunda, it's on the other side. It's brand new and real nice. It's the talk of the town. Everyone's comin' to see it. At least, everyone who can afford it."

He leads the way. She follows.

They cross the magnificent rotunda that she hadn't had time to admire when she arrived, all marble and gold, with the largest chandelier she's ever seen hanging from the ceiling. Beautiful? Well, impressive at least. Lots of wrought iron. A huge lamp shaped like a flame, electrified and glowing amber, undoubtedly to flatter the ladies' complexions, filled the lobby with a soft, soothing light. The employees are in their positions behind the reception desk – the cashier who just made a little fortune off her greets her with a bow – the concierge is deep in conversation with a cigar-smoking man talking in a loud voice – might he be looking for a woman like her, is there a Ti-Lou on one of the upper floors of the Windsor waiting for the phone to ring so she can grab her prophylactics and don her most indecent garb? – other guests are strutting around like birds in a cage. Priceless birds in a gilded cage. What are they looking for? The bar? The restaurant?

At the end of the hallway called Peacock Alley that is lined with shops and separates the two immense ballrooms is the famous bar.

Ti-Lou realizes she never could have found it by herself. Do people feel they have to hide to drink at the Windsor?

"You have a dining room as well, don't you?"

"We have two, Madame. One for the morning only and the other for the rest of the day."

The door to the bar is so ornately decorated with wrought iron, grape vines, varnished metal, and artfully set false gemstones that Ti-Lou feels like she's approaching the screen of a North African seraglio.

"It's still open, isn't it?"

"Yes. They keep the door closed to show it off, and to be able to open it individually for each customer. Will your husband be joining you in the bar soon?"

She stops in her tracks.

"What's got into you all today, always talking about my husband? I told the guy at the reception desk that I'm a widow, Widow Georges Desrosiers. Don't tell me you expect my dead husband to join me for a martini in the bar at the Windsor!"

The bellboy hesitates before answering.

"I'm sorry. I had no way of knowing."

"That's true, but do you have to mention their husbands to all the women who show up alone at the bar?"

Another hesitation.

"In fact, yes."

"What do you mean, in fact, yes? Why?"

The bellboy looks around, as if he didn't want to be heard saying what he was about to say.

"Well … women are not allowed on their own in the bar."

The sentence has been pronounced. She hears the gable slam down on the priceless carpet between her and the bellboy, the sound of irreversible, definitive rejection. Has Victorian censorship, the chronic illness Ottawa has always suffered from, reached Montréal? And yet Montréal has the reputation of being an open-minded city. Open, yes, but only to men? A Ti-Lou upstairs, but never there for everyone to see in the bar? Anglo-Saxon hypocrisy has invaded the French realm in the Americas?

"We seem to have a problem here. I told you. I'm a widow. Don't widows have the right to enjoy a drink before dinner?"

"Not in the bar. If they're unaccompanied."

"So what're they supposed to do? You want them to drink alone in their rooms because their husbands made the mistake of dropping dead too soon?"

"I don't know what to say, Madame."

"I can see that. Your mouth is hanging open like a dead fish."

"I'm sorry."

"You're not sorry at all. You don't mind sending a poor woman back to her room to drink alone, like an alcoholic, like someone who hides to drink! I've never hidden to drink, and I'm not about to start tonight. This is my only evening in Montréal and I want a drink before dinner. Surrounded by other people. If you don't open the pretentious gates to your damn paradise for me, I'll do it myself."

She reaches out to push the screen. It doesn't open. There must be some mechanism controlled by the bartender.

Are they going to leave her here, outside an iron gate, humiliated simply because she is unaccompanied?

The bellboy leans over to her.

Ti-Lou raises a hand to her forehead. Here comes the final blow.

"There's something else … You're not really dressed like a widow."

She turns to him and places a hand on his arm.

"I know there's a disguise for widows, I've been stuck with it for years. I'm supposed to hide behind a black veil and sniff as if I had a sinus infection, but my husband's been dead for a long time, I was fed up looking like an old crow, and I didn't want to wear black until the day I die. Is that so hard to understand? All I want is a drink before dinner. Don't tell me it's going to be the same problem in the dining room. Do widows have the right to eat here?"

The bellboy signals to the bartender. There's a click and the door opens ajar.

"Tell them your husband's on his way. They don't know you're a widow. That will give you time … time for a drink. And don't worry about the dining room. It's just the bar, you know, because of the kind of woman who could show up …"

"Maybe your bar would be livelier with the kind of woman who could show up..."

"You don't know that!"

"No, but I suspect it. I bet it's even worse than I imagine. I should've had a drink in my room. If your guests can't tell the difference between a widow and a floozie."

"The door's open, Madame. You can go in now."

Ti-Lou backs up a few steps.

"Will I be able to leave on my own? Or will I have to ask permission? Will I be a prisoner in a bar in a fancy hotel where the bartender and the bellboy get to choose the customers, then release them when they please? Have they lost their minds?"

"That's what they call an exclusive bar."

"That's what I call a useless bar. If I lived in this town, I'd spoil your reputation!"

She thinks that she does live in Montréal now, but she wonders whether she'll have the courage to denounce the policies at the Windsor Hotel. She doubts it.

The bellboy holds the door open.

"Don't worry about leaving, Madame. There's a button for the customers inside."

"That's reassuring. Floozies have to be able to escape."

"Few of them manage to fool us."

Ti-Lou laughs.

"You underestimate them. Maybe there are more than you think who manage to sneak into your bar under false pretenses. Take me, for example, I could be one."

"That's why we're careful, Madame."

"Does that mean you don't believe I'm a widow?"

"I didn't say that."

"Would you like to see my papers?"

"I wouldn't dare ask you that. I'm just a bellboy."

"All this makes me want to go have a drink in my room. You don't prevent women from getting drunk in their rooms, I hope?"

"What you do in your room is none of our business."

"But what I do in the bar is your business? That's absurd."

"The hotel's image is our business, Madame."

The bellboy is about to walk away, without asking for his due – he doesn't dare extend his hand for a tip – when a voice calls from the hotel lobby.

"Joséphine! Who would have thought I'd meet you here!"

They both turn to see.

A magnificent specimen of a man, dressed in the latest style, is heading towards them, his hands extended, all smiles, but, Ti-Lou notices immediately, the look of a predator and the canines of a scavenger.

A gigolo on the prowl. If he thinks he can fool her, he's wrong. She'll use him more than he could hope to use her. He called her Joséphine? We'll see about that!

"Althéode! My friend! Where have you been, for heaven's sake! I've been stuck here, like at the gates to paradise, because widows aren't welcome."

Did he understand the allusion to widowhood? If he's a pro, he did. And it's obvious he hated the name she gave him. Good!

"It seems to me, my dear Joséphine, you used to have a more affectionate name for me …"

"My bunny? That's not a more affectionate name, it's the name of a pet. Our petting days are far behind us, I'll stick to Althéode."

He blushed. Good. His name is probably Roger. Or Raymond. But his varnish is thick and well applied enough to create an illusion. He's a handsome beast. And she's known her share of animals.

She takes a dollar out of her bag, hands it to the bellboy.

"There you go."

"It's too much, Madame."

"You earned it. You defended the Victorian honour of your hotel and you almost saved me from drinking alone in my *sweet*."

He takes the money, bows deeply, and leaves.

Ti-Lou turns to Althéode.

"What should I call you? Lucien? Fernand? I hope you're going to spare me the sweet overtures. I've known hundreds like you and I'm too tired to play the game. I just want to use you to get into this bar, I hope that's clear, and the flirting ends there."

He is clearly stunned but tries hard to conceal it.

Ti-Lou smiles.

"I don't know what kind of swindler you are, but watch out, I've known all kinds and never in a hundred years can you prey on me without losing some feathers, but if you want to have a drink with me, just one, be my guest. I told them I was a widow, I'm not, but I do want to have a drink in their damn bird cage."

While the lobby of the Windsor Hotel strives to look bright and modern, the bar, on the other hand, looks like a nineteenth-century London club: leather armchairs, upholstered booths with brass tacks, a bar carved out of what seems to be a single slab of precious wood, false gas lamps that run on electricity, dark corners for private meetings or clandestine dates, a more open central area for those who want to be seen – already full at this hour of illustrious nobodies and wannabes constantly looking to see who has noticed them – and the smell of priceless cigars that drowns the scent of wealthy women's expensive perfume that could make the place more welcoming. It is anything but welcoming. It would like to be, but everything, from the heavy draperies on the windows to the ornate Turkish carpets, the panelling with overly bevelled two-way mirrors that reflect nothing, suggests repressed pleasure, the reluctance to be seen drinking in public, and what the Anglo-Saxons call British wit or irony to hide gross ignorance and the lack of any true sense of humour. If they laugh, it's too loud, to hide the idiocy of what was just uttered, and otherwise, they drink in silence. Bottoms up. Even the women, who are clearly bored stiff. And have been for ages.

Victoria has been here, and her puritanism is hanging on for dear life.

Althéode leads Ti-Lou to one of the comfortable but anonymous armchairs set on either side of a low coffee table where a pretentious menu with a gold cord and tassels is prominently displayed.

"This is my favourite place. We can see everything without being noticed."

Ti-Lou removes her gloves and places them on the menu.

"Good Lord, are you a professional thief? Do you dress up like a black cat to sneak into hotels? Have you read too many Arsène Lupin novels?"

She notices that he hesitates a few seconds before answering and she assumes that she has hit the nail on the head and is facing a hotel burglar. A very handsome hotel burglar. Perhaps he takes her for a pickpocket or for ... what she is.

He gestures to the bartender.

"A thief, no, but I do have a profession."

After ordering – a double martini for himself and a Between the Sheets for her – he looks her in the eye.

"I recognized you. Even from behind."

She prevents herself from reacting. How can he recognize her? An ex-client? No. She'd remember.

"From Ottawa. In case you're wondering."

"Did we meet in Ottawa? When was that?"

"No, we didn't meet in Ottawa, but that's where I saw you at work."

She blanches. A policeman? A hotel policeman who traps women like her who dare to force their way through the fancy doors to this damn bar? Will he grab her by the nape of her neck and throw her out? In front of everyone?

He leans over to her and places his hand on her arm.

"Don't worry. I work the same trade as you."

A gigolo! What are the odds of meeting a gigolo her first night in town! Certainly he can't think ...

Their drinks arrive. They toast each other like old friends. The Between the Sheets is delicious, both velvety and tart.

"Whenever I went to Ottawa, for work, I managed to run into you, Ti-Lou. So I could watch you. Admire you. Observe your every gesture, your repartee, the way you hold your head, smile, laugh ... your elegance, Ti-Lou, at all times and in all company. The more vulgar the man, the more divine you were. I've never been able to imitate you. The more vulgar they are, the more I want to disappear. Not you. I've never understood how you do it. To operate in that scene and remain the most beautiful woman in Ottawa.

A heart of stone? If that was the trick, I envied you. Whenever they were handsome, or somehow attractive, I was proud, but I was so ashamed when they were too vulgar."

Ti-Lou frowned and he noticed.

"Yes, I said *handsome*. I'm a prostitute ... for men ... just like you."

Ti-Lou registers the shock.

She takes a sip of Between the Sheets to buy time, to regain her composure.

"Well you're pretty frank, I must say."

"I wanted you to know who you were dealing with right away."

"Why? So I wouldn't think you were flirting with me?"

"Yes. So you didn't think –"

"I just retired, Althéode, and I would have rejected you anyway."

"My name is Albert."

She smiles, finishes her drink with her eyes closed.

"I prefer Althéode. It's more original."

"It's more ironic, too. You were mocking me. You couldn't mock someone named Albert, it's too ordinary."

"That's true."

She had met a few like him in Ottawa. Older ones whose reputation was known for years and who, for the most part, carried their burden with discreet shame. If they were affluent, powerful (ministers of justice or of the church), they were left alone, their situation simply hinted at, they were referred to as "confirmed bachelors," and high society in the federal capital draped itself in hypocritical propriety and pretended not to know. Especially when it came to priests. People referred to the young men who accompanied them as "secretaries," and would burst out laughing behind their backs and imitate effeminate gestures, usually imagined because most of the time there was no such behaviour. On the contrary, these men often felt obliged to demonstrate a certain virility, they courted women, sometimes with almost ridiculous ardour. They knew that people knew and they exploited hypocrisy and ruses to be accepted. If they were younger, however, people didn't hesitate to make fun of them openly, hinting broadly, because everyone was convinced they were incapable – too weak or fearful – of reacting like real men, and that sometimes led to violent confrontations in the middle of a ball or a gala. The truth was never mentioned, the word never spoken, but everyone knew why so-and-so were arguing or insulting each other. If these men had no connections, no protection, they were promptly excluded, they disappeared, even when they were qualified for the tasks they'd been assigned to. If they were the "secretaries" of powerful men, people resorted to jostling them in the hallway or giving them sly smiles clearly meant to be interpreted as warnings or obvious threats.

The young secretaries were not, however, considered prostitutes, but protégés. While the magnificent specimen of a man sitting across from her, his legs crossed, holding a glass, comfortable in his tailored suit and his probably Italian shoes, had just admitted to a trade she'd never suspected existed.

She throws her head back and laughs because she doesn't know what else to do.

"So, if I understand correctly, you're one of my competitors."

He laughs in turn. His laughter is less forced. He looks amused by her reaction.

"But my clientele is different from yours."

She feels like taking off her hat without asking permission, just as she did at the tea salon earlier. She feels hot, a bit short of breath.

"If I had known you existed, I could've sent you some of my clients over the years. Because sometimes ... you know ... I sensed something in them –"

"– that you disapproved of?"

"Not at all! I'm not narrow-minded! Not in my line of work! That's yours as well."

He's standing and bows to her.

"Excuse me. I didn't mean to insult you."

"Sit down. And order us another round of drinks."

He signals to the waiter who hurries over to the bar.

"Did I shock you?"

"Don't be silly. With the life I've led ... You didn't shock me, but you surprised me."

"Would you like to know more?"

"Yes, I want to know more."

"You're apt to be disappointed. My experience probably isn't very different from yours."

Indeed, what he tells her is surprisingly like her own experience over the past thirty years: the boorish behaviour of men would seem to be the same, no matter what their sexual preference. Albert experienced the same humiliations, the same adulations, adoration so outrageous it was frightening, deceitful flattery, and the post-coital sadness or shameful guilt because of the client's profession – family, wife, and children – and violence even, but less often than her because Albert is a well-built, muscular man no one would want to provoke. And money, of course, but in his case, money quickly spent because it always burned a hole in his pocket as a young man.

"I've reached the age where I should think about retiring like you, with dignity and no regrets, but I never thought about the future, never looked ahead, I began saving too late so now I have to haunt hotels and dark corners and parks looking for potential clients because I don't have enough money to feel secure. I still find lots of clients, bunches, because there aren't that many of my kind, and I can hardly meet the demand, but I'm not what I used to be, as they say, and I know it, I can see myself aging, I'm horrified to think about the day when the appeal's gone, when I can't create the illusion. It might be the oldest profession in the world, but it's no life."

She has finished her second Between the Sheets. She sipped on it listening to him talk. This is the first time in her life she has been the confidante of someone who, like her, earned a living as a prostitute, and it's a man.

"It's true. It's not very different. We've had the same life –"

"– except I didn't spend more than thirty years in a gilded cage on the top floor of a fancy hotel. I've known lots of fine hotels, the fanciest, the most elegant, in Montréal and elsewhere, but always one night at a time."

"Would you have liked to have a gilded cage?"

"When I thought about you, during my trips to Ottawa, in your famous suite in the Château Laurier, and the … let's call it the stability of your situation, for lack of a better word … yes, I envied you. Is it true what they say, about the Cherry Delights?"

"How do you know that?"

"Everyone knows. It's one of Ottawa's most famous legends. Even people who never met a floozie in their lives have heard about it. The suite, the Cherry Delights … Do you realize what that meant for someone like me? Me, with my little downtown apartment. That's where I bring my clients who can't afford better. The ones who pay me less because I'm attracted to them, the ones I pick up at the end of a night when nothing better has shown up. Ten bucks is ten bucks, right?"

He uncrosses his legs, leans over to her, puts his empty glass on the table.

"When I saw you a while ago, I couldn't believe it! Ti-Lou, in person! I recognized you from behind. Just goes to show you. I was coming from the fifth floor where I left a family man in tears because of what he just did with me, I needed a pick-me-up before going on the prowl again, and I saw that stupid kid stopping you from entering this bar."

"He wasn't stopping me. He was explaining what the hotel policy was. You don't have that problem, nobody stops you from entering a bar."

"They'd stop me if they knew what I was up to."

"But it doesn't show with you."

"It doesn't show with you, either. You have too much class."

"Anyway, thank you for coming to my rescue."

"It's an honour. One of the highlights of my last few years. Would you like another drink?"

"No, I drank enough. I should eat something. I just hope they don't stop false widows from eating alone in the Windsor dining room."

He hesitates before answering. He lifts his hand to his neck, like a woman who wants to hide the nascent wrinkles or the ugly folds that have begun to appear under her chin.

"Would you do me the honour … would you do me the honour,

Madame Ti-Lou, of dining with me? Their chateaubriand bouquetière is famous in Montréal and I've never tasted it. Let me treat you. Please."

The dining room looks like a wide corridor that has been transformed to accommodate a huge wedding party: four very straight rows of tables under a high ceiling outrageously decorated with pastel coffers and featuring the inevitable chandelier, the emblem of wealth and good taste in some circles. Everything is showy, so the food must be good.

Ti-Lou hated the decor immediately. She feels as if she's eating in a military armoury disguised to create the illusion of a chic restaurant.

It's true, however, that the food is excellent.

The chateaubriand was perfect: the meat rare, the vegetables crisp, the sauce neither too thick nor too liquid. And the wine, chosen by the snobbish, condescending sommelier, was a divine match for the menu. Ti-Lou spoke very little during the meal, she let Albert wander through his memories so similar to hers. He made her laugh describing the sometimes amazing eccentricities of certain clients, moved her when speaking of the solitude of individuals like them, golden pariahs, condemned by the very people who adulate them, powerful in an underground society of intrigue and betrayal, but helpless in the official world where everyone acts as if they didn't exist. Phantoms of the night – or early morning – forgotten as soon as their visitors closed the door behind them. Ti-Lou felt as if she was listening to herself speak, as if she was looking into a mirror and seeing a sort of masculine twin, younger but also aware of what awaited him, relating her own story. How often she had needed to confide in someone, as he was doing now, without ever finding an interlocutor because the company she kept – all men, without exception – only wanted one thing from her.

After dessert and coffee had been served, he lit a cigarette, having asked her permission.

"I had another reason, other than wanting the pleasure of your company a bit longer, for asking you to join me for dinner."

She takes a last sip of coffee, cold and bitter, puts down the pale green cup of china so fine light shines through the swirls of the floral motif.

"If you want to borrow money from me, let me stop you right there. I've got some, it's true, but I saved it for my old age and I'm afraid that time has come. My money is for my old age, not someone else's."

He puts out his cigarette in the ashtray that's as delicate and ornate as Ti-Lou's coffee cup.

"You don't know me, Madame Ti-Lou, it's true, but still, I'm surprised you see me like that. Do I look like a profiteer?"

"I didn't say I thought you were, I just said that in case ..."

"Well, don't worry. I can take care of myself. Even if I started a bit late, I'll manage. No, listen ... I wanted to talk to you about something else. I've always thought we'd make a great team, the two of us."

"A great team? You want us to work together? I've been telling you all evening that I've retired. For good. I haven't come to Montréal to work with someone, I've come to Montréal to hide, to disappear, to live the boring life of someone who hopes to be able to rest, even if I'm not sure I can. I came to croak anonymously, like someone who's so alone, she doesn't even remember that others exist! I'm fed up with people, Albert, I've had enough."

"Listen to me before getting on your high horse."

"I don't want to listen to you, can't you understand that?!"

"Just two minutes."

"Okay. In two minutes, I'm going to raise my hand to ask for the bill."

"I'm the one who's supposed to do that. I'm paying."

"Well, I'll do it, if I can't stand it anymore, and I'll pay myself."

She leans over and places her hand on his forearm.

"I think you're really nice, I'm actually happy to have met you, you're amusing, full of vitality, but I've had enough, I don't feel like meeting people anymore."

"Why?"

"What do you mean, why?"

"Why? There's no reason –"

"You've been in this profession long enough to know there are lots of reasons."

"Listen to me. Since we came into this dining room, I noticed at least two men looking at you, and one who was looking at me."

"Don't you think I noticed them, too? I can tell you where the ones who were looking at me are sitting. I can even describe the hats their wives are wearing. But yours, I don't know where he's sitting, because I'm not interested in him. So if we were associates, what would we do? Eh? I never stooped to doing that in a restaurant and I'm not about to start today."

"It would be easy for me, all I'd have to do is get up and head for the men's room."

"Right, everything's easier for men. Even that, apparently."

"The two of us could have a plan … You could pretend to want to make a phone call, or whatever, while I'd sit here, twiddling my thumbs, looking innocent. You'd let him follow you, approach you and make a date …"

"Your two minutes are almost up, Albert, and so far, they haven't been convincing."

"You keep interrupting me."

"Speaking of interruptions, there's the maître d'. Do you want something else?"

Albert simply asks for the bill.

"I guess there's no point, you don't want to listen to me."

"No, I don't want to listen to you, that's obvious. Why would I? I'm not interested in what you have to offer."

"You're not interested in making more money?"

"No. I think I have enough."

"We never have enough."

"Maybe at your age it's true. But I can get by on less from now on."

"Are you sure? After the lifestyle you've had?"

They fall silent because the waiter is returning with the bill. Which he places in front of Ti-Lou.

A brief moment of embarrassment.

Albert grabs the bill.

"I'm paying!"

The waiter bows, red as a tomato.

"I'm sorry, I thought..."

And he backs away, still practically bent in half.

Albert puts the money, apparently a lot of money, on top of the bill.

"Is that what you want? To look like the one who's paying from now on?"

He shoves the bill aside and it falls on the floor along with the bank notes. He doesn't lean over to pick them up.

"We wouldn't have to work all the time, Madame Ti-Lou. Maybe I would, yes, because I need to, but not you. Just a bit of extra spending money, as they say. Wouldn't you like that? We could... we could meet in a fancy hotel on the pretext of having supper together, not just here, there's the Ritz, the Mont-Royal, there's lots of them!"

"I never worked the hotels, and I won't start at my age."

"What difference would it make, you're not close to home."

"Sooner or later, they'd recognize us... in the hotels and restaurants."

"We'd go to a different place every time. And only go back after a few months..."

"We'd do it right there? We'd go to the rooms upstairs with the clients?"

"That's what I already do."

"I never had to do that, Albert! Never!"

"Try, just for fun. Don't take it seriously."

She starts to stand up. She's leaving. Albert holds her back, taking her hand.

"I know what you're going to tell me. You've always taken your work seriously. I'm not asking you to change. What I meant is... It's the way you approach it that could change, Madame Ti-Lou. You wouldn't have to do it every day, we'd call each other, we'd make an appointment, you could say yes or no, we'd go for dinner in a fancy hotel or a fancy restaurant ..."

She withdraws her hand and turns to leave the table.

"People are starting to look at us. Follow me, we can go for a walk outside if we want to go on talking ..."

It's a mild April evening. Soon it will be May, with the buds bursting, the scent of lilacs that brings tears to your eyes, at long last, the hope of longer days – warmer, dry, or slightly humid – light jackets, and the pleasure of aimless walks like this.

They had already walked around Dominion Square twice. And twice they had run into the man walking his dog Ti-Lou had seen from the window of her suite earlier. Ti-Lou thought that he took really long walks with that dog ... Was he actually looking for a woman like her, or a man like Albert? Was Dominion Square a hangout for men like Albert? And how could anyone leave with someone picked up in a park? Especially given the look that one had given her when they walked by each other. This was the first time she'd thought about men like Albert. Until tonight, they'd been rather unreal entities she'd never had any contact with. She glanced at him several times. Many a woman would have given anything for him. She herself, younger ... She leaned on his arm. No sexual tension passed between them. And that was a relief.

Meanwhile, Albert was making plans. He was planning crazy outings that always ended with a little fortune to be shared between them, the money spent in the restaurant reimbursed three or four times by what he laughingly called "the evening's earnings." They'd have fun and earn so much money!

She let him ramble on. What he was offering was quite ingenious, and tempting, but she remained adamant. At least so she thought. She would see him again, however, she'd give him her address, let him know when she had a phone, but as for the rest ...

Perhaps, once in a while ... for some extra spending money ... for fun ... No. Don't even think about it. Not right now, at least.

She knew it wasn't nice of her to let him dream, let him hope. Something was preventing her from sending him off, discouraging him, telling him NO, irrevocably, definitively. For the first time since her first visits to Dr. McKenny, she had the feeling she'd stumbled on the rare treasure that life rarely offered: a friend.

FOURTH CHANCE ENCOUNTER

A Virago from Ottawa

Stepping out of the elevator on the ground floor, she stops the first bellboy she sees.

"Excuse me, where is the dining room?"

"We have two, Madame. One for the morning only, and the other for the rest of the day."

"It's obvious I'm not looking for the morning one, isn't it?"

Ti-Lou immediately regrets her words. Especially the tone she used.

"I'm sorry, I'm hungry and that puts me in a bad mood."

The bellboy lifts his little red cap.

"This has to be the first time a guest has apologized to me! ... I'll take you there, just follow me."

She follows his lead.

"It's not very crowded at this hour. Will your husband be joining you?"

She shrugs.

"How come everyone keeps asking me about my husband? My husband's dead. Don't tell me they won't let me in the dining room because I'm alone!"

"Of course, not. That's not what I meant ..."

"I'm sorry, again, I don't know what got into me."

"My God, twice in the same day!"

The two dining rooms and the bar are at the end of a hallway called Peacock Alley that is lined with shops and separates the two immense ballrooms. Ti-Lou realizes she never could have found it by herself and she hands the bellboy a dollar bill.

"That's too much, Madame."

"No, it's not too much. I was rude with you."

He takes the money, bows deeply, and leaves.

After being asked once again, this time by the maître d', if her husband will be joining her, Ti-Lou is led to a table in a far corner of the dining room. Obviously, women on their own are not welcome. Or let's say they're "frowned upon."

She orders a glass of white wine and a dozen oysters. For starters. She'll see afterwards. The waiter, for menu-management reasons, he claims, insists that she order her entire meal right away; she replies that she might not order anything else, and, since the dining room is almost empty, she hardly thinks there could be a menu-management problem. This time she doesn't regret her words. Or her tone.

He leaves in a huff. That one won't be getting a big tip, she thinks, smiling to herself.

The wine arrives promptly. Good. Cool. She closes her eyes briefly. Sighs. Trying not to think about what's in store for her the following morning. The new life. Real solitude after a false public life. She was often seen in public but was rarely taking part. Goddess in the bedroom, pariah everywhere else. When she closes the door behind her in her new apartment tomorrow ... a little shiver. Isn't all this a bit radical? Her decision? She could have done it gradually, why did she feel obliged to drop everything and disappear? Was she really that fed up? Yes. Oh, yes. She thinks about what she'd be doing if she were still at the Château Laurier and expects a little shiver of anticipation that fails to happen. The leisurely bath before all the lotions and the gardenia perfume that men can't resist. The wait for the phone call announcing her first visitor. The disappointment, most of the time, as she faces what she'll be subjected to in the following hours. The sickening smell of cigars, afterwards, the lewd laughter, the bawdy jokes, the slap on her buttocks as if she were a mare, the money left on the night table ...

She picks up her glass of ice water and holds it to her forehead.

Finished. All that is finished. But to be replaced by what? A woman at the window, or curled up on a sofa, rubbing her leg that is beginning to hurt more and more? Books falling from her hands? Magazines whose superficiality no longer interests her because she no longer has to think about her appearance?

When the oysters arrive, she is about to order another glass of wine and does so, because she knows she won't have enough to see her through the platter of oysters on the half shell.

They're delicious, plump, juicy, and, most important, not at all milky like the ones in most Ottawa restaurants. The first one, with a touch of wine vinegar and minced shallot, tickles the inside of her mouth. It tastes of the sea. And she sees herself at the beach in Kennebunk, with … with whom? She can't even visualize his silhouette. She remembers they were both wearing white linen, but –

She starts. Someone has just taken a seat across from her. She saw a shadow, a hand withdraw the chair. She looks up.

And sees a matron. Massive. Shoulders as square as her jaw. An arrogant bust and a haughty mouth. Skin the colour of lard. Everything she's wearing, meant to appear young and fashionable, underscores this ridiculous woman's pathetic attempt to look modern: the cloche hat sporting one stiff, black aigrette that seems to want to escape to the ceiling, the emerald green sequined dress too tight under the arms that emphasizes the rolls of fat, her numerous necklaces spilling loosely over her vast bosom, the pale makeup that makes her look like a clown, and the ruby-red lipstick that suggests a mouth chapped by the cold and unable to thaw.

This is the wife of one of Ti-Lou's most faithful clients, an anglophone senator who frequented the Château Laurier for close to twenty-five years and who, over those years, must have spent a fortune on Cherry Delights, on flowers and tumbles between the sheets.

Ti-Lou can't remember this woman's first name. And yet, she'd often heard talk of her, nothing good, for the better part of her life. Theresa? Madeleine? Connie?

Whatever. Theresa, Madeleine, or Connie is staring at her so furiously, Ti-Lou realizes that she knows everything, that perhaps she always knew everything, and that her hatred for her is limitless. Almost comical, in fact. If they weren't in a public place, Ti-Lou would tell her to relax, to get over it, that she had done her a favour because, according to her husband, she didn't enjoy that business, that she, Ti-Lou, had spared her years of the assaults that she feared and found disgusting. In fact, she should be thanking Ti-Lou ...

Juanita! Juanita St. Clair! How could she have forgotten a name like that? She almost shouts it out loud but catches herself. How did she come up with a name like that? She must be the only senator's wife in Ottawa named Juanita. A Latina – Cuban, Mexican, Guatemalan – who renounced her origins and her customs to embrace the toxic, unhealthy ways of her husband? Or a huge dowry from Brazil or Argentina who found her way to Ottawa to seal come dubious deal?

Juanita St. Clair hasn't said a word yet. She is simply looking daggers at Ti-Lou. Perhaps she's searching for the words to express her supreme contempt.

Ti-Lou, a woman who doesn't cower easily, decides to taunt her, just for fun. She picks up an oyster, adds a few drops of wine vinegar and says, in French:

"*Si vous permettez*, Juanita, I'll continue to enjoy my oysters. I prefer them cold and the ice is beginning to melt. I have eleven to go, and I wouldn't want them to taste of sludge."

On the heels of this provocation, as soon as she opens her mouth, Juanita St. Clair becomes lyrical. The words that escape her mouth are amazingly precise: not only does she know about her husband's assignations with Ti-Lou, it's as if she had been present! It's almost as if she perversely enjoys describing them. Her disgust for Ti-Lou's profession erupts in immense waves, in convoluted, endless sentences, she uses English adjectives Ti-Lou never heard before, she is both vulgar and virtuous, vulgar with this vocabulary surprising for a woman of her standing and virtuous in her obviously sincere reactions to her own words. She gets everything off her chest once and for all and what she reveals to her husband's once or possibly still mistress is incredibly ugly. A vicious mix of rancour and disgust and contempt. She stammers occasionally, she fulminates and belches, but always in a low voice. The few other diners around them must think that two old friends who hadn't seen each other for a long time have just met here by accident. Because throughout her monologue, Juanita St. Clair has been smiling. From up close, it's clearly a forced smile, it's clear she wants to bite her interlocutor, but from afar, it's probably convincing.

During this entire time, Ti-Lou is savouring her oysters. She even goes so far as to slurp a bit, to further enrage Juanita. She succeeds because at one point she sees her catch her breath, to prevent herself from scratching out Ti-Lou's eyes in front of everyone. Ti-Lou almost wishes she would. She would love to hit this fat dowager, suddenly, to make her fat flesh jiggle, rip off her aigrette, and wipe the ruby-red off her lips with a good slap in the face. Then she thinks, as she swallows her last oyster, in the end, Juanita is just a woman betrayed, undoubtedly humiliated, who for years had to swallow her rage and her pride, a victim, Juanita St. Clair is a victim. Another. Like the wives of all her clients. So many women betrayed to whom she had never given a thought.

Should she try to explain? There'd be no point.

So Ti-Lou lets Juanita talk as she finishes her second glass of white wine, without interrupting her, even smiling along with her.

She's almost beginning to like her and wonders how Juanita would react if she offered to be her friend.

The waiter comes to ask whether she would like to order another course, she answers no, but has the nerve to ask Juanita if she would like a glass of wine. Then she requests the bill. Senator St. Clair's wife pauses in her harangue during the waiter's brief presence, then resumes the minute he turns away from the table.

At the end of her monologue, she remains seated instead of promptly standing to leave the table, draped in her offended dignity. She was looking at Ti-Lou the entire time she was speaking to her, she even leaned across the table occasionally to emphasize what she was saying, but now that she has said everything she had to say, she seems to have run out of energy, as if the strength required for her declarations of hatred and frustration had suddenly disappeared, leaving her incapable of even standing up. Ti-Lou feels as if she is watching her deflate before her very eyes. All that's missing is tears, shoulders wracked with sobs, the lace hanky held to her eyes, a runny nose. Should she go to her rescue? Facilitate an honourable exit by leaving the table before her, once she has paid the bill? No.

Ti-Lou allows silence to descend between them. If Juanita regrets certain things she has said to her, or if she really doesn't have the strength to stand, that's her problem. And if she hopes her presence will weigh on Ti-Lou like a living reproach that refuses to go away, she's wrong. Ti-Lou doesn't have a guilty conscience, she's not in a hurry, and she will not leave the dining room until Juanita St. Clair has left.

A war of the nerves? So be it. She is prepared to spend hours sitting across from Senator St. Clair's wife. She'll have another glass of wine, she'll yawn, she'll toy with the silverware, fold and unfold her napkin, touch up her makeup, but she will not stand up first. She refuses to look like the one who wants to escape or is being chased away.

The bill arrives, Ti-Lou takes the money out of her purse, places it on the tablecloth. The waiter leaves, frowning. The woman who was talking is silent, the one who didn't say a word still hasn't said a word. What is going on at table eight?

After ten long minutes – which seemed longer than she ever could have imagined – Ti-Lou realizes how ridiculous the situation is and decides to make a tiny concession. They can't spend the night sitting in the dining room at the Windsor Hotel dumbly staring at each other! Everything has been said, the scene is over, a satisfactory ending for both protagonists has to be found. She sits up straight, takes out the gloves she'd neatly folded in her purse and starts to slip them on. She speaks to her in English, to make sure Juanita will understand.

"Listen, Madame St. Clair. I don't want to look as if I'm being chased away, you don't want to be the first one to stand up, so why don't we do it together? Like children, we'll count: one, two, three, go … And on go, we will both stand, turn our backs to each other, I'll leave the dining room, and you will go back to the meal that has had time to congeal in your plate … Agreed?"

Juanita St. Clair doesn't answer.

Ti-Lou leans over the table.

"Madame St. Clair, I just found a solution for both of us. I know you don't want to give in, but I'm warning you, I'm capable of holding my ground as long as it takes. I'm pigheaded, and I won't let you win! And I know you want to avoid a scandal..."

Juanita St. Clair lowers her head after nodding in agreement.

Ti-Lou has finished slipping on her gloves and adjusts the hat she wore during her entire meal.

"Good. Thank heavens. Because it would have been long. But before I leave, I want to tell you something. I understand your reaction, I probably would have done the same thing in your place. If it made you feel better, I'm glad. You did it with a lot of elegance and discretion. But you have to know, it didn't change a thing for me. I've never had any regrets, never felt any remorse, and what you told me doesn't change that. I have never solicited anyone, the men I've known have all come to me, and if you, their legitimate spouses, wanted to keep them, you should've figured out how to do it! My entire life, all I've done is meet a demand, period."

She pushes back her chair, leans on the table.

"Okay, now ... One, two, three ... go!"

It's a surprisingly mild spring evening, although it had been quite cool most of the day.

A scent that couldn't be the smell of flowers, it's too early in the season, tickled Ti-Lou's nostrils the minute she stepped outside the hotel. Too unnerved by the scene with Juanita St. Clair to go directly upstairs to her room, she decided to take a walk in Dominion Square across the street.

The doorman lifts his red cap with the khaki visor.

"Do you want a taxi, Madame?"

"No, thank you. I just want to take a walk around the square –"

"I don't recommend that, Madame."

"Why, is it dangerous?"

"No, but a beautiful woman like you, walking alone in a park at this hour ...".

She smiles and taps him on the arm.

"Are you afraid someone will mistake me for a floozie?"

He tips his cap a second time.

"That's not what I said."

"But it's what you meant to say."

"What I meant to say is ... There's a madman who goes around downtown attacking women these days ..."

"I can defend myself."

"... with a razor. They call him the Razor Maniac."

She laughs and walks down the concrete stairs.

"Sounds like a bad murder mystery ... Montréal policemen must think they're Sherlock Holmes! Montréal's too small to have a Jack the Ripper, honestly! I promise I'll be careful."

She can see the stars, many and bright, through the still-bare limbs of the trees in Dominion Square. In a few days, the buds will appear, in a few weeks they will burst. Cheerful tender green will replace the sad greys and browns of early spring. The lawn will grow, people will want to stretch out on it.

She recalls the magnificent May evenings on the banks of the Rideau River. The leisurely calèche rides, the outbursts of laughter, the illicit things that took place in her phaeton that titillated so many men, the lights of Ottawa going off, one after the other, always too early ... All this reminds Ti-Lou of Juanita St. Clair, the poor woman who'd had the courage to confront her, but hadn't dared go so far as to insult her out loud, in front of everyone, or to hit her, a well-placed slap in the face to erase once and for all the years of betrayal and humiliation. How does she feel now? Frustrated not to have gone farther in her abuse or violence?

For years, her clients' wives had been no more than furtive shadows glimpsed at balls or at the theatre, like a single woman, in fact, blurry, ethereal, a prototype who undoubtedly considered Ti-Lou an enemy, or at the very least a rival, but they remained faceless, with no real personality, a threatening silhouette – frightening because she heard the hateful comments that followed her everywhere – but never a victim. Whereas listening to Senator St. Clair's wife … What was this new impression, this new feeling? For women like Juanita St. Clair? How to name it? Compassion? She'd often made fun of these betrayed women she'd enjoyed imagining as silly, ridiculous, so why, all of a sudden … She stops in the central walkway of Dominion Square, at the foot of the monument to the heroes of the Boer War. Is she beginning to find Juanita St. Clair likeable? What's come over her? Finding that pathetic harpy with her ridiculous aigrette, bursting the seams of a dress meant for someone else, touching, moving, while she, Ti-Lou, should be offended, outraged even, that she dared accost her! She turns back to the hotel all ablaze on the other side of Peel Street. Is Juanita St. Clair eating a chateaubriand bouquetière or a seafood platter? And with whòm? Surely not with her husband, she wouldn't have dared approach her. Ti-Lou feels like crossing the street and rushing back to the dining room, to insist that the shrew apologize … or to sit down with her and offer her friendship.

Suddenly, she notices a silhouette on her left. The man walking his dog – for hours, since she'd seen him from her window earlier in the evening – is approaching her, his head down. She walks right over and addresses him:

"You've been walking that dog for hours! How long does it take for him to do his business? If he's constipated, give him something, for heaven's sake! And if you're looking for company, go walk somewhere else! Boulevard Saint-Laurent is full of loose women. This is the third time I've run into you in fifteen minutes, and you're bothering me! Is that clear?"

The dog began to bark at her. Furiously. But his master didn't look up. He even seemed to withdraw, as if he were afraid of Ti-Lou.

"Didn't I make myself clear? You want me to draw you a picture? I told you to leave me alone. Go away. Can't a woman take a walk after dinner? Tighten the leash on that damn dog and get out of here! Right away or I'm going to scream bloody murder! You see, the doorman at the Windsor heard me and he's looking this way! Leave before he calls the police!"

The dog was still barking and the man jerked on the leash. As he turns to leave, Ti-Lou hears him mutter:

"I'm sorry, Madame, I can't help myself."

When she reached the hotel entrance, the doorman tipped his cap once again and told her:

"There was a lady looking for you. She said she saw you leave the hotel. I told her you went for a walk. Did she find you?"

"No, but I'm sure a bit of fresh air will do her good."

The following morning, the front page of all the newspapers featured the same headline: THE RAZOR MANIAC STRIKES AGAIN!

The story reported the murder, the night before, of an Ottawa Senator's wife, Madame Juanita St. Clair, in Dominion Square at the foot of the Lion of Belfort.

Ti-Lou, who had left the hotel early that morning and hadn't read the newspapers, never found out.

FIFTH CHANCE ENCOUNTER

A Helpful Police Officer

Peel Street and rue De La Gauchetière are jammed with cars. The smell of horse manure no longer fills the air, automobiles must have taken over since Ti-Lou's last visit to Montréal. Taxis are parked outside the station entrance. The station doorman picks up her suitcases, his whistle has already attracted the attention of a driver. Ti-Lou hands a dollar bill to the porter, who tips his cap.

"That's too much, Madame."

"No, it's not too much. You waited while I went for tea, you earned it."

"I took my break while I was waiting."

"Well, you can have another drink on me with that."

He executes an almost comical bow and turns to leave.

Her bags are already in the trunk of the car, the doorman is holding the back door open, cap in hand.

But something is wrong. A doubt. She can't put her finger on it, a slight dizziness. Everything around her starts to spin. A doubt, that's it. A doubt cripples her.

The young porter is puzzled.

"Aren't you going to take your cab, Madame?"

She hesitates, looks at the driver, then the doorman. What is she feeling? A threat? No, it's more like anxiety, vague but disturbing. She tries to imagine herself arriving at her new apartment just as night is falling, the strangeness of an unknown place, a big apartment after the relatively compact size of a hotel suite, all those doors opening onto empty rooms located more or less at street level, after living for so long in the heights ...

The driver tucks his cap beneath his arm and approaches her.

"Did you have a good trip, Madame?"

"Excellent, thank you."

"Are you returning to Montréal or just here for a visit?"

"I'm arriving. To live here."

"Really? You don't have much luggage."

"My things will arrive in a few days."

"So where are you going, Madame?"

The moment of truth. She has to decide. She could take refuge in a fancy hotel suite – a world she knows – or muster her courage and... She decides without further thought.

"Boulevard Saint-Joseph, between Fabre and Garnier."

She finally gets into the cab, the doorman closes the door, and the car takes off.

It's quite a long way from Windsor Station to boulevard Saint-Joseph. As they cross a considerable section of the city where she'll be living from now on, Ti-Lou feels that slight dizziness again, something akin to doubt or a vague uncertainty that upsets her. She came to take refuge in Montréal, that's true, to lose herself here, to find peace and quiet and rest, but will she find that in this crush of humans rushing every which way, in this constant bustle – is it possible to rest in the middle of perpetual effervescence – perhaps she should have stayed where she was, found herself a little house in a remote neighbourhood of Ottawa where no one knew her and happily watched life go by from behind the lace curtains of a window, veiled in the mystery of her disappearance, a clandestine resident of a city where she had enjoyed a certain celebrity for so long?

No. Ottawa is definitely behind her, she will never set foot there again. She had no regrets as the train pulled out of the station, she shouldn't regret it now that she has reached her destination. Nevertheless, this crowd rushing around, the noise...

As they drive up Avenue du Parc she admires the brand new cross at the top of Mount Royal, the luminous cross that had been promised and took the city fifty years to deliver. They say

Mount Royal is one of the most beautiful parks in North America. Some day she must take a walk there. She's curious about shops along avenue du Mont-Royal, thinking that is undoubtedly where she'll go shopping, that she'll go as soon as tomorrow morning to reassemble her wardrobe. From head to toe.

She smiles. She feels like one of the queens of France who in days of old, upon crossing the border to get married, had to undress completely and change their clothes, leaving behind everything that came from their homeland, even the most intimate undergarments. Ti-Lou assumes that they kept only their dowry, to be given to their new husband, the king. She glances behind her. She is bringing her dowry with her as well. But to be kept for herself.

And yet, in a way, she has changed country, too: she has left the Anglo-Saxon rigidity of Ottawa to be immersed, at least she'll try to be immersed, in the Latin atmosphere, the unruly turbulence of Canada's metropolis, the city whose reputation is as scandalous as hers.

The driver is looking at her in his rear-view mirror.

"I'll go up Fabre and turn left on Saint-Joseph so you don't have to cross the street to your house."

She thanks him with a nod.

Rue Fabre is lined with huge trees that have yet to bud. Through the bare branches, she can see the sun about to set behind the rather drab houses.

The house where she'll be living on boulevard Saint-Joseph, three storeys, with balconies decorated with wrought iron railings, is made of dark brown bricks, more austere looking than she remembered. It's true, it was a lovely summer afternoon and the façade of the house was hidden behind the leaves of the trees, but this afternoon, although mild for this time of the year, it looks morose, stripped of any lively colours. No green anywhere, only grey. And the brown of the bricks. Cars are speeding by her house, honking horns. She wonders whether she'll be able to stand it. But after a while, you manage to ignore them, even forget their existence, she thinks. And if she remembers correctly, her bedroom is at the back of the apartment.

After paying the driver, she pushes open the little iron gate that surrounds the tiny front yard and walks up the four steps to the porch. She sets down her two suitcases, her overnight bag, and opens her purse. In one of the two compartments in her wallet, she finds the slip of paper folded in four where she noted the address and the owner's phone number, but not the key to the apartment. In a bit of a panic, she frantically searches through her purse. Everything is there, gloves, handkerchief, lipstick, compact, gardenia perfume, a second wallet she didn't realize she had … but no key.

She tries to recall her last gestures before leaving her suite in the Château Laurier. She doesn't see herself checking to make sure the key was there, she can't even remember the last time she saw it. Could it be in another purse, another wallet? Among all the things she left behind? What purse did she have when she rented the apartment? And why is the slip of paper folded in four there, but not the key?

Was she stupid enough to have forgotten the key in Ottawa?

Now she is truly panicked.

She sits down on the top step and empties her purse on the porch floor. No key. She searches inside, the lining is not torn, there is no false bottom. She can't very well knock down the door on her first evening. She takes her hanky and wipes her forehead, blows her nose. She has to find a solution, otherwise she'll have to spend the night in a hotel. She is about to stand up and go to ring the upstairs doorbell and ask the tenants permission to use their phone – in the hope that the landlord will be at home and doesn't live too far away – when a voice startles her.

"Is something wrong, my little lady?"

A policeman on horseback has just reined in his horse in front of the house. Too preoccupied by her ridiculous mistake and her growing panic, she hadn't heard him arrive, even though the horse's hoofs must have clattered on the asphalt of the boulevard. But with all the noise …

She immediately thinks of the two bags of money she put down by the apartment door. How to prevent him at all costs from dismounting and offering to help her, send him away claiming everything was fine.

"I can't find my key, but I'm sure it's here somewhere. Don't bother about me, I'll be fine ..."

He is already leaning forward, he has raised one leg and is about to dismount and join her on the porch.

"Really, don't worry, I'm always losing my keys and I always find them."

He ties the reins to a small tree. The horse snorts and whinnies. The policeman offers him something. A cube of sugar? An apple? Then he scratches his muzzle.

Ti-Lou can't help but notice that he's one hunk of a man.

"What will you do if you can't find them?"

She suddenly gives in, forgetting her bags of money, and proceeds to tell him her entire adventure, the train trip from Ottawa, the taxi ride through the streets of Montréal, her arrival at this apartment she's rented for one year, her panic when she realized she might have forgotten the key ... She's talking too much, too fast, too loudly. Will he find her suspect?

When she finished her tale – unnecessary except for the last bit – he smiles and shakes his head.

She points to the neighbour's door.

"I was going to ring the neighbours' bell and ask to use their phone. I have the landlord's number."

He pushes open the gate and walks towards her.

It's not just the panache of the uniform, he has the kind of face she likes: a square jaw, lively, intelligent eyes, a sensual mouth. A kind of youthful naïveté lights up his features, although he's certainly a few years over forty. Not much younger than her.

She closes her eyes briefly. Don't tell me she's going to succumb to a policeman's charms in a moment like this!

"You've come to live in Montréal for a year and that's all the luggage you have?"

She stands up and heads for her bags. If he asks to see what's in them, she'll scratch his eyes out!

"The rest is on its way … it will arrive tomorrow. This is just …
just the essential."

He has leaned against one of the columns supporting the roof
of the balcony.

"Go make your phone call, I'll guard your treasure for you."

If only he knew …

She pretends to laugh.

"My treasure, some treasure, really. It's just old stuff, some
old rags."

Shut up! He's going to think something's fishy.

She rings the doorbell upstairs. No answer. She tries the neighbour on the top floor. She explains her situation to a crotchety old
woman who refuses to let her in because she doesn't know her. The
policeman has to intervene and reluctantly the old lady lets Ti-Lou
use her telephone. It all takes place so fast, Ti-Lou can't believe it's
happening to her: the phone call, the landlord who lives a few minutes away, his promise to come immediately although he clearly is
not pleased – she has disturbed his supper, he claims – the old shrew
who is sizing her up as if she were a slab of meat on the butcher's
block, her return to the porch outside the apartment, the handsome
policeman who hasn't moved and who doesn't seem to want to leave
when she tells him everything's all right, the key is on its way, it's
all settled. The situation is absurd, she's confused, convinced this is a
bad dream, that she'll wake up any minute tucked into her big bed
at the Château Laurier and she'll burst out laughing.

"Do you mind if I wait for the landlord with you?"

What to say? She can hardly refuse, she nods. A strange smell
tickles her nostrils. She looks up and realizes that the horse has just
deposited some road apples. That's all she needed.

The policeman blushes.

"So sorry. I'll clean it up before I leave."

She finds his embarrassment touching. She's about to ask him
how he'll go about it and where he'll dispose of what he picks
up but thinks better of it. It would be cruel to embarrass him
even more.

"Don't bother ... there must be people who are paid to do that?"

"Well, yes ... but right in front of your house like this ..."

The landlord arrives at that moment. Ti-Lou had forgotten how ugly he was. Overweight, wobbly, badly shaven, a mean look in his eye. When he comes closer, she wonders if he has taken a bath since the last time she saw him, the year before.

"I've got better things to do than open doors. I have a plate of pork kidneys waiting for me."

The mention of pork kidneys makes Ti-Lou shudder with disgust.

The landlord notices.

"Here we go, someone else who thinks they're disgusting. I'll have you know they're delicious. Maybe not pretty, but really good."

"I believe you, but I'll give you my share."

"I didn't offer you any."

"I know, it was a joke."

"Stupid joke."

He opens the door and pushes it open without another word. She thanks him with a nod.

"I guess this means you left the key in Ottawa?"

"I'm afraid so. I'll bring this one back to you once I've had a copy made."

"Don't bother, I've got others. I keep a few for every apartment. Unfortunately, you're not the only one to lose her keys. I just hope you're not the kind who loses them all the time."

He turns towards the policeman who wrinkles his nose when he walks by.

"You really didn't have to call the police."

"I didn't call the police. He was passing by the house when I was searching in my purse. He offered to help me."

The landlord shrugs and as he goes down the steps, he notices the presents the horse has left on the street.

"If that hasn't been cleaned up by tomorrow morning, I'm gonna file a complaint with the city. It smells to high heaven!"

He leaves, limping.

The policeman takes off his cap, wipes his forehead, smiling.

"Pleasant character. And he's the last one who should complain about the smell. I hope his wife smells the same 'cause otherwise, I feel sorry for her."

A brief silence ensues. An awkward moment for both of them. The policeman clearly doesn't want to leave. Ti-Lou has just stolen a look at his left hand. No wedding ring. Surprising that a handsome man like him isn't married. She'd like to invite him in, but she can't find a pretext. Then he's the one who finds one.

"So now, let me help you with your bags."

She is about to refuse but realizes that might seem suspect. He leans over and lifts the two bags.

"Good Lord. These are heavy! What are you transporting in there, gold bars?"

She pretends to laugh.

"No, don't worry, my fortune is secure ..."

She has no idea why she said that, stops short in middle of the hallway, afraid he might ask her what she meant by that.

He arrives behind her. A bit too close. Apologizes.

The landlord did not smell good, but the policeman smells of fine-quality aftershave, the scent of pine, and the outdoors.

She walks down the hall to the kitchen and turns on the ceiling light.

"You rented the flat furnished?"

"For the time being. I intend to replace everything. If I stay long enough ..."

"You said you rented for a year."

"But I'll give myself the freedom to leave if I don't like it."

"Do you do this often?"

"What?"

"Move, on a whim, leave everything behind."

"It's the first time in my life. No, actually, it's the second time. The first time was when I left home, and believe me, I had good reasons. But I hope I'm going to like it here in Montréal, that I'll be happy here. I came to rest."

"You've chosen the right place. Boulevard Saint-Joseph is the most restful part of town."

"You mean it's boring?"

"I mean it's not the liveliest place."

"Maybe that's what I want. Lie low here …"

"A beautiful woman like you? That's criminal!"

He blushes suddenly. She acts like she didn't notice and goes to open the kitchen window, then the door.

"It smells musty. I'll have to air the place out."

She turns back to him a bit brusquely, extends her hand.

"I'd offer you a cup of tea or coffee, but there's nothing in the house. So, thank you for helping me … It was very kind of you …"

He seems to hesitate, blushes a second time, and takes the plunge:

"Uhhh … listen, since you've got nothing in the house, I feel sorry for you, all alone like this, the first night … What are you going to eat? I was thinking … don't get me wrong, but I was thinking … I know a good Chinese restaurant on Mont-Royal, not far from here. If you're not too tired … I finish work in an hour, I could come to get you … If you'd like, I don't want to insist … If you don't want to, that's fine."

Is this what she's been waiting for? Why is her heart beating so fast, like she was eighteen years old? She feels flushed, her hands are damp, she feels as if the She-Wolf of Ottawa has disappeared, leaving in her place a schoolgirl ready to fall into the arms of the first handsome guy who appears. Is it fatigue? Nerves? The fear of being alone?

She removes her hat in a gesture she knows is seductive, places it on the table, starts to remove her gloves.

"I have to warn you, I'll be wearing the same dress. Like I told you, my things will be arriving tomorrow."

He glances at her two suitcases.

"No, I don't have a change of clothes in there … just a nightgown … I realize now, I forgot … Well, okay … come back in an hour or so, and I'll do my best not to embarrass you."

His smile is devastating, a flash of straight, white teeth. He is visibly delighted.

"You won't embarrass me. I'll be proud to have you on my arm, Madame …??"

"Louise. Louise Wilson. From Ottawa, like I already told you."

He lifts his cap, bows his head slightly, she thinks he's about to kiss her hand. No, he turns around to leave.

"See you soon, Louise Wilson from Ottawa."

She hears the front door close.

She sits down on one of the chairs around the table, calls herself an idiot, and bursts out laughing.

The clawfoot tub, chipped in places, is enormous and deep. It takes up half the space in the bathroom. Undoubtedly a mistake, bought by someone who had no sense of proportion. The hot water comes from an old gas hot-water tank that protested a bit when Ti-Lou lit it, but it seems to work well. Soaking up to her neck, the pain in her leg somewhat eased, Ti-Lou allows herself to daydream. At first she chided herself for accepting the policeman's invitation – she doesn't even know his name – then she tells herself, for once she had the choice, she could have said no and she chose to say yes. For the past thirty years, she has made herself available to whomever would pay the price, she could never refuse, she waited, lying in her bed or languishing in her bergère, for the phone to ring to announce the arrival of a visitor whose whims she would have to satisfy. Or she would consult her gold-bound appointment book where she had noted the name or pseudonym of those who had taken the trouble – they were rare – of arranging their visit in advance. But now, on this evening in late April, and for the first time in a very long time, she could have replied with a firm but polite no, and the man undoubtedly would have left without protesting. Why did she accept? She stretches out her painful leg and vigorously massages her foot. To increase the circulation, to prevent the blood from coagulating or thickening, she can't really remember. A small, bitter smile. She will certainly have to find herself a Dr. McKenny here in Montréal. The neighbourhood is full of them, she noticed the nameplate of a Dr. Sanregret a few doors away when she came to rent the apartment.

Someone who will scold her when she's eaten too many sweets, someone who won't be too shocked by her past – although she could simply not reveal it – and who will try in vain, like his predecessor, to make her listen to reason. The same diagnosis, the same advice, the same reproaches. She adds a bit of hot water. She accepted the policeman's invitation because she was attracted to him, that's clear. She also accepted, she can't deny it, so she wouldn't have to spend the first evening of her voluntary exile alone. She would've had to have supper in a restaurant anyway, so why not in the company of a handsome man? She doesn't know the neighbourhood, he'll be able to show her around, tell her where to buy her meat, her fruits and vegetables – the thought of needing to cook for herself makes her panic briefly – and where to go shopping for clothes and shoes. She leans her head back and slides down into the tub. No excuses, no idle justifications, she simply doesn't want to be alone, why deny it? She thought she'd had her fill of men, forever, when she left Ottawa just hours ago, and here she is ... No, it's not true, she didn't throw herself into his arms, she did absolutely nothing to provoke this surprising proposal. It happened and she took advantage of it, period. Better than spending the evening wandering around this apartment, wondering whether she made the right decision, if retirement, so young, is really what she wants, if she won't go crazy all alone hibernating on boulevard Saint-Joseph after all these years of countless distractions to help her forget that she was alone. She was alone surrounded by men, and now she's sentencing herself to be alone without them. She steps out of the tub quickly and dries herself with an old towel hanging on a hook behind the door. So many things to buy! Linens because she refuses to sleep in sheets that belonged to people she doesn't know, pots and pans, because what she found in the kitchen was battered and scorched, along with everything else, everything else ... She mustn't let herself get discouraged, she should think about the time she's about to spend with her policeman, shy but bold enough to dare ask her out with him, even if he did blush. Fortunately, she does have a change of underwear in her overnight bag. Why is she thinking of that?! She has no intention of asking him to come home with her. None whatsoever! Now she has another half-hour or so. She hurries into what is now her bedroom, a lugubrious room with no personality. She will try to press her dress if by any chance the previous tenants have left an iron behind. Otherwise, she'll hang it up in the bathroom so the steam from the hot water can remove the creases.

They walked south on rue Fabre and crossed Gilford and then Mont-Royal. Ti-Lou kept stealing glances at Maurice – that's his name, Maurice Trottier – while they were walking. An intelligent profile, a high forehead, a straight nose, interesting mouth. Less impressive without his uniform, but a fine presence nevertheless. Not well dressed, however. In fact, he apologized, saying he wasn't expecting to go out for dinner with a beautiful woman after work. She took advantage of the moment to ask him why he wasn't married. He glanced at his left hand and replied that his wife and his daughter had died of the Spanish Flu in 1919. And he hadn't kept his wedding ring. He had buried it in his wife's coffin, on her hand. A memory of him for her to take along into the next world. He said "next world" as if he wanted to avoid the word "heaven." A freethinker? Or perhaps his faith was shattered the day of the unjust, cruel death of his wife and daughter? She apologized for her indiscretion, he said there was no offence, she couldn't have known. He added that he hadn't really sought the company of women since. That healing – if there is such a thing – had been long and difficult.

They entered a Chinese restaurant located above the Passe-Temps Cinéma – three films and an ice cream cone for ten cents – on Mont-Royal. The ceiling is low, the decor awful, the lighting brutal, the carpet worn, and the smells from the kitchen make her slightly nauseous.

Ti-Lou doesn't really care for Chinese cuisine, but she doesn't dare say so. The waiters greet Maurice with a smile, the hostess is beaming at him, he must be a regular customer, he seems to know the menu by heart and offers to order for both of them, and she accepts, thinking she'll barely touch what they serve her.

Much to her surprise, everything is absolutely delicious. She says so and he explains that he always orders what the Chinese customers eat, not the others who only know chow mein, chop suey, or chicken fried rice. He explains that what people usually eat in Chinese restaurants isn't remotely Chinese, it was invented in North America and is only a North American version of what the Chinese really eat.

"When you order a po-po platter, you should know there's nothing Chinese about it."

He leans a bit closer to say:

"It might not smell appetizing, but now you can see, it tastes pretty darn good!"

They laugh, the meal is pleasant, even though the lighting, too harsh for a woman who cares about her appearance, is dreadful.

After the fish served with a spicy, almost black sauce that burned Ti-Lou's mouth but she loved it, Maurice coughed into his fist and wiped his lips.

"You'll have to excuse me, but I have to speak to you as a policeman."

Ti-Lou has a moment of apprehension. Has he figured her out, has he guessed about her past, what she has in her suitcases? Has news of her disappearance preceded her? No, that's impossible, he wouldn't have invited her out to dinner.

"What do you mean?"

He folds his napkin and places it on the table.

"We won't order dessert. It's true, the Chinese aren't great with desserts."

She laughs.

"Is that what you call 'speaking as a policeman'?"

He still looks very serious.

"I just want to warn you about something. And tell you to be careful, you shouldn't go out alone at night. There's a guy who's been attacking women lately. With a razor. They call him the Razor Maniac. It's true that so far, he's only been operating downtown, but be careful. You never know ..."

Now she places her napkin on the table.

"Don't tell me you invited me out to supper to tell me this! You could've told me back at my apartment."

He blushes so deeply she has to hide her laughter behind her hand.

"No. I invited you because I wanted to. I ..."

He stops in the middle of his sentence. Ti-Lou realizes he'll say no more, that it would be too hard for him, that he can't find the words or he's too shy.

He goes back to the subject of the Razor Maniac, a field where he is more at ease, and as a good policeman who loves his work, he gives her more details, the number of victims, where and how they were found, the danger this represents for women who live alone, even far from downtown. She is looking at him with feigned concentration, because she is no longer listening. She has just realized the ridiculous situation she has put herself in. Perhaps they'll be searching for her by tomorrow morning, if not the police, at least the managers of the Château Laurier whom she failed to inform of her departure and who will suddenly find themselves without a resident floozie, an important source of revenue because her clients paid a handsome commission to the hotel which covered much more than the price of the suite. She left Ottawa with two huge bags of money that she's going to hide in the back of a closet like a thief – she has no intention of renting safety deposit boxes in Montréal banks – she has always lived like an outlaw, on the fringes of society, she is, what's the word? A renegade? A rebel? A hothead? And here she is in a Chinese restaurant on Mont-Royal in the company of a policeman she hardly knows, who obviously has a crush on her, whom she wouldn't want to manipulate or hurt. Suddenly she feels totally disarmed and impotent. She didn't do anything to encourage him, that's true, but she didn't do anything to discourage him either. On the contrary. Because she was looking for a distraction on this first evening of solitude, something to keep her mind off the thought of the life ahead of her. She should have refused Maurice's invitation, stayed at home, eaten the crackers she stuffed into her overnight bag before leaving in case she was hungry on the train, and waited until the following day to leave her apartment.

She should have begun her life as a recluse the night of her arrival, instead of postponing everything till the next day.

"You're not listening to me, are you?"

She is startled.

"I'm sorry. I'm tired. I had a big day, I should've stayed home."

"Do you regret accepting my invitation?"

"No, I simply regret that it was tonight."

"We can try again, if you want ..."

"We'll see, we'll see ..."

Another thing strikes her as he raises his hand to ask for the bill.

This is the first time, yes, she can safely say the first time that she has eaten in a restaurant with someone who was not part of Ottawa's elite. She looks around her. She is used to the flashy decor of fancy restaurants in the nation's capital, to the pretentious chandeliers, the thick carpets or the shiny hardwood floors, to the bouquets of fresh flowers between her and her hosts, to the annoying maître d's, the annoying sommeliers, the annoying customers. To rare chateaubriand bouquetière or filet mignon. And most of all, to the hostile looks from other women. Here, she noticed, the women looked at her with envy. Because she's beautiful and because she's accompanied by a handsome man.

Instead of feeling anxious, she feels a kind of relief she doesn't quite understand. Then a real excitement she can barely hide. If she's going to break loose, why not go all the way? Why lock herself up? Why worry about what Maurice Trottier might represent for her? Why not try to be ... happy?! She realizes that she didn't flee Ottawa to be happy, that hadn't even occurred to her, but simply because she'd had enough. She wasn't thinking about her well-being, or eventual happiness, she was content simply to flee without further thought, and here she is with a simple policeman who, although he never could have afforded to pay her a visit at the Château Laurier, is opening up new horizons.

New and enticing.

What if she were to devote the rest of her life to trying to be happy? She feels both ridiculous and exalted. This is childish, the dream of a pimply teenager, but good heavens it's exciting.

After leaving the Café Banquet, they casually tour avenue du Mont-Royal. Ti-Lou has allowed herself to take Maurice's arm, Maurice is showing Ti-Lou where she can go shopping the following day: L.N. Messier, the only department store on the street, with its windows full of clothes that she doesn't like – shapeless dresses that are too short and cloche hats – but will have to buy if she wants to look remotely modern in her new life. And Giroux et Deslauriers, next door, for shoes.

"I know Giroux et Deslauriers ... at least I've heard of it."

"Really? Giroux et Deslauriers is known all the way to Ottawa?"

"No, but I have a cousin who works there ... My cousin Teena."

"You know Teena Desrosiers?"

"Her mother and my mother were sisters."

"It's a small world!"

"You know her, too?"

"Everyone knows her. She's a great saleswoman. And she's the most amusing old maid in the neighbourhood."

He stops short and adjusts his raincoat.

"Sorry, I shouldn't talk about your cousin like that."

"Don't worry, it's true that she's an old maid. I saw her three years ago at my second cousin Nana's wedding and she was going through her change of life. She was something else, believe me."

"Well, we all want her to serve us when we need shoes. She knows her business. And she's so nice. Talk about a coincidence, eh?"

She smiles and takes his arm again.

"Yes, really, what are the chances?!"

She simply hopes Maurice won't mention her to Teena the next time he goes to buy shoes. Although she'd be surprised if Teena carried on about her cousin's previous profession.

"I'll go to see her tomorrow morning."

"Maybe she'll give you a discount ..."

Ti-Lou glances at the shoes on display in the window.

She never thought she'd have to face a member of her family

so soon after her arrival in Montréal. What will she say? I quit because I was fed up with earning my living on my back? Will she want to speak to her? Let alone serve her? But she was friendly at Nana's wedding. Unlike the other sister, Tititte, with her uptight airs. Unless there's another shoe store nearby. But what if Teena finds out she went somewhere else …

"Why the big smile? Do you really like those shoes in the window?"

"No, I just had a funny thought."

"You want to tell me?"

"You wouldn't find it funny … it's just that … no one in my family knows that I've arrived in Montréal."

"Do you have lots of relatives here?"

"On the Desrosiers side, yes. Quite a few."

"And you didn't tell them you were coming?"

"I left on a whim. But that's a long story, we can talk about it another time."

She realizes she just gave him reason to hope they'll see each other again. She glances at him. She catches a beautiful smile. The involuntary allusion hadn't escaped him.

They walk back up rue Fabre, in no hurry, and stop at the corner of Gilford.

"You see, there's two grocery stores here on the corner of Gilford and Fabre. Soucis and Provost. You'll find everything you need there: meat, fruit, vegetables … and it's right around the corner from your place. They both deliver, so once you have a phone, you can call. Monsieur Soucis still delivers by horse-drawn cart, but Monsieur Provost bought a car for deliveries. It's their sons who take care of that. And since they're right across from each other, they have a price war that works out fine for the customers."

"Do they open early? I don't have anything for tomorrow morning."

"Seven o'clock, they're open for business."

They walk the rest of the way in silence. The breeze is mild. The month of May isn't far away. Ti-Lou wonders if there are lilacs in the neighbourhood. She'd love to fill the apartment with armfuls.

To change the smell. And liven things up. In the meantime, she'll spray some gardenia scent.

When they arrive at her house, she wonders whether she should invite Maurice in for a few minutes, even though she has nothing to offer him to drink. Maurice hopes she will.

Ti-Lou pushes the little gate open.

"I'd invite you in for a nightcap, but as you know, I have nothing to offer you."

"Listen, I have an idea. If you'd like, I could come tomorrow morning with coffee, bread and butter and jam ... there must be a percolator in your furnished apartment. We could have breakfast together before I go to work. I work from eight to six. But if you want to sleep in, I understand ..."

After accepting his offer with a big smile, she extends her hand which, this time, he kisses.

"See you tomorrow, Mademoiselle Wilson."

"See you tomorrow, Monsieur Trottier. And don't you worry ... I'll watch out for the Razor Maniac."

EPILOGUE

MONTRÉAL, MAY 1926

"You still seeing your policeman?"

"You still seeing your Monsieur Rambert? When's the wedding?"

The tea set is on a little table between their two chairs. Maria brought a cake from a new Belgian patisserie on Mont-Royal near De Lorimier. She was on her way back from visiting her sister Teena who's been on sick leave for several weeks with terrible back pain, and she couldn't resist the temptations displayed in the window: single-crust apple pies, strawberry tarts with the fruit drowning in pastry cream, maple éclairs, and raspberry trottoirs, things that were unknown to Montrealers – at least those living in the Plateau-Mont-Royal neighbourhood – until the arrival of Monsieur Broekhardt. She hesitated for a long time before finally settling on a fraisier that struck her as the epitome of culinary decadence.

Marie licks her fork one last time, then takes a sip of her tea where cake crumbs and bits of sugar-coated strawberry are floating.

"One thing's for sure, you did a great job on your apartment."

The sky has begun to cloud over. Maria cranes her neck. Yes, it's going to rain. That will be welcome because it's been a dry spring and the young leaves on the trees are already a bit stunted.

"We should probably go inside, rain's on its way."

They're sitting on the balcony that the landlord has recently painted and that still smells of fresh paint, Ti-Lou in her rocking chair, Maria in a little wicker armchair they've brought out from the living room. Chirping birds are pecking at the young grass in the wide median strip on boulevard Saint-Joseph.

"No. The rain's coming from the west, arriving sidewise like that, it never reaches the balcony. Besides, I like watching it fall. Finish your tea."

"It's good."

"I found it in a store on Mont-Royal that's always empty. No one goes there, don't know how they manage to stay open. I swear I'm their only customer."

Maria clinks her spoon on the rim of the pretty, almond-green china teacup.

"You'd do anything to change the subject, Ti-Lou. You haven't answered my question."

"You didn't answer mine."

"You know very well I'll never marry Monsieur Rambert, but I don't know if you're still seeing your policeman."

Ti-Lou gives herself a little push with her feet and rocks in her chair, her teacup in her lap, for a good minute before speaking. The whole time she manages not to spill a single drop of the hot drink.

The rain arrives. The smell of wet asphalt fills the air. Passersby pick up their pace, a horse pulling a wagon full of blocks of ice for sale tosses his head and whinnies, with what sounds like pleasure.

"When I arrived in Montréal last year, there were no horses outside Windsor Station, so I thought there weren't any left in the city."

Maria sighs in exasperation and pours herself another cup of tea. Soon it will be time for her to leave, to get ready for her shift at the Paradise Club.

"Okay. I get it. Anyway, congratulations on what you've done to the apartment, pretty incredible compared to what it was the first time I came to visit."

Ti-Lou stops rocking and pours herself another cup of tea.

"I have to admit, Maurice helped me a lot."

Maria freezes. Did Ti-Lou just let that slip, or is she finally ready to talk about her policeman?

"That's right, his name is Maurice. I forgot."

"Yes, Maurice Trottier. And yes, I'm still seeing him. Actually, I'm seeing a lot of him."

"Is it serious?"

"We never talk about that. It'll last as long as it lasts."

"But it could last for a long time…"

"Yes, it could last for a long time."

"Do you hope that it will last for a long time?"

The rain is falling like a liquid curtain that separates them from the world outside. Maria figures she'll have to take a cab home. Ti-Lou feels like she's in a confessional at the bottom of a lake.

"I'm afraid to talk about it. Afraid it'll bring bad luck. You know, Maria … at my age, Maurice is the first man of my life. After the thousands of men I've known, thousands, Maria, Maurice is the first one who's not doing it with me because his wife is frigid, or because I'm a present courtesy of the Canadian government, or just to treat himself to a one-night stand. I'm not complaining, I chose that life for myself and I don't regret my years at the Château Laurier, that's not what I'm saying, but I'm having my first serious relationship at fifty! Other men have fallen in love with me, but I rejected them all. I never wanted to be in love, I never missed that. Maurice is different… I don't know how to put it. I had to change my life, change cities, to meet him. A crazy chance meeting that changed my life. And he arrived on horseback, like a real Prince Charming in a fairy tale. Sometimes I think he's too nice, too perfect… I don't mean I don't deserve him, I'm as deserving as anyone else, but… it's all about fate, Maria! I never thought about fate before today! Fate has been kind to me this year, but what does it hold in store for me next year? I don't want to be negative, never have been, I'm just… I don't know… cautious, I guess. He repainted the entire apartment, he helped me choose my furniture, he treats me like I'm the most important woman in the world, he's too perfect, Maria, it's impossible, such a perfect man. For the other men I've known… I was just… just a trinket, for my whole life, I was a trinket, then suddenly… I'm just a woman in love. And I'm scared. Because I feel like I'd die if he left me…"

Maria leans over the table and reaches out to place her hand on her cousin's hand.

"Does he know …?"

"About my past? Of course, not. I was the spoiled daughter of a senator in Ottawa who never got married because someone broke her heart when she was young."

"And he believes you?"

"That's right. He's naive to boot! Or else he makes himself believe he believes me. All he knows is that I'm diabetic. He even cured me of my Cherry Delights, imagine! I don't eat them anymore because he convinced me not to eat them. I'm laughing, but I'm not sure it's funny. He practically put me on a diet, Maria, I've almost accepted to eat reasonably, for him."

She puts her hand on her heart.

"Am I giving up my hard-earned freedom for a Montréal city policeman?"

Maria has to laugh at how serious Ti-Lou is.

"Why not? Just don't let him take over."

"Like you with Monsieur Rambert?"

"Like me with Monsieur Rambert. Does he have any kids, your Maurice?"

"No. Why?"

"If he doesn't have kids, he won't ask you to marry him. And that's just as well."

She stands up and brushes the crumbs from her skirt.

"It's stopped raining, I'm going to catch my tram."

Ti-Lou stands up and repeats her cousin's gestures.

"Come back soon. We don't see each other often enough."

"Maybe we should introduce our beaux to each other."

They laugh.

"I can imagine the scene …"

Marie pushes back her chair and picks up the tray with the tea set.

"I'll get my hat. By the way, you know … It's not true that the latest style doesn't suit you. Stop saying that. You look beautiful in what you're wearing. Besides, you'd look beautiful no matter what you wear."

"That's what Maurice tells me."

Maria turns back to her before entering the house.

"Maybe you're right. Be careful, he might be too nice."

Ti-Lou gives her a little slap on her bum.

After adjusting her hat in the big mirror still hanging on the back of Ti-Lou's bedroom door, Maria slaps her forehead.

"Oh! I forgot. Did Maurice tell you? They finally caught the famous Razor Maniac who's been killing women for the past year. Can you believe it? He'd go around pretending to walk his dog, so no one suspected him. One less madman in this city!"

She kisses her cousin on the cheek.

"Meanwhile, enjoy your Prince Charming."

Key West
January to April 2012

DESTINATION PARADISE

In memory of Claude Gai who was,
on stage, a fabulous Duchesse

*Religion, love, and music are the triple
expression of the same reality, the longing
to expand that haunts the human soul.*

—HONORÉ DE BALZAC
La Duchesse de Langeais (1834)

*In the soul of every one of us, there is a
singing blackbird. Life is about taming it.*

—METIN ARDITI
The Conductor of Illusions (2012)

The Carmelite in the Garbage Can

MONTRÉAL, DECEMBER 1930

He closes the book. Places it on his stomach. He's not sure he really likes the end. He expected something more positive, almost like the happy endings in American movies. After all, twelve sailors who spend twenty-four days fabricating a ladder of rope and metal on a cliff beaten by the waves of the Mediterranean, a bluff considered impregnable, in order to kidnap a barefoot Carmelite who took refuge in a convent to die there, of love, in the throes of deprivation and poverty, deserve a small reward! He raced through the last fifteen pages of the novel imagining the reunion of the Duchesse de Langeais and her Général de Montriveau, their true kiss, at last, their first, the soldier's trembling hands as he unfastens the nun's veil, opens her robes, and slips inside while she swoons because this is what she has been waiting for, dreaming of, for the past seven years ... and the pleasure that would follow, of which Édouard knew nothing and which he promised himself he would experience as soon as possible, despite the rules and restrictions of his religion. But no. The general bursts into Madame de Navarreins's cell when she has just died, and all he can retrieve from the inhuman demands and the mental torture of the convent is the corpse of his mistress, or rather the woman who, braving all the hypocrisy and meanness of Parisian high society, could have become his mistress, had she waited for him a few hours longer.

The story ends in the middle of the Mediterranean, somewhere between Barcelona and the Balearic Islands, as the general wonders whether he shouldn't simply dispose of her body by throwing it overboard since he achieved his goal and now La Duchesse de Langeais has escaped him forever. Quite disappointing. Édouard thinks, however, that a happy ending would have clashed with the fabric of this dark, melancholic, pessimistic novel. Still ... He feels as if the writer has let him down, left him hanging.

And the last line, spoken by the Général de Montriveau's friend, Monsieur de Ronquerolles, was perplexing:

"... and only a woman's last love can satisfy a man's first love."

Many things were over his head in this book (he knew nothing of the Terror, the Restoration, nothing about French aristocracy and the mores of Faubourg Saint-Germain at the beginning of the nineteenth century, he had never read a novel in which there were only two protagonists who, page after page after page, spoke of love, surrender, restraint, honour, and lovers who were lovers in their imagination only, so he concentrated, he was learning, he was trying to retain the thousands of facts that bombarded his mind, he was trying to *understand*), but this, really, he couldn't figure out what it was supposed to mean ... that men should only love women who have lived? And what about the virginity lauded by the Catholic Church?

There's no point in wracking his brains, he's tired, his sisters, Albertine and Madeleine, will be home from the movies soon and if they see the light in his bedroom, they'll insist upon telling him the story of the film that he intends to see before Friday night when Cinéma Saint-Denis will be changing the program. He puts the book on his night table and turns off the light. He is lying on his back, his eyes wide open. He takes his right hand out from under the covers, traces what he imagines to be the gesture of a society lady from Faubourg Saint-Germain in Paris at the beginning of the nineteenth century, something airy yet controlled. He speaks out loud, attempting to speak in a nasal voice and a French accent (failing on both counts).

"I am Antoinette de Navarreins, La Duchesse de Langeais and a barefoot Carmelite. But I shall never die of love."

He smiles and falls asleep.

He found the novel among the potato peels in the garbage can belonging to Monsieur Béliveau, the bachelor on the fourth floor who always displays fine manners and whom Victoire mistrusts because she doesn't like his fancy gestures or his prying eyes.

A week earlier, Victoire had asked him to take out the garbage. His father was once again too drunk to do it, and she had a terrible backache after scrubbing down the inside staircases covered in slush from the tenants' boots after the first snowfall of the year. The tenants of the twenty apartments in the building were required to bring down their garbage cans every Monday morning, but they were not obligated to take them out to the sidewalk. That was the janitor's job. Or that of his wife, as it happens, since Télesphore, too full of himself to accept his role as everyone's servant, had been letting her handle almost all the work for years. Édouard hated it when his mother asked him to help her and complained that his sisters could show some good will and roll up their sleeves from time to time. Victoire would answer that Albertine and Madeleine were girls, and you don't ask girls to take out the garbage from twenty apartments before leaving for work. One day Édouard dared comment that she, his mother, was a woman and it wasn't a woman's job either; she replied that if she stopped doing a man's work, they'd all find themselves out on the street from one day to the next. He'd lowered his head and apologized.

That morning, however, seeing his mother's drawn face and her obvious exhaustion, he hadn't dared protest. He'd put on his coat, his tuque and gloves, and his boots and headed for the shed where the garbage cans were stored.

It had snowed part of the night. In the semi-darkness of early dawn, ruelle des Fortifications looked like a Christmas card, painted in blue and white, sprinkled with sparkling diamonds that hid the poverty for a few hours, until the sun melted the snow and revealed the true dreariness of this dead-end street. The tenants' names were written on the cans. He found the inevitable beer bottles of Madame L'Heureux, the widow on the second floor who claimed she didn't drink, the fashion magazines of the French woman on the ground floor (sometimes he'd put them aside and thumb through them before falling asleep – he had saved stacks of them without knowing why), kitchen leftovers that had begun to stink, and, when the cover of Monsieur Béliveau's can fell into the snow, a dog-eared, yellowed book discarded in a nest of potato peels.

Honoré de Balzac. *La Duchesse de Langeais.*

A forbidden book. A novel on the Index!

When he was going to school, the teaching brothers were adamant about forbidden reading, they became almost lyrical when they attacked the subject of books on the Index. Pointing his finger, raising his voice, Brother Paul, the most twisted of the brothers, shouted the names of the damned nineteenth-century novelists, the Russians, the English, the Germans, as well as the French who were, in his opinion, the most perverted and reprehensible of all. He would spit out the words *Balzac*, *Hugo*, *Zola* like cannon balls, speaking of the corruption that saturated their work, the repudiation of religion, the gravest sin they had all committed, the fallen women they constantly wrote about, and the illicit relationships they praised with no respect for the holy sacrament of marriage. In fact, he made the thirty pupils in his class want to race to find these books if only to verify whether all his accusations were justified. Without realizing it, he was the origin of a passion for reading in many young men who otherwise might never have opened a book in their lives.

Édouard retrieved the novel from the garbage can, wiped it on his parka in the hope that it wouldn't smell of potato peels for long. A hard-bound edition from Les éditions Nelson. He went to check the end (his big brother Gabriel is a printer and has told him that all books carry the date and place of printing on the last page). *Printed in France.* So why state that in English? Mystery. He hid the book in his pocket and finished his chore, grumbling because the garbage cans were particularly full that week, heavier and smellier than usual.

That same evening he began to read the prohibited book, expecting to commit sins whose existence he didn't even suspect and licking his chops in anticipation. He hoped that *La Duchesse de Langeais* would be as racy as promised and he would soon be able to boast that he was the only one in the household, aside from his father who read the romantic and symbolist poets, to have read a book on the Index and to have discovered all sorts of surprising, disturbing, and shameful things. Without mentioning it to his mother, of course, for fear of receiving the worst verbal lashing of his life.

He almost gave up ten times during the first twenty-five pages. The author's socio-political and religious considerations didn't interest him – he knew absolutely nothing about the history of France, especially the aspects that involved Spain and Italy – and he got lost in the labyrinth of endless sentences, often trying in vain to find the subject so he could follow the gist and emerging exhausted and dizzy from the web of words some of which he didn't even recognize and whose order escaped him. Why make it so complicated? The books he had read before – for the most part, insipid novels written in a simple style, sometimes a bit too simple – were easy to follow and never sent the reader searching for the subject or the direct object just to lay claim to the snobbish label, "literature." What he wanted was a story, not a tricky, convoluted puzzle.

Then, in the middle of a paragraph he thought would never end, where the author was again holding forth on useless topics, the first protagonist finally appeared, a general in the army who had been sent, who knows why since he was French, to one of the Balearic Islands to "charter" (Édouard went to check the meaning of that word in his father's dictionary) an important fleet leaving for the Americas.

The general is searching for a woman he loved – that's more interesting – and who was believed to have taken refuge here, on this island, in a convent led by barefoot Carmelites – that's actually fascinating – to end her days in penitence observing the strict rules of this cloistered religious order to expiate her sins – which sins?!

And the definitive breakthrough, the moment when Édouard understood that he would read to the end no matter what, came when during a religious service, one of the barefoot Carmelites sits down at the organ and Général de Montriveau recognizes the woman he loved from the way she plays.

He was dumbfounded. He lay there in his bed, immobile, blown away by the idea that one could recognize someone from her way of touching the organ. Are there so many ways of interpreting a piece of music? Isn't music always the same? You follow the score and you play what's written, right? And in her parlour in Paris, the Duchesse de Langeais had a piano, not an organ! Can you play a piece of music the same way on the piano and the organ?

To lend some credence, it must be said that the music the nun played was "Le chant du Tage," their favourite piece when they got together socially, and the Duchesse always had a very personal way of interpreting it ... still, quite a coincidence. Furthermore, we will soon learn that the nun had guessed who the visitor was, that she'd been hoping he would appear for years, and this was how she'd let him know she had recognized him and still loved him. At last there was a whiff of scandal in the air (a virtuous nun in love with an army general!). Now Édouard had to keep reading ...

Suddenly, a return to the past. The author recounts the first meetings between the duchess and her general.

Édouard drank in the dozens and dozens of pages where the two characters spoke of love without ever making it. He both admired and detested the duchess's duplicity, exploiting all her assets (and corsets) to charm the general, to wrap him around her little finger, make him suffer by constantly refusing to surrender to him, pushing him away whenever he became too enterprising, always taking refuge behind the screen of the virtuous married woman while she did everything to drive him mad with desire. When at last the general understood who she was and what a cruel game she was playing with him and, humiliated, he finally abandoned her, of course she realized that she truly loved him (Édouard had actually seen that coming) and, after going to wait for him on the doorstep of his house, weeping for hours on end, while all of Parisian high society looked on, destroying her reputation forever, the Duchesse de Langeais entered the barefoot Carmelite order to expiate her sin.

Page after page, Édouard allowed himself to be carried away by the descriptions of the settings – Faubourg Saint-Germain with its balls and salons, the opulence recovered by the French aristocracy who had lost everything during the Revolution and who once again enjoyed wallowing in privilege and abundance – and the endless conversations between two witty minds constantly vying to convince or dominate each other with complicated arguments that weren't always clear, at least not to him. No subject was too vast: life, death, society, love, God. Édouard adored – even if he didn't understand everything – this verbal merry-go-round where no one ever emerged as the winner. The style was convoluted, the vocabulary sometimes impenetrable, but everything was so beautiful and elegant that as the days went by, Édouard began to identify with the Duchesse de Langeais, her mood changes, her outbursts, her mind as dazzling as her gowns. Every night, before falling asleep, he would floor Général de Montriveau with murderous arguments while allowing him to kiss the hem of his gown and his fingertips. Occasionally, the general even managed to unfasten his gown and remove it ...

For a long time now, he had accepted the fact that he always identified with the heroines in movies – Theda Bara, Mary Pickford, Gloria Swanson – and that in novels he was the one to whom the Danish prince or the English pirate or the immensely wealthy American businessman would offer his heart, his body, and his fortune. He was no longer ashamed of this. Of course, he kept it a secret, he didn't want people to know, but that was as far as he went: he had decided that if he was different from other men, he should accept it as a privilege and not feel guilty.

Assuming, of course, that he'd find others like him.

Unless he was the only one.

Which would sentence him to loneliness and perhaps, ultimately – who knows – to madness.

But he was seventeen years old, and although, in his search for pariahs like himself, he was eager to explore the world – more precisely, boulevard Saint-Laurent where apparently all of society's rejects could be found – for the time being, all he could do was dream.

That night, after mulling over the end of the novel, he dreams of Général de Montriveau and not of the Duchesse de Langeais. For the first time he doesn't see himself as the duchess and she is not the object of all the flowery compliments and very precise caresses because the general finds in him, a hundred years later and on another continent, a less resistant, more willing partner than the worldly duchess.

He is lying in his bed, in his pyjamas, sound asleep when the door to his room opens … Whether that dream lasts a few seconds or all night, it doesn't matter, when Édouard wakes up in the early morning, he is in heaven and he thanks Monsieur Honoré de Balzac.

PART ONE

The Carmelite Is Selling Shoes

"Tell his mother to send him to see me."

Teena pours herself a last cup of tea, blows on the burning hot liquid, makes a face because it's too strong.

Maria is putting on her coat. It's been a good evening. She won a dollar at cards – a rare occasion, since she's not a good player – she'll be able to go home by cab. She even offered to give Tititte a lift.

"You realize that boy's never worked in his life, eh? This'll be his very first job."

Tititte appears in the kitchen at that point. Wearing gloves and hat, her scarf neatly tied and her makeup touched up, she creates an illusion: she looks fifty at the most, when in fact she's closer to sixty. Forty is her goal, but as her sisters often say, wrinkles can be hidden but not erased. She consoles herself thinking that at least she looks like the youngest of the Desrosiers sisters. And recently she has had another reason for disguising her appearance.

"Did you call the taxi?"

Teena is emptying her cup into the sink.

"You're sure in a hurry to leave! You so ashamed you want to lick your wounds in private?"

Teena and Maria chuckle. Tititte shrugs.

"One bad-luck night is no cause for me to feel ashamed. I'm not at all ashamed! I played a good game, but I was unlucky."

Maria pinches her cheek, the way she used to do with her kids when they misbehaved.

"Admit that you played a lousy game! It was like you were somewhere else. How come you're so distracted, you have a new beau?"

Tititte shrugs her shoulders.

"I'm going to ignore that comment."

She turns away and heads for the telephone on the kitchen wall.

"If you're not going to call, I'll call myself."

Maria steps between her and the phone.

"Wait a minute, we haven't finished."

"If it's too long, I'll order my own taxi."

"It won't be long, just give us five minutes."

Teena and Maria pull up two chairs.

"If you sit down, it'll never end."

Maria stands up, puts her fists on her hips.

"Go ahead, call your damn cab, and let us talk. Go on, leave, you pain."

"Gooood Lord, don't raise your voice like that. I'll wait."

She unbuttons her coat and takes it off, but not her gloves or her hat. And remains standing in the doorway.

Teena rolls her eyes at Maria and hides her giggles behind her hand. Maria sits down beside her.

"Besides, that Édouard doesn't look like much of a worker…"

"It's not a very demanding job."

"I know, but he's fat and –"

"Maria! He's what, seventeen, eighteen years old? He has to be capable of kneeling to help people try on a pair of shoes! I need a salesman as soon as possible because it's almost Christmas and Monsieur Villeneuve is leaving! He didn't stay long, it wasn't his cup of tea. But anyone can do this job, c'mon, you don't need a university degree! And you're the one who mentioned him to me, Maria, so why are you suddenly backing off?"

"I mentioned him to you because his mother told me he's looking for work. At least, she's looking for work for him 'cause she's fed up seeing him lolling on the living room sofa doing nothing."

"Let's just hope he's not as useless as his father."

"That's what I was thinking too. Never mind, forget it. It probably was a dumb idea."

"No, no. I've met five candidates and I'm telling you, they weren't too bright. At least with him, I know he's not dull, he can hold a conversation. Sometimes hours go by without a single customer in the store. At least he's someone I can chat with."

"That's not what I call chatting. You can't shut him up once he's started. Believe me, he'll talk your ear off!"

"So you won't have to stay tuned to CKAC radio for a change."

Tititte lets out a sly laugh. Her sisters turn to her. They know a mean comment is coming.

"At any rate, if you ask me, that kid won't be fathering lots of children."

Her sisters look at each other and smile.

"Are the two of you thinking what I'm thinking?"

Teena is fiddling with the edge of the tablecloth.

"You wondering if he'll always be ... a *confirmed bachelor*? I've been wondering since I first saw him at Nana's wedding. He was pretty young, but he already looked like a sissy."

The three sisters know what the expression *confirmed bachelor* signifies, but they don't dare say more because homosexuality remains a total and incomprehensible mystery to them. All three of them have met such men in their respective jobs: Maria at the Paradise Club on the Main that recently became a refuge for them, Tititte at Ogilvy's where most of the salesmen are what she calls *delicate gentlemen*, and Teena who has certain customers whose feet are fine and perfumed – who in God's name perfumes his feet? – and whose wrists are limp.

Teena fans her face with her hand.

"Maybe he'll be celebrating Saint Catherine's Day on November 25."

Maria jumps up and goes to the phone.

"Enough of this! Don't forget we're talking about my daughter's brother-in-law. Who cares if he's a *confirmed bachelor* or a sissy, he needs a job!"

The taxi is on its way and she's buttoning up her coat.

"Pansy or not, he needs to find work."

Teena accompanies her sisters to the door. They stand in the entrance, looking out for the taxi. Teena pushes aside the lace curtain and her breath leaves circles of steam on the glass.

"More damn snow."

Tititte taps her on the shoulder.

"Don't start swearing now, we've got another four months of it."

"My God, four months!"

"I thought you liked snow."

"When we were young, sure. And a bit at Christmas ... but now ... listen, last year the snowbanks came up to the second floor! We had to walk down to Dorchester to cross the street. Pretty soon we won't be able to see the other side of the street because of the snowbanks."

"Right. If this was February, we'd have to go outside to see if the taxi arrived 'cause we couldn't see the car coming down the street."

"Climbing over the snowbanks, falling, getting up soaking wet, slipping on the sidewalk ... I can't take it anymore. Sometimes I feel like locking myself up inside and waiting for spring."

"Like a mama bear, Teena? Maybe you'd lose a few pounds that way, they say bears lose weight when they hibernate."

Tititte opens the door and takes off before her sister can catch her.

"Taxi's here!"

"It's not even true!"

"I'll shout and have him back up to Dorchester ..."

As she walks around her apartment, turning off the lights, Teena realizes she forgot to ask her sisters to listen to something. She'd even taken it out, left it in full view on the pouffe in front of her favourite armchair. But they were in such a hurry to start the game, they hadn't even entered the living room. She picks it up and turns it over before taking it out of its plain brown envelope. Madame Bolduc's latest record. She puts it on the gramophone turntable. She'd wound the machine up before Maria and Tititte arrived, so they could listen to the new song by the remarkable woman who'd become an idol for the Québécois who adored her lively, comical lyrics. In the heat of the action – their enthusiasm, the laughter, the pleasure of seeing each other again, and the always exciting card game – she had forgotten. She lowers the needle onto the record.

She chokes up at the first measures.

The harmonica, the piano, the rapid rhythm, so sure of itself, almost boastful and then the nasal voice of Madame Bolduc ...

> *Mademoiselle, voulez-vous danser*
> *La bastringue pis la bastringue...*

It's not so much the lyrics she finds moving – they're actually quite banal – it's more what the music stirs up in her. Something deep inside from her childhood and her parents' childhood, from the countryside, the countryside of faraway Saskatchewan, it makes skirts swirl, sets feet to tapping, it makes you want to stand up and dance, it makes you want to love everyone and laugh and cry at the same time. This is music that makes people who aren't the nostalgic type feel nostalgic. You can't figure out what you're missing, but you're missing something, listening to this crazy mix of instruments and voices, so joyous sounding, but sad in the emotions it arouses.

All of a sudden, Teena's living room smells of pipe tobacco, sweat, and apple pie. And the toe-tapping urge takes over.

She taps one foot, then the other, and starts following the beat of the song, tapping her heels on the wood floor. She doesn't know what she misses, yet she misses something. Yes, she does know. Her father, her mother, her childhood in Sainte-Maria-de-Saskatchewan, Christmastime on the Prairies. How she'd like to erase everything. And go back to where it all started. Choose another path, no matter which path, certainly not one that leads here, to Montréal, the misleading paradise of those who abandoned that place and who dream of returning.

The song is over, she rewinds the machine and puts the needle back at the beginning of the record.

Pond's Cold Cream gives your skin a soothing sense of freshness, as promised on the little jar. She wipes her face with Kleenex. Fatigue and fear have etched deep circles under her eyes. So far she has managed to hide them with makeup, but one day soon this will no longer be possible. The three-sided mirror on her dressing table reflects the image, twice from a three-quarter angle and once from the front, of the anxiety in her eyes, of her skin previously so smooth, now striped with tiny wrinkles, especially at the corners of her eyes and her mouth that she holds closed to repress a scream. Her smile, once lovely, has become a grimace, her face has closed down. She is less patient with her customers at Ogilvy's and, try as she might, no longer manages to sing the praises of the supple leather gloves she's been selling to wealthy Montréal women for years. She has lost what she used to call her *sparkle* that made her such a good saleswoman. Her sales record has tumbled in recent weeks and her boss has noticed.

She shrugs.

What is a pair of kid gloves compared to what is threatening her?

The doctor told her not to worry until she has the test results. But how can she not be sick with worry when a lump under her arm, that she touches a hundred times a day, constantly reminds her that the body she pampered for so many years is letting her down? The oils, the diets, the sea-salt baths, and even, when her budget allowed, one or two massages a year to attack the fatty tissue and the accumulated fatigue – was all that for nothing and will she learn, from one day to the next, that a horrible thing she dares not name has invaded her body and is going to kill her?

She slips her hand under her right breast.

It's hard. A bit harder every day, it seems. The doctor advised her not to think about it, not to panic, to hope and pray to God that it's nothing rather than fearing the worst. After all, it could be a benign tumour. She felt like standing up and shouting, do you have a lump under your arm? no? then you don't know what you're talking about! don't try to put me to sleep with your comforting words, and let me wail if I want to wail! She held her tongue. The poor man. He was simply trying to encourage her. How many times a week did he have to announce this bad news to women? And how many of them wanted to scratch his eyes out as she did? Yet he was not to blame, it was fate, goddamn fate that never leads us where we want to go. Or the Good Lord himself who rewards us, at the end of a life that wasn't always easy, with sicknesses, each one uglier and more serious than the other.

She stands up and leaves her bedroom to make sure that all the lights are out and the doors locked.

Why bother? Why bother to save on electricity and lock the doors to protect yourself from thieves if everything, if life, life, life, is coming to an end? To hell with the cost of electricity, welcome, thieves! If it weren't so cold outside, she'd sleep with the door wide open. She would court danger if she could count on a catastrophe. Immediately. Fast. No long agony in a depressing hospital where unlucky women like her are crowded six to a room, waiting for the end they long for. One good stab in the heart is much faster!

She collapses on the sofa and starts to cry, hiding her face in her hands.

And soon it will be Christmas.

Maria found her two daughters in the kitchen. Alice was making coffee while Béa was cutting two enormous slices of apple pie. They insisted upon telling their mother about the film. She refused the offer of coffee and pie and listened, pretending to be interested in this story of pirates and treasure hidden on a desert island hit by a devastating cyclone that the girls were describing with emphatic gestures and in minute detail. Béa waxed almost poetic talking about Douglas Fairbanks, his moustache, his skill with a sword, his stunning leaps among the sails of the ship, his smile, his swagger, and his fearless attitude. *The Black Pirate* was incredible!

After more than five years behind the counter at the Pâtisserie Ontario, Béa has become a plump, listless girl who only perks up when talking about the movies. She dreams of cinema, she devours it, she has made it the centre of her life and lives for the evenings when she and her sister go to the Cinéma Saint-Denis to see two silent French films or to one of the few theatres in the west end of Montréal (still rare at the time) where the American talkies are first shown. The talkies interest her less. She finds them hard to follow because everyone talks too much and too fast. Her English is far from fluent and that frustrates her. Fortunately, that evening the film was silent but early in the new year they'd be showing, according to Béa, a strange German talkie dubbed in English called *The Blue Angel*, forbidden to people under twenty-one, and it looked pretty boring.

"Doesn't seem to have much action. I like it when things happen! Battles, races … or beautiful balls with beautiful gowns. But not a cabaret singer with a beaver top hat on her head …"

Maria worries about her. She rarely talks about boys, who seem to terrorize her. She lowers her eyes in the presence of her sister's many beaux, only peeks at them when they've turned their backs and are leaving the house. Maybe Maria should talk to her about this. But she's still young, she has time.

Maria dreads the moment when she'll have to organize weddings for the two of them. She doesn't feel like reliving the experience of Nana's wedding, a fabulous party, that's true, but it caused her so much trouble.

Meanwhile, Alice has found work as a waitress at the Geracimo, a restaurant on rue Sainte-Catherine, near Saint-Denis. It's the first job she's appreciated since she left school (her two horrible years as a tobacco shaker are now behind her), she's more conscious of her appearance, more likeable, and, surprisingly, she teases her sister less about her chubbiness. The direct contact with the public is good for her. As for boys, many show up at the house every month, some quite presentable, still at school or even college – eternal students who seem in no hurry to enter the job market – and some suspect types who worry Maria, all of them, Maria assumes, met at the restaurant. Passing shadows, in her life and at the restaurant. Flings that never last long and seem to leave little impression on her daughter's memory. She talks endlessly about the current beau, the handsomest, the nicest she's ever met, then, when it's over, mum's the word, total amnesia. He is replaced by the next one, with no comments and no regrets.

Two daughters, so unlike each other, who raise very different concerns.

Once the story of the film is over, the Black Pirate victorious and the damsel in distress rescued, the dishes done, the good-night wishes pronounced (hugs are rare in this house), Maria finds herself alone in the kitchen. It's too late to call Nana's mother-in-law. She's not even sure she still has her number.

The phone is on the wall in her kitchen, too. She approaches it and studies the spiderweb of names and numbers scribbled on the wallpaper all around the phone. She thinks she jotted it down somewhere ... All the relatives are there, along with services and emergency numbers. Always in lead pencil. To be erased if necessary. But they never are erased and they accumulate. And the web becomes bigger and bigger. The first ones, her sisters, her brother, the grocery store, the police, the fire department, are close to the phone, written down first; the others spread out in concentric circles. On the perimeter, Alice's beaux, numbers used only once or twice but still there, useless forevermore.

While looking for Victoire's number, Maria reviews all the important people in her life. It looks like a lot, seen from afar, so many names, but when you read them one by one, you realize that ultimately you don't know that many people. Although not everyone has had a phone installed ...

Ah, there she is. Instead of writing her name, Victoire, she had written: *mother-in-law – Nana.*

She'll call her tomorrow morning to say that her sister will be waiting for Édouard at the shoe store. He can simply ask for Mademoiselle Desrosiers. Anyway, he knows her.

Let's hope it works out.

"Did you have to choose such a flashy tie?!"

"I'm going to a job interview, Ma, not a funeral."

"And your knot is huge!"

"Right! The knot on a tie is meant to be seen."

Édouard is leaning over the little mirror hanging over the sink. He tightens the knot on his tie a bit, wets his index finger and passes it over his eyebrows. Then he washes his hands with the big bar of brown soap.

"My turn to criticize you ... When are you going to buy us some decent soap? This one scrapes our skin off."

Victoire, who was gathering up the crumbs left by four people, her and her three children, who had just finished breakfast, straightens up and looks at her son from behind, this soft, overweight teenager whom she loves more than anything in the world but is constantly nagging, possibly just to hide her preference. And also because their quarrels are invigorating. Recently, those with her daughters, Albertine and Madeleine, are always about the same subject – Albertine accuses her sister of stealing her beau, which isn't true – while those with Édouard, more serious and more colourful, cover an almost inexhaustible variety of subjects and are often amusingly absurd. An argument with neither head nor tail will counter the one just made, things heat up and get a bit out of control and they'll say anything to prove they're right even when they know they're wrong. It's fun, inconsequential, and quickly forgotten. On the other hand, the fights about that damn Alex are going to drive her crazy. Fighting over such an insignificant drip!

"I'll buy better quality soap when you start paying some rent, Édouard. Maybe next week, you never know!"

Édouard dries his hands, smells them, and makes a face.

"C'mon, we're not that poor ..."

Victoire drops the crumbs into the garbage and comes to stand beside her son to wash her hands. She pushes him aside with her hip.

"Oh yes, Édouard, we are that poor."

She expects a sharp retort. No response. He doesn't have time this morning, he has a long tramway ride ahead of him to get from Vieux-Montréal to Plateau-Mont-Royal. The Giroux et Deslauriers shoe store is at the other end of the world, at the corner of Mont-Royal and Fabre. Édouard will have to take two trams. Almost an hour of travel. Will he have the courage to get up every morning, winter and summer, and take those two trams to go sell shoes to people – to quote Teena Desrosiers – whose feet don't always smell sweet? He'll have no choice. This third contribution to the rent, added to those of Albertine and Madeleine, will improve their living conditions.

She runs her hand over the back of her son's jacket. The fabric is starting to wrinkle.

"I told you to iron your jacket. The back's all wrinkled."

"I did iron it. But it's so cheap and so worn, it wrinkles just looking at it."

He heads for the kitchen door, in his pitter-patter gait that people always make fun of, especially his classmates who nicknamed him *Édouard Petitpas*.

"No kiss for me?"

"I'm not five years old anymore."

"You weren't five when you kissed me at least three times yesterday."

He turns back to her, hands in his pockets, like a real man for once. He even goes so far as to rattle the change in his pocket.

She smiles.

"I have to act like a man. That's what you're always telling me."

"And acting like a man means no longer kissing your mother?"

"From one day to the next! And rattling the change in your pants pocket."

Another great subject for an argument. If only they had time …

"I might not come straight home from my meeting with Mademoiselle Desrosiers, Ma. The shoe store is right next to Messier and I've always wanted to see that store."

"Just make sure you're home by noon."

"I can't promise …"

"I've got some leftover shepherd's pie."

He turns away and heads down the hallway, his heels clicking on the linoleum.

"That's an offer I can't refuse …"

"So you'll be home?"

"Give me a break, Ma. I'm eighteen."

"Seventeen."

The front door. Bang! Whenever anyone leaves their place, the whole building shakes.

She hears him climb the stairs to the ground floor. In a few seconds, she'll see the hem of his pant legs pass into front of the tiny window near the ceiling in their kitchen that overlooks ruelle des Fortifications. There. Her son goes pitter-pattering by.

And she's left alone. With Télesphore who's still sleeping.

When they're not fighting, Albertine and Madeleine are ignoring each other.

Yet they take the tram together every morning and every evening. They both found work, at the same time, at the Dupuis Frères department store, Madeleine in household appliances on the fourth floor, Albertine in the bargain department in the basement. So they feel obligated, despite their serious bone of contention, to travel together, even though ignoring each other during the half-hour trip between their home and the store seems ridiculous and childish. But they don't speak. And they avoid looking at each other. An old couple who no longer have anything to say to each other.

Not so long ago, before the misunderstanding about Alex, they would walk arm in arm, chattering away, laughing, making fun of passersby, especially the men they never found handsome or interesting enough. They'd become serious when one shared a secret with the other and would resume laughing as soon as they noticed something unusual. Like everyone else, they'd complain about the overcrowded trams in the morning, coyly thank any man who offered them a seat, and chat in loud voices to attract attention. In fact, they almost believed they were happy because they were earning a living and men were beginning to show an interest in them.

After a difficult adolescence spent criticizing everything – the basement apartment in ruelle des Fortifications, her family, especially her parents, Télesphore because he was lazy and Victoire because she was too long-suffering and was killing herself doing the janitor's job in her husband's place, her brother whom she found useless, and her future that looked so grim since nothing interested her – Albertine was transformed as soon as she began working at Dupuis Frères. Finally leaving school where she learned nothing and kept engaging the teaching nuns in endless arguments, escaping the dark, suffocating apartment where frustration and unspoken resentment reigned, meeting new people and proving that she could do more than complain and brood about her disappointments, had, virtually from one day to the next, turned her into a young woman who, if not beautiful, was vivacious and almost charming. A positive period in her life that had begun when she met Alex, a tall, charming guy, considerate and talkative – a rare commodity in a society where men tended to shut up and let the women do the talking – who had lots of plans and with whom she'd fallen madly in love. Undoubtedly too madly.

Possessive and demanding, she spun a web of suffocating attention around him and he quickly felt imprisoned. Blinded by passion, Albertine was incapable of seeing the damage she was doing to her budding love with her excessive demands. Without realizing it, she had become an emotional tyrant, demanding vows he didn't want to make and promises he found pointless.

And he turned his attention to Madeleine.

Victoire had seen it all coming.

To begin with, she hadn't liked Alex when Albertine first introduced him. Too friendly, too sure of himself, too eager to please. Not handsome but convinced he was and he acted accordingly. Too attentive to Albertine, to Madeleine, to her, excessively gallant, too quick with facile, often superfluous compliments, he paraded around their living room like a rooster in the barnyard, telling his travelling-salesman stories as if they were exceptional adventures. Victoire, seeing through his game and shocked by her daughter's blindness, had remained indifferent to what she considered his Don Juan antics. Seeing that his charms had little effect on Victoire, he attempted to win her over with even more effusive compliments and even flowers. She had almost sent him packing on more than one occasion but had restrained herself. After all, he was the first boy to be interested in Albertine. As the months went by, she couldn't help but wonder what he saw in her daughter. Dark, not pretty, full of complexes, shy with strangers – although heaven knows she wasn't with her family – Albertine was really not the type of woman who would attract a talkative, exuberant travelling salesman like him. Was he looking for a docile little lady he could park in a cute little house full of legitimate children, while he, the peacock, went traipsing around the province? Wasn't he a cliché, a walking travelling-salesman story himself?

Before it became too serious – she certainly didn't want to see a depressed Albertine moping around the house if Alex tired of her – she had tried to have a conversation with Albertine who was clearly allowing herself to be so taken in by the young man's attentions she'd been heard humming in the bathroom on more than one occasion. Albertine singing! That could only lead to trouble. But Albertine wasn't interested in advice from her mother who was too nosy and too mistrustful, and the conversation ended badly, with her accusing her mother of wanting to ruin her life and her mother saying that she was doing exactly that herself.

Yet Alex's interest and his affection for Albertine seemed sincere, so Victoire had decided to wait before intervening more energetically, while keeping an eye on the situation. With a heavy heart, she saw Albertine make mistake after mistake, falling into all the traps that lie in wait for a woman who loves too much, becoming more and more demanding, even capricious with Alex – undoubtedly out of fear of losing him, while it was the best way to chase him away – taking for granted that they were officially a couple even though they had just begun their relationship, acting, with no real justification, like a married woman who suspects her husband of looking elsewhere and making accusations he probably didn't deserve. Acting like a shrew who'd caught a big fish and wouldn't let go of her catch. She couldn't imagine he would consider spending his life with the hysterical woman she was becoming! And when Albertine started making scenes with Alex in front of the whole household, leaving speechless this man usually so talkative, Victoire realized the end was near and that Albertine was about to experience her first big heartache unless she changed her attitude.

Especially since she'd noticed the furtive looks Alex was giving Madeleine, clearly a less-stubborn prospect, while Albertine, too caught up in her recriminations, didn't notice a thing.

And on the fatal evening when Alex broke up with Albertine, claiming that her demands were suffocating him, that he wasn't prepared to commit to the serious relationship she was trying to impose, showering her with as many compliments as reproaches, acting the insincere asshole to the very end, the household capsized in a maelstrom of complaints and curses.

Crying fits followed outbursts of rage, clothes were ripped, dishes thrown around the kitchen. Albertine wasn't only angry with Alex, she was lashing out at everyone, she was accusing her mother, her sister, and even her brother – although Édouard had only run into Alex on a couple of occasions – of sabotaging her relationship, her only hope of ever escaping this damned house. She threatened to leave home with no forwarding address, to rent a room the way Gabriel had done before her, until one evening, Victoire, tired of hearing the same recriminations and frustrated by Télesphore's repeated refusal to get involved in "women's matters," headed for the door to the apartment, flung it open, and told Albertine to take her shouting somewhere else, that she'd had enough, she wanted her out of her sight. Outraged, Albertine froze in the middle of the living room.

"Are you kicking me out?"

"You are kicking yourself out."

Albertine had locked herself up in her room for days – she almost lost her job at Dupuis Frères – licking her wounds, plotting acts of revenge each crueller and more violent than the next; she spent countless sleepless nights picturing herself reigning over a pile of tortured bodies, victorious and free at last. She constantly rehearsed in her mind cruel murders and sprees of vengeful insults that brought her no satisfaction. And that enraged her even more.

When, pale and defeated, she finally emerged from the bedroom she had turned upside down, it was only to learn that Alex had invited Madeleine to go to the movies with him.

A shadow leaning in the doorway to the kitchen.

Dishevelled, stooped, head lowered, his eyes undoubtedly blood-shot, reeking of sweat and undigested alcohol, Télesphore has made an appearance in all his splendour.

"You want somethin' to eat?"

No answer.

"Cuppa tea? It'd be good for you."

Slight nod of the head.

"You're gonna kill yourself."

"That'd make you too happy."

His voice is hoarse and weak, his breath ragged. He coughs and heads for the sink where he spits without bothering to turn on the faucet.

"I've told you a hundred times not to spit in my sink. I'm the one who cleans up after."

He lets the water run, wets his hand, and rubs the back of his neck.

"I could run you a bath."

One of the few advantages of being the janitor in a building, beside the telephone they wouldn't have otherwise, is unlimited hot water, not included in the tenants' leases, but free for them.

Another nod of the head.

"Gotta eat something after."

He shrugs.

"I'll fix something while you wash."

She enters the bathroom and starts to fill the tub.

How she'd like to scald him.

As she butters his toast, just golden, almost white, the way he likes it, Victoire has a frightening thought. Albertine and Madeleine are both old enough to get married. What if Alex proposed to Madeleine, and Paul – Albertine's new beau, another drip but this one's spineless – did the same with Albertine?!

Two weddings! How could they ever pay for them?!

Rather than going directly to his appointment with Mademoiselle Desrosiers, Édouard went into L.N. Messier, the store he'd heard so much about, right next door to the Giroux et Deslauriers shoe store.

His dutiful attempt to stamp the snow off his boots in the doorway made the woman at the perfume counter smile.

"You don't have to do that, Monsieur."

Monsieur? He looks like a "Monsieur"? He's flattered that he looks older than his age.

"I'm used to doing it at home, otherwise my mother would kill me! Besides, I don't want to track slush all through the store."

She laughed.

"The store pays someone to clean the floors."

"That's no reason to make more work for them."

He waved to her and went to stand at the end of the central aisle. Here, in the back, in the middle of the Ladies Intimate Apparel section, is where his uncle Josaphat came before he disappeared, to play his fiddle twice a day to entertain the customers. It was Victoire who told him that when he'd asked how Josaphat earned a living.

There and at weddings, funerals, and family get-togethers.

The manager thought it would attract customers, but certain saleswomen – the ones who didn't like his music or were frightened by his piercing eyes and his bohemian appearance – claimed that he chased customers away. That simply wasn't true. Over the years, he'd won over a group of women admirers who stopped by L.N. Messier several times a week just to listen to him play Massenet's "Méditation" or Dvořák's *Humoresque*, two of his big hits.

If they left without buying anything, it wasn't because Josaphat and his music repelled them but simply because they didn't have any money to spend. Listening to music on CKAC or CHLP was fine and good, but listening to a real violinist who stirred your soul, right there, two feet away from you, was a very different feeling. And to watch an artist while listening to him was an experience for these women who had never seen the inside of a concert hall. So they pretended to need something – a spool of thread, safety pins, whatever – so they could come to listen to him.

Édouard imagines his uncle standing there, the way he did at their family reunions, his eyes closed, concentrating. He places his chin on his instrument, raises his arm, positions the bow above the strings. Édouard can almost hear him. Tears fill his eyes. It was so beautiful. The sudden calm in the middle of the noisy Christmas or New Year's parties, a moment of peace that even the worst drunks enjoyed, closing their eyes, holding their glass of beer in one hand and the other often on their heart.

They haven't heard from him for a long time. Victoire thinks he might have gone back to Duhamel because the city suffocated him. But he doesn't call them. He doesn't write either. One day Édouard asked his mother if something had happened, an argument that would explain his disappearance. She had simply stared at him and shaken her head. He came to the conclusion that there were lots of things he didn't know about his family and he was determined to uncover them.

Édouard walked around the store quickly. Nothing interesting. Everything was cheap. Shoes that looked like they were made of cardboard, flowery housecoats, gaudy prints, no plain colours or anything that might attract a buyer with a bit of good taste. Ugly. Affordable. Pots and pans that wouldn't last a year, flashy glass jewellery, stinky perfumes. The kind of thing he'd grown up with, in fact, and that he longed to leave behind.

Oh! Morgan's, Eaton's, or Ogilvy's, that was another story!

He loved to linger there admiring the folds of a dress or a string of soft grey beads. Or watching Tititte Desrosiers, Nana's other aunt, sing the praises of the loveliest kid-leather gloves in the world to dazzlingly chic ladies from Westmount.

Here poverty cast a pall over everything.

He tried several times to imagine the Duchesse de Langeais walking down these aisles: the horrified look on her face, her dismissive gesture waving this worthless, ugly merchandise out of her sight.

A twinge of remorse. No disdain. No judgment. This is where his mother would shop if she lived in the neighbourhood, and his mother is above reproach.

As he is leaving to go to his appointment, near the entrance to the store, he notices a painter leaning over a painting he is finishing, his brow furrowed, his eyes squinting. Having signed his name, he backs off and studies his work briefly before taking it off the easel and replacing it with a blank canvas.

Édouard approaches the painting.

A forest in the fall. All the details: red and yellow leaves, the conifers always green, the muddy ground, the deep ruts, the gnarled roots of a tree, the inevitable bird perched on a broken branch, you can almost hear it singing. It is neither beautiful nor ugly. It is ordinary. Like everything for sale in this store. Glancing at the other canvases, Édouard realizes they all look alike, all based on the same model, as if the artist constantly repainted the same scene, simply changing the seasonal colours. The same forest, the vegetation in the foreground, the roots, the bird. Pale spring green replaces the deeper green of summer, followed by the flaming colours of autumn.

Édouard turns to the painter.

"You don't have a winter scene?"

The painter who was holding his brush between his teeth removes it from his mouth and wipes it on the sleeve of his stained shirt.

"No. 'Specially not this time of the year. People see enough snow in the streets, they don't want to hang it on their walls!"

"You do winter in the summer?"

"No. I don't do it anymore. Winter doesn't sell. I had two left last summer and I ended up selling them at a discount to foreigners.

Frenchmen who didn't believe a winter like that could exist ...
I think I'd had those two paintings for years, can't tell you how
happy I was to get rid of them!"

He picks up a kind of shaving brush, dips it in a gummy solution
that he spreads over the blank canvas.

Édouard coughs into his fist and clears his throat.

"Did you know a fiddler who used to play here twice a day –"

The painter interrupts him with a burst of joyful laughter.

"Monsieur Josaphat? Of course I knew him! We used to go for
a beer at Taverne Normand on the corner. A great guy. Played like
a god. Really talented!"

"Has it been a while since you've seen him?"

"He disappeared a few months ago. One morning he didn't show
up and we never saw him again. At first, I found the store really
quiet. I'd become used to his visits twice a day ... Maybe he died.
But I don't think so. He didn't look sick. Tired, unhappy, but not
sick. Maybe he was fed up."

"Did you know where he lived?"

The painter turns to him.

"You lookin' for him?"

"He's my uncle, my mother's brother, and we haven't heard from
him either."

"He's your uncle and you don't know where he lives?"

"Well ... he moves around a lot ... and he doesn't always tell us
where ..."

The painter picks up the canvas and shakes it up and down.

"Has to dry before I start ... I remember once he said he had
a little place on rue Amherst at the corner of De Montigny.
I remember, last winter, he told me his living room was over a
passageway between two houses, really damp, impossible to heat
in the winter ..."

"Would anyone here know where he's gone?"

"Doubt it. Like I said, he disappeared from one day to the next.
And he never talked to people, just me, and that was probably 'cause
I often bought him a beer. I get a good price for these paintings,

you know. You'd be surprised. That one I just finished ... at least two bucks!"

"People who shop here can afford to pay that?"

"No, but they find my stuff real beautiful. And I'm a good salesman!"

He places his blank canvas on the easel.

"'Cuse me now, there's another masterpiece waiting for me to paint it ..."

Although he doesn't know him well, Édouard has always been fascinated by his uncle Josaphat. Perhaps because there's a kind of mystery surrounding him: Édouard knows he is not welcome at their house – in fact he can't remember ever seeing him there – and his father blanches every time his name is mentioned; or possibly also because whenever he has heard him play his instrument, especially at his brother Gabriel's wedding five years ago, Édouard felt as if he was in the presence of something grand that he couldn't name but that moved him deeply. A chubby little guy different from the other kids, not remotely curious about the things that interested his sisters, his cousins, or his friends, who preferred to put bits of fabric on his head to imitate the hats worn by the ladies in the magazines his mother sometimes retrieved from the tenants' garbage, or to mimic the songs he heard on the radio, Édouard often felt lonely, the word "reject" not being part of his vocabulary yet. But the sounds that rose from his uncle Josaphat's fiddle propelled him into an unknown world, at least to the threshold of this world, because he felt stuck outside the door, still closed to him, but through which music managed to touch him like a promise. An invented world that conjured freedom. He had observed Josaphat, a rickety old man one moment, shabbily dressed and not too clean, then suddenly a demigod the next moment, bathed in a mysterious light that emanated from him, from his gestures suddenly agile and precise, and from his concentration and what he drew from his violin, these long devastating laments or the cascades of laughter executed at dazzling speed. At Gabriel's wedding, Édouard had spent part of the day sitting at the musician's feet and without knowing where it came from had suppressed his desire to cry, not from sadness but joy. And the rare times Josaphat spoke to him, he inevitably said, "You're your father's son. You got poetry in your blood and that'll be your downfall." What did that mean? Especially since he didn't want to resemble Télesphore, the heartless wannabe-bard who preferred to recite odes to the moon than accept his job as a janitor. Édouard had learned very young to judge and detest his father. Because of Victoire who broke her back doing his work, of course, but also because he recognized in himself the tendency to dream rather than act that he sensed in his father, the tendency to take refuge in a fuzzy cocoon where he was inaccessible, almost within the reach of happiness. And when he saw his father drink – beer when money was scarce, hard liquor when he somehow managed to get his hands on some cash, maybe stolen from his wife's wallet – he wondered whether that was the secret, the key to the door that led to the other world. Because he had also seen his uncle Josaphat drinking all day at Gabriel's wedding. He was too young to enter a tavern or a nightclub – he had to wait until he was twenty-one – but he promised to make up for lost time to enter the world not of his father, but of his uncle.

On his way out of L.N. Messier, he puts on his tuque and his gloves, then he remembers that the store where he might have his very first job is right next door.

His mother told him to be polite with Mademoiselle Desrosiers, to show an interest in the job, to answer her questions carefully – as if he needed this kind of advice, he had good manners, didn't he? – and not to forget to ask for news of her sisters to show that he remembers who she is. Of course he remembers who she is! Gabriel's mother-in-law's sister, right? And the other one, the lady he finds so chic at Ogilvy's, you know, the one who sells kid-leather gloves ... Yes, yes, he remembers. She also advised him to be vague if Teena Desrosiers asked too many questions about his family.

"She doesn't have to know how poor we are. You can tell her you left school because you were fed up ..."

"That's the truth."

"... but especially because you wanted to earn your own living.

That's not so true, but she doesn't have to know that. And show her you know about shoes, that you haven't been looking at all those magazines for nothing."

He takes a deep breath, adjusts his coat, threadbare but clean, turns right at the entrance to the shop, takes a quick look at the display in the windows. Brooks Brothers shoes. At least they don't sell junk. Brooks Brothers is real quality.

He plasters a smile on his face and pushes the door open.

Teena hates people who arrive late.

As a child, she was always the first to arrive at the little school in Sainte-Maria-de-Saskatchewan. She never waited for her sisters who were both dawdlers – Tititte took her time with her cereal, Maria played with her food – she'd leave the house early so she could be the first to greet their teacher. Sundays she often had to wait on the church steps for the deacon to open the doors. And as for her first beaux, her family would make fun of her when she began waiting for them at five o'clock in the afternoon.

Her whole life she has always arrived early for appointments, even if it's meant twiddling her thumbs outside a closed door or on a busy street corner where she felt like she was in everyone's way. But better to be in everyone's way than to keep someone waiting. She was the one kept waiting, the one twiddling her thumbs waiting for someone else or for the doors to open or for the bus to arrive, she had accepted that and no longer gave it any thought.

In the past half-hour, she has looked at her watch every two minutes, tapping her foot impatiently, letting out annoyed sighs. Not a single customer came to occupy her time. If Nana's brother-in-law turned out to be not only overweight but the lazy type who always arrived late, he wouldn't last long at Giroux et Deslauriers!

When the little bell over the door tinkles, she doesn't even bother to make sure it's him before shouting to the store at large:

"If there's anything I hate, it's people who are late! I said ten o'clock, not half past ten!"

He freezes in the doorway, terrified. Looking so ridiculous in his tight coat, wide-eyed and tight-lipped, possibly to hide his trembling mouth, Teena has to prevent herself from laughing. Two seconds earlier, she wanted to send him packing, and now, suddenly, seeing how taken aback he is, she's sorry she frightened him and feels like giving him a big hug.

But she has to appear strict.

"You hear me?"

He unbuttons his coat, almost trembling, takes off his tricolour tuque and unties his scarf.

"I'm sorry. I didn't realize we had a precise appointment... I thought it was around ten o'clock, not ten o'clock on the dot."

She goes over to him and sizes him up.

"Are you darn sure, with your corpulency, you can kneel at the customers' feet forty or fifty times a day?"

Édouard feels like turning on his heels and leaving the shop, slamming the door behind him. He's not used to being treated like this. Mentioning his weight before they even know each other! This is a bad start. He should've stayed in bed with his head under his pillow instead of crossing half the city to meet this dragoness whom he'd found so nice the few times he ran into her. His fear was promptly replaced by rage, the kind he's often sensed in his sister Albertine that makes her so unpredictable.

He is no longer afraid, he's fuming.

He puffs up his chest and looks Teena straight in the eye.

"I might be fat, but that doesn't mean I'm not flexible."

In less than five seconds, he had time to kneel at her feet and stand up again.

"Is that flexible enough for you? You want me to jump over the chairs or do cartwheels?"

She has taken a couple of steps back. He realizes she's about to laugh.

"We'll see if you're that flexible once you've spent hours running around the store finding shoes for people who don't know what they want and try on ten different pairs before leaving and telling you they'll think about it."

He takes off his coat and folds it over his arm.

"Does that mean I'm hired?"

"That means that we'll chat for a while, then maybe I'll take you on trial."

Édouard doesn't even know if he's happy. Spending day after day with her ... but as he gets closer to his possibly new boss, he realizes that she smells nice.

"You smell nice. What perfume do you use, Mademoiselle Desrosiers?"

"Good heavens, men don't usually notice things like that."

"They notice, but they're too embarrassed to ask."

Teena holds back another smile.

Definitely a *confirmed bachelor*.

"It's not much, but I can't offer you more. This is your first job, you know, and you don't have any experience."

Édouard is disappointed. Of course he didn't expect a fortune, but so little ... he had dared to dream about going to the movies, maybe even the theatre, from time to time, eating in restaurants, buying decent clothes, Brooks Brothers shoes, like he'd be selling if he accepted Mademoiselle Desrosiers's offer. But with this pathetic salary ... once he'd contributed to the rent – his mother had insisted on that – he'd hardly have enough left to pay for transportation and little daily expenses. He might not have more money than he has now but he'd have to travel back and forth morning and evening and he'd be working all day, six days a week.

"Couldn't you pay a couple of bucks more?"

"Not even a couple of quarters more. Once we've seen how you do, how you manage with the customers, if you're good salesman, if you lose patience, because sometimes, believe me, you need *a lot* of patience, we'll see. Meanwhile ... take what I'm offering, or go look for another job. But you won't find better. You're better off helping people try on shoes for low pay than breaking your back chained to a noisy machine for not much more. Think it over."

No more familiarity between them. Teena had rebecome the boss, cold, a bit distant. She'd been quite lively while she showed him around the store and explained what was expected of a good salesman, the schedule he would have to follow strictly, but as soon as it came to money, she sat up straighter and the look on her face and her tone of voice became harsher. You would've thought she was the manager of the department store next door, not Giroux et Deslauriers that had only one other employee.

"Can I tell you tomorrow?"

"No. You must already know if you want to stay. If you're not interested, that's okay, there are others. But if you're interested, jump on it now 'cause jobs are few and far between these days. The Depression has reached us, you know, and jobs are apt to get rarer."

"Do people have money to buy shoes during a depression?"

"People always need shoes to go to work."

She stands up, walks over to a display to rearrange a shoe that didn't need to be rearranged.

"It's eleven o'clock. You can think about it until noon. Then I'll turn to someone else."

He practically jumps on her and extends his hand.

"I don't need a half-hour. I'll take the job."

"You sure of your decision?"

"I'm sure. And I have the feeling we're going to get along fine."

It's a reflex, she wipes her hand after shaking Édouard's and he is slightly offended. Without knowing it, never having thought about it, all her life Teena has insulted every person whose hand she has shaken. And if anyone ever pointed it out to her, she would have been stunned.

"Don't be so sure, kid. And never forget one thing: I'm the boss, I'm in charge, I'm the one who decides around here."

Without another word, Édouard, the new employee at Giroux et Deslauriers, puts on his coat and gloves and his tuque.

That she takes off brusquely.

"Go buy yourself a hat. Now you're a man, not a schoolboy. People in the tram have to know you're travelling to work."

He blushes to the roots of his hair.

"I don't have money to buy myself a hat."

She bends over behind the cash register, picks up her purse, and fiddles with her wallet.

"Here's an advance. Two bucks. Go next door to Messier's, they've got good hats at decent prices."

He hesitates, heads for the door, then turns back to her.

"My mother knitted that tuque for me. I'll have to tell her I lost it."

She hands it back to him.

"Okay. You can take it home. But I never want to see it again."

"You got the job!"

"You bet, and it was easy."

"I'm so happy."

She covers her mouth with her hand, sits down.

"C'mon, Ma, don't cry."

"If you knew the difference this will make."

He crouches down in front of her. When she's like this, vulnerable, letting down her guard, when she lets her children see her real feelings, or her real thoughts, most of the time in spite of herself because she's just had a shock or the pressure is simply too great, he'd go to the ends of the earth for her. Deep down inside, he knows, beneath the strong woman who makes all the decisions, who produces miracles from nothing, there is a core of fragility, weakness not strength, compassion not heartlessness, the opposite of the image she imposes on her family.

"Those two bucks will change everything, Édouard!"

"Don't exaggerate!"

"Well, it will change lots of things."

"If it's that important, I can give you more."

"Don't be silly..."

"I can give you five bucks instead of two."

"Now you're the one who's exaggerating. You'd have nothing left."

"Four? You want four, Ma?"

She hesitates, shakes her head.

He's tempted to offer her his entire salary. Just to see her happy. To feel for once, just once, that she wasn't juggling insoluble problems, that she could rock in her favourite chair and not think about a thing. At least nothing negative.

"If you could give me three. But I don't want to insist. I don't want you to go broke for us."

He smiles and kisses her on the cheek.

"I won't go broke. Almost, but not completely. Okay, three bucks every Friday night. Now don't go wasting them."

She slaps him on the arm.

"Don't you worry! We can't afford to waste anything around here! We'll be able to eat better."

"And don't tell Pa."

"I'd cut off my right hand before telling him we'll have three bucks more a week for our regular budget."

"Where are you going to hide them? He knows all your hiding places."

"Don't kid yourself... He doesn't know all of them. Neither do the rest of you ..."

She stands up, opens the icebox, and leans over.

"The icebox is good for lots of things."

It's like Ali Baba's cave, kept in the dark. That's what Maria thinks every time she comes to visit her cousin Ti-Lou in her apartment on boulevard Saint-Joseph.

When she arrived in Montréal five years ago, Ti-Lou hardly had a thing. Two suitcases and the clothes on her back. But the suitcases contained a fortune in cash that Ti-Lou, without wasting it, enjoyed spending on knick-knacks and trinkets, on furniture and kitchen accessories, on paintings and decorations not always in good taste, all the things she'd never possessed because she'd spent most of her life in a hotel suite. When Maria suggested she was spending too much, too fast, she told her not to worry, that her money was well invested, it was making good returns and that when she had finished filling her apartment with objects she fancied, she would stop. The furniture was heavy, massive, the rugs were thick, the paintings enormous – only one canvas depicting an autumn scene with colourful trees and a bird perched on a branch was a normal size, even rather small – the ceiling light was cumbersome and the Bélanger stove that reigned in the kitchen was gigantic. Ti-Lou often told her cousin that she loved cooking for one person on a stove that could feed a family of fifteen.

"I make little meals that I cook in big pots on my big stove. And I always eat off big plates."

And when the house was full, leaving hardly enough room to move around, Ti-Lou had heavy drapes hung in the windows to prevent the light from entering. She had bought fifty-watt light bulbs. She spent her days in a dark place filled with things she found beautiful but could barely see. One day, screwing up her nerve, Maria had asked her why.

"It resembles my life. There are lots of things I keep in the dark, but I know they're there."

No further explanation. Maria had to be satisfied with this cryptic answer.

And when the Depression of 1929 hit, Ti-Lou stopped spending her money on useless things, just as she'd promised.

A single spot in her huge apartment was well lit. Next to her favourite armchair in the living room, Ti-Lou had set up a floor lamp with a hundred-watt bulb. A bright circle of light in the darkness. To read. Her passion since she retired. The bookshelves behind her armchair had gradually filled up over the years. She loved the grand sagas of the nineteenth century, she had devoured all twenty volumes of Les Rougon-Macquart by Zola, one after another, one a week for five months in a row, part of La Comédie humaine by Balzac whose old-fashioned, convoluted style she didn't always appreciate, Hugo's weighty tomes – Les Misérables, Notre-Dame de Paris and even Les travailleurs de la mer whose subject didn't really interest her. The bookseller on avenue du Mont-Royal had told her about Proust, but she hadn't yet dared tackle him for fear she wouldn't understand. To see her through the winter, she had ordered War and Peace, Anna Karenina, and The Brothers Karamazov. After France, Russia. The bookseller warned her that Tolstoy and Dostoevsky weren't easier to read than Proust, but she simply replied that she didn't like Proust's looks. For her, circles under the eyes were proof of a lack of sexuality in men. She thought Proust must smell sour.

The evenings when Maurice Trottier, whom she still called her Prince Charming, came to visit, she turned on all the lights to make the house seem brighter. He nevertheless often remarked that the apartment was too dark and that she would ruin her eyes. To which she would reply:

"With everything they've seen, if my eyes were going to be ruined, it would've happened ages ago."

He was afraid she'd suffocate in the jumble of knick-knacks that he found overdone and overwhelming, she'd reply that it was in his arms she wanted to suffocate, appealing to his male ego in the hope of changing the subject, and she always succeeded. And they always made love in semi-darkness.

She hadn't hidden her past from her suitor for long. She was afraid he would find out from another source – he was a policeman, after all – and she thought he'd react better if the information came from her.

The night of her confession – to minimize the risks, she had donned her most revealing nightie, a light, diaphanous creation that seemed almost invisible – Maurice had heard her out, then taken her hand and said:

"What happened in Ottawa happened in Ottawa and stayed in Ottawa."

Period. No discussion. No judgment.

Ti-Lou thought it was too good to be true, a man like him couldn't exist, he must be hiding something. No. As the months and now even years went by, she had learned to appreciate her handsome suitor who had appeared from heaven the night of her arrival, like a welcome-to-Montréal present, and had chosen to forget, or rather, ignore her past. He was upright of mind and of body, didn't waste energy on useless speculation, and lived in the present, enjoying everything they had to offer each other.

Because he loved her?

That she didn't dare believe.

It's too hot in the living room. Maria has already taken off the wool sweater she was wearing under her winter coat, but she's still suffocating in her little cotton dress. Ti-Lou, who's always been sensitive to the cold, has set up two auxiliary heaters that must cost her a fortune in electricity. On top of the heat from the big cast-iron radiator under the window, the dry heat they generate smells of burned old dust and makes the air in the room unbreathable.

"I hope you don't find it too hot in here?"

Ti-Lou has just covered her legs with the wool blanket she'll keep by her all winter.

"Actually ... yes. You've always been sensitive to the cold, Ti-Lou, but this is ridiculous!"

"Listen, let me tell you something. I'm not even sure I feel that cold. It's just that ... you'll laugh ... it's as if ... I spent so much time undressed, I like feeling cozy and warm ..."

"You mean you felt cold when you were –"

"No, that's not what I meant. The hotel was well heated. It's hard to explain ... but it's as if I can never be covered enough. Now don't go thinking there's some guilt related to my profession, that's not what it is. Don't repeat this to anyone, but, when I feel nice and warm, I feel protected. Crazy, eh?"

"But when Maurice comes to see you, do you keep the heat like this?"

"No. That's the point. When Maurice comes, I turn it off and I don't feel cold, which all goes to show you, right? And he still finds that it's too hot in here. Too hot and dark! I wonder why he keeps coming to see me!"

"You're a beautiful woman, Ti-Lou."

"Correction ... I'm still a beautiful woman."

"Don't start in on that again."

"The French have an expression for it: lovely leftovers. How awful! Being compared to leftovers."

Ti-Lou waves her hand in the air as if to chase away the notion of aging and the horror and humiliation it entails.

"Imagine if he showed up now, unannounced, he'd think I was crazy for sure!"

She blushed.

Maria takes a cookie from the plate placed on the pouffe between their two armchairs.

"So sounds like he should come to live with you to cure you of this ..."

"That's out of the question! It's like you with Monsieur Rambert, you each have your own house, your own things. And you see, it's lasted for five years, and you fifteen years, right?"

"What does Maurice have to say about this? The same as Monsieur Rambert? I can't believe that a policeman suffers in silence."

"He doesn't say anything. We've never discussed it. I guess we both like our independence. Besides, where would he put his horse?"

She laughs, throws back the blanket, and stands up with difficulty.

"But... you probably figured out I didn't ask you to come to talk about that. There's something I didn't want to talk about on the phone."

"Are you going to the bathroom? Do you need help?"

"No. I just need to stretch a bit... while I still have both legs."

Maria starts and stands up herself.

"Why are you saying that? Did you get bad news?"

Ti-Lou leaves the room, walks down the hallway to the kitchen limping, and returns.

"I don't mean to make you wait, Mària, it's just that when I go too long without walking, my leg really hurts. Even at night I have to get up..."

"That must worry Maurice."

"Maurice sleeps like a log. Thank heavens."

She plunks herself down in her armchair, pulls up her blanket and turns on the floor lamp that sheds a harsh light on her. Maria can finally assess the changes in her cousin since her last visit. Circles under her eyes, dull skin, new wrinkles around her eyes. Her cheeks, once so high, an actress's cheekbones, have fallen, her neck has withered.

"You wonder why I keep the house so dark. If I showed this to Maurice..."

"Maurice doesn't know?"

"He knows about the diabetes, about what's in store for me. He doesn't know what's happening to me already. In the semidarkness, I can still create an illusion, Maria, but not in broad daylight. And that's why I called you. If you can't, don't worry, I'll make other arrangements, I'll take a taxi alone... but if you could... I hesitated till the last minute before asking you. I'll be getting my final results tomorrow and that's when they'll tell me if I need an operation. And I don't want to go alone. You work at night..."

Could you come with me tomorrow morning? It's far from here, on Drummond below Burnside ..."

Maria remains silent, her eyes wide open. She can't find the words to express her shock, her compassion, the big lump of tenderness mixed with pity that rises in her throat.

"I told you, if you can't, I can make other arrangements."

"No. It's just that ..."

"If you're trying to find words to console me, forget it. There are no words. I'm inconsolable. Just say yes or no."

"Yes. I'll go with you. Of course. You could've asked me on the phone, you know."

"No. Not on the phone. In broad daylight. I want you to know what you're getting into, and I wanted to see in your eyes if you were sincere. Tell me there's more than pity in your response, Maria."

Maria leans over to take Ti-Lou's hand, careful not to brush up against her sore leg.

"There's more than pity, Ti-Lou. We've been through too much together, and each on her own, for there to be just pity."

When she arrives at the shoe store, fifteen minutes before opening time, Teena finds Édouard leaning against a store window.

"You don't have to arrive before me, Édouard. That's not what I meant yesterday."

Has she ended up with someone more punctual that she is? Yesterday she thought she was dealing with a dawdler.

"I didn't mean to arrive too early, but I caught the 52 car and it brought me straight here. It was so fast, I arrived earlier than I meant to."

It's a beautiful December day, mild, it feels like late March. Unfortunately, the snow began to melt at sunrise and there's slush as far as the eye can see. Puddles of black mud cover the streets and sidewalks and if you don't watch where you step, you'll have dirty boots and the bottom of your pant legs or your nylon stockings will be wet all day.

When he left home, nervous, terrorized by the idea of arriving late on his first day of work, Édouard hurried to catch the 52 tram – the one that goes up Saint-Laurent, turns right on Mont-Royal and travels east until the Iberville terminal – to avoid wading in the cold slush. The tram stops right in front of Giroux et Deslauriers. But only every sixty minutes. So Édouard arrived a bit too early at the corner of Fabre and Mont-Royal. The following tram would have arrived too late.

"Tomorrow, I'll take the connecting two cars. I'll be able to calculate the time better."

He is sporting a new hat to replace the tricolour tuque he was wearing the day before. It makes him look less like a young kid but nevertheless fails to meet with Teena's approval. She clucks her tongue as she opens the door.

"Honestly, you could've bought a better hat than that. Yesterday you looked like a child, today you look like a little old man."

Édouard sighs in exasperation.

"Who cares what my hat looks like! The customers won't even see it."

She turns to him as she pushes the door open.

"No, but I will. That hat doesn't look good on you, Édouard!"

"I bought it with your money … and I spent it all."

"Next door?"

"Yes."

"We'll go exchange it during our lunch hour. They know me, they can't refuse. We'll find one that suits you better. Right now we have to start our day."

It's cold in the shop. And damp. The owners have ordered Teena to lower the heat at night, just warm enough to prevent the pipes from freezing. She's tried in vain to explain that this only saves pennies, the shop takes hours to heat up every morning, that it would cost less to keep the thermostat at the same temperature, day and night, during the winter, but they refuse to listen and there are days, especially in January and February when the saleswoman has to keep her coat on during her first hours at work. She takes it off when customers appear, but they notice and some even protest loudly. She shrugs and pretends to be fighting something, a cold or a flu. They are not fooled, even though they pretend to believe her.

"The switches are in the back of the store, near the restrooms. Turn on some lights, we can't see a thing in here. Good God, it's cold!"

She watches him waddle towards the back of the store. She spent part of the previous evening wondering if she had made a mistake, if she hadn't hired him just to make her sister happy, and to help the woman forced to work as a janitor, a woman she doesn't even know but whose tribulations Maria has told her about. Does she really feel like spending eight hours a day with this overweight teenager who's never worked a day in his life and who might prove to be a bad salesman? And will she have the heart to fire him if it doesn't work out?

She shrugs. Him or someone else ... experienced sales personnel cost a lot of money, don't listen to her because she's a woman, and do as they please, and that's no better.

When she was named manager at Giroux et Deslauriers – which doesn't mean much because she only has one employee under her – she felt important, held her head high, and added a bit of spring to her step. That didn't last long when she realized that her assistant – he had a fancy title, too – couldn't accept that they had made a woman manager of the establishment and chose to leave rather than follow her orders. And all the others she had hired since then, even Monsieur Villeneuve who had seemed so nice at first, had the same problem. They didn't all admit it, some cited ridiculous reasons for leaving the shop, but Teena knew why, after only a few months or a few weeks, they would arrive one morning with some excuse for leaving her in the lurch.

She didn't think she was a difficult boss. But *she* was the boss, and that was the problem.

When she spoke to the administration about hiring a young woman as her assistant, she was told they couldn't possibly leave two women alone in the shop. As if Édouard could defend her if a bandit showed up at Giroux et Deslauriers!

Did she hire this thought-to-be *confirmed bachelor* because she believed she'd have the upper hand with him, that he wouldn't have the courage or the strength to resist, unlike the others who'd almost always done as they pleased?

Perhaps.

Even certainly, yes.

The lights go on, the shelves lined with shoes emerge from the dark, along with the customers' chairs and the little stools the sales people don't always use because sometimes it's easier to crouch down at the customers' feet than to sit down in front of them.

Édouard takes off his coat and looks at her.

She freezes. She doesn't know what to ask him, what to tell him to do.

Then the bell over the door tinkles.
Someone has just come in.
This early?
Who buys shoes at nine o'clock in the morning?

This is the sound she's been waiting for. It must be quarter to ten. She stays bent over behind the display case where she has placed the cookies she just unwrapped, a tempting new kind called Marsh-mallow Dreams – vanilla cookies with a choice of pink or green marshmallow, sprinkled with coconut – she hasn't dared taste yet because her boss is still in the back of the shop. But as soon as Madame Guillemette leaves to go to the bank, Béa will, as she always says, "test" the cookies, one of each colour, so she can recommend them to customers. Or suggest that they choose something else. The perfect excuse she's been using for years, totally justifiable and convenient. Madame Guillemette isn't fooled but she tolerates it since over the years Béa has become an expert taster she can trust. She is never wrong. Madame Guillemette continues to buy the cookies her salesgirl likes and doesn't hesitate to reject the ones that don't win her favour.

She waits until someone coughs into his fist to attract her attention and she knows that when she straightens up, she'll be red as a tomato. He has this effect on her, this Arthur Liasse who for the past two months has been finding a pretext to stop by every morning for a cookie or two and a wee bit of courtship.

She tries not to think too much about this wee bit of courtship, for fear of taking it too seriously and getting her hopes up. It's obvious that Arthur likes her – he's told her several times that he finds her attractive – but she can't let herself assume it could go farther than that. She doesn't want to be too optimistic, she prefers not to fantasize and avoid disappointment.

"Do I have to sing 'O Canada' to get your attention, Mademoiselle Rathier?"

Should she play independent and keep him waiting, just a bit? Why not?

"I'm sorry, Monsieur Liasse, but I have to finish arranging my cookies."

"I start work in fifteen minutes, I can't wait long ..."

"That's true, I'm sorry."

She straightens up too quickly and has one of the dizzy spells that have been bothering her recently – her mother, her sisters, her brother all say she eats too much and doesn't do enough exercise – and she braces herself on the counter. Arthur walks around the display case and takes her by the shoulders.

"Are you sick, Mademoiselle Rathier? You look as if you're going to faint."

She pushes him away, for appearance's sake, because she'd really like him to leave his hands on her shoulders and even pull her closer to him.

"No, no. I'm fine. I just stood up too fast."

She turns her head to him. His beautiful green eyes. She's never seen eyes so green. And so beautiful.

He approaches his forehead to hers.

"What would you say if I kissed you?"

She replies without the slightest hesitation. As if that's what she was waiting for. In fact, she was waiting for just this.

"Just try and you'll see."

He kisses her. His mouth closed, almost tight-lipped, shy, an attempt at a kiss, not a skillful demonstration. Perhaps he's as inexperienced as she is.

Is this the culmination of all those evenings spent listening to radio dramas or reading those French and American magazines, dreaming, not of a Prince Charming, she knows that Prince Charmings are invented to make young girls dream – her mother says it's to promote the sale of wedding gowns – no, of an ordinary young man, like him, like Arthur Liasse, with his godawful name and his breath smelling of cigarettes, someone who would notice her, who would take care of her, make her feel important. Madly in love? If possible, yes, otherwise she'd be content with deep affection. In a big house full of children.

It tastes a bit of tobacco. It's neither pleasant nor unpleasant. In fact, it's a bit disappointing. But better than nothing.

She pushes him back, smooths her hair that didn't need smoothing.

"Go back behind the counter, Monsieur Liasse, you don't belong on this side."

He coughs into his fist and moves away. Now he's the one who's red as a tomato. Did the kiss have more of an effect on him than on her?

"I think I'll splurge this morning, I'll take two gateau royals."

"Don't look. He just came in."

Alice leans over the cash register, pretending to count the money. Not him again!

The Geracimo Restaurant is almost empty at this hour. The breakfast rush is over, and there's a good hour and a half before the mad noon hour when the place is invaded by a loud mob who demand to be served ASAP because their lunch hour is short. This is the moment when the waitresses can relax and chat while they fold the paper napkins and smoke their cigarettes. And stretch their tired legs. The older women complain of their varicose veins – the result, they claim, of the thousands of steps they take, year after year, on a hard floor – while the younger women use the time to touch up their makeup. As noon approaches, they scatter, chattering as they head for the sections they've been assigned for the day.

"He sat down at one of your tables."

Alice curses and slams the drawer of the cash register.

"How does he always manage to know which section is mine? If you ask me, he's got a spy in the restaurant. He must pay someone, it's unbelievable!"

Claudette, a friendly girl everyone likes, always more tired than the others because of her weight, everyone's confidante who as a result knows all the secrets of these women who have to work to earn their living and don't always appreciate it, this girl some of the customers call *Auntie* because they've known her for so long, takes a few steps back and glances at the man who has just arrived.

"It's true, it's strange …"

Alice picks up her pad, her pencil – she has no choice, the

customer is in her section, she has to wait on him – and walks down the aisle to the back of the restaurant. She is convinced that every time he enters the restaurant, someone, one of the waitresses or the manager, signals discreetly to this silly man to tell him where to sit. Every morning, at ten o'clock on the dot, he parks the huge truck he drives for a furniture company outside the front door of the Geracimo and sits down in Alice's section and orders his coffee and the restaurant's morning special, pancakes with maple syrup, pepper steak being the evening special and the hot chicken sandwich the special at lunchtime. He has never declared his interest in Alice, but she can tell from his insistent looks and the flush on his neck when she approaches him that one of these mornings, he'll make his move and say what she doesn't want to hear. She is not interested in him. Not at all. She doesn't want to be impolite with him – besides, she doesn't have the right – but she knows that she'll send him off, and probably not diplomatically, if he makes one too-flattering comment or, even worse, if he dares ask her to go out with him some evening. He's probably too shy, but she doesn't want to take any chances, and weeks ago, she prepared a couple of cutting sentences that she hopes she'll dare deliver if the occasion arises. In fact, she might never have to, if he's as timid as she suspects from his behaviour ...

He's pretending to read the menu.

She feels like slapping him on the back of his head. She knows very well, and so does he, that he will order the usual.

"Same thing as usual?"

He looks up brusquely, redder, if possible, than usual.

"Why not? Why change, it's so good ..."

He wants to say more, add a comment, but she doesn't give him time and hurries off, her heels tapping on the terrazzo floor. Perhaps she just avoided what she's been dreading for so long and she heaves a big sigh of relief.

Just before going through the swinging doors into the kitchen to place her order, she turns to Claudette, not knowing why, maybe to let her know she escaped again and catches the bitch, the damn hypocrite, exchanging a sign of complicity with her customer. She rushes over and almost throttles her.

"So you're the one, damn you."

Claudette is startled and raises her arms to protect herself as if Alice were about to hit her.

"What are you talking about? Now what have I done?"

"You know damn well. You gave him a signal!"

"Gave who what?! Who was I signalling?"

"To him, the creep, my customer."

"Signals! I wasn't signalling –"

"Liar! I saw you."

"I wasn't signalling to him! I smiled at him because he smiled at me, but I wasn't signalling! You're crazy!"

"I saw you!"

"You saw me smile at him. I've got a right to smile at people."

"Well not to him. And don't say it wasn't a signal."

"A signal of what? What kind of signal? What d'ya mean?"

"You know very well. If I ever find out that you're the one who's always showing him where to sit so I can wait on him every morning, I'll poke out your eyes with your lead pencil!"

"What's going on here?"

Jean-Guy Gagnon, the day manager, is a man you don't argue with. His assertive tone and the veiled threats behind everything he says have settled more than one dispute since Alice has been working at Geracimo. The girls fear him like the plague. This time, however, Alice doesn't want the argument to be settled with a friendly handshake. She refuses to think that she and Claudette will feel so threatened by his fierce looks and his vague words, whose dangerous implications they sense, that they'll promise to bury the hatchet.

"We can hear you yelling all the way to the entrance. Do you think customers will stay here if they see two waitresses scratching each other's eyes out? No way, they'll go across the street to the Select and we'll never see them again!"

Claudette adjusts her skirt and smooths her apron.

"It was no big deal. It's over. Excuse us, Jean-Guy."

"It better be over. 'Cause you could find yourselves settling your problems on the sidewalk, and there'd be a sign in the window, saying, just for the two of you, HIRING WAITRESSES! Understand?" Alice is fuming. She doesn't want to pretend that everything's fine just to avoid getting fired from Geracimo. She knows that this job is precious, that hundreds of young women would like to be in her place, that her mother would make a terrible scene if she came home without a job, she knows all that, she doesn't want it to happen, so to avoid any unfortunate aftermath, she should turn on her heels and head for the kitchen to give her customer's order to the cook, but she stands there, stiff as a rod, with blue veins visibly throbbing in her neck and across her forehead.

Control herself... How to control herself?!

Claudette and Jean-Guy are staring at her, undoubtedly expecting her to explode.

No.

They would be too happy to get rid of her. Him, the gawky guy who disliked her the minute she entered the restaurant, and Claudette, the traitor, the sneak who'd probably like to take her place. Alice runs a hand over her face. Wait, no. Her usual paranoia. No one hates her, no one envies her place, it's all in her head. When she gets angry, she sees red and distorts the situation she's facing. It has cost her several jobs over the past couple of years, and some good ones. She mustn't give in to it, let it take over again. It mustn't cost her another job.

She takes a deep breath and looks Claudette in the eye.

"Let's say I believe you. But if I learn that I was right, I'll shove your apron down your throat, along with your pad, your pencil, and waitress's cap. In the meantime, I'm going to order the pancakes with maple syrup for that loser."

She takes a few steps towards the kitchen then returns to her colleague.

"And if he shows up in my section tomorrow morning, even if it costs me my job, both of you will be sorry. I told you, Claudette, I don't want a boyfriend these days, I'm fed up with men, how clear can I make it?!"

Édouard has never seen such a well-dressed man.

Everything about him is perfect, from his felt hat to his well-pressed pants, the gabardine overcoat, and the supple, natural-leather gloves. In the fashion magazines he consults whenever he can, men are rarely portrayed in colour, creating the impression that every elegant man wears black, grey, or white. Or possibly beige or brown, the only shades that occasionally appear in clothing catalogues.

But this man ...

His hat is grey, but it's as if that's the only concession he makes to the usual magazine illustrations – and in fact, the material of his hat reflects a subtly green sheen when the man moves his head – the gabardine of his coat is a magnificent bottle green that accentuates the butter yellow of his gloves, a tiny silk flower, more orange than red, adorns his buttonhole, the pants, if Édouard had to name a colour, would be prune, and his watery-green silk scarf, in a final refined touch, is worn casually over one shoulder, like in the films from France. More like an ascot than a scarf.

A foreigner lost on Plateau-Mont-Royal? A French Canadian who wants to forget his roots and does everything to pass for a Frenchman? An actor! Maybe he's an actor! Édouard will listen carefully to his voice, maybe he's heard him on the radio, in a radio drama or an ad. Whatever the case, he is superb and Édouard is in awe. A good thing he's still in the back of the shop and the gentleman hasn't spotted him with his gawking eyes and gaping mouth.

"Mademoiselle Desrosiers, I have a problem."

A superb voice as well!

Teena approaches him, rubbing her hands together. The reflex of a saleswoman who senses a good sale, or simply because her fingers are still stiff from the cold? They know each other, and well, because the gentleman kisses her on both cheeks with obvious pleasure.

"What can I do for you, Monsieur Lacroix?"

Lacroix? That doesn't ring a bell. He can't be an actor. And his accent isn't French. A wealthy businessman or a professional. What would a lawyer be doing here? And he doesn't have a satchel with him so he's not a doctor.

In a dramatic gesture, the customer collapses onto one of the chairs, while removing his gloves with an elegant flourish.

"Simply save my life!"

A strange smell, both sweet and musky, has reached Édouard at the other end of the shop. He would love to wallow in it forever. His aunts and his cousins smell good, sometimes they are even a bit too exuberant with their perfume. But this chic man with the ascot exudes an unfamiliar scent as intoxicating as the gardenia perfume Nana's aunt Ti-Lou wears, but different: this smells of freshly cut grass, rather than flowers, more like the forest than flowerbeds. Édouard's heart skips a beat as he thinks, this might be what a man smells like. A clean man.

"I made the stupid mistake of leaving the house wearing my rubbers and my pant legs are already wet, almost up to my knees … Do you by any chance have something that comes higher up the leg, maybe something like those rain boots with the little metal clips in front that women wear? They're ugly but they'd protect my pants."

Teena sits down on the little stool in front of him. She removes his rubbers covered with slush and drops them on the floor.

"Wouldn't you rather have a nice pair of winter boots, Monsieur Lacroix? Some new ones have come in. They'd be better in the snow as well."

He raises his hand in protest, a first truly effeminate gesture, and Édouard blushes to the roots of his hair.

A *confirmed bachelor*. A real *confirmed bachelor*!

"I've never seen a decent pair of winter boots in Montréal! I'm not a lumberjack! I'd rather wear rubber boots that don't try to be anything but ugly than lumberjack boots that simply destroy a silhouette it took hours to gauge and perfect."

Drawn to the unusual scent of this strange man, and by his bizarre comments, Édouard has tiptoed closer.

As she gets up from her stool to head for the back of the shop, she notices him.

"Oh, I forgot to introduce you to my new assistant, Monsieur Lacroix. Édouard, come, let me introduce you."

Monsieur Lacroix scrutinizes Édouard from head to toe, without extending his hand. And he doesn't seem at all impressed by what he sees.

"Where did you find this specimen?"

"He's my sister's daughter's mother-in-law's son..."

"Stop. You're giving me a headache. I do hope he smells better than your last assistant! I felt like I was stumbling into an ashtray when he was here."

Édouard is so impressed – and humiliated to be dismissed like this – that he can't manage to say a word.

Monsieur Lacroix breaks out laughing.

"Don't tell me he's deaf and dumb! If he stutters, Mademoiselle Desrosiers, I order you to fire him immediately."

This is too much. Until this moment, Édouard admired the arrogance, the smug tone of voice, the grand gestures of a fine lady in a man who could have been his father, but this last comment is going too far. Suddenly the cup spills over before Édouard even realized it was full.

He places his fists on his hips, like his mother when she's about to give him a piece of her mind, and a flood of words bursts out of his mouth with an ease he didn't know he had. It almost burns his lips, and he can read on the other man's face the effect his words are having: on his forehead first, frowning, then his eyebrows, down to his nose wrinkling and his mouth, pursed like that of a stuck-up old lady. Who cares if what he says makes him lose his job on his first day – in the heat of the action, he utters things he doesn't even think – he can't let a poser size him up like merchandise and look down on him.

This is the first manifestation of the Duchesse de Langeais, the Antoinette de Navarreins of Plateau-Mont-Royal, who was slumbering inside him and waiting for an occasion like this to explode, and the relief it brings him is a revelation.

"Hey! Just a minute! That's enough! I might not be dressed like a fashion plate, and I might not have the money to buy myself fancy rubber boots with metal clasps, but I'm a real person and I deserve to be treated like one! I'll show you that I'm not deaf and dumb, and I don't stutter! No one should look at someone the way you looked at me! I'm not garbage, I'm a human being, and if you feel like laughing at me, make sure I don't see it, wait until I've turned my back! This is my first morning working here and the first customer I meet treats me like a dirty rag. I'm risking my job talking to you like this, I know that, but tough luck, I can't just sit back. If my Aunt Teena wants to fire me when I've finished, I'll be upset, but at least I'll feel that I was right to answer you back. I don't know who you think you are, some fancy foreigner or a Hollywood actor, but believe me, we know where you come from the minute you open your mouth. If you were the man you pretend to be, you wouldn't be buying galoshes at Giroux et Deslauriers, you'd be buying leather boots at Ogilvy's! You might spend your entire budget on your wardrobe, but get this straight ... Outside of Plateau-Mont-Royal, you'll look like a beggar."

He stops short. Suddenly he is teetering on the brink of a void, a black hole has formed in his brain, and all his vocabulary abandons him. Along with the use of his limbs. He stands frozen in front of Monsieur Lacroix and all he can do is continue to look him in the eye. Nothing else. He is fuming, he'd like to add to what he just said, be even meaner, more cutting, more ... to the point, however, the first outburst from the character he's created for himself since reading Balzac has stopped in mid-flight, someone picked up a rifle, a shot he didn't hear rang out, and there he is, in mid-air, wings extended, before plummeting to the ground where shame and death await him. Shot dead at the very moment of his birth. How sad! What to do now? Go out into the cold, slamming the door behind him, and run to take refuge in his mother's apron, without demanding his due?

No, no. He has to find something else before the silence that has descended on the shoe store is broken. He can't let his Aunt Teena or the despicable Monsieur Lacroix speak!

Antoinette! What would Antoinette say? What would she do? There's no time for thought, he has to act, fast. Fast, the Duchesse de Langeais to the rescue!

He places his hand on his heart, raises his head, closes his eyes.

And when he speaks, this time, another voice has replaced his, a great lightness fills him, and he has become the barefoot Carmelite imprisoned in a fortress in the Balearic Islands, and nothing, no one can resist him now. No matter what he is about to say. In an unlikely accent.

"You are a barefoot tramp, Monsieur, and you always will be. You don't deserve to be shod. Be gone!"

His eyes closed, his index finger pointing in the direction of the door, Édouard expects to hear the sound of the guillotine, the squeaking of the blade on the oiled wooden frame being lowered towards his neck, the unpleasant shlack of his head being severed from the rest of his body.

Nothing. No one says a word. If Mademoiselle Desrosiers is stiff as a rod beside him when he opens his eyes after what feels like two lifetimes although it only lasted a few seconds, Monsieur Lacroix, on the other hand, while obviously taken aback by what he just heard, is almost smiling and Édouard could swear that he can detect a little twinkle in his eyes.

The customer crosses his legs, plays with his butter-yellow gloves, slapping them against his knees as if he were keeping time. Even his foot covered in slush keeps the beat.

"If I hadn't already asked you where you found your unusual assistant, Mademoiselle Desrosiers –"

She interrupts him, her body practically bent in two. Like a vassal expecting to be punished by her master, forever banned from his estate.

"I hope you'll excuse him, Monsieur Lacroix, I had no idea he could be so rude."

She turns to Édouard.

"Where are your manners?!"

Monsieur Lacroix raises his hand to stop her.

"Don't scold him. I've never met anyone with such a sense of repartee. It could be quite an asset if he learned to control it better."

He stands up and approaches Édouard who takes a few steps back, convinced that Monsieur Lacroix is stalling before giving him the lesson he deserves. A good slap in the face, for instance.

"Your imitation of an offended lady was remarkable, young man. Have you rehearsed it often?"

Édouard doesn't know what to say. He can't possibly admit that it's the first time it's happened, that until that day, it had all been in his head, that he imagined dramas, dreamed up tragedies in which he was the heroine, never thinking he would ever dare address someone that way, in that tone of voice! It came out on its own. And he would give everything in the world to erase this unfortunate incident. Especially since Mademoiselle Desrosiers, his aunt or at least his relative, could tell on him! Making his mother cry even harder, giving his father yet another reason to wave his bottle in the air and shout. No.

"You're not answering. It's difficult to talk about these things, you're right. I've been there myself."

He takes a piece of paper out of his pocket and jots something down.

"You know the Paradise Club on Saint-Laurent?"

Teena reacts.

"The Paradise Club? That's where my sister Maria's been working for almost fifteen years."

He turns to her with a big smile, as if she just said the most wonderful thing in the world.

"Maria is your sister?"

"Yes, she is."

"What a small world! She's a wonderful woman!"

"You bet. Everyone knows she's a wonderful woman, you can't imagine how wonderful! But why did you ask Édouard that?"

Monsieur Lacroix turns back to the young man who wishes he could disappear between the cracks in the floor or run to escape.

"I wrote down the address. Come see us some evening, we're a group of ... a group of friends who gather there almost every night after supper."

Teena places her hand on his sleeve.

"He isn't twenty-one yet ..."

"I'm sure he can manage to pass ..."

Édouard doesn't like being spoken of as if he weren't present.

"Why would I want to go there?"

Monsieur Lacroix sits back down and extends one foot to Édouard.

"I think you would find it interesting ... There's a section reserved for us, someone will show you ... Meanwhile, young man, if I am really your first customer, go find me an acceptable pair of rubber boots!"

It's been said out loud.

Ti-Lou saw the words land on the doctor's desk like a gob of spit.

Maria placed a hand on her arm. She didn't reject it. Had she even felt it?

She should cry, scream, and insult someone, demolish everything in the office, including herself, she should become a whirlwind of rage, a devastating hurricane, but she remains immobile. Only a wrinkle on her forehead and a slight trembling of her lips betray the anxiety and the fury welling up inside her.

"When will it take place?"

The doctor closes the yellow file folder holding the severe warnings, noted in blue ink on official forms, accumulated over the years, followed by the threats he recorded and that she chose to ignore, every passing day representing for her a small victory over destiny, and she'd shrug and reply, arrogant and so lovely, we'll see, one day at a time, tomorrow is another day, or, even worse, it might never come to that, why should I worry? A shrug of the shoulders, a wave of the hand, the rustling of a silk dress, and everything was forgotten. Or denied.

Now he just said it. It's official. It has happened. The time has come. The doctor didn't mince his words because his warnings in recent months had become more peremptory and his threats, one might say, more desperate. On more than one occasion, Ti-Lou had even had the feeling he wanted to shake her and yell in her face.

"As soon as possible. Before it gets worse and the situation becomes even more dangerous. Gangrene is pitiless."

"Before Christmas?"

"Not that soon. Early January."

She opens her handbag, takes out a lilac lace hanky that smells of gardenias, and dabs at her first tears. She is managing to control herself, but the doctor realizes the slightest thing could set her off.

"Tell me ... umm ... I'm not sure how to say it ... When I have only one leg, I'll have to walk with crutches, I know that, but ... Will I be able to live a normal life?"

"Yes, of course. You will be able to move around as you wish, go anywhere you want, no problem, don't worry about that ... After an initial period of adaptation, of course."

"Yes, but ... it's silly to ask, but ... oh, never mind ..."

"No, please, go ahead, if I can help ..."

"I don't know how to say this, Doctor ... When I say a normal life, I mean ... For me, a normal life is unthinkable without ... without beauty. I'll never be able to find myself beautiful after that, you know, only one leg and two crutches ... How can I manage? I find aging difficult as is ..."

"You must let time take its course –"

"Oh no, please, not that sermon! I've got less time now, and if it's going to take me a while to accept all this, my body will have aged even more, and my face, too! What will I have left?"

"I don't know what else to say to you, Mademoiselle Desrosiers. You are a very beautiful woman and you will remain a very beautiful woman despite it all ..."

She stands up in a flash, her handbag falls onto the floor, Maria bends over to pick it up.

"You don't understand! A beautiful woman! When I step out of my bath – how will I step out of my tub anyway? – how do you expect me to find that I'm beautiful with a stump! A stump in place of my leg! Oh, we know, that's not your problem! Your job is to saw off my leg, throw it into the garbage, then leave me to work things out!"

"Mademoiselle Desrosiers ..."

"Mademoiselle Desrosiers says go to hell, Doctor!"

"I can refer you to a specialist who can help you with those problems afterwards. It's not my field, Mademoiselle Desrosiers, I don't have the right to get involved."

"You don't have the right to help me!"

"Help you to heal, yes. And to learn to live with the handicap. But for the rest, that will be up to someone else."

"I don't want someone else. I want you! You've been following me for five years! I know you. That specialist you want me to consult, I don't know him, I won't know what to say. I'll have to start all over with him. I don't feel like telling my life story to someone new, someone I don't know, can't you understand that?"

She takes her purse back from her cousin, turns her back on the doctor, and limps towards the door.

"We have to set the date, Mademoiselle Desrosiers. There's a protocol to be followed."

"Forget your protocol! You can call me at home this afternoon. I've had enough of this for now, enough and then some."

She leaves the door open and doesn't even say goodbye to the secretary with whom she's always so nice.

The doctor leans back in his chair.

Maria stands in turn.

"You can expect me to answer the phone. I'll keep her company for the rest of the day."

On her way to the brand-new Drummond Medical Building where she has an appointment with her doctor, Tititte Desrosiers thinks she sees her sister Maria's silhouette a hundred feet ahead of her. She's with someone who is limping. Their cousin Ti-Lou? What are they doing in this neighbourhood, two women who never leave the east end of Montréal? Ti-Lou must have an appointment with her doctor whose office could be in the same building as hers, and Maria decided to accompany her ... What a strange coincidence.

She decides not to call out to them, it's already after noon and if she's delayed, she won't have time to eat before going back to work. Ogilvy's is close by, but Tititte doesn't know how long her appointment with Dr. Woolf will take. Although ... if the news is bad, she won't feel like eating.

She pulls open the heavy door, stamps her feet on the braided jute carpet to remove the dirty snow from rue Drummond. Suddenly it's very hot. Almost too hot. The central heating must still be working. The doorman raises his cap to greet her. He comes out from behind his art deco wood-and-brass desk and heads for the elevators.

"I believe you're going to the fifth floor, Mademoiselle Desrosiers?"

They're very stylish at the Drummond Medical Building, everyone is polite and solicitous, it smells new and clean, everything is chic but not flashy. Almost enough to make you forget why it exists.

As she arrives at the door of Woolf & Chapman, she shudders. Within the next few minutes, she will learn the truth, the die will be cast, her destiny, her life, decided upon, settled. A reprieve or not, survival or ...

Her relief is so great, she promptly begins to sob. She doesn't have time to fish a handkerchief out of her purse before the tears start to pour down her cheeks and neck. Dr. Woolf – who rarely has the occasion to share good news with his patients – is flushed with pleasure.

"I'm very happy for you, Mademoiselle Desrosiers."

Tititte's conversations with Dr. Woolf always take place in French. He insists. A declared francophile in Montréal's anglophone society, he is happy to practise his French whenever possible, usually with his patients, and he finds this patient, this Mademoiselle Desrosiers, with her fancy airs and her rather forced manner of speaking with him – deference or fear? – particularly pleasant. She's a beautiful woman, she has lovely posture, her manner of speaking is clear, her comments lively and interesting, and she smells delightful. He knows she sells gloves at Ogilvy's and he often finds a reason to pass her counter – Ogilvy's is a short walk from his office – just to have the pleasure of greeting her.

She dabs at her eyes, blows her nose, and apologizes.

"No need to apologize, your reaction is totally normal. You were probably expecting worse, and this feels like a gift."

She puts her handkerchief back into her purse after wiping a last tear.

"I can't tell you. I'd stopped living after our last appointment ... I was so scared –"

He interrupts her, raising a finger.

"Excuse me, but you were my last patient before noon. It's time for lunch and I hope it's not presumptuous of me ... Would you like to accompany me? We could have a bowl of vegetable soup" – his English accent makes Tititte's heart flutter – "and a plum pudding next door."

She has lost control of her hands that have started fidgeting on their own. They're opening and closing her purse, smoothing her skirt on her lap, replacing locks of hair that haven't moved. She feels like a sixteen-year-old girl who's just been invited out on her first date.

"Uhhh ... ummm ... I'd love to join you, Dr. Woolf, but I have to be back at work at one o'clock."

Her arm jerks up, even too close to her eyes for her to read her watch. It falls back on its own without knowing where to land. It finally lands on the arm of her chair with an unpleasant thud.

They are both equally uncomfortable and the intervening silence is terribly embarrassing.

He should tell her that their consultation is over or she should take the initiative of standing to leave his office, but neither one dares to move.

After a long pause, during which both of them blush like shy sixty-year-old teenagers, the doctor takes a deep breath and dives in.

"Well then, perhaps ..."

He coughs into his fist, seems to hesitate, then continues.

"Perhaps you would accept a dinner invitation? Are you busy this evening?"

"He's an actor."

"Are you sure? That's what I thought when I saw him walk in, but his voice isn't familiar ... or his name."

"I don't think he gets a lot of work."

"Well if he was on the radio, I would've recognized his voice. I know all the actors who play in the radio dramas."

"No, he works in the theatre. At the Arcade, with the Giroux sisters."

"I know them. They're great. They do lots of radio. I'd recognize their voices anywhere ... especially Germaine, she always sounds like she's got a cold. A funny voice, but I like it. Sometimes I try to imitate her, just for fun."

Teena stared at him for a few seconds. Édouard thought he might have said too much – a young man who has fun imitating an actress's voice – and he fell silent.

"I just said he wasn't getting much work ... But that's not true. He's working but we don't hear about it because he just does theatre. Once he told me he does a play every week! Imagine, learning a whole play by heart every week! They rehearse the play for the following week during the day, and they perform the play of the week at night. That's no life. But he says he loves it. My sister Tititte went to see him perform once. She told me he was good, but she didn't think he seemed virile enough to play a hero. At one point, he had to fight with another man and looked like he was having trouble. Anyway, he's a far cry from Douglas Fairbanks, that's for sure."

Xavier Lacroix turned out to be the only customer to show up in the shoe store between ten o'clock and noon. Teena used that time to explain to Édouard what she expected of him: to welcome people cordially, ask them what type of shoes they were looking for, bring them what they wanted to try on, and never, absolutely never, make any comments about the state of their feet, the shoes they were already wearing, and especially about the smell when they removed their shoes. And there would be smells! Some disgusting, some worse than others, some unbearable. Most of the customers were clean, of course, but the ones that stank could ruin the air in the store for hours. That meant airing out the store frequently. Winter and summer. After waiting until the offenders left so as not to insult them.

"Sometimes, in the summer, it's worse. Because there's no air circulation. When it's really hot, like in August, and it stinks, believe me, it's something else! You have to breathe through your mouth ... or smoke lots of cigarettes. Do you smoke?"

"No, it costs too much."

"Well believe me, you'll start pretty soon."

"But wouldn't we be doing them a favour telling them to wash their feet?"

"Sometimes they wash them, but they stink anyway. It's like a sickness. I'm not sure they can do anything about it."

Once Teena finished her presentation, Édouard declared that being a shoe salesman seemed like an easy job. She told him to wait before drawing a conclusion, wait until he dealt with a woman who tries on dozens of pairs of shoes – sometimes out of boredom, just to pass the time – and walks out without making a purchase, leaving the store turned upside down. And smelling a bit strange.

"Can't we tell them off?"

"You're here to serve them, not to give them a piece of your mind. They won't all react like Xavier Lacroix! They want to try on shoes, you help them try on shoes. You know the expression: *the customer is always right*? Unfortunately for us, that's true. If you have trouble accepting that, you better tell me right now. I saw that you can be pretty temperamental, don't think I'll let you get away with it every time you feel like telling someone off, this is no place for that, it's not *your* place to do it."

Édouard had listened to her description of his duties and promised to do what she wanted, while telling himself he certainly wasn't going to put up with people whose feet stank. He'd find a way to make them aware of their problem.

Sitting in the chairs of the customers who were yet to arrive, they began chatting about this and that. Teena obviously wanted to know more about him, he'd picked up on that quickly and remained evasive. Until the conversation came back to Xavier Lacroix.

"Is that his real name, Aunt Teena?"

"Don't call me Aunt Teena here! First of all, I'm not your aunt. I am your brother's wife's aunt. Call me Mademoiselle Desrosiers, like everyone else.

"Is that his real name, Mademoiselle Desrosiers?"

"Whose real name?"

"Xavier Lacroix. Especially Xavier. I don't know anyone named Xavier."

"Your father's name is Télesphore, Édouard. You know anyone else named Télesphore?"

"You're right there. If my name was Télesphore Lacroix and I wanted to be an actor, I'd look for another name."

She stands up and puts her hands on her hips and arches her back.

"Does your back ache?"

"I'm old, Édouard. Everything aches."

"You're not that old."

"No, it's true, I'm not that old. Let's just say I'm worn out. When you reach my age, I hope you will have stopped needing to sell shoes to earn your living."

"I won't be doing this all my life."

"That's what I thought, too. And look at me after all these years. What would you like to do?"

"I dunno. Maybe rehearse a play that I'll perform the following week during the day, and go on stage evenings, performing with Germaine or Antoinette Giroux."

"Dream away. Besides, by the time you become an actor, the Giroux sisters are apt to have been dead and buried for years."

"Dreaming helps pass the time. And you never know ... with the right connections ..."

"You think becoming an actor is all about connections?"

"Why not? You have to go looking for your chances, instead of waiting for them to find you."

She falls silent for a few seconds, then bends over to pick up a fleck of something on the waxed maple floor.

"You're going to go there, aren't you?"

He understood perfectly what she was referring to, but plays innocent.

"Go where?"

"To the Paradise Club. You're going to go?"

"I'm too young."

"But you're tempted."

"Sure I'm tempted by the clubs, like everyone my age. I can hardly wait to be twenty-one."

"Most don't wait until they're twenty-one."

"Do you think I could look older if I fixed myself up a bit?"

"You don't have to fix yourself up to get into places like that. Especially the Paradise. Ever since the new owner took over, my sister Maria says they turn a blind eye."

"That's right, your sister works there. I'd be embarrassed to show up at the Paradise knowing she'd be there."

"Don't worry ... she's seen all kinds ... especially recently."

"What do you mean?"

She slaps his knee.

"You'll see if you go. Meanwhile, it's time to eat. Did you bring a lunch?"

"My mother made me a sandwich with crushed olives and cream cheese."

"Never heard of that."

"It's good. And cheap. You take a jar of crushed olives and spread some on bread, with butter and cream cheese. My favourite is

Chateau pimento cream cheese. The bread soaks it up, the sandwich gets soft. We eat that every Friday. I asked my mother to make me one today because I had a craving."

"Does your mother satisfy all your whims?"

"Just about. Would you like to taste it?"

"Thanks, but I'll pass …"

One section of the Rougemont store – to be precise, the left-hand corner near the entrance – has recently been turned into a restaurant, and every noon some thirty people crowd around the W-shaped counter to eat hamburgers or steamed hot dogs served by inexperienced waitresses on the verge of hysteria. Or to gulp down the daily special that is never very good but is popular because it only costs twenty-five cents. The rest of the day, idle housewives treat themselves to a caramel sundae or greasy, soggy French fries with vinegar. Or simply a glass of soda water. That they make last as long as possible. The kids won't be home from school until four thirty and supper is still a long ways away.

The saleswomen in the neighbouring sections – especially in the cosmetics and perfume department – complain in vain about the smell of grease that permeates their clothes and their hair. The manager – the man they all hate and call Fat Taillefer – tells them the restaurant is there to stay because it attracts customers, something they claim remains to be seen. They are far from sure there are more people in the store since the W-shaped lunch counter opened, but that doesn't prevent them from eating there themselves because it's practical. And cheap.

It's 12:35, Albertine and Madeleine are attacking their dessert, a tasteless green Jell-O into which the cook threw some canned fruit salad and pompously named *Tropical Gelatine*. Madeleine added a bit of milk and her sister bluntly tells her that makes her sick to her stomach. Madeleine, maybe out of pure bravado, picks up her bowl and gulps down the rest of her Jell-O and milk combo.

Slurping to boot. Another small provocation. Albertine, who has just received her bill, slaps it down on the wooden counter.

"Well that's the limit! I can't take it anymore."

Madeleine is startled.

"What's wrong with you, shouting like that in public?"

"What's wrong is I'm fed up, I'm suffocating, I'm going to explode!"

Madeleine gestures that she should lower her voice.

"Everyone doesn't have to know you're going to explode, Bartine. Nobody's interested."

Albertine stands up, grabs her coat that she was sitting on, and starts to put it on.

"Well I want everyone to know that I'm stuck twenty-four hours a day with my hypocritical sister who stole my beau and plays holier-than-thou while she slurps down her Jell-O!"

"Don't start that again. First of all, I did not steal your beau."

"No? Then, how come you're going out with him?"

Madeleine stands up in turn. If Albertine wants to make a scene in front of everyone, tough luck.

"I'm going out with him because he couldn't stand you anymore, is that clear?"

All heads have turned to the sisters. One waitress has frozen, coffee pot in hand, the other one has stopped in the middle of preparing a bill.

"I've told you that dozens of times, but you don't want to understand. You were suffocating him, Bartine, can't you get that through your head once and for all? I told you, Ma told you, he told you himself."

"Well no, I don't understand. I don't. Even when he tried to explain, I didn't understand. Because I didn't know I was suffocating him. I still don't know what I could've done to suffocate him. That will always be the big mystery in my life! But I might've been able to accept it, make my peace with it, if I didn't have to see you leave with him, twice a week, to go to the movies or out to eat in a restaurant! There's stuff you don't understand, either! Unless you're just pretending. Eh? Don't you feel ashamed sometimes when he's so nice to you in front of me, when he helps you on with your coat or when he kisses your neck, Madeleine? Two months ago, he was doing that with me."

"You could make sure you're not around when he comes by."

"Sure! Now I should disappear because Mademoiselle has done me the honour of stealing my beau! Maybe you'd like me to move?"

"Stop that. You're always threatening to move."

Fat Taillefer has shown up, waving his arms to calm Albertine.

"Please ladies, go settle your family feuds somewhere else. This is no place for that. We can hear you shouting all the way to the middle of the store. Pay your bills and leave. And don't come back until you've settled your problem."

Albertine stands up on her tiptoes so she is nose to nose with the store manager.

"I've been holding it in for months, Monsieur. I didn't mean to explode here, but this is where it finally happened! And if I don't get it out of my system, it'll kill me. You understand? Would you rather hear me shout or see me collapse right here on the floor?"

"Neither, Mademoiselle. What I want is to see you disappear from here."

"You too? Like her? Is everyone against me? Should I stop living because my beau left me for my sister? And now I'm the guilty one? Is that it? I'm the one who has to pay for it? Haven't I paid enough already? Aren't I unhappy enough? You want more? How's this?!"

The slap is well aimed and loud. Everyone holds their breath. Clearly, Fat Taillefer is struggling not to slap Albertine in turn. She takes a few steps back.

"I hope you realize that you're not the one I want to hit. It's her. Little Miss Perfect. The perfect saint. The thief. Now you can call the police, go ahead, I'd rather go to jail than back to the basement at Dupuis Frères to sell last year's useless stock."

The manager's cheek is beginning to swell. A big red mark on his left cheek. He leans over to Albertine and speaks to her quietly, almost kindly.

"Leave, Mademoiselle. That's all I'm asking you."

Albertine finishes buttoning her coat and takes her wool tuque out of her purse.

"Thank you. I'm sorry. If you only knew ... I know what I just did won't change a thing, and that kills me! Because it didn't even make me feel better."

She walks out of the store, her chin tucked into her scarf.

Now Madeleine is getting dirty looks.

The hypocrite. Who steals boyfriends.

She picks up her sister's bill, places a dollar bill on the counter, and leaves in turn.

"It's not just about me, Maria! There's Maurice, too. How's he going to take it?"

"He must've known it might come to this?"

"Yes, but like me, he must've hoped it wouldn't happen. Maybe not as much as me, but ... a stump of a leg! Who would want to go out with a woman with a stump of a leg?"

She took refuge in her favourite armchair as soon as they entered her apartment. Maria wanted to open the curtains to let some light in, Ti-Lou stopped her, saying that after her return from the hospital, after the amputation, she would never open the curtains again, she'd never turn on the lamps in the evening, she would live in total darkness. Hidden and blind. So she couldn't see what had become of her body.

"I've been trying to prepare him lately, but he doesn't want to know. He said he'd be there for me, if it happens or doesn't happen."

"You see, he must know he can face it."

"No, he doesn't! He's a man. He might think he can, sure, but ... when I come home from the hospital, when he finds me in my bed, what will happen? How do you look at a woman who only has one leg? How do you handle that? Will he be able to act like there's no problem and not look there, not see what ... not see the damn stump?"

She raises her arm and punches the back of the armchair. The frame is wood. It hurts and the pain makes her feel better.

"I won't be able to put him through that, the body of a crippled woman, the body of a woman who earned her living with her body that has just been butchered. I won't be able to watch him pretend that he doesn't notice, that nothing has changed, that everything's the same as before. That he still desires me! I won't be capable of seeing him pretend that he still desires me, Maria!"

Maria is taken aback by her cousin's distress. She knows she is there to listen, that nothing she could say would help, that Ti-Lou, who wouldn't even listen to her, needs to express her anger, to shout her pain and sorrow, and that she's undoubtedly right to be worried. Men are what they are and their promises are promises. Even the Prince Charmings. If perfect men are looking for perfection...

"Try not to think about that. You have to prepare for the hospital, that's what matters now. The doctor told you it can't wait anymore, Ti-Lou. You put it off too long and you didn't take care of yourself."

"He's been telling me that for years. Why's he in such a hurry now? Does he want to chop it off any old way? C'mon, you floozie, lie down and let us have our way, you're used to that. But this time it won't be to earn your living but to put an end to it!"

Ti-Lou struggles out of her chair and rubs her leg.

"You know what I feel like doing sometimes? Eh? More and more often? I want to drop everything! Yes, everything! The insulin, the operation. The rehabilitation that will follow, the months of adaptation, the pain of the phantom limb! To hell with it all, I'll just let myself rot away! Rotting, but standing on my own two feet!"

"You can't mean that."

"I mean it."

"The doctor won't allow it."

"It's my leg. My diabetes. I can do what I want with it."

"That would be suicide, Ti-Lou."

"Don't try to tell me that I'd risk spending eternity in Hell. You don't believe that stuff anymore than I do, Maria!"

"I'm not worried about eternity. Just think of what your life would be like! The suffering! The gangrene that could spread through your body! The deterioration, day after day. That would give Maurice a reason to abandon you."

"That might be what I want, actually. Just let me rot in peace!"

"No, that's not what you want. You're a strong woman, Ti-Lou, you always have been."

Ti-Lou shouts at the top of her lungs, her voice breaks, sobs stifle her words, rendering her sentences incomprehensible. She's no longer shouting, she's roaring.

"I'm not a strong woman! How can you say that? I'm about to lose everything, Maria, everything! This is just the first piece I'm losing, the rest will follow! Do you think I can't see that in the doctor's eyes, and in yours and in Maurice's eyes? The amputation won't solve anything, it's too late, the poison has already spread everywhere in my body!"

She crosses the room, limping, opens the curtains wide, and turns to her cousin in the bright afternoon sunlight.

"Take a good look at me, Maria! You wanted more light, you've got it. Is this a strong woman you see, eh, do you really see a strong woman standing here? Yes or no?"

Maria goes over and takes her into her arms.

"Yes, it's a strong woman I see. Yes."

Ti-Lou breaks down.

The first week went by quickly. With Christmas approaching, the store has been constantly busy, with everyone wanting to wear new shoes during the holidays. Teena and Édouard were on the go from morning to evening, kneeling in front of customers dozens of times a day, rushing back and forth to the storeroom. Édouard was a bit lost when he had to serve two or three not-always-patient people at the same time, he was almost running, breathing heavily, perspiring profusely, while wanting to please everyone and prove to his boss that he could become a good salesman. Teena often signalled to him to calm down, she'd spend their entire half-hour lunch break offering advice on how to save his energy while appearing to serve everyone. And since she did not yet allow him to prepare the bills, her work load was heavier than ever. When she wasn't crouching in front of a customer, she was busy at the cash register. Telling herself that her fifty-odd years were beginning to take their toll.

As for Édouard, he was learning the hard way, and to his great surprise, he was enjoying it immensely. He was meeting lots of people, he was always busy, time went by faster than staying at home doing nothing, and at the end of the week, he would receive what represented a large sum of money to him, although he pretended the opposite to Teena.

As far as the smells went, it seemed that everyone had decided to wash their feet before going to buy shoes that week, because no bad odours had infested the store. Had the customers realized that the shoe shop would be busy and decided to avoid the humiliation of exposing their noxious exhalations? Whatever the case, from

Monday afternoon to Saturday evening, Giroux et Deslauriers had only smelled of new leather and shoe polish.

The women loved Édouard. They found him polite and efficient, although a bit flustered, and most of all, amusing. Amusing in his way of being, moving, and speaking. Most of them had never met a *confirmed bachelor* – they sensed immediately that he was one, not realizing however that, unaware of it himself, he was still innocent – and he intrigued them. His gift for quick retorts, some almost insolent, always pertinent and especially amusing, made them burst out laughing. They undoubtedly never went so far as to think about his sexuality – a taboo subject at any rate – and they saw him as a friendly clown, inoffensive, almost like a pet animal. They would have loved to stroll around Plateau-Mont-Royal with him, arm in arm, making jokes and licking ice cream cones. Totally safe.

The men, on the other hand, were promptly put off by him. They found him pretentious – his retorts were cleverer than theirs – effeminate, and too loud because he was too talkative. They tried to avoid him and preferred to be waited on by Mademoiselle Desrosiers, sighing with exasperation when they reluctantly ended up with this fat young man whose manners they disliked and who aroused their suspicion. And those who guessed that he was a *confirmed bachelor* in the making, or worse, an accomplished one, showed their disdain, tightening their lips and raising their noses. They let him handle their feet but never shook his hand.

At nine o'clock on Friday night, right after closing time, Teena handed Édouard a small plain brown envelope with an amount written on it.

"Here's your first pay. Cash. Don't spend it all in one place. Go straight home for supper, no celebrating. Don't forget you have to work tomorrow."

Édouard sits down beside his mother on the living-room sofa. He takes off his shoes, wriggles his toes, and sighs with pleasure.

"I was beginning to worry ... Then I remembered it's Friday."

"Right. We closed at nine."

"Were there lots of customers?"

"Oh, yes! Tons, ever since Monday afternoon. Christmas is around the corner, right ... Mademoiselle Desrosiers, I mean, Aunt Teena took out the Christmas decorations. She says we'll try to put them up tomorrow. Otherwise, if we're too busy, she'll go in on Sunday. I offered to go help her. I love decorating for Christmas."

He leans to the side, takes the little brown envelope out of his pants pocket, and empties it onto his lap.

"I've never had so much of my own money in my whole life. My first pay. And here's my first room and board."

He hands three one-dollar bills to Victoire.

"There'll be more like that every week. I've found a profession, Ma."

That night, in his bed, just before falling asleep, Édouard says out loud, in his phony French accent:

"I am Antoinette de Navarreins, Duchesse de Langeais, barefoot Carmelite and shoe saleswoman."

PART TWO

The Carmelite Steps Out into the World

He appeared at the main entrance of the Saint-Jean-de-Dieu Hospital on a windy October afternoon. It had been raining all morning, the ground was slippery because of the fallen leaves – red, yellow, some green – that created a pretty carpet, perfumed but perilous; you could easily miss a curbstone and lose your balance or slip and find yourself with a sore, wet seat for the rest of the day.

A sister had come to open the door. He had immediately held his violin case up in the air and shouted:

"Sanctuary! Sanctuary!"

The nun had tried to close the heavy wooden door, saying:

"This isn't a church."

He'd raised a hand and held the door open.

"Haven't you read Victor Hugo, Sister? *Notre-Dame de Paris*? Quasimodo takes refuge in the cathedral, shouting: 'Sanctuary! Sanctuary!'"

She had tried to push the door shut. He had blocked it with his foot, like one of the gangsters he'd seen in American movies.

"I don't need to have read Victor Hugo to know what sanctuary meant in the Middle Ages! I've never read a single book on the Index in my life. And I have to ask you to remove your foot before I crush it."

"This hospital isn't a church, I know that, but it can be a refuge. Especially this one. How many unhappy madmen have found shelter here, Sister? In the Saint-Jean-de-Dieu lunatic asylum?"

He'd nevertheless obeyed with a sigh. The door was heavy and his foot hurt. To his great surprise, the nun hadn't promptly closed it.

"You could've asked for shelter without quoting Victor Hugo! Honestly!"

"Do you hate him that much?"

"I don't 'hate' him, I've never read him. I just know his books are forbidden."

"You don't know what you're missing."

She squared her shoulders and tried again to push the door shut.

"Have you come to my door to talk about Victor Hugo or to ask me for a bowl of soup?"

He smiled. He had a beautiful smile, his teeth seemed white for a beggar. And he didn't smell bad.

"You think I'm a beggar? I'm not a beggar, Sister, I'm crazy. Like everyone else here."

"You don't look crazy at all. And the madmen I know don't quote Victor Hugo."

"Thanks for the compliment. But ..."

He'd become serious again. He'd held his violin case against his coat, a bit flimsy for the season, and looked her straight in the eye. His eyes were beautiful, too, but the sister, faithful to her religion, and especially to her order, didn't have the right to notice men's eyes. Nor their smiles, for that matter, nor their teeth. Accordingly, she'd looked away from the old man's face and set her gaze on the bare branches of the trees that line rue Hochelaga on the far side of the hospital grounds. A gust of wind had lifted her veil that she held down after grasping the crucifix that hung around her neck.

The man gave her a pitiful look as he shoved his bare hands into his pockets, having slipped his violin case beneath his arm.

"I can't take it anymore, Sister. I'm tired of seeing things no one else sees."

She turned her gaze back to him. Perhaps he was having a crisis. She couldn't ignore a man in crisis.

"You have visions?"

"I don't know if that's what you call it, but ... Do you see the four women at the foot of the staircase? No, eh? Well, those women have been following me since my childhood. They're the ones who introduced me to Victor Hugo. Among other things. And I wish that someone here, a doctor or a brain surgeon, could get rid of them. 'Cause I can't take it anymore."

She opened the door a crack.

"You shouldn't have come to this door. There's another entrance, out back, for emergency cases. But come in. All I can offer you is a hot meal, and I can try to arrange a meeting with one of our doctors. But I can't promise anything, you hear, today's Sunday."

They climbed the broad interior staircase side by side. The man with the violin had removed his hat as if entering a church and taken in the dark woodwork, the austere paintings, and the pale marble of the steps. An impressive place that looked more like the lobby of a hotel than a hospital. Montréal's madmen had fancy accommodation.

"Don't you have family doctor?"

"If I had the money, I'd buy myself a good meal before I'd pay for a doctor, Sister."

"You play the violin?"

"It's not a machine gun I have in this case."

She didn't even smile at his attempt at humour. And he wondered if there was room for humour in an insane asylum.

"Are you an artist?"

"If you wish. And if you don't wish, I'm just a fiddler."

"But you earn your living with your violin."

"If you call that earning a living."

"But not enough to pay for a doctor ..."

He had stopped at the top of the staircase.

"Why are we talking about this now, Sister? I came here because I need your help and I didn't know where to go."

Then he turned around and spoke to the four women who were following him silently.

"Are you going to follow me in here, too?"

Startled, the nun looked behind her as well. No one, of course.

"If you're acting, you're a good actor. And if you're not acting ..."

The man smiled again.

"I'm crazy as hell?"

"Maybe not crazy as hell but you certainly have a problem."

And that is how Josaphat-le-Violon made his entry at Saint-Jean-de-Dieu.

Through the main entrance.

But that day, a Sunday, the sister had warned him, he didn't get to see a doctor. The one on duty wasn't a specialist, the others all had the day off, and it didn't seem necessary to contact them because Josaphat wasn't in crisis, contrary to what the sister had thought at first, and he didn't seem dangerous. They offered him a hot meal that he found delicious, even if nothing tasted salty enough to him — he hadn't eaten barley soup since leaving Duhamel, years earlier, and it brought tears to his eyes: Victoire watching over the pot, constantly going back to add a little something, Gabriel blowing on his spoon so he didn't burn his mouth, him salivating because it smelled so good, and the taste of fresh vegetables and stewed beef, happiness, happiness! — and a bed for the night, after he had enchanted everyone with his fiddle, the nuns, the male nurses, and the patients alike.

After the meal, he'd gone to stand in the middle of the refectory, taken out his fiddle, and said:

"This is to thank you for your welcome. Afterwards, I'll be on my way …"

He had played the "Méditation," he'd played a *Humoresque*.

Relative calm had descended upon the big hall while he was interpreting Massenet and Dvořák. The deeply disturbed, the incurable, the ones who had lost all sense of their surroundings, went on complaining, whining, laughing, shouting, but the others, the less-severe cases whose crises were not permanent and who found their confinement painful because they knew they were confined, had listened attentively, some had cried, others beamed with joy.

The hospital employees couldn't get over it. They hadn't seen a meal end so calmly for ages. No intervention had been necessary, no punishments either.

After the applause, encouraged by the many requests for more, more, Josaphat had improvised for another quarter of an hour, passing from one composer, one century, to another, from gigues from his childhood to more modern tunes he'd picked up in Montréal's taverns. His repertory from L.N. Messier performed in a very different atmosphere, for a very different audience. This place didn't smell of perfume sold in fancy bottles and of clean housewives, it smelled of convent cooking, not very tasty and never spicy enough, with overcooked vegetables and meat stewed for hours. The blandness of the nuns' cooking matched the blandness of their existence as servants of the Good Lord. And it also smelled of human beings incapable of taking care of themselves. Sweat, and something else.

After thanking him and praising his skill with the bow, they had offered him shelter for the night. It was dark outside, and cold. Coifs were fluttering, faces pink with pleasure, there was laughter, tension had disappeared from the big common room. Perhaps, people hoped, he'd repeat this tour de force at breakfast time, the following morning … Josaphat had approached the sister who certainly hadn't spared her praise and murmured with a smile:

"Sanctuary! Sanctuary!"

She'd promptly retorted:

"May I call you Monsieur Quasimodo?"

"Yes, but I'll never call you Esmeralda!"

The nun's laughter was shrill, very different from her speaking voice, as if a young girl were hidden inside this massive body and behind this face disguised by her pointed coif.

"I certainly don't look like a gypsy."

"You're not supposed to know who Esmeralda is, Sister."

"You don't have to spent time with someone to know their reputation, you know."

They had laughed. A moment of complicity.

A man in his fifties, grey hair, a well-trimmed moustache, one of the patients who had listened to him most attentively, had come closer and extended his hand:

"I recognized the 'Méditation' from *Thaïs*. I hadn't heard it for such a long time. My mother used to play it on the piano."

It's hard to say why, but Édouard finds that the Christmas decorations make the shoe store look sad rather than merry. The coloured lights, most of which, burned out, needed to be replaced, emphasize the outdated, dull aspect of the dusty garlands that Teena almost decided to leave in their cardboard box, telling her assistant that for years now, she's been asking to have this pathetic assortment of old ornaments replaced once and for all. She and Édouard had to dust off everything, piece together the so-called gold garlands that should have ended up in the garbage, now greasy and more brown than yellow, and fight with the strings of lights that were hopelessly tangled and gnawed on by mice.

"Someday, the place will go up in flames and they'll blame me. Damn owners, too cheap to spend a penny. It's Christmas, for heaven's sake, not a funeral!"

No jolly, plump père Noël, no angels with or without trumpets, no representation of the Holy Family, nothing but garlands about to give up the ghost and lights that risk setting Plateau-Mont-Royal on fire. The scene of the manger in Bethlehem would look wonderful in one of the big show windows, the one on the left. They could drape a white sheet over empty shoe boxes to represent the village – even though snow never falls in Bethlehem, everyone knows that but no one gives a damn – Teena could bring her collection of Provençal Christmas figurines from home, she could dust them with flour to make them white, along with the woolly sheep with matchstick legs tucked away in a kitchen drawer, and get out her glass ornaments, the cardboard angels, the false snow – laundry soap flakes – and the aluminum-foil icicles. She put all that away years ago because she thinks there's nothing sadder than an aging woman who decorates her house at Christmas for herself all alone.

She offered to do all that for free, but her bosses told her that a shoe store isn't a family enterprise like the one next door and that what mattered to the owners of Giroux et Deslauriers wasn't pleasing children with flashy decorations, but selling as many pairs of shoes as possible before December 24.

"Next thing we know, you'll be offering to dress up as Santa Claus, Mademoiselle Desrosiers!"

No matter how much she protested that it could be an incentive, that decorations in the windows might attract customers, they remained unconvinced and on the Sunday before Christmas, Édouard contemplated sadly what Teena and he had managed to do with the little they had on hand.

"If it was up to me, I'd take it all down, throw it all in the garbage, and pretend this was a week like any other."

Standing behind her cash register, Teena shrugged.

"It has to look like Christmas for everyone."

"It looks like the poor man's Christmas."

"That's what it is for most of our customers, anyway. You're not in the west end of rue Sainte-Catherine, here, this isn't your Aunt Tititte's counter at Ogilvy's."

"My mother always says, 'We might be poor but we're clean.' With this stuff, we don't look clean at all."

"As far as that goes, you're right. Next year, I'll throw it all away without even opening the boxes. They can say what they want."

"They won't even notice."

"They'll notice, don't worry. They have to come bring our Christmas bonuses."

"They can keep them and buy new Christmas frills with the money."

They had a good laugh, exhausted and dirty.

Teena invited Édouard to eat at Larivière et Leblanc, open on Sundays during the holidays thanks to special dispensation from the Montréal diocese, and they hatched plans for new decorations, the most beautiful, the most sparkling ones they could imagine. For the following year.

"Does that mean I'll still be here a year from now?"

"That means you'll still be here a year from now, if you behave yourself, Édouard. You can become a good salesman, if you want, but you're often impatient with the customers. Got to work on that..."

If by chance Édouard has the necessary talents to become a good salesman, on this cold dark Monday morning he's about to prove the opposite. And come close to losing his job.

All because of one customer.

Well-groomed, pleasant, smiling, his fur hat low on his brow, a bit of frost in his moustache, he entered whistling cheerily.

"I got a big Christmas bonus and I'm going to buy myself the most beautiful Brooks shoes you have! I saw a superb pair in the window. Brown."

Édouard asked his size and headed to the storeroom while the customer began chatting with Teena. He could hear him carrying on while he sorted through the boxes of Brooks shoes: a mechanic, married, two children, far from rich but comfortable, obviously in good spirits every hour of the day and night, probably the life of the party in his family ... By the time Édouard had found the shoes he wanted, he had told his life's story and was beginning to get on Édouard's nerves. This much good humour so early in the day was hard to stomach for someone who had trouble dragging himself out of bed every morning.

The customer was lolling on one of the chairs, legs apart, blowing smoke rings from the cigarette he'd just lit.

And it was while removing his first shoe that everything fell apart.

This wasn't an unpleasant smell, it was an unspeakable stench, something between dead rat and clothes rotting with dampness. Édouard couldn't prevent himself from backing off; he straightened up after dropping the customer's shoe on the floor.

The man burst out laughing.

"Something else, eh? But you're lucky, you only have to put up with it for five minutes. And it will disappear fast. At home, everyone scatters like cockroaches when I threaten to take off my shoes. And my wife makes me wash my feet twice before I can join her in bed."

Édouard couldn't control himself, it came out on its own, like a nervous reaction that defies control:

"I wouldn't want to be your wife. Poor woman! How long has she had to put up with this?"

Teena, horrified, glares at him.

The customer stood up, hoisted his pants that sat below his burgeoning belly, tugging on his suspenders.

"I bet you would like to be in my wife's place! Eh? Stink or no stink, you'd love to be in her place, eh, you damn faggot!"

Édouard neither broke down nor fled. He stood up on his tiptoes – the other man was more than six feet tall – and held his nose.

"No human being would like to be in your wife's place, Monsieur, not even the damn faggots!"

The outburst was so powerful, it sucked the air from his lungs. He fell over backwards, almost hitting his head on a chair, and ended up on his back at Teena's feet.

The customer stuck his foot near Édouard's nose.

"Here, stick this up your nose. The smell of a man, a real man! And you can stick your Brooks shoes up your ass! Along with other things."

He grabbed his coat, didn't bother to put on his shoe, and headed for the door, limping. He turned back, just before leaving.

"And you're lucky I didn't smash your face in. If I ever see you again, if I run into you in a dark alleyway, I'll make you regret the day you were born."

They watched him as he leaned against a store window and put his shoe back on.

The quarrel that followed was epic.

Teena went to open the door to air out the store, and to make sure the customer had left, then she sat down on a chair and for a good ten minutes delivered a blast of reproaches and threats, going back and forth between the two with little or no transition, as if she couldn't control what she was saying, regularly banging her fist on the arm of her chair. Édouard protested in vain, claiming he was right to react, that it was inhuman to submit other people to such a stink, that soap and foot powders existed, she replied that was none of their business, they were there to sell shoes, not to give their customers hygiene advice, that she had warned him after the incident with Xavier Lacroix, that he had promised to be careful, that he'd never succeed in life if he didn't learn to control himself.

He finally lowered his head and crossed his arms like a sulky child.

"Well really, you should fire me if I'm that awful!"

She tugged on the sleeves of her jacket that had slid up during her gesticulations.

"That's exactly what you deserve ... But it's Christmastime, and I won't have time to find another salesman. Consider yourself lucky and thank the Baby Jesus for being born this week! Any other time of the year and you'd be sitting in your number 52 streetcar, believe you me!"

He promised, cross his heart, and hope to die.

But Teena began to mistrust his promises.

He went to cry, out of sight, in the storeroom. The emotional overload was suffocating him, torn between pride and shame, the pride of having dared to stand up to an imposing man who should have frightened him and the shame of having been humiliated, called a faggot – what, in fact, was that, what was a faggot? – and demolished within seconds, the distress and the impotence in the face of physical violence, and mostly the incredible discovery, twice within a few weeks, that his gift for retorts would prove to be as effective outside his home as it was with members of the family, all that had shaken him and left him sobbing. Tears were pouring down his cheeks, he was sniffling and uttering little snorts like a stuck piglet, he was trembling, he felt as if his heart was going to explode in his chest, and at the same time, he was proud of himself and wished he could jump up and down with laughter.

Now all he had to do – and this was perhaps the most difficult –

was learn to be tougher, not let himself be carried away by his emotions, learn to use his big mouth while remaining cool and never giving his target the time or the occasion to retort or react. A worldly woman. La Duchesse de Langeais. Every time. Every time he had to floor someone, he would have to remain calm and attack straight on, regardless of the impact or the consequences, hold his head high, give the opponent no leeway, make every word an uppercut, a bullet, a cannonball. Antoinette de Navarreins was piercing her shell, breaking out of her chrysalid, still weak and a bit terrified by the road ahead, but determined, yes, and full of hope.

La Duchesse de Langeais was his only salvation.

When he emerged from the storeroom, two ladies were squealing with delight as they tried on shoes undoubtedly too expensive for them.

Teena, crouching at their feet, looked up. He signalled that he was fine.

He was fine, indeed. The world would see just how fine he was.

Maria asked Béa to bring home some cookies, two pounds chosen among the new specialties at the Biscuiterie Ontario, the ones no one knew yet if possible, and otherwise, fall back on their favourites with the royal icing and the cinnamon sister's sighs.

It's her turn to host her sisters for their weekly card game and she didn't have the time or the inclination to prepare the snack they shared at the end of the evening during their lively, endless discussions that sometimes turned sour because the Desrosiers sisters would argue about the money, where it had gone, who had won and who had lost and how much. (There are often small amounts missing because Tititte doesn't willingly admit defeat, like that time not so long ago when she denied having played badly, even though it was obvious.)

They are sitting around the kitchen table. The game is almost over, the coffee is percolating on the stove, the tea is steeping, there are only a few cards left to be played.

Nana had joined them at the last minute – a neighbour agreed to babysit – and they were able to play Five Hundred, a game that requires four players, and they were delighted because this was the first time in a long time, in fact, since Nana's last visit a few months earlier, the night she admitted that she was expecting again. They had congratulated her effusively, and she had said that she was happy, although this child came as a surprise. The first two had been planned, but not this one. Tititte had let out one of her dramatic sighs that amused everyone:

"Oh, men! They can't control themselves."

Nana smiled as she lay down her ace of hearts.

"What would you know about that, ma tante?"

Tititte had blushed so deeply they wondered if she was bordering on apoplexy.

Maria noticed that they were calmer than usual. There was no talk about movies or radio dramas, no gossip about anyone whatsoever, the multiple games of Five Hundred had taken place without a hitch, without the usual shouts of protest or sarcastic insults, they had accepted their bad hands and boasted less about their good moves; in fact, the evening had been a bit subdued, lacking in the usual energy and excitement. Maria, who was rarely the one to host, thought at one point the get-together had been a failure, but her sisters and her daughter looked serene and didn't seem to have any complaints. And no mean comments about her had been uttered all evening. It was almost worrisome.

"I think it's ready ... Tea or coffee? Béa brought home some new cookies that look like dog turds but they're supposed to be delicious."

The table was cleared in seconds, the oilcloth back in place and the plates set out.

"Thanks, Maria, for hosting us on your only night off."

"You host us so often, Teena, I figured it's about time I made an effort. And it's a nice change from my nights at the Paradise."

The coffee is steaming, the cookies – they really are ugly – grace the middle of the table surrounded by petits fours for Tititte who will limit herself to nibbling on one or two because, much to the amusement of her sisters who don't believe she'll have the willpower, she has decided to watch her waistline.

Ever since she received the good news, she has been taking care of herself, taking long winter walks, watching what she eats, and the flabbiness threatening her body during the long wait for her results from Dr. Woolf is gone. She has recovered her creamy complexion and her regal posture. Tititte is back and she wants people to know it. What she doesn't want them to know about, however, is the many evenings and lunchtimes spent recently with Dr. Woolf. An idyll? Maybe not. But some delightful moments.

When she saw her arrive at Maria's earlier that evening, Teena teased her:

"You back to walking three inches above ground, Tititte?"

She answered:

"A resuscitated woman levitates, didn't you know that?"

Maria joins them.

"Go ahead, *dig in*, as they say in English."

The cookies – which Teena has christened *dog turds*, although their pompous name is *chocolate teardrops* – are declared delicious, the coffee well brewed, the tea not too strong, and the evening interesting. Maria hates the word *interesting*; what does that mean, *interesting*? Dull? Deadly boring? They didn't laugh, they didn't shout as usual, they didn't argue, but they had fun, didn't they?

Teena swallows her last sip and reaches for the teapot to pour herself another cup.

"So Nana, how are you doing? Not too tired given your ... condition?"

Nana looks down, passes her hand over her round belly that she doesn't try to camouflage like most of the women she knows who consider pregnancy a shameful thing to be hidden and ignored. The priests insist that women should welcome being in a family way, then they demand – in the name of decency, modesty – that they hide the results.

"Besides spending half of every morning on my hands and knees by the toilet, I'm fine. My other two kids keep asking questions, I tell them that sometimes mums feel sick in the morning and they want to know why. I guess I'll have to tell them soon. I'm fed up with mothers who are rushed to the hospital 'because the Indians broke their legs,' then they come home with a baby in their arms. It's stupid. And insulting for Indians."

Teena swallows a bit of chocolate teardrop that she washes down with a sip of tea.

"They're good, Maria, but a bit dry. Could do with some icing."

Then she turns to her niece.

"There's always the story of babies delivered by storks ... But that's stupid, too."

"It's worse, because there are no storks in the province of Québec! So all that's left is the truth."

"Well how are you going to tell them that?"

"I don't have to tell them everything. I can tell them I have a baby in my belly, they don't have to know how it got there."

They laugh. An embarrassed laugh. Memories surface in the minds of the three older women, the youngest needs only to think back to the day before.

"I was worried at first. Two kids is already a big responsibility. So ... we were scared for a while, Gabriel and me, that the Depression would affect us, too. But no. So far, so good. Money's not too scarce right now. Gabriel says that as long as they're printing religious material, we don't have to worry. People will never cut back on that. He's been working almost fifteen hours a day for the past three weeks, just to finish the Sacred Heart calendar in time for Christmas. He brought one home the other day."

She dips a chocolate teardrop in her coffee – she's the only one who drinks coffee – before popping it into her mouth.

"It's true, they're a bit dry, Ma."

Maria shrugs.

"Next time, I'll float them in milk, or bury them in whipped cream. In the meantime, dip them in your cups."

"You've never been able to whip cream, Ma ..."

"Well you'll help me!"

"Don't get mad. It's not your fault."

"Just stop criticizing!"

"We're not criticizing ..."

"So what are you doing? If these cookies are inedible, I'll throw them in the garbage, period!"

"Never mind, Ma, let's change the subject."

Maria takes a bite of cookie, chews it, swallows it.

"I think these cookies are really good!"

Nana knows she'd better change the subject before her aunts chime in and the chocolate teardrops become another end-of-the-evening tragedy, a Desrosiers sisters specialty, since they like nothing better than to turn simple chit-chat into a national tragedy for the mere pleasure of an unending discussion. So she goes back to the subject of the Sacred Heart calendar, without really knowing what she can say about it.

"I hung it on the kitchen wall over the sideboard. I know I shouldn't say this, but ... I think it's really ugly. I'm not rejecting the Sacred Heart, I'm not rejecting my religion, but after a while I can't take those looks of suffering and pain, I don't know why ... I feel like his eyes are following me around the kitchen!"

Actually, she found the calendar quite pretty, it adds a splash of colour that will change every month, but she's managed to avoid an argument. The three other women start talking about everything that scares or bothers them in the Catholic religion, a fascinating, vast subject that promptly monopolizes their conversation.

No stone is left unturned, from the atrocities of the Stations of the Cross – the poor man who hadn't done anything wrong – to confession, the humiliating obligation forced on them every third Friday of the month, including Lent – forty days of fish is punishment for women born in a province where fish is hard to come by – and the bombastic, terrifying sermons delivered by the parish priests who specialize in guilt and veiled accusations, especially when it comes to avoiding being in a family way. The sisters get carried away, they fume and criticize and condemn, they're happy.

Once the subject has been exhausted – it was long, passionate, exhausting – a rare silence descends on the kitchen. It's time for them to separate, they don't feel like it. They're content, they'd gladly stay there sipping their beverages, staring at the oilcloth or their hands briefly unoccupied, ignoring the snow outdoors and Christmas approaching with the tree to be decorated, the gifts to be wrapped. Four women suspended in time, drifting between dreams and reality, choosing the charm of dreams. Or perhaps simply enjoying this vacant pause. For the first time in a while, Tititte isn't thinking about her good fortune, the reprieve life has offered her, and her friendship with Dr. Woolf, Teena isn't worrying about the decision she'll have to make after the holidays about Édouard, Nana has forgotten that she must insist that Gabriel find them a new apartment for May first since their current home is too small for a family of five. And forgotten about their money worries that she hid from her mother and her aunts. As for Maria ...

She pours herself a last cup of tea. It has steeped too long, she knows it will be undrinkable, but she needs a prop because what she has to say is touchy.

"The other day I was thinking about how ... we used to be scattered all over the place, I was in Rhode Island, my daughters and my parents in Saskatchewan, my two sisters and my brother here in Montréal, the rest of the family in Calgary, Winnipeg, Ottawa ... We never saw each other, hardly ever spoke on the phone, we all dreamed of living in the same place, preferably here, because Montréal is big, it's French, Québec is our ancestors' home ... Now, for almost twenty years, most of the family has been here, I have a good job, I have a handsome seventeen-year-old son I love so much, a man who loves me, my oldest daughter is married, we play cards once a week laughing our heads off, but ..."

She takes a sip and grimaces.

"I don't want you to take this as criticism, it's not, it's just an observation, but I thought to myself ... Is this all life has to offer me, to offer *us?* Was this really our dream? Don't go thinking I'm unhappy, I'm not ... I'm not unhappy, it's just that I feel like I'm missing something, I don't know what, there's something I didn't do or something that never came my way. Do you ever have the feeling that ... you're incomplete? I'm not sure that's the right word. Sometimes I look at myself in the mirror and I think, maybe that woman I'm looking at had things I haven't had ... adventures, that's what I mean, adventures. Like I wasn't meant to always stay in the same place. Sure, we all know I've always been like this, when I was twenty I left Saskatchewan to travel around the world ... But today ... today I'm over fifty and that part of me is still present! I'm sorry to say this in front of you, Nana, but sometimes I'd like to disappear, like when I was twenty, disappear, there's no other word, to end up somewhere else, far away, alone, I don't dare use the word *free* because I don't know if I would be, but ... elsewhere, that's the point, elsewhere ... It's not about all of you, I don't want to be far away from you, I love you too much, I just need ... *need* to be somewhere else. That's how I am. Who I am! I suffocate when I'm stuck in the same place too long. I have to move my butt. It's been more than fifteen years since I made a move."

The silence would have gone on forever if Béa hadn't arrived bringing reality with her, along with an unpleasant sample of the cold air outside.

"Good Lord, you're all so serious! Did a chick from your brood die, or what?"

Her cheeks are scarlet. Not because of the cold, but because Arthur Liasse kissed her on the doorstep. Not a tight-lipped little peck, a real long kiss like in the movie they just saw, a serious, disturbing kiss, the kind that leaves you weak in the knees and breathless, a far cry from the quick furtive kisses stolen behind the cookie counter.

Despite Madame Guillemette's warning – that boy's not right for you, he just wants to feel you up in the balcony of the movie theatre – she finally accepted his invitation to go out some evening, to go to the movies or for supper in a restaurant. She got both: a meal at Geracimo and a movie at Cinéma Saint-Denis. At the restaurant, their waitress was her sister Alice who couldn't believe her eyes when she saw them arrive, then frowned when they sat down on the same side of their booth. During the whole meal, she kept making faces to let her sister know she didn't think much of her date. Béa pretended she didn't notice and she laughed too loudly and let Arthur kiss her neck in front of Alice.

After the movie, Arthur offered to walk her home to rue Montcalm, a ten-minute walk from Cinéma Saint-Denis. They walked hand in hand in the hard snow that crunched under their footsteps, then, outside the door to the apartment ...

Maria stands up and starts to clear the table.

"Look how red your face is, is it that cold outside?"

Béa takes off her coat that she'll hang on the hall tree in the entrance but for the time being she leaves it on the back on Nana's chair.

"No, but it's windy."

The three other women have pushed back their chairs and stood up, stretching after sitting there for hours except for quick trips to the bathroom, and are preparing to leave.

"My face might be red, but have you seen the dumb look on your faces?"

Did they have an argument? About the card game? Did her aunt Tititte get carried away again because she can't stand to lose a few pennies?

"It's not a dumb look, we're just tired."

"Probably from shouting too loud, I bet. When I walked in, no one was saying a word. Always a bad sign."

Nana kisses her on both cheeks.

"We weren't saying anything because we had nothing left to say."

"Impossible! You always have something to say. Except after a fight..."

Nana is heading for her mother's bedroom where she'd left her coat on the bed with those of Teena and Tititte.

"How was your movie?"

Béa follows her down the hallway, almost skipping.

"It was a movie with Gloria Swanson. She has huge eyes and believe me, she knows how to use them!"

Once they're both inside the bedroom, Béa grabs her sister by the sleeve of her dress.

"Nana, I've got a beau. He's not really handsome, but he's really nice."

Nana is tying her scarf around her neck and starts to put on the coat she has trouble buttoning because of her round belly.

"Alice told us that when she got home from work. So needless to say, you better get ready for a serious conversation with Ma."

Alice and Théo spent the evening in the big bedroom across from the living room that the two sisters share. They listened to the radio and smoked cigarettes – Alice is twenty-one and can do what she wants, but Théo, at seventeen, although he smokes wherever he pleases outside the house, has to hide it from his mother who claims, who knows why, that smoking might be bad for your health.

The young woman thumbed through magazines, and Théo read twice, cover to cover, a comic book that depicted the story of an anthill hidden in a park in a big American city and the adventures of its inhabitants who were planning to swarm the whole world. She gushed over the women's outfits, he burst out laughing a few times, his laughter sounding more like snorts than outbursts of joy. They daydreamed, lying side by side on the big bed, they confided in each other a bit, not too much, just enough to pique each other's curiosity, stopping on purpose at the best part of the story to create suspense – so, so then what happened?! – and promising to tell the rest some other time … They accused each other of lying, or at least exaggerating – he didn't dare do that!, didn't I tell you Charlotte Dubé was no goody two-shoes! – then, having exhausted their imaginations, they resumed their silent daydreams.

Earlier in the evening, they had quickly withdrawn after greeting the three visitors. (Théo paused for a moment in Nana's arms, because even after five years he still misses her, her kindness and her generosity. He no longer dares call her his second mother, he's too old, but he really misses the days when she was in charge of the household.)

They kept the door open for a while, hoping to catch bits of conversation, then, tiring of the inane comments, stories of old-lady sicknesses, of customers whose feet stink, and of women so snobbish they have no manners, they closed the door and turned up the volume on the radio.

Of course, Alice told the story of Béa's visit to Geracimo with the beau Alice called a *loser* because she found him so homely and uninteresting. Théo laughed at the description of his sister salivating over her pepper steak while fluttering her eyelids to seduce her beau.

"A loser…"

He wanted to know in what sense, and Alice made him laugh even more.

But by the time Béa opens the door to the bedroom, they're absorbed in their daydreams. Théo is startled because he was on the verge of falling asleep. Alice gets up.

"So tell us, did he feel you up? Slip his hand inside your blouse, pull up your skirt?"

Béa shrugs and flops down on the bed beside her brother.

"Not everyone's named Alice Rathier and lets the boys go to town on the balcony at Cinéma Saint-Denis."

Alice is on top of her in less than two seconds. They wrestle and laugh, deliver slaps and pinches and pull each other's hair. Used to these loud but inoffensive games he's been watching since he was a little kid, Théo doesn't interfere. He simply looks on, shaking his head. If he got involved, they would both gang up on him and he'd have an array of bruises to show for it.

"C'mon! Admit it! How far did you go, eh? Did you go all the way?"

Béa pulls away, gives her sister a good push, and Alice lands flat on her back on the floor.

Everyone is laughing.

The door opens again and Maria charges in.

"Enough of this racket! It's late. It's bedtime, you have to work tomorrow! Get to your room, Théo! How many times do I have to tell you, you got no business in your sisters' room. You're not four years old now! And I'm not working myself to the bone so you can arrive late for your classes. Or too tired because you laughed so hard with your sisters!"

Théo leaves the bedroom without saying a word, flushed because his mother gave him hell, and also because he caught sight more than once of his sisters' underwear.

The girls are already undressing. Alice is sulking.

"Théo's not the only one who's not four years old now, Ma! Stop treating us like kids."

"I'll stop treating you like kids when you leave here to get married, not before."

"Oh gawd, we're in for a long haul. Especially since I've decided I'm not interested in guys."

"Alice, stop saying that! You know you're only saying that because you're too interested in guys! And Béa, I need to have a serious conversation with you!"

"C'mon, Ma. I know what you're going to say to me."

"Well, you'll listen to me anyway. When you're old enough, you'll do what you want. But as long as you live in my house, you're still a minor, and you'll follow my rules."

She has disappeared as fast as she appeared.

The two sisters wait a few seconds before they let out their hilarious laughter. The last thing they want is for their mother to show up again.

Alice slips into her flannel nightgown, the one she calls her *old maid's nightie* that she saves for winter nights.

"Get ready for a real sermon ..."

Béa sighs and slips under the covers.

"Did you have to go through that?"

"Yes, when I was about your age."

"And ...?"

"It's embarrassing. Rrreally embarrassing."

Béa falls asleep anyway, thinking about Arthur Liasse's long kiss.

The Saint-Jean-de-Dieu Hospital took in Josaphat the way people adopt a lost cat or a stray dog.

No one, however, was fooled about the state of his mental health: they didn't believe in his visions, or his stories about having to save the full moon, or his spontaneous talent for interpreting the classics without ever having studied them, the nuns and the doctors simply saw a clever scheme for finding shelter for the winter. Josaphat was much too articulate and his conversation too brilliant for them to give credence to the ravings of this clever storyteller in the old tradition of the beggars who used to roam the roads of Québec inventing unlikely tales to earn their keep. Josaphat was undoubtedly a trained classical musician who was going through a rough patch and had found refuge at Saint-Jean-de-Dieu the way others retreat to a monastery for a while. In fact, how many patients in the history of the hospital had shown up like him, one fine afternoon, asking to be interred because they were crazy? None. They struggled, they scratched, they screamed that they did not have dementia, they demanded to be discharged, they threatened to throw a bomb or set the place on fire, never had they asked to be held prisoner at Saint-Jean-de-Dieu. Except for him. Who had shouted: "Sanctuary! Sanctuary!" like in the Middle Ages, more proof that he was educated. And cultured.

Unless, as some of the nuns had suggested, Josaphat was telling the truth and they were dealing with an exceptional individual, a gentle madman who was experiencing what he claimed to be experiencing. Or, at least, who believed he was. And who needed help. Something the doctors had rejected with a wave of the hand

and a shrug of their shoulders: this Josaphat-le-Violon – that's how he introduced himself – was a clever liar, albeit likeable and talented, who turned out to be very useful during the holidays with his romantic melodies that brought tears to the eyes and his jigs that made you tap your feet. His violin soothed the patients after meals, a moment when they were often agitated and hard to control. So much the better! They would use him just as he was using the hospital. They should give him a patient's uniform, give him room and board, let him think they believed his tall tales they considered the colourful, touching poetry of a peasant, and they should use him. Play your violin, Josaphat, share this unexpected panacea!

The hospital director had even said:

"This is a serious bending of our rules, I know that, but I'm prepared to face the consequences. If there are any. After all, perhaps no one will ever know that this Josaphat-le-Violon was once among us like a shadow from the Québec of yesteryear ... We're not holding him against his will, he insists upon staying. And the patients will benefit from his presence as much as we will ... In January, we'll see ... we'll see ..."

When the sister suggested – another serious bending of the rules – that it would be cruel for them to turn him out in January, the coldest month of the year, he replied:

"This probably won't be his first January on the streets if he really is homeless. I'm sure he knows how to take care of himself. Furthermore ... if, as we believe, he is not what he claims to be, he will soon return to his family and his profession. Maybe there's an orchestra out there looking for him ..."

So to pay for his garments, his food – a bit bland but the best he's eaten in a long time – and his bed in one of the wards, every evening and sometimes during the day when the atmosphere at Saint-Jean-de-Dieu is particularly febrile, Josaphat takes out his fiddle and plays music, like the Pied Piper with the children of Hamelin. Not to chase away the rats, but to soothe souls, ease anxieties, calm uncontrollable fits, and bring tears to everyone's eyes.

And he has made a friend. Slowly but surely, the patient who came the very first evening to tell him that his mother played the

"Méditation" from *Thaïs* on the piano has become an inseparable companion, sometimes silent, occasionally eloquent, always moody and intense. They both work in the laundry room, located in another pavilion of the vast hospital, they spend part of the day in the steam of the huge pressing machines, then emerge drenched in sweat, weak from the heat, and, after taking the little electric train that connects the pavilions through the basement, they begin to distribute from the metal conveyor belts clean sheets and carefully folded clothes to the various dormitories, those reserved for men as well as those for women.

Monsieur Émile, that's how everyone refers to him, is a poet whose parent had him interred thirty years ago, first in a retreat at the Saint-Benoît monastery, then for the past five years in the Saint-Jean-de-Dieu asylum, because they didn't understand him and thought he was crazy. He always looks as if he's carrying the weight of the world on his shoulders and walks hesitantly, his back stooped, his head bowed. He is a gentle, polite man who speaks quietly, as if to apologize for his very existence or for fear of disturbing others. He always carries with him a little notebook that contains all the poetry he wrote as an adolescent, superb verses, the most beautiful that Josaphat has ever heard, inspired by the Parnassian poets, his idols. Like Rimbaud who wrote his "Bateau ivre," he wrote his magnificent "Le vaisseau d'or" before he turned twenty. But he was not allowed to complete his "Récital des anges" which he considered his masterpiece. Deprived of his muses, possibly overwhelmed by medication, he is constantly rewriting the same poems, changing the occasional word or even a line, but incapable of creating new work. In his night table, he keeps his most precious treasure, the edition of 107 of his poems that Louis Dantin, the man he knew as Father Seers who had been his mentor, had published by Beauchemin in 1904, proof that his genius had existed in another life, that he had been a teenage prodigy whose wings were clipped because he shocked the society whose versifiers tended to be prominent citizens, without talent and imbued with self-importance, who wrote poetry as a hobby. He had wanted to live the life of a true bohemian and had paid the price.

Josaphat was horrified by the life story of this brilliant man, destroyed by his obtuse and ignorant social milieu. Two misunderstood madmen, two outcasts. And in turn, he confided his story in murmured gasps and outbursts of emotion. Duhamel, Victoire, his sister and their two children, Gabriel and Albertine, her unhappy marriage with Télesphore who more than them deserved to be locked up here in an insane asylum, and of course, the knitters, Rose, Violette, and Mauve and their mother Florence, everything they had given him, culture and especially music, and the burden that had plagued him for years, that he was unable to cast off: the full moon that had to be released from the sky, the rescue of the horses who without him, without his fiddle, would be tortured to death.

Monsieur Émile believed everything. Everything. Occasionally he would even ask Josaphat, in the middle of a meal or while they were pressing white cotton pants:

"Are they here, with us now?"

Josaphat would answer yes.

"Where, exactly?"

Josaphat would indicate a corner of the room where the knitters were standing, alert, their eyes filled with infinite compassion. For both men.

Monsieur Émile would bow.

"*Mes hommages, mesdames.*"

Their friendship was sealed a week after Josaphat arrived at the hospital, in a moment when Monsieur Émile was reading, as he often did, one of his poems in the recreation room. Josaphat had picked up his fiddle and accompanied the poet, unobtrusively, simply trying to underscore the verses in long, languorous chords that were something other than music, more like a discreet commentary, a fraternal embrace. Monsieur Émile had looked at him, smiling, his voice trembling. When he finished reading, he approached the musician, placed a hand on his shoulder and murmured:

"'Le Récital des anges.' That was my 'Récital des anges.'"

Today, however, the angels' recital wasn't as good as yesterday or the day before.

The poet has a miserable cold that muddled his usually clear reading and, to avoid burying his voice, Josaphat had to mute his violin and play almost inaudibly. It was a jig popular in his childhood that he had taken to interpreting slowly, almost like a lullaby, because he loved the melody that he rendered like a long soothing ribbon of rubato that the patients, especially the most agitated, seemed to enjoy. They were less attentive to the poems, the nuns were scowling, several anxious cries rose above "La romance du vin," one man burst out laughing at the end of "Devant un portrait de ma mère." For the first time in weeks, the half-hour following the noontime meal was so chaotic the wardens had to intervene.

Monsieur Émile left the huge hall as soon as he finished reading and took refuge in the men's room where he thought no one would disturb him. He was wrong. Josaphat, his fiddle tucked under his arm, was waiting for him at the door. Monsieur Émile appeared, drying his hands on his pants.

"There are no hand towels. We should tell the sisters ... or bring some ourselves, before we distribute the sheets."

Josaphat was walking slowly, forcing his friend to turn back to him.

"What just happened isn't your fault, Monsieur Émile. Not mine either. You have a cold, you're less focussed and have trouble talking ..."

"I don't like it when people don't listen to me. Those poems are important, Monsieur Josaphat! Before you arrived, I felt like a voice in the wilderness, I had the feeling no one was listening. But with you ... you calm them down, Monsieur Josaphat, and thanks to you, they listen to me, even if most of them don't understand what I'm reading. They listen to my words through your music and when I stumble, because of a cold or whatever, you stumble too because I'm hard to follow ... And that's what happens ... The angels' recital is a failure. The high point of my day, the focal point of my existence, the sacred moment that should never fail ..."

"There'll be another one tomorrow."

"Yes, but the day after tomorrow? Where will you be the day after tomorrow, Monsieur Josaphat? You're not a patient at

Saint-Jean-de-Dieu, you can disappear whenever you want. And you see, I'm admitting that I need you."

"Who says I want to disappear?"

"You. I heard you talking in the dormitory with your four companions last night. You were talking about escape, about a duty to be done, a gift for someone."

Josaphat stops and sits down on a bench against the wall of the narrow hallway leading to the laundry room.

"Come sit down. I have to explain something to you."

Monsieur Émile remains standing in front of him.

"I prefer to remain standing to learn bad news. Sitting there, I'd see you from the side. I want to look you in the eye."

Neither one will lower his eyes while Josaphat speaks. Neither the feverish look in the fiddler's eyes, nor the imperative need he'll express will change the disappointment, the discouragement visible on the poet's face: the dashed hopes of a possibly permanent collaboration, the "Récital des anges" reduced to its initial half that had been unsuccessful for so many years, the return of the shouts, the fits, the insults while he was baring his soul through texts revised a hundred times, then returned to their original form a hundred times over, texts that he will continue to try, always in vain, to share with the world. His bequest. His legacy. Irreversible solitude. What the clever man facing him is saying, trying so hard to be convincing, is false, he knows it, he feels it, it is sentencing him to a gradual death, to a slow but definitive decline to the ultimate void. After thirty years of solitude, a few weeks of companionship, then again the terrible isolation surrounded by the insane.

"I know I made a prisoner of myself when I came to take refuge here. I needed it. I still need it. No one except you believed me, no one tried to treat me, cure me, because no one believes me. They offered me asylum, without offering help. In an insane asylum where no one believes I'm crazy. I still have my visions that make me happy and are killing me at the same time. They're right here, on either side of you, listening to me, I know they're even trying to help me make myself clear and be as gentle with you as possible because they know how important you are, they recognize your genius and they would probably stay with you if they didn't have to take care of me until someone else, I guess you could say another chosen one, appears. A child who, like me, will be seduced and allow himself to be shaped, taught things he won't understand and that will do him no good. I'd love to leave them with you, Monsieur Émile, leave you in their care, leave them in your care, but I know they're going to follow me. Maybe not forever, maybe just for a while. Because there's one thing I want to do. Not before I die, I'm in fine health, I know I'm not about to die ... but before I abdicate completely. I have a gift to give, a tiny gift, a silly gift, but one that's really important to me. After that we'll see. Maybe I'll come back to accompany you here, because I enjoy that, because we make a good team, we help each other survive. But maybe not. I've come from the backwoods, maybe I should go back. Even if I'm far from sure I could find happiness there. For the time being, I'm going back to my apartment on rue Amherst. I haven't paid the rent for two months, I hope they haven't changed the lock. And I'll prepare myself. It will take place on Christmas Day. I told you, it's no big deal, it's even silly, but if I don't do it, I'll die."

When Josaphat has finished explaining what he intends to do at Christmas, Monsieur Émile comes to sit beside him.

"Take me with you."

"You know that's impossible."

"If you only leave for a few hours, take me with you. I'd like to be there."

"You can't leave here without people knowing. But I can."

"I can ... I can disguise myself, I can –"

"No, Monsieur Émile. People would know right away. That might jeopardize my plans."

Monsieur Émile lowers his head, wipes his forehead.

"Yes. That's true. It might jeopardize your plans. If they find us before you've had time to pull it off. I understand. But I'm the one they'd bring back here. Not you. If you decide afterwards to stay in the outside world, promise me someday you'll come back to tell me how it went."

"There probably won't be much to tell."

"Yes, there will. There'll be what it meant to you."

"I could explain that to you right now. I know what I'll feel. As for the rest... I might not survive, Monsieur Émile."

"Why do you say that?"

"Because I gave Télesphore permission to kill me if we ever ran into each other again."

She left the decoration of the tree's lower branches to her two children who are laughing as they struggle with the ornaments and the tinsel icicles. They keep dropping the ornaments, which fortunately don't break, putting the shiny metallic ribbons in their mouths, then spitting them out, complaining that they taste bad. They yank on the branches of the tree that almost tipped over on the living room rug more than once. Each time she saved it in the nick of time, pretending she found it amusing. She doesn't feel like dealing with two children who complain and snivel while she decorates the Christmas tree.

Nana knows they're too young, they don't know what they're doing – neither one remembers the tree from the previous year – but they insisted upon helping her and she figured she could always help them if the task proved to be too difficult. She showed them, as if it were a game, the little metal hooks that would allow them to attach the ornaments to the end of a branch and the little metallic strips they had to handle carefully because they're fragile. They do their best, concentrated and serious, they stick out their tongues, shout triumphantly when they manage to attach an ornament or an icicle, and ask her if she's happy, if they'll get a reward when they've finished, maybe some Whippet cookies with milk or a piece of chocolate. She says yes, thinking that at this rate, decorating the tree will take the entire afternoon.

When Gabriel arrives home from work, around six thirty, the tree is decorated and the children have eaten. As soon as he's taken off his winter coat and his muddy boots – a mild spell has melted the snow – he goes to ruffle his son's hair, pinch his daughter's cheek, and kiss his wife.

"You smell of beer, Gabriel."

"It's payday, we went to have a beer next to the print shop. Now that I know sign language, I can talk to the guys. I make a lot of mistakes and that makes them laugh. It's funny, when the Deaf laugh, they hardly make any noise. Before, we just worked together, now we're getting to know each other a bit…"

He leans over and places his ear on her belly.

"Has he started to kick yet?"

"No, not yet."

"I can hardly wait."

"Well, not me."

He straightens up, takes her in his arms, and kisses her again.

"What's wrong? You usually give me a better reception on payday."

She pushes him away and heads for the kitchen where she's warming up their supper.

"I can't help it. Every payday, I'm afraid you'll arrive home carrying your tool kit."

"How many times do I have to tell you not to worry? We're not going to run out of work."

"The Depression's hitting everyone, Gabriel. People might start cutting their expenses even for religion."

He catches up with her, grabs her by the arm, and hugs her.

"People will never cut back on religion. Some printers are having a hard time, I know that, there are guys at the tavern who have lost their jobs and are real discouraged, but as long as we have the archdiocese as our customer, we'll be fine. People will stop going to the movies, but they won't stop going to church."

"Anyway, I see that some people don't stop going to the tavern."

"Once a week, Nana, once a week I go to the tavern for one beer, there's lots of guys worse than me."

"I still don't like it. It starts with once a week –"

"Listen, you don't want to nag me about something so silly, it's Christmastime and I've got good news."

He sits down at the table while Nana fills their bowls with the beef soup she's been stretching out every afternoon since Monday, adding some broth, vegetables, or little noodles. There's no meat left, but it's as delicious as ever.

The children have come to join them. Nana gives them a slice of bread and butter and they go to sit near the stove where it's warm. But not too close, they know they have to be careful of the oven door that can get boiling hot.

"It better be good, your good news."

He takes a few spoonfuls of soup before answering.

"The proof that everything's fine at the shop is that the boss is giving me a turkey for Christmas. A big twenty-pound turkey! And I thought ... We could invite your family. Not mine, they won't come because of my father, but yours —"

"Maman will probably be working."

"So we'll eat earlier than usual. Besides, your mother never goes to work before nine o'clock. Your sisters and your brother would be happy, right?"

"We'll see."

"You could invite your two aunts, too. They're always alone for the holidays. Béa will help you, she's already a good cook. We can afford it, Nana, stop worrying all the time."

She pushes her bowl away and takes a sip of water.

"I can't. I can't stop worrying. A turkey is great, I'm glad, but you can't serve a turkey on its own! There's all the stuff that goes with it. The tourtières as a first course, the apple pies and the doughnuts for afterwards. A bit of wine, some hard-liquor toasts. And the truth is, the turkey isn't what costs the most. You men have no idea, you think food arrives on the table by itself —"

She stops in the middle of her sentence.

"I'm sorry. It must be my condition that's making me like this ... but ... We're going to have a third child, Gabriel, a child we didn't mean to have, that's taken us by surprise. I can't help but worry, don't you understand?"

He stands up, walks around the table, and places his hand on her neck.

"Another mouth to feed, it's not the end of the world."

She blows her nose, wipes her eyes, and pats her belly.

"That's what you think. But it's not just the mouth to feed, it's everything that goes with having a baby in the house. The diapers, the clothes. I guess it's not up to you to think about those things. You didn't even notice that we decorated the Christmas tree, it took us the whole afternoon."

He hurries over to the kitchen door, rushes down the hall, and enters the living room.

"It's so beautiful! What a beauty! It's the most beautiful tree I've ever seen!"

Delighted, the children stand up and run to join their father.

Nana brings her bowl closer and takes another spoonful of the soup that's had time to go cold.

Make herself eat, even if she doesn't feel like it.

Her mother had warned her that men were irresponsible, that they really have no sense of reality, they get caught up in their daydreams instead of facing their problems. And they often drown it all in alcohol. Maria sees proof of that every night at the Paradise Club where men avoiding their responsibilities spend the evening, laughing too loud to forget what's waiting for them at home, family life that was supposed to be so wonderful, a quiet little existence, the comforts of home, when what they often find is disappointment and anxiety.

Her love for Gabriel is still intact, the thrills he awakens in her haven't lessened with time – five years already! – she adores the children he has given her and is prepared to welcome others despite their precarious financial situation that borders on poverty, but some tiny thing, some vague misgivings, cast a shadow on the admiration she felt for him at the beginning of their marriage. He is hard working, yes, he is courageous, but the daydreaming side of him, possibly inherited from his father – Josaphat, who he stills believes is his uncle – and the way he often refuses to face reality and takes refuge in drinking, something he always denies – he doesn't only smell of beer on Fridays as he claims – all of that worries her more and more, and sometimes, especially in the middle of the night when her damn insomnia triggers dark ideas she can't escape, she finds herself wondering, she's ashamed to admit but she can't help it, if perhaps he isn't the man she believed he was after all. And perhaps she's the one who will always have to struggle to keep their heads above water.

She is listening to them laugh and sing in the living room, the three most important people in her life. That's what she should concentrate on, these moments of pure joy that fill the household because Gabriel is a good man she shouldn't allow herself to judge, and he loves her and would do everything in his power to meet their needs.

She stands up, puts the soup pot back on the stove, and opens the oven door to make sure the chicken isn't overcooked.

"Gabriel, the chicken's going to be dry!"

More laughter, a race down the hallway, Gabriel bursts into the kitchen, a child on each arm.

"Tell your chicken to wait!"

A bad dream. He woke with a start, reassured to find himself in his bed. What did he just escape? He feels as if a furtive shadow is sneaking away from him. He almost ran into something or someone threatening, he resisted, he cried out, he must have run because his heart is pounding and he's hot. Yet it's cold in his bedroom, it will be a while before his mother gets up to start the coal furnace. He's thirsty. He reaches out for the glass of water on his night table and takes some long gulps. It's cold. Feels good. He lies there on his back, his arms by his side under the covers. He stares at the ceiling that he can't see because it's too dark in the room. His eyes will become accustomed to the dark, first he'll detect the outline of the little window, high on the wall because they live in the basement, then slowly the furniture will appear, the closed door, the posters on the wall whose subjects he can't see: Josephine Baker, his latest discovery, who dresses in tropical splendour and sings the praises of her two loves, her country and Paris, beside an Ipana toothpaste ad featuring a gentleman with a moustache and a lady with permed hair about to kiss ... He'd like to fall back to sleep fast, otherwise he'll spend the rest of the night tossing and turning and will get up exhausted. His days at the shoe store are demanding, everyone seems to want new shoes for Christmas. He wants to stay at Giroux et Deslauriers with Mademoiselle Desrosiers, and he has to prove his worth. Breathe in deeply, exhale. Repeat until his heart calms down. Vague images resurface. He's not trying to remember his dream, he rarely manages to do so, but traces of silhouettes appear, flashes of sensations grip his heart. A party is taking place around him. There are lots of people, and suddenly, he's alone with someone. Someone dangerous? No. Not yet. That will come later. For the time being, this someone ... a name seems to want to emerge ... A name that flashes by his eyes so fast he doesn't have time to read it ... Léon? Léo? No, Léopold! Cousin Léopold. Why, in the middle of the night, is he suddenly thinking of cousin Léopold, a vague acquaintance on his father's side of the family, was he a relative or just a family friend? Is he alone with cousin Léopold? In a room with a closed door? An arm reaches out in the dark. A hand strokes his cheek. Then memories – of the dream but also of the day of his sister Albertine's first communion, more than ten years ago – unfold, confused, both precise and blurry, a mouth on his, the taste of rye and cigar, words murmured, caresses becoming increasingly precise, he wants to cry out but he's not sure whether it's to call for help or ... express what? Fear? Joy? No, arousal! He's aroused. What cousin Léopold is doing is exciting! He knows it's wrong because the door to the room is closed and that he ... he's only a child, that cousin Léopold has placed his hand on a forbidden part of his body, but ... He turns in his bed and pulls his knees up to his belly. Why is this jolt of memory, brought on by a bad dream, giving him an erection? He never thought about cousin Léopold again after that incident, he buried that memory in an inaccessible corner of his mind, even when he imagines himself in the place of the woman in the Ipana toothpaste ad, even when he imagines that he is Antoinette de Navarreins, even when he dreams of meeting someone like him ... Did he go back, in the course of a nightmare, a memory, to the source of all this? Is cousin Léopold the cause or was it latent within him? Without cousin Léopold, would he have this poster of Josephine Baker on his wall, this fantasy of being a barefoot Carmelite? He knows he's going to masturbate and that he'll regret it immediately, because the priests preach constantly we should feel soiled and guilty when we indulge in this ugly, but so gratifying, activity. If he resists, he won't fall back to sleep; if he succumbs, after a brief moment of guilt, his body will relax, a drowsiness will overtake him, his eyes will close on their own. He turns onto his back again and folds the covers below his knees.

A few minutes later, just before falling asleep, he raises his arm above him and makes what he considers an elegant gesture in the dark.

"I am Antoinette de Navarreins, Duchesse de Langeais, a barefoot Carmelite, I sell shoes, and I am a dangerous woman."

"To help you, to support you, but mostly because I can't live without you."

As she does whenever Maurice comes to visit, Ti-Lou has placed a piece of pink tulle over the lamp on her night table. It's flattering for him and for her. He won't see her wrinkles blurred by the soft light, nor will she see how age has begun to leave its mark on his face, too. Especially because of his concern for her. They made love ever so very gently – Maurice avoided brusque movements to spare his partner any pain – they lay there for a long time afterwards, in silence, short of breath, their limbs entwined. In two days, Maurice will have to leave for Charlevoix – a monstrous Trottier family reunion to celebrate New Year's – and they won't see each other again until he joins Ti-Lou on the morning of her admission to the hospital on January 4. Something Ti-Lou refuses to accept.

And they picked up the discussion where they'd left off last time.

Ti-Lou has once again forbidden her policeman to accompany her to the hospital, she has even gone so far as to forbid him to come visit her after the amputation which she calls her *operation* because she can't utter the word that makes her tremble, and she almost broaches the subject of separation but she simply doesn't have the courage to tackle it. That decision should come from him, she wishes he'd abandon her, that he'd find some reason, anything, a trifle, some stupid pretext to stop seeing her, let him be a lout, play the heartless role, make her pay for everything that they will no longer be able to share, for the complications of a handicap, the ugliness, especially the ugliness of a once-beautiful woman nailed to an armchair or confined to her bed. She wants to spare him the disgust he's bound to feel at the sight of her stump, the damn stump at the end of a now-useless leg. Remain irremediably alone with her single leg. Not so she can become accustomed, she knows she'll never become accustomed to it, but to give herself time to assimilate and learn to accept the loneliness she will have imposed upon herself, as well as the long tunnel that will lead irreversibly to her death. Be it rapid or slow.

He has guessed her intentions and understood her reasons. He protested, encountered a wall of arguments that he found ridiculous and that Ti-Lou shot at him like so many hurtful arrows. She wanted to provoke his departure and only succeeded in reinforcing his intention to stay by her side. Maurice, his hand on Ti-Lou's stomach, unable to really express himself because they had agreed never to speak of love, struggles to counter her attacks and feels defeated, when he thought they had settled the matter the last time. It's exhausting. And it's pointless because, whether she likes it or not, he will be there when she wakes up in the hospital.

"Stop saying that. You can easily get along without me."

Something in her eyes that resembles, if he's not mistaken, a glimmer of hope, makes him think that he should insist a bit more, that Ti-Lou refuses to admit it but is flattered, that under the cover of pride, buried beneath arguments repeated so often they've become ineffective, there is a desire she probably finds shameful, although it really isn't, and that he must convince her, get her to surrender. Does he detect in this last stand an unacknowledged call for help? A last spark of resilience that hides a secret desire to abdicate?

It is so fragile, so tenuous, he should take a thousand precautions. But he chooses honesty instead.

He lays his head on her belly, dares extend his arm towards her sick leg, strokes it carefully.

"Whether you like it or not, I'll be there. I'm going to skip the family reunion. I didn't want to be away from you anyway. I'll be there to take you to the hospital, I'll help you settle into your room, I'll be there when they come to take you for the operation and when you come back from the recovery room. I'll be the first person you speak to and I'll hold your hand so you don't panic.

And if you panic, I'll have them bring you medication to calm you. When you do your first rehabilitation exercises, I'm the one who'll help you. If you get discouraged, I'll give you a push. And I insist upon buying you your first crutches, I will be there the first time you leave the house in the spring ... I don't want any more objections or threats. If I really felt that you no longer wanted anything to do with me, I'd leave and you'd never hear from me again. But that's not what I feel. Stop being afraid that I'll leave you. Because of an amputated leg. An amputated leg won't change what I think of you, what you give me, what I feel for you. We won't even have to change how we live. I promise. Everything will be like before. At least, that's what I want."

She runs her fingers through Maurice's hair. The slightest pressure from her fingertips lets him know she accepts, and she withdraws her hand.

Finally.

He knows there's nothing more to be said, the pact is concluded. He lifts his head and gives her one of the sly grins she finds so beautiful, so disarming and amusing.

"In the meantime, I have a surprise for you."

He doesn't even bother to cover up, it's almost too hot in the bedroom. He crosses the room naked, walking on his tiptoes, imitating the cat-burglars in the cartoons – a bad actor, his imitation is so bad, it's touching – he goes into the hallway and returns a minute later with a package wrapped in lilac tissue paper that Ti-Lou recognizes immediately. It's the paper Madame Carlyle used in the shop at the Château Laurier in Ottawa. Is she still there behind her counter of useless trinkets, the Made in Canada souvenirs each one uglier than the next, stiff in her severe dress, with the mean look of a woman who has never accepted her sad fate? Ti-Lou hasn't thought about her for five years and she imagines her, aged, stooped, but still frustrated and bitter behind her varnished wood showcase.

She sits up in her bed, propping the pillows up behind her.

Maurice places the present on her lap.

"My boss went to Ottawa last weekend and I asked him to buy this for you at the Château Laurier."

She immediately guesses what it is, not just because of the wrapping, but especially because the smell that comes from the box, through the tissue paper, makes her salivate and fills her eyes with tears.

"You didn't! Are you trying to kill me?"

She undoes the red bow and tears the paper.

A box of Cherry Delights.

Maurice sits down at the foot of the bed.

"I figured, at this point, one more box of Cherry Delights won't change a thing. Enjoy a last splurge, it'll do you good."

She opens the box. The intoxicating smell of rich, dark chocolate promptly fills the bedroom. She removes the sheet of glossy paper covering the first layer of candy.

"You didn't!"

Delighted, Maurice looks at her and laughs.

"I knew you couldn't find them in Montréal and that it would make you happy, even if it could kill you! If you fall into a coma, I'll call the ambulance."

She takes a chocolate without hesitating and pops it into her mouth.

It's even more delicious than she remembered. Really dark chocolate, almost bitter, that explodes in your mouth, the cherry liqueur that coats your tongue, the flesh of the fruit she doesn't dare bite into, so she can make the pleasure last ... It's so sweet, it's almost salty. She chews slowly, swallows the juice, waits until the rest melts on her tongue and her palate.

She has leaned back against the headboard, her hand on her heart.

"How did I manage to go five years without that and not go totally crazy?"

She pushes the box over to Maurice.

"Have one, at least."

He fiddles in the pretty box as if looking for a particular chocolate.

"Take any one, they all taste the same."

"I know, but I like the sound of the paper. It reminds me of my childhood."

"Did you eat lots of chocolate when you were a kid?"

"No. That's the point. Whenever we had some, my mother would keep the empty box for months because the little paper cups held the smell for so long."

He savours the chocolate-covered cherry, nods appreciatively, and swallows it.

"You don't look too impressed."

"It's delicious, but I think it's your memories of Ottawa, as much as the chocolate, that make you feel that way ... For me, any chocolate would do ... Now don't go thinking I don't like them, they're delicious!"

She slaps his hand.

"Those chocolates are the best thing I've eaten in my whole life, PERIOD! And my memories of Ottawa have nothing to do with it. It's the taste of that chocolate I adore."

She takes a second one and closes her eyes.

"If I fall into a coma, don't call anyone! At least I'll die happy!"

"You sure you're just going to the movies dressed like that? You look like you're going to high mass!"

Madeleine, Albertine, and Victoire are sitting in the living room. Victoire is mending her husband's wool socks, Madeleine is polishing her nails, with a magazine open on her lap – Alex won't be coming tonight so she can let her hair down a bit – and as for Albertine, she's been staring into space for at least a half-hour. No one knows if she's sulking or planning some mischief. Ever since she made a scene at the Rougemont, she hasn't spoken to anyone at home, she answers her mother's questions with monosyllables, goes to bed early, leaves for work before Madeleine so she won't have to travel with her, and withdraws to her room sighing like a lost soul whenever Alex comes to visit her sister.

Victoire is worried, Madeleine is relieved.

Albertine is dead weight in the apartment, her presence – a silent ghost wandering from room to room like a living reproach – is sometimes unbearable, she knows it and does nothing to change it. On the contrary. Frowning, tight-lipped, she eats the meals her mother prepares with no apparent pleasure, never so much as looks her sister in the eye – although she occasionally glares at her when her back is turned – and she has even stopped making fun of her brother whom she had terrorized during their entire childhood.

Whose appearance, this evening, borders on the ridiculous.

At least in her opinion.

Stiff in hand-me-downs too small for him, awkward, distracted, hypersensitive, Édouard always seemed like a child who wanted to go unnoticed. That's her brother Édouard, it's the only image of him she has. A clumsy, overweight boy easy to ignore because of his lack of personality. But tonight, thanks to an advance on his pay courtesy of his boss, he's dressed in new clothes from head to toe, polished shoes, a flashy tie, a felt hat on his head instead of his eternal wool tuque, and he looks more like a bad boy who's off to make trouble, a look that doesn't suit him. Like a grown man just emerged from her kid brother's body. But Édouard isn't a man yet. And furthermore, he'll never be a real man. He looks like he's wearing a disguise, she'd like to say so and tell him to change back into his old clothes, to don his old reassuring identity.

But Madeleine is the one who spoke out.

Édouard doesn't answer. He simply blushes as he pulls on his wool gloves.

Victoire puts her handiwork in her knitting basket and stands up, holding her lower back.

"I don't like seeing you leave for the movies at this hour. Must be a pretty late showing."

Édouard answers without looking at her, and Victoire thinks there's definitely something suspicious about this outing.

"There were two films tonight, Ma, and I wasn't interested in the first one. This one doesn't start until nine thirty ..."

"It'll finish at eleven, Édouard, what time will you get home? You have to work tomorrow."

"When we go for two films, we get home after eleven and you never say a thing! Why do you care that I'm only interested in one of the movies?"

"Don't change the subject, Édouard! That's your usual trick when you don't feel like answering our questions."

"I answered your questions, Ma!"

"You answered beside my questions, that's different."

She's gone over to him to tie his scarf and button up his coat. He better not catch cold.

"And you smell of perfume!"

"It's not perfume, it's aftershave."

"You've started shaving more than once a week. Where? Behind your ears? You hardly have a beard."

"That's enough, Ma! Leave me alone! I'm not a child anymore. I'm going to turn eighteen soon, I'm earning my own living, I've got a right to go to the movies once in a while! And to the late show if I want!"

Madeleine bursts out laughing. Even Albertine seems to be paying attention to this exchange between her mother and her brother. Madeleine stands up and goes to kiss her brother on both cheeks.

"Have a good time at the movies, Édouard. And come home late if you want. It's about time you came out of your shell. But it's true, that aftershave doesn't smell great ... The girls aren't going to like it ..."

A deathly silence descends on the living room. All four family members blush at the same time. Are they all thinking the same thing? Has the word *girls* put an awkward stop to all conversation? No one is looking at anyone as Édouard heads for the staircase that leads to the ruelle des Fortifications.

His mother follows him up the stairs. At the top, she grabs him by his coat sleeve.

"I'd like to ask you something ..."

He turns back to her and strokes her cheek with the back of hand.

"You want me to go get Pa at the tavern, right?"

She lowers her head, runs her hand over her hair as if to tighten the topknot she wears when she has to tackle a heavy chore – today it was the floor in the vestibule that needed a good scrubbing – which hasn't budged since morning.

"Well I'd like you to stop by to see if he's there. And in what state."

"I won't have time to bring him home."

"Ask someone else, one of his buddies to do it."

"They're all as drunk as him."

"Okay, forget it."

"No, I'll go. But I can't promise that he'll be home soon."

"S'alright. I'll leave the door unlocked. I think he forgot his key."

He leans over to give her a kiss. She whispers in his ear:

"Are you really going to the movies, Édouard?"

"Of course, Ma, I'm really going to the movies. I'll tell you all about it tomorrow morning."

Silence reigns in the living room again. Madeleine is applying nail polish to her right hand, Albertine is pretending to read. Madeleine feels like telling her that she's holding her magazine upside down, just to get a reaction.

Maybe the moment has come. The moment she's been avoiding since they finished supper.

At first, she'd decided to wait until they'd gone to bed. Just after they turned off the light. Take advantage of the dark to avoid seeing the effect her news would have on her sister. Who might decide to turn over in her bed and cry. But that would be cowardly. She should speak to her now and face the storm, hoping that it won't last all night.

Good heavens, life is complicated.

She waves her hand, blows on her nails.

"I have something to tell you, Bartine."

"I don't feel like listening to you, Madeleine."

Albertine closes the magazine, throws it on the floor, and crosses her arms.

"Besides, I know what you're going to tell me."

"No, I don't think you do."

"Anyway, I'm sure it's about Alex."

"Of course it's about Alex. What else is there between the two of us?!"

"No wonder."

Madeleine tightens the cap on the bottle of nail polish she's holding in her fingertips.

"Good thing we don't put it on often … It smells so strong."

She sets the bottle down on the side table, trying to decide how to broach the subject. What she has to tell Albertine is touchy and she has to choose her words. She turns to her sister who has withdrawn, her eyes closed. If she fixed herself up a bit, some lipstick and a touch of makeup, got rid of that stubborn look on her face, especially, she could be pretty. But her obstinate forehead, her perpetual frown, her nervous almost brusque gestures discourage anyone from approaching her. And when she relaxes a bit, lets down her defences, and becomes interested in someone, Alex was proof of this, she becomes excessively possessive, she suffocates the person she's chosen and ends up smothering him with too much attention. No talent for solitude, no talent for love. Her sister Albertine in a nutshell.

"I have to tell you something, and I don't want a scene like at the Rougemont, okay? You might not like it, but ..."

Albertine will undoubtedly jump up, shout, pace back and forth, kick anything in her path, the sofa, the armchairs, the rug, maybe even herself.

"Listen, it had to happen sooner or later ... I invited Alex to Christmas dinner. After asking Ma's permission, of course. I'm sorry to subject you to this, but we have to go on living, you have to understand, just because you used to go out with him ... We have to put that behind us, all of us, that's the past, not about to return, so there's no point rehashing it over and over ... Alex will be sitting at the table with us, he'll eat turkey with us, he'll stuff himself with tourtière and doughnuts, and you won't say a thing. Because you have no say in it."

No reaction. Albertine kept her eyes closed, her arms crossed, it's as if she hadn't heard a word. Not even a twitch on her face.

Maybe she's asleep.

"Say something! Don't just sit there! If you're going to make a scene, go ahead, do it now, don't wait until Christmas dinner in front of everyone!"

Albertine turns her head slowly towards her sister. But she doesn't open her eyes to speak.

"What do you expect me to say? One more stab in the back doesn't hurt any more."

She stands up, takes her magazine and leaves the room.

Not a single tear.

Not one.

She often dreams that she's crying. Salty tears running down her cheeks, she can taste them as they run down her neck. Her mouth is open, about to scream. Not a sound comes out. Just the tears. That make her feel better. Her heart is in shreds, her brain on fire, she wants to scream, but unlike what happens when she's awake, she spills tears and remains mute. In real life, she screams, she doesn't strike out with her hands but with words, not always relevant words, she doesn't choose them, she takes them as they come, flailing blindly, without taking aim, she screams just to scream, improvises monologues, often unending, that have neither head nor tail, that remain the only possible expression of her frustration. Tears might stifle them. But they never come. Her mother once told her that she had a dry heart and she felt like telling her she didn't know how right she was.

So why didn't she make a scene earlier? Why did she limit her reaction to a single sentence – very effective for once – instead of assailing her sister with insults, as she usually would have done?

Fatigue. Tired of it all. Alex. Love. Being abandoned by a man who, in the end, probably wasn't worth crying over. Wounded pride. The ironic twist of fate, the sudden reversal – her sister who has no qualms about taking her place – damn bad luck, the stamp of bad luck that seems to have marked her life for good. And will follow her everywhere and always, she senses it, if she doesn't shake it off, if she doesn't react as soon as possible.

Get away. Leave this damn house that nurtures unhappiness and pain, where everyone – except her sister, but for how long? – seems to be destined to suffer: her father punishing his lack of talent by drinking; her mother, a voluntary martyr for who knows what reason – to punish herself? for what? – her homely brother, secretive and hypocritical, who spies and judges people without realizing how repulsive he is himself; and her, with her uncontrollable fits and the rage devouring her soul.

Latch onto the first candidate, that Paul something, for example, she can't even remember his family name, who asked her to go to the movies with him one evening. Yes, accept anyone, get pregnant if necessary, to be shunned, to get kicked out of the house, forced to marry a man with no name, just to get away from here. To get away.

And go be unhappy elsewhere?

Yes.

To exchange one pain for another.

Madeleine is snoring quietly in her bed. Alex is the one who'll be subjected to that in the future. In addition to living with the most boring woman on the planet, he'll have to put up with her sonorous assaults every night.

She rolls over in her bed.

She smiles.

Small consolation. But still…

He walked by the door to the Paradise Club a dozen times before finding the courage to push it open.

He has no idea what awaits him inside. The invitation of an actor past his prime, the vague feeling that this invitation contained something, a promise, that concerned him, that spoke to what he was concealing deep down inside himself ever since he read *La Duchesse de Langeais*, an important, imperative message – come join us, be part of us, we're waiting for you – that's what he was counting on as he rushed here, his heart pounding, after several weeks of hesitation, disguised as a mature man although he still looks like a child, wading through the wet snow that has begun to fall again. Undoubtedly a crazy idea, an illusion, a tenuous hope that will dissolve the minute he crosses the threshold of this place that is probably disappointing, not deserving of its name. At least not for him. A nightclub like any other where they'll kick him out as soon as they see that he's underage. Now it's too late to go to the movies, he'll have to wander through the streets for a good hour before heading home to tell his mother about a film he hasn't seen.

He checks to make sure that his pant legs aren't dragging in the slush. They are. He slips his hands under his overcoat, hoists them up and tightens his belt one notch. A kid losing his pants. Here's hoping no one saw him.

The front of the building is spiffy, it looks as if it was recently repainted in an attempt to spruce up this rather drab section of boulevard Saint-Laurent by spreading a splash of bright red over two storeys. Farther north, near rue Sainte-Catherine, it's brightly lit, there's already a lot of activity – the nightclubs have just begun to open, the French Casino will fill up slowly; here, closer to rue Dorchester, a few furtive shadows hug the walls. Two or three women, Édouard guesses they are probably prostitutes, stroll by, holding their winter coats tightly closed. He blushes as they walk by. Will they accost him, laughing, like the women in movies? No. Too young? Or because, as he dares hope, he is standing outside an establishment whose customers are not interested in them and they'd be wasting their time?

Postponing once again the moment when he'll have to push open the door if he doesn't want to spend his evening in the snow, he goes to inspect the fairly big poster advertising the invited artist of the week, framed by small blinking light bulbs that remind him of Christmas-tree lights. On a small, square table, a man wearing roller skates seems to be spinning rapidly, holding his arms above his head. The image is blurred because of his speed, impossible to say if he is young or old, but he seems really thin, almost sickly. His sequined costume reflects the glare of the spotlights. Below the poster, in capital letters: SAMARCETTE, THE LIVING TOP. Samarcette? What a strange name. And what a weird way to earn a living! What else does he do? Does he spin like that on his little table during his entire number? How boring!

Édouard moves closer, almost glues his nose to the picture. Those pants are really too tight. In the halo of light, you can see the curve of his back, the shape of his buttocks …

It happens so fast he doesn't have time to think about what he's doing. Without really deciding – he would swear – he steps up to the threshold of the Paradise Club, pushes open the door, and enters.

The first thing that strikes him is the smell. It smells of beer, like the tavern where, an hour earlier, he went to tell his father that his mother was waiting for him at home. A warm scent, both bland and sweetish, a bit sickening. Another refuge for the disenfranchised, with one difference: women are allowed here. But unlike the tavern, with its woodwork and marble and bright lights, a kind of faux palace where men can get drunk and imagine they're kings of the world, the Paradise is a big, square space with a rather low ceiling, dark, almost cave-like. And at this point, almost empty. Édouard is disappointed. He expected a feverish atmosphere, a haze of cigarette smoke, music, maybe jazz played by musicians in suits – more movie images – on a big stage where scantily clad dancers might appear, or at least a crooner. But instead, in one corner, he sees a little wooden platform featuring an old upright piano, heavy and nondescript. No room for an orchestra, let alone scantily clad dancers. He even wonders how the living top will manage to roller skate there. And where are the spotlights that will make his body-clinging costume sparkle?

It's so dark, Édouard hesitates before making his way through the deserted tables and remains by the door, almost hidden, wondering whether he shouldn't escape right away, before his disappointment becomes more acute.

Did he misunderstand Xavier Lacroix's words? Being the incurable dreamer he is, did he magnify what someone had said – which was, in fact, simply an invitation – turning it into an unlikely promise, a utopian dream in which he could wallow, out of sight from the rest of the world, with men like him, even if he doesn't yet know what that really means? Did he, as usual, push aside harsh reality to take refuge in an easy illusion because it was more convenient?

This place is clearly not worthy of La Duchesse de Langeais.

Not even his Duchesse.

Someone shouts that he can sit wherever he wants, the tables in this section aren't reserved. He takes a few timid steps, surprised to hear talk of reservations, pulls out the first chair he sees, and sits down. He stands up again to take his coat off and hang it on the back of another chair. He won't stay long, but it's hot inside and he doesn't want to leave this place covered in sweat. Enough to catch his death of cold. And have to face his mother's annoying questions.

Loud laughter reaches him from the other end of the club, followed by shouts and applause. He can't say whether it was a man or a woman who laughed. He can make out a group of people in the dark. They seem to be having fun, good for them. He looks at this watch. Ten past ten. If he decides to stay, he'll have to leave by eleven o'clock if he wants to arrive home at a decent hour without alerting his mother to this first escapade.

A waitress is approaching him. He doesn't raise his head, so she can't see his face.

"What can I get you, my dear? A beer, or a shot of something?

He orders a beer, disguising his voice. Hoping the waitress won't realize that her customer is underage ...

"Édouard?! What are you doing here?"

He looks up and faces her.

He had forgotten that his sister-in-law Nana's mother has been working here for years. In fact, he hadn't forgotten, he'd simply chosen to ignore the fact because it interfered with his dream and his illusion that he could avoid facing a potentially embarrassing situation. He'd decided that she'd be absent the night he showed up at the club, or that she wouldn't recognize him with his disguise, or that he'd manage to avoid her.

He doesn't know what to say. For the simple reason that he actually doesn't know what he's doing there.

"You're underage. Sure, sometimes we let people under twenty-one come in, all the clubs on the Main do that, but you're practically a kid!"

Will she take him by the scruff of the neck and throw him out? Call his mother to squeal on him? And cause a disaster in his life he could happily do without?

She sits down across from him. Sighing and shaking her head.

"Listen ... I just might know why you're here. But still you're underage."

He looks so pathetic, she takes one of his hands.

"I know it must've taken a lot of courage for you to enter, and it'll take even more for you to cross the club, to join the others on the other side of the red rope, in the ringside. But you're just a kid, Édouard."

"I'm not a kid, ma tante."

"Don't call me 'ma tante.' I'm not your aunt. And yes, you are still a kid. And not even precocious kids are allowed in a place like this."

"I can't wait another three years!"

"We're not asking you to wait three years. Just wait till you don't look like you've just received your first communion. What if there's a raid!?"

He sits upright.

"There are raids?"

"Not so far, but that doesn't mean it can't happen. You never know with the cops. Despite the brown envelopes that are passed out."

She stands up and gestures for him to leave his seat, too. He doesn't budge.

"Édouard, don't make me mad. Try to find another way to arrange some encounters."

What kind of encounters? Did she guess?

More shouting and applause from the ringside. Someone shouts in a falsetto voice that "booze and ass rule the world" and is greeted with wilder applause.

Heads turned, shoulders shrugged, a few sarcastic comments rose from the tables located outside the space enclosed by the red rope, then apathy redescended upon the Paradise Club. Except in the ringside, of course, where more lascivious laughs and strident shouts were shared.

Maria wipes her hands on her apron.

"I'm sorry to ask you to leave, Édouard, but ..."

A fat man has come over to them and placed himself between Maria and Édouard, hands on his hips.

"What's going on here? This customer making trouble, Maria?"

"He's not making trouble, Monsieur Vadeboncœur, he's just too young."

She stands up and fusses with the handkerchief she keeps in the pocket of her white blouse.

The newcomer studies Édouard's face and smiles.

"You bet! You're pretty young to come drinking in a club, son."

Édouard raises his head.

"I didn't come here to drink."

If it weren't so dark in the club, the other two would have seen him blush.

"So why did you come?"

Despite himself, Édouard looks over to the ringside. Monsieur Vadeboncœur understands immediately.

"Ah, I get it. I've never seen you here before. Is this your first time?"

Édouard nods. His heart is pounding, he wishes he were anywhere else, anywhere but the Paradise Club, he'd like to grab his coat and run out the door, it's all so humiliating, they understood, even his aunt who isn't his aunt, they'll laugh at him, point their fingers at him, and … what's that word you read in French novels … *decry* him! They're going to decry him! And he'll never be able to set foot here again.

Monsieur Vadeboncœur, who's a good foot taller than Maria, leans over and says:

"Let him join them, Maria, just this once."

Here we go, she's going to say she knows him, she'll insist that they kick him out, she's going to condemn him to his ignorance and unanswered questions. If only he dared explain that he came here to find answers, maybe she'd understand.

"Just think about what might happen, Monsieur Vadeboncœur. They'll devour him. You know how they can be …"

With a wave of his hand, Monsieur Vadeboncœur dismisses her concerns. Then he gestures to Édouard.

"Okay. You can stay. But if there's the slightest fuss …"

A customer at a nearby table raises his hand.

"Go back to work, Maria. Forget all this."

Maria leaves. Monsieur Vadeboncœur sits down opposite Édouard.

"I hope you know that's a reserved section. For the likes of you. And it costs a quarter to pass that red rope. It's expensive, I know. But privileges are expensive. And the Paradise is the only club in Montréal that offers that privilege. So good luck."

He stands up, a sly smile on his lips, and heads for the bar where a man as fat as he is seems to be waiting for him.

Édouard remains alone. He's both relieved and nervous. All he has to do is stand up, cross the club, pay his twenty-five cents – twenty-five cents, a fortune! – to whoever asks him, and go beyond the red rope. Perhaps that red rope is the only thing that stands between him and the answers he's looking for.

He leaves his table, checks to make sure no one is watching him, and shuffles across the Paradise. He realizes that the club has begun to fill up during his conversation with Maria and Monsieur Vadebonœur. Talk is livelier now, and the cigarette smoke thicker. Maybe he'll go unnoticed.

When he reaches the red rope, his courage fails him, and he sits down at one of the tables closest to the ringside.

Maria, who's been keeping an eye on him, frowns.

"Maybe he won't have the courage to go through with it. Too bad, he should. Now that he's come this far, he may as well go all the way."

She goes over to Rita, the new waitress, everyone says that she's the boss's mistress and she reports everything that goes on in the club to Valdémar Vadebonœur. Maria doesn't like tattletales and she usually avoids her, but this time she needs her help.

"Rita, can I ask you a favour?"

Rita is a plump girl, not much good on the floor because she tires easily and doesn't seem to like her new job she undoubtedly finds beneath her. She was a salesgirl at the cosmetics counter at Morgan's before she met Valdémar and she lets everyone know that.

"Good Lord, Maria, you're talking to me tonight?"

"We're not here to chat, we're here to work ... And you can stop using *vous* with me, even if I'm old enough to be your mother."

"I was taught to respect my elders."

"I hope it wasn't Monsieur Vadebonœur who told you that."

"No, 'course not, I can think for myself, you know."

Maria sighs impatiently and points towards Édouard who's facing away from them.

"That kid's in your section, but don't go take his order. He won't be there long, he wants to get into the ringside."

"I thought you and Valdémar were about to kick him out over there. He's much too young! Especially too young for the ringside. Does he know what's in store for him?"

"I think he only has a vague idea … And if it's adventure he's looking for, he'll find it there."

She takes a quarter from the pouch where she keeps her tips and passes it to Rita.

"Go give this to Jean-Paul. Tell him it's from me and ask him to let the kid go through without paying the cover charge … if he dares make the move."

"That's what they call encouraging vice."

"No, they call it opening the door to adventure. Something I know a lot about."

Meanwhile, Édouard is all eyes and ears as he takes in everything happening on the other side of the red rope.

There's a dozen of them and they all know each other, that's clear. They've pushed the tables closer so they can sit together, they're chattering and shouting, they keep getting up to change places, some seem to be miming deep voices to say outrageous things that their companions find hilarious, while others imitate high feminine voices and pose and gesticulate excessively, possibly to mask the inanity of their comments. In the middle of this motley, noisy group reigns Xavier Lacroix, the only element of calm in this choppy sea. Doesn't he have a performance tonight? Don't the Giroux sisters need a hero or a haughty butler? The actor has taken his rightful place at the head of the table and is observing the spectacle with an attitude that could be interpreted as scornful or appreciative. Their leader? The minor celebrity who doesn't hide his reality, while remaining relatively discreet in his own behaviour.

Édouard recognized him immediately and tried to attract his attention, raising his hand, until he was afraid a waitress would think he wanted to order and promptly lowered his arm. If he decides to make his move, it will cost him twenty-five cents to go beyond the red rope and he'll hardly have enough left to buy a beverage.

While the rest of the Paradise clientele seem engulfed in quiet boredom, the lethargy produced by alcohol that will only get worse as the evening goes by, the mood in the ringside is effervescent and explosive, hyper and loud.

Someone shouts:

"The show starts in fifteen minutes, girls. The Top is coming!"

Hands go up immediately and Jean-Paul, waiter as well as ringside guardian, comes to take the last order before the show.

Édouard had forgotten Samarcette, the living top. He glances towards the tiny stage. A huge lady has sat down at the upright piano and begun to play popular tunes.

A man at the far end of the club shouts at the top of his lungs:

"Oh, no, don't tell me he's gonna make us dizzy again doing his somersaults on roller skates."

Someone in the ringside answers:

"Just look the other way!"

The other one pushes back his chair and raises his arm, as if proposing a toast.

"Sure, he's all yours!"

Everyone laughs happily.

Édouard can't believe it. Instead of an argument, or possibly even a fight, strangely enough, it seems like an understanding has been reached between the ringside and the rest of the club. Is that what the red rope is for? Separation? You do your thing, I'll do mine. With no animosity between them.

Jean-Paul passes by him.

"You can join them if you want. It's free for you, tonight."

Maria watches Édouard stand up, check the crease in his trousers, brush back his hair, and turn to Jean-Paul.

The waiter unhooks the red rope and Maria thinks of a pen being opened to welcome back a lost sheep. Or a victim thrown to the wolves. Will he bleat with fear, try to escape, succumb to the blows and sarcasms of the cruel inhabitants of the ringside?

Édouard has taken the few steps leading to the other side of the red rope. Also thinking of a sacrificial lamb headed for slaughter, for the humiliation that might eliminate in him any urge to work his way up, starting from so far down, from the bottom of the barrel, and some day appear as a barefoot Carmelite, the product of French high society. To work his way up. At least a bit! And not just in his mind! Enough to prevent himself from drowning in the dark waters of anonymity.

He doesn't have the polish. He'll never have it. He might not even have the polish needed to be accepted by a gang of misfits kept in a fenced-off pen so their sickness doesn't spread.

Why try? Why not turn on his heels while he still has time, take refuge in the mediocrity that's his lot in life, the shoe store, people whose feet stink, impolite customers, bowing before legs that aren't always clean, with an old lady as a boss and a miserable salary? His lot in life, his fate.

All the heads have turned his way, as if the dozen people sitting around the table sensed that something was about to happen, a revelation – but given the new arrival's appearance, clearly so young, that seemed unlikely – or a repudiation, the heartless, irreversible kind the regulars at the Paradise Club made their specialty and never failed to enjoy.

After a brief silence, someone said:

"Good lord, the Little Match Girl."

To which another quipped:

"No. It's Little Orphan Annie."

A few malicious sniggers are exchanged.

Édouard, who has heard everything, wants to die. Maybe if he collapses in front of them, they'll take pity ... No! He hasn't come this far for their pity. But for what? Certainly not for their admiration. There's nothing admirable about him. Nothing admirable, nothing touching. Nothing special at all, so why would they be generous with him? Despite Xavier Lacroix's invitation. That dirty dog who does nothing to come to his rescue.

He takes a deep breath while his eyes tear up and a lump grows in his throat, suggesting that he won't even be able to talk. He can't just turn around and flee like a miserable wretch in front of twelve people who might represent his salvation! He can't waste the only chance he might ever have to escape ... escape what? Mediocrity? That's what he's meant for, isn't it?

No.

No!

Later, he will never boast about finding the strength and working up his nerve because he'll have no memory of the few seconds that turned him into the famous Duchesse de Langeais, the terror of the Main and of Plateau-Mont-Royal, first within this small circle of crazies, then in the entire scene of *confirmed bachelors* in Montréal. He puffed up his chest, placed his right hand on his heart, took another deep breath, and in a burst of energy fired by despair or an involuntary death wish, he said in the bad French accent that became his signature and the source of so much laughter over the following forty-five years:

"I am Antoinette de Navarreins, Duchesse de Langeais, barefoot Carmelite, I am dangerous, and I've stooped to gracen you with my visit."

The ensuing triumph will remain famous in the annals of the Main. They are fewer than fifteen to give him a standing ovation, but several months later, closer to a hundred will claim to have been present. Everyone, especially the other members of this clandestine brotherhood who had the misfortune of not showing up at the Paradise Club that night, the prostitutes who sometimes frequented the club, the drinkers who were unaware of what happened until they were told the story and therefore hadn't participated – they will all have their tale to tell, an anecdote, true or false, experienced or imagined and increasingly detailed to seem more authentic, to prove that they were there and witnessed La Duchesse's debut. Thus the little outburst delivered awkwardly by a child who recognized a chance to save his life will become a declaration of self-affirmation often cited, later on, to those who can't find the courage when faced with the choice of revealing themselves or remaining anonymous.

The ovation is long and powerful. They ruffle his hair, kiss him on both cheeks, tap him on the back, and sit him down in the place of honour, to the right of Xavier Lacroix who extends his surprisingly damp and limp hand. He doesn't seem to recognize Édouard.

Someone asks what he wants to drink.

Someone else leans over, places his hand before his mouth to attenuate the comment meant to be a pathetic attempt at bitchiness:

"A glass of milk for the little boy."

Édouard, still reeling from the shouts ringing in his ears, hears the remark and places his hand on his neck, as if toying with an imaginary necklace, undoubtedly a cascade of diamonds, and retorts:

"La Duchesse only drinks champagne!"

Another ovation.

The wise guy swallows his words.

No one asks his name, that will come later. He is already and will remain for the rest of his life La Duchesse de Langeais, even though most of the men around the table have never heard of Balzac's novel. (Later, Édouard will try, on more than one occasion, to explain the origin of his name to certain friends but he'll quickly realize that no one is interested, and he'll drop the subject.)

Xavier Lacroix, for one, understands everything.

He leans over to the new arrival and raises his glass. He speaks to him in a low voice, the voice one uses to be heard by only one person in the middle of a crowd:

"I assume your use of the verb 'gracen,' instead of 'grace,' was deliberate?"

Édouard flashes him a big smile, the first he's managed to attempt since he entered the ringside, and he's so terrified, it takes a huge effort.

"I had to end with something funny."

"How did you know that?"

"I just knew, I sensed it."

The faux champagne arrives and everyone raises a glass to the young – so very young – Duchesse de Langeais.

At the opposite end of the club, Maria has followed all this carefully.

Édouard notices her beyond the hilarious faces surrounding him. He raises his glass.

She raises her hand in response.

"Well who would've thought, looks like one member of the family has found his place in life."

Valdémar Vadeboncœur took over the Paradise a year ago. Bought it for a song, because the previous owner wanted to unload it as soon as possible, having lost his fortune in the Great Crash of 1929, and as he said himself, he was too old to start over again. The nightclub had been neglected, the roof leaked, there was dust in every crack, the air was unbreathable, and there were fewer and fewer customers. At first, Valdémar wanted to turn it into a chic establishment – without trying to compete with the French Casino, the indisputable gathering place of the city's high rollers – a quiet oasis where serious drinkers who preferred to avoid noise and action could come to drink in peace. Alone or accompanied. Women, beautiful, distinguished, and most of all, discreet, would be available to solitary customers, for the price of a bottle or two of champagne, and everyone, especially him, would profit. But people advised him against trying to change the profile of the Paradise. Its reputation and obvious usefulness were firmly established on the Main – a friendly, no-fuss place for the hard up – and there was the problem of its location: the real action took place farther north on boulevard Saint-Laurent, the well-healed habitués wouldn't want to go south where the Main bordered on Chinatown. Valdémar still wanted to find a new vocation for the Paradise, something unusual – a specialty? – something that would make his nightclub different, a place that offered something that couldn't be found elsewhere. He thought about *confirmed bachelors* one evening walking by the Midway Cinema, a meeting place for those outsiders who went there hoping to find in the dark what society shunned in broad daylight. In recent years, night life in the city had been exploding. Catholic to an extreme and prudish by day, after nightfall Montréal became shameless, irreverent, and wild. Since segregation hardly existed, American jazz musicians – who were welcome in the cabarets where they were playing, could stay in any of the city's hotels, and drink as much as they wanted because Prohibition didn't exist north of the border – were happy to settle in Montréal and their tunes redolent with alcohol and cigarette smoke could be heard up and down the Main and throughout Old Montréal. To the delight of Montrealers who welcomed them with open arms. But the *confirmed bachelors*, increasingly tolerated, especially on the Main, still didn't have a gathering place where they could relax, they were still forced to meet and grope their way in the dark, always worried they'd be caught and end up disgraced. What to do about them? It made no sense to open a bar exclusively for them, it would take too long to build the clientele and it might prove to be insufficient... Studying the plans for his future establishment, Valdémar got the idea of a roped-off section. Why not designate the section closest to the stage "the ringside" and reserve it for these men – or these women – whose tastes were different, and why not make it a reserved section, accessible for a price? They might be prepared to pay to meet without having to hide! Of course, it would be a kind of segregation, but – given the fat brown envelopes that circulated between Valdémar Vadeboncœur and the police on the Main, with a little help from city hall – also a kind of protection. It hadn't been easy, the *confirmed bachelors* were suspicious at first, then, slowly but surely, once they realized it really was safe, those who have since become pillars of the place adopted it, told their friends about it, and the Paradise is now their official spot, the only one where they don't have to hide. They take advantage of it, they carry on, they laugh, they have fun, and the money comes pouring in. But the women, the *bachelor girls*, haven't yet shown an interest in the new Paradise Club. There's talk of a clandestine cabaret on rue Sanguinet, in the red-light district... As for the other drinkers, the old habitués along with the new arrivals attracted by the flashy red storefront, they focus on their drinks and rarely pay attention to what's happening on the other side of the red rope, aside from the occasional shrug and sarcastic comment.

The only element that hasn't changed during these transformations is Maria, whom Valdémar thought he wanted to get rid of because of her age, but he quickly learned to appreciate her warmth and efficiency. The old customers are fond of her, the new ones adore her, although it's Jean-Paul – a *confirmed bachelor* himself – who serves them in the ringside. Especially since Valdémar imposed his girlfriend Rita as the second waitress and he knows she's useless and that Maria does all the work.

Xavier Lacroix takes charge of the introductions.

Among the dozen people around the table, glasses in hand, smiles on their lips – some jovial who laugh too loud, others more discreet, showing a certain restraint in their gestures and comments, preferring to be amused by the others – Édouard remembers two names. First, that of a fat man nicknamed La Vaillancourt, curly blond hair, flushed, incredibly likeable, whose claim to fame is that he's the ticket taker at the Cinéma de Paris on rue Sainte-Catherine, the fanciest theatre in town, wearing the supplied uniform, with cap and epaulettes, and Lady Rolande Saint-Germain, a classical musician who plays wind instruments, especially the English horn, in the ensembles that form from time to time while waiting for Montréal to finally have a symphony orchestra, something that apparently is in the offing. He also plays occasionally with the marching band in parc Lafontaine. His friends always give him a loud ovation whenever he has a little solo, much to his embarrassment. One day he asked Miss Vaillancourt to try to moderate the group's enthusiasm, to which he replied: "Enjoy our ovations, the only ones you'll ever get." Édouard doesn't understand why Xavier Lacroix tells this gratuitously mean anecdote as he introduces them and thinks he should beware of him in the future, while Lady Saint-Germain, a scapegoat who probably needs a defender, studies the bottom of his glass. The others are nondescript, interchangeable, in many ways simply the spectators of La Vaillancourt's antics and Xavier Lacroix's cutting ripostes. Édouard quickly understands that they gather here solely to have fun, their carrying-on is harmless, inoffensive, that they talk a lot but do little and, without grasping why, he is disappointed.

Once he's gone around the table, Xavier turns to Édouard.

"And do I dare ask with whom we have the pleasure?"

Édouard, who hasn't said a word since he began drinking his faux champagne, raises his glass, smiles and resumes his French accent:

"I just told you who I was. Shall we leave it at that for now, my friend?"

More applause. Glasses are raised. Hand on his heart, La Vaillancourt croons:

"I adooore mysteries! And French actresses!"

Xavier Lacroix leans over to Édouard.

"Drop the accent, you've got it all wrong."

Édouard looks him straight in the eye, and says in broad Québécois:

"You think you've got it right?"

Xavier puts a hand on his shoulder.

"Listen kid, you might not know who I am, but you should know that nobody talks to me like that! I'm in charge here, at the Paradise ringside! Don't think you can come and take over!"

Édouard shrugs off his hand, raises his glass, and drinks.

"You're the one who invited me, so you havta put up with me now."

"I invited you here?"

"You don't remember?"

"If I remembered, I'd regret it!"

Well, well. He's afraid. Good.

At that point, a chorus of protest fills the club and La Vaillancourt shouts: "Oh no, not him again!"

Xavier Lacroix promptly turns away from Édouard and addresses the group:

"Time for a round of To Tip the Top."

This is a game they invented a few days ago, after the pathetic performance of Samarcette, the acrobat on roller skates: the goal was to guess the number of mistakes Samarcette would make during his act and how many times he would fall. It's a two-phase game. Everyone gets two slips of paper and writes a number on each one: one for the number of mistakes and one for the falls. The slips are signed and placed in two separate piles in the middle of the table.

If someone guesses the right number twice – it hasn't happened yet – he can order the drink of his choice and the others will pay. The insignificant prize isn't important, what matters is the pleasure they have counting out loud the number of mistakes and falls. Samarcette is totally aware of their game, it upsets him, and his act, bad to begin with, is getting worse every evening.

No change in lighting, no announcement, no applause. Samarcette gets up on the stage, wearing his roller skates, carrying his props – a little square table on which he'll attempt to execute a few pirouettes and a sequined cape for his grand finale – while the fat lady at the piano plays some vaguely circus music. He places his table beside the piano, puts his cape on it, and faces his far-from-enthusiastic audience. His smile is frozen, his eyes full of terror. He knows they're going to boo him, that he deserves to be booed because his act is awful, yet he goes on. Undoubtedly to earn a living because this is all he knows how to do.

The following minutes break Édouard's heart. Samarcette, hardly older than him, stuffed in his tight costume, isn't simply bad, he's pathetic. A little bird trapped in a cage stalked by a band of voracious cats. His pirouettes are awkward, his gestures are stiff, he has very little space to move, and constantly risks hitting the pianist or landing on her lap. He trips, he falls, he struggles to his feet. When he climbs onto the table, he looks like he's climbing the gallows. He almost breaks his neck several times and at the end, when he dons his cape for his grand finale, his hops and lunges are so embarrassing, Édouard would like to go up on the stage to console him. To take him into his arms and help him leave the stage, whisper that he should try to do something else, that he's still young, he has his whole life ahead of him, that he must have a dream, an ambition…

And what about him, with his shoe store and his delusions of grandeur? La Duchesse de Langeais de la Main? Shoe salesman by day, duchess by night? Is that his future? Stinky feet but his head in the clouds to avoid smelling them? The Paradise Club, with Xavier Lacroix who has already turned on him because he can hold his own, the effeminate ticket taker and the French-horn player?

And the others, the anonymous *confirmed bachelors* who come here every night to drown their solitude? What did he think he'd find here? A revelation? Happiness? Salvation? In a paid-entry pen? Yes. Perhaps. Because it's better than nothing.

At any rate, he refuses to become the Samarcette of the ringside.

During the entire act, of course, the drinkers were counting Samarcette's mistakes and falls. Someone shouted his disappointment when the total became greater than what he'd written on his slips of paper, while others encouraged the acrobat to fall when his score was below their predictions.

Édouard lowers his head during the acrobat's brief bow. It's too sad. The boos, the mockery, the mean comments about the tight costume and the insignificance of what it revealed. Somebody even shouted that Samarcette should stuff his crotch to give them something to look at.

Édouard entered the Paradise precisely because of that tight costume, the curve of the back and the shape of the buttocks, the sequins sparkling in the floodlights, and all he felt during the act was pity for the poor, failed artist.

Things have calmed down, he looks at the time. Eleven thirty. His mother will kill him.

He says good night to everyone, stands up and walks over to the red rope, and leaves the pen. Someone asks when they'll see him again and he simply shrugs.

As he walks past Maria, she takes his arm.

"Did you find what you were looking for?"

His mouth smiles, but not his eyes.

"Perhaps. Unfortunately."

"You smell of booze, Édouard! And cigarette smoke! Don't try to tell me you went to Théâtre Saint-Denis. I'm not stupid!"

"People are allowed to smoke during the film! The theatre's full of smoke ..."

"But they're not allowed to drink! You can't kid me! Where were you?"

"Okay, fine. I went for a beer at the tavern after the movie. That's why I'm home late."

"What tavern? You're underage! I'll report them to the police! They're not allowed to serve you beer until you're twenty-one. It's almost midnight! A seventeen-year-old kid doesn't come home at midnight."

"Ma, it was with friends, we gave it a try and they let us in. It's no big deal!"

"What do you mean, no big deal?! Look at your father!"

"Don't compare me to Pa! You can see I'm not drunk."

"Not true. I can't see that you're not drunk. Maybe you're like your father when I first met him, maybe you can hold your liquor ... Or at least you're still able to limit yourself to one beer ... That's how it starts, kid, with one beer ..."

"That's what you're always telling me and my sisters, to scare us."

"Your sisters are old enough to do what they want."

"Not Madeleine."

"And she doesn't drink, either."

"So I suppose the day she turns twenty-one, she'll dive into booze and you won't say a thing?"

"Don't change the subject, Édouard! I know you. You'll drag us into an endless argument just to prevent me from bawling you out. This is the second time you've tried that tonight."

"Sure I want to prevent you from bawling me out. I go to the movies with some friends, we decide to try to get into a tavern on our way home, I drink one little beer ... So? I'm telling you, it's no big deal! It doesn't mean I'll do it again tomorrow night, and the night after, and every night of my life, just because I did it once."

"Your father probably said that to his mother when he was your age. And look at him now! I don't want that to happen to you. I'm just trying to protect you, Édouard."

"I don't need protection."

"Besides, let's get back to tonight, who are these friends? Eh? You're always complaining that you don't have any friends."

"So you should be happy I finally found some friends, right? I've got a job now and I meet people."

"Does Teena Desrosiers know these people?"

"Ma! I don't need Mademoiselle Desrosiers to make friends! By the way, speaking of her ... You see, I had some good news to tell you, and you've spoiled it all."

"Good news? Go ahead, tell me! I could use some good news!"

"Since our hard work paid off, apparently we set a new sales record, Mademoiselle Desrosiers decided to give me a little holiday bonus, even though I haven't been working with her long ... And I thought I could pay for the turkey, actually, for the whole Christmas dinner with it. Isn't that good news?"

"Édouard, don't try to butter me up with a turkey! I know you. You just invented that, to get out of trouble."

"No, I swear it's true."

"You think I'm going to forget that you came home pissed because you promise me a turkey? You think you can buy peace with meat pies and cranberries?"

"I don't think any of that, Ma, I'm just offering to pay for Christmas dinner. If you're not interested, I'll keep the money for myself."

"To go drinking? No way! A promise is a promise. You pay for Christmas dinner, you thank Mademoiselle Desrosiers from me, and you don't go drinking in a tavern for another three years! You hear me?"

"I can't promise that, Ma."

"Édouard!"

"Well, that's how it is. I'm a man, I'm earning my living, and if I have to buy my independence, that's what I'll do."

"Oh really? Listen to me, kid. You must've noticed that your father's not the boss around here, I am. And the boss is telling you that if you come home again with your hair smelling of smoke and your breath smelling of booze, you'll get a beating you won't forget."

She turns on her heels and heads for the kitchen, fanning her face.

"I don't want my kids to stink like their father."

Left alone, Édouard thinks that the next time he comes home from the Paradise Club – because he knows he'll be going back, it's his destiny as a faux duchess – he better remember to chew half a box of Chiclets.

He uses his own disenchantment to hurt La Duchesse. He's not the one who is disappointed, who just experienced a failure, she is. She is pacing back and forth in her immense bedroom in her home in Faubourg Saint-Germain. She is furious. She told her… her – what's the expression… her charwoman? no! her chambermaid, that's it! – she told her chambermaid that she was feeling faint, that she didn't want to see anyone, she asked her to bring her smelling salts, her laudanum, she added that she would undress on her own, thank you, my dear, and she plunked herself down at the window overlooking the boulevard where the most beautiful women in Paris pass in their carriages. Except for her, distressed and disenchanted. These… these peasants are not worthy of her company, that's obvious. Proletarian beer drinkers! A ticket taker! A mediocre actor! An English-horn player! An acrobat on roller skates! And yet, she has to admit, she is attracted to them. And to their hangout. By what she believes she can find and experience there. Really. She raises a hand. Makes her usual gesture of a grand lady who scorns everything and fears nothing. "I am Antoinette de Navarreins. Duchesse de Langeais. Barefoot Carmelite. I am a dangerous woman. And I will once again lower myself and deign to visit those ignoramuses. I'll show them what I'm made of. Because I belong there. And if that mediocre actor is the enemy to be vanquished, *watch out!* – No, La Duchesse wouldn't say 'Watch out!' – Beware! Beware, Xavier Lacroix, here I come!"

Édouard is lying on his back, with his arms at his side...

La Duchesse moves her chair closer to his bed.

"You need some advice, my friend. You still haven't spent enough time with Honoré de Balzac. Read him. Before going back to the Paradise Club. Refine your style, learn manners. Only then will you be in a position to mock them. One has to understand things before daring to ridicule them. Never strike out in the dark, strike in broad daylight, and take aim. Careful aim. With no scruples. Make note of these titles: *Father Goriot, Lost Illusions, A Harlot High and Low.*

Édouard raises his head.

"I already have those three books. Three more books on the Index. That I bought behind everyone's back. With my own hard-earned money, believe me! I'm not that stupid, you know."

"And please drop that dreadful Canadian accent..."

"Never. I'll use my accent when I need it, and yours when it suits me. La Duchesse de Langeais will frequent rabble like no duchess ever did before her! Is that the right word: the rabble? You see, I'm more well-read than you thought."

He sits up in bed and places his hand on the duchess's shoulder.

"I haven't found my Général de Montriveau yet, but believe me, when I meet him, I won't waste my time theorizing with him about love, life, and death for hours on end. And I won't end my days in a freezing convent in the godforsaken Balearic Islands, pining away, always playing the same tune on the same organ, no matter how romantic. No, thanks! In the meantime, you can go retire, go stew in your pain, I might need you tomorrow. From this moment on, you are my chambermaid, and don't you dare forget it."

Farewell to the Poet

They are facing each other on two long, varnished benches in the entrance hall of Saint-Jean-de-Dieu Hospital. They could have shared one bench, sat beside each other, but they feared the emotions that closeness might have triggered. Their farewell should take place in calm and serenity.

Josaphat has placed his violin case on his lap. Monsieur Émile is holding one of the little notebooks in which he continues to jot down the same poems he wrote at the end of the previous century.

"I can't promise that, Monsieur Émile. I might not feel like coming back here afterwards."

"Just to tell me if you succeeded..."

"Oh I'll succeed, for sure, but I don't know how it'll end..."

"You still don't know what you'll do afterwards?"

"No. Maybe I'll go back to the woods, back to Duhamel. Maybe people will remember me there. Otherwise..."

"If you decide to stay in Montréal, Monsieur Josaphat, come back here. People appreciate you here."

"Yes, I know. But... You know, if I come back, I'll feel like staying, that's the problem. I asked for sanctuary, they granted it, I needed to have decent food, to stay warm, and to rest, but now I have to move on. Or go back to the same as before."

"Why?"

"If only I knew why..."

"You're like... like a panacea here, Monsieur Josaphat. A balm on the soul of all the patients, including me."

"You'll carry on like before, Monsieur Émile. You'll read your poems to them, and that'll do them good."

"No. Not without you. It won't be the same. Think about what's awaiting you out there, the winter, the cold, the horrible cold. The horrendous cold in the month of January!"

"Maybe I'll go back to my old apartment. Maybe they haven't changed the lock."

"You said your apartment was impossible to heat."

"Please, Monsieur Émile, don't insist. It's hard enough as it is."

"You know … You shouldn't think I'm being egotistical. I sense that you're about to make a serious mistake, for a reason I don't understand, and if only I could convince you –"

"You've tried, lots of times over the past week, but I've decided and nothing can change my mind now. In the meantime, I'd like you to recite 'Le vaisseau d'or' for me one last time, and I'll accompany you on the violin."

"One last time. What a horrible phrase."

"When you read your poems to the patients, imagine that I'm accompanying you, and that's what I'll do when I play the 'Méditation' or a *Humoresque*. In Duhamel, or at L.N. Messier where I just might have to go back to earn my living."

He takes out his instrument and strokes it before taking out the bow. He lifts it to his shoulder, places his chin, and lifts his arm.

"Go on."

Monsieur Émile opens his notebook, finds the right page, and clears his throat.

He reads the poem, taking his time, articulating, savouring every word, "Venus," "bare flesh," "disgust," "hatred," "neurosis." And when he murmurs the last two verses, his head down: "What has become of my heart, an abandoned ship? / Alas, it sank in the abyss of dreams!" – Josaphat modulates a last strain of the melody, a last breath, a barely audible sigh.

Then he wipes a tear as he looks at Monsieur Émile.

"In the abyss of dreams … That's where my heart is, too. In the abyss of dreams."

Florence came to sit beside him while he was playing. Her daughters remained standing to the left of the bench, at the very top of the stairs leading to the exit.

Monsieur Émile stands and bows slightly.

"One last time, my respects, Ladies."

Three Christmas Dinners

He arrived at Ti-Lou's with a table for breakfast in bed. A rectangular wooden tray with four little whorled legs. When he first showed it to her, she protested – she refused to have him treat her like a patient – and he convinced her, saying that serving Christmas dinner in bed was original, certainly something he'd never heard of. She tilted her head back and laughed, revealing her lovely throat, releasing, as always, the strong scent of gardenia.

"So we can boast about having done that together!"

She didn't dare mention that for years, she'd had breakfast in bed at the Château Laurier. But he wasn't at the Château Laurier with her...

He placed the little table between them.

The shadow of a frown clouded Ti-Lou's forehead.

"I'll be eating in bed at the hospital, too."

"Don't think about that."

"You're right. And the table won't be as pretty as this one."

"Wait till you see what we're eating. No way you'll get this at the hospital."

He bought everything at a fancy grocery store on Sainte-Catherine Ouest, in the heart of Westmount. Glistening foie gras, red caviar, black caviar, lobster salad with a macédoine of vegetables, and for dessert, a Paris-Brest that looks like a huge cream puff the shape of a doughnut. The Veuve Cliquot and the red Sancerre come, of course, from the liquor commission.

It all cost him the equivalent of a week's salary, but who cares!

The tray is laden with specialties he'd known only by name, aside from the Paris-Brest he'd never even heard of.

"I don't know how to eat this stuff. I don't even know where to start."

She laughs again and takes his hand.

"Don't worry, I know how!"

They begin with the foie gras and the caviar spread on black bread. Ti-Lou closes her eyes, savours each bite, wipes her lips, and takes more. She doesn't say a word, simply grunts with pleasure. They move on to the lobster that she buries under a layer of macédoine. She looks up between two sips of Sancerre.

"You almost killed me with the Cherry Delights. You'll finish me off with this!"

They laugh, toast, and kiss.

Maurice doesn't dare say he prefers canned Paris Pâté to the foie gras, that the Sancerre irritates his throat, the caviar is too salty, and the lobster that he finds a bit stringy slides around in his mouth. Because for the first time in many months, she seems happy. Almost happy. Only her eyes, as they look around the bedroom during the meal, betray the anxiety she feels, her despair about what the coming days will bring, the mutilation that she put off for as long as possible and that she considers a punishment. Her body manages to create an illusion – big, graceful gestures, smiles of satisfaction, loud laughter between sips – but her eyes can't lie.

She finds everything delicious, says so, and asks for more. She tells him he had a wonderful idea, that it's the loveliest Christmas dinner she's ever had, that he's a love, and that she's the luckiest woman in the world to have him at her side. She doesn't tell him she loves him, they decided a long time ago that they wouldn't talk about such things, but the tone of her voice thrills Maurice's heart.

His surprise, that he took such trouble to prepare, is a great success.

It's at dessert time that Ti-Lou breaks down.

Maurice just popped the cork – it's the first time he's ever opened a bottle of champagne and he pulled it off and is proud – he wipes the overflowing froth and is about to fill Ti-Lou's flute glass when he realizes her attitude has changed.

She has frozen and is no longer smiling. Tears fill her eyes. He doesn't know whether the emotion he reads on her face has been triggered by the pleasure of what they've just shared, the food, the laughter, the jokes, Christmas in bed, or whether something else, something terrible, devastating, is about to happen.

She looks at him without saying a word.

The tears finally run down her cheeks, her neck.

Maurice places the bottle of champagne on the night table, leans over, and takes Ti-Lou in his arms.

"Say it, Ti-Lou. Don't hold it in. Even if it's ugly, really ugly, say it, don't hold it inside you."

She speaks into his neck, her mouth almost next to Maurice's ear.

"I can't do it. I'm incapable, Maurice. Incapable. I know I'll become a monster. You'll suffer because of me! And you're the one person in this world I don't want to see suffer, and you'll suffer because of me!"

The turkey weighs twenty-five pounds.

Nana screamed when she saw it.

"It's a monster! It'll never fit in the oven!"

It fit in, just barely.

Now it is in the middle of the table. Gabriel carried it on outstretched arms, to the applause of the guests who spared no compliments: the most beautiful bird we've ever seen (Maria), perfectly browned (Tititte), it smells sooo delicious (Teena), makes you want to stuff yourself (Théo), I could eat only the skin it's so beautiful (Alice), to hell with my diet (Béa). Sitting at a card table next to the big table, Gabriel and Nana's two children, a boy and a girl, simply sit there wide-eyed in the midst of all this excitement. It's their first turkey dinner, they think it smells good, but they wonder what all the fuss is about.

Béa spent the day with Nana. Preparing the stuffing – Grandma Desrosiers's recipe, a Saskatchewan tradition they will never betray, followed to the letter – thawing the tourtières and the apple pies baked the previous week by frantic Nana and kept out on the back balcony because there was no more room in the icebox, peeling and boiling the potatoes, mashing them – Béa had to borrow some savory from the neighbour because they'd run out – whipping them with a generous lump of butter, opening the cans of peas and the jars of stuffed olives, filling the celery sticks with pimento cream cheese, setting the table, placing a glass of tomato juice at each setting to add a splash of colour, basting the damn bird every half-hour so it didn't get dry ...

The young woman, looking pretty in her pink dress with blue

flowers over which she wore an apron, seized the opportunity to confide in her sister. She told her about Arthur Liasse who was becoming more and more insistent, about her fear of embarking on what might be her first serious relationship, about wanting to say yes to everything he wanted, and about her scruples as a devout Catholic. They blushed when they used certain words, they laughed making fun of men who only have one thing on their minds – something they were too modest to call by name – and they became more serious when Béa asked Nana more precise questions about marriage. They chattered away without really looking at each other, because of the touchy aspect of some subjects. Béa came out of this conversation both better informed and more confused than ever. She now knows what to expect without having answers to all her questions. What can she allow? What should she forbid? Her conscience and her feelings are waging a battle that Arthur Liasse just might win.

The turkey has been declared delicious, the stuffing sublime, the tourtières equal to the best, legendary pies of Joséphine Desrosiers. Teary-eyed, Teena and Tititte recall their memories of Christmas in Sainte-Maria-de-Saskatchewan. The frozen fields, the intense, almost violent cold, the sky, blue as far as the eye can see, that takes your breath away. Maria shrugs, pretending to remember none of that. Nana confesses that she took her grandmother's recipe book after her death. Everything on the table comes from her. The stuffing with the turkey giblets folded into the bread cubes, as well as the cranberry jelly sharpened with lemon zest. Gabriel says he never saw such a feast at home with his parents. They stuff themselves, they laugh, they tease Béa about Arthur Liasse – when are you going to introduce us, when's the wedding – and Alice who continues to claim she's not interested in men, and they warn her about becoming a mean old maid. She retorts, looking at her two aunts, that old maids are independent. Teena replies that independence can come with a price. People take another helping, even if they're no longer hungry, but it's so good. The skin crackles, the meat isn't too dry, the gravy is delightfully smooth. And the cranberry jelly adds a nice touch of acidity that tickles the tongue. Nana reminds

everyone that the apple pies and doughnuts are still to come, everyone protests, they fan themselves and loosen their belts. Tititte
suggests that they wait a good half-hour before serving dessert and
the children protest. She looks very pretty this evening in her purple
dress with the white collar. She looks well again and younger than
she has in a long time.

Between two bites, Teena raises her hand, as if asking permission
to speak.

"By the way, Béa isn't the only one who has a new boyfriend."

Tititte almost chokes on a gulp of Kik Cola.

"Pleeaase, Teena, really!"

Teena smiles maliciously and takes her time chewing a bite of
turkey before adding:

"Imagine, everyone, Tititte has found herself an elderly beau."

There are cries of surprise and bursts of applause around the table.

Tititte hides her face in her napkin.

"How can you say things like that, Teena?"

"Well it's true, isn't it?"

Her sister wipes her lips, her forehead, and puts down her napkin
as if she had finished her meal.

"I didn't find myself an elderly beau. You make it sound like I've
been hunting for a boyfriend all my life. You don't have to start
rumours just because Dr. Woolf asked me to go to the movies with
him once or twice!"

Maria pours herself a cup of tea. Bitter. It steeped too long.

"Where did you meet your Dr. Woolf? You're not sick, are you?"

Tititte doesn't want to talk about the period of terror she went
through recently, especially not during Christmas dinner. She'll have
to make up a story. Think fast.

"Well... he came to Ogilvy's to buy some kid gloves. We got
along, so he came back."

"How many pairs of gloves did he buy before he asked you out?
I hope he wasn't buying gloves for his wife!"

Everyone laughs. Even Tititte.

"He didn't buy anything, he just came to chat... Besides, he's a widower. Has been for a long time. He'd pass by my counter, stop to say hello and ask how I was ... I'm telling you, it's not serious."

Théo has trouble swallowing a big mouthful of food. His mother has told him not to talk with his mouth full, and since he always has something to say, he has trouble changing this bad habit.

"If it's not serious, ma tante, why's your face so red?"

More loud laughter and applause and congratulations for his witty comment, and Teena musses his hair.

Tititte pretends to be concentrating on what's left on her plate. She's clearly on the verge of tears.

"My face is red because this is none of your business and I don't want you to get involved."

Nana stands up and goes around the table to stand behind her aunt and give her a hug.

"Don't worry, ma tante Tititte, we're only teasing because we're happy for you."

"I don't want people to make fun of me. I know I'm too old to start ... dating."

Everyone protests.

"Not true!"

"No, you're not." (Maria)

"You're not old, ma tante ..." (Alice)

"And you're so pretty ..." (Théo)

"Never too old for love." (Béa)

"Anyway, I understand Dr. Woolf, you're a pretty attractive woman!" (Gabriel, a bit tipsy)

"I guess it depends on what you mean by *dating*!" (Teena)

Tititte slaps the table.

"I knew it! Here come the bad jokes. You can't help yourself, can you Teena? You couldn't resist making a dumb comment."

"No reason to get upset like that. You heard what Nana said, we're just happy for you."

Sensing the conversation might turn sour and spoil the meal, Gabriel decides, as he often does when he's had too much to drink, to entertain everyone. He stands up, all flushed, and raising his right arm, like the opera singers he's seen in magazines, breaks into "Vive la Canadienne," in the nasal, off-key voice of a Sunday tenor.

Everyone feels obliged to join in for the chorus ("*Et ses jolis yeux doux, doux, doux, et ses jolis yeux doux...*") and calm returns around the table. Tititte wipes her nose with her napkin, Teena places her hand on her sister's, to say she's sorry.

As soon as he finishes that song, leaving no time for the discussion to resume, Gabriel launches into "Sous les ponts de Paris," the tune he considers his hit, which, in fact, has been driving everyone crazy for years.

While Gabriel is singing "*ils sont heureux de trouver une chambrette,*" Maria pushes her chair back from the table and crosses her arms. She looks at them, one after another. The most important people in her life. Her children, her sisters, her first two grandchildren. If she had to decide right then and there, she would choose to stay, she'd go on serving beer to drunks and watching the *confirmed bachelors* carry on in the ringside at the Paradise Club, night after night, playing cards once a week with Teena and Tititte, and waiting for Nana and Gabriel and their children to visit on Sunday afternoons.

She couldn't name her angst, that word isn't part of her vocabulary, but what she feels when she thinks about the life she's made for herself over the past fifteen years, the lump in her throat and the heaviness in her heart make her want to stand up, leave the house, and take the first train to anywhere. Why? Was it really better in Providence? Was she happier? More independent? Is it movement that interests her, the idea of moving, the illusion of advancing? Towards what? Yes, that's what it was in her youth, the dream of changing everything for the better, and especially elsewhere, because she had her whole life ahead of her and she didn't want to waste it in the back of beyond in Saskatchewan. Now that most of her life is behind her, what would she do elsewhere? Can you reinvent your existence when you're over fifty? Doing what? Serving beer to drunks somewhere else? In Québec City or somewhere in the States? Just to keep moving? And how long would it take before she realized that nothing had really changed and that something was missing? The Paradise Club, the card games with her sisters, her grandchildren? How long before she dreamed of coming back, knowing full well that soon she'd be dreaming of leaving again ...

Here we go again. Her heart is beating faster, she feels like crying. She should get up and go out on the balcony for a breath of fresh air, maybe smoke a cigarette. To calm herself down. But then she'd have to explain, justify, reassure. No. Too tired. She'll stay there, put up with the song to the end, listen to the chatter until everyone gets up from the table because it's getting late, thanks so much, lovely Christmas Eve, we must do it again next year. Next year. Same place. With the same people. The turkey as Gabriel's bonus. A third grandchild.

The opposite of freedom.

And yet, she loves them so much.

"You daydreaming, Maria?!"

Think fast. Find something to say.

"Don't ask me why, I was thinking about Édouard. Weird, eh? Do you think you can keep him at the store?"

Teena turns to Nana who has started to clear the table.

"Nana, you can tell your mother-in-law not to worry. I think Édouard will become a good salesman."

Nana nods and places a hand on her husband's shoulder.

As long as he doesn't stand up and launch into "O Canada," the way he does every time he wants to bring an evening to an end.

He looks at her. And smiles.

"Don't worry, Nana. No 'O Canada' tonight. I'm not pissed enough."

Albertine has spent part of the day sitting on her bed, arms crossed, head bowed, fuming and crying. She barely greeted Alex when he arrived and promptly fled to the bedroom she shares with her sister, without even bothering to pretext a migraine or stomach ache. She couldn't imagine spending the afternoon watching the recently engaged couple hold hands and exchange silly smiles. Everyone understood, no one protested when she stood up and left the living room. Her ear glued to the door, she listened to them laughing, Alex, Madeleine, and Édouard. It's Christmas, time to have fun or at least pretend to have fun, gushing about how beautiful the decorated tree is (even if theirs is, in her opinion, hideous, a poor man's Christmas tree with decorations ugly beyond words), while munching on stuffed olives and celery sticks stuffed with pimento cream cheese Victoire was preparing in the kitchen. Ridiculous. Their laughter was forced, she's sure, for her benefit alone, so she'd believe they were having a good time. They weren't having a good time, they had no right to have a good time.

She's convinced that her mother spent hours in the kitchen, also sulking, because she doesn't like Alex, never trusted him, even when he was going out with Albertine. She thinks he looks shifty and never knows what to say to him. She's right, Alex is a … a … Albertine can't find the words to describe him and resorts to little laughs she hopes are suitably mean and mocking. As for her father, he's probably having a nap, nodding off in an armchair, or he's off in some corner reading Victor Hugo or Lamartine, already oblivious to their presence. And their very existence.

They sat down to dinner around six o'clock, politely applauding the arrival of the turkey after downing their tomato juice. Albertine can imagine them silently bent over their plates, chewing the turkey she hopes is too dry and tasteless, along with the mashed potatoes that could use more butter. Only Édouard's voice can be heard occasionally, but she can't hear what he's saying. Nonsense, as usual. Télesphore kept his promise and hasn't had a drop to drink all day. He's undoubtedly grouchy and impatient, the way he always is when he's sober, and that must make the atmosphere even heavier. So much the better!

But it does smell delicious.

She's hungry, she hasn't eaten since her two slices of toast around nine o'clock this morning. Her stomach is growling.

She looks up.

She can't let them prevent her from eating.

She jumps up, crosses the room, and opens the door.

She hurries down the hall, almost runs into the kitchen, walks around the table without saying a word, and grabs a plate from the cupboard. Stunned, everyone has stopped eating, waiting to see what she does. She goes over to the table, leans over the turkey, tears off one wing, then the other. She serves herself mashed potatoes, peas, stuffing, cranberry jelly, tops it all off with a thick layer of gravy, takes a slice of bread – a soft, white loaf, her favourite – with a generous helping of butter.

Still without uttering a word, her head held higher than upon her arrival, she leaves the room, clicking her heels on the linoleum.

Back in the bedroom, she stops short beside her bed.

She forgot to take a knife and fork.

Victoire almost applauded her daughter. She usually disagrees with everything Albertine says or does, the shouts heard throughout the house every day testify to that, but now, this display of courage by the young woman from whom they might have expected anger, accusations, and insults rather than this show of bravado, this affirmation of independence delivered with total sang-froid, has won her admiration and even made her feel a bit excited. Stubborn as a mule. And totally uncompromising. Not only does Victoire understand her daughter and her remarkable gesture, but she wishes she had the courage to follow behind and congratulate her.

Madeleine and Alex simply stare at their plates as if nothing had happened, Édouard briefly emerges from his lethargy to watch his sister's brusque moves and seems to have found it all funny, and Télesphore probably can't believe that Albertine didn't ask him to serve her. Christmas is the only time of the year when he plays his role as the father and despite his lack of skill, he always insists upon carving the turkey and serving it to his family.

Victoire pushes back her chair, gets up, takes a knife and fork out of the chest of silverware she received as a wedding present and rarely uses because their meals are never worthy of it, and heads for Albertine's bedroom.

They don't speak to each other.

Albertine, devastated, is staring at the plate she placed on the night table.

Victoire goes over to her, places the cutlery beside the plate, runs her fingers through her daughter's hair, and leaves the room, carefully closing the door behind her.

In Édouard's mind, a duchess is simpering and coy. She is surrounded by aristocrats, all men, who court her with compliments on her exquisite gown, her attractive hairstyle, her creamy complexion, her dazzling teeth, and her enchanting laugh. Her cascade of diamonds sparkles to the far ends of the room, the enormous emerald on her finger flutters from her shoulder to her forehead to her glass of red wine, her last, she swears, otherwise she'll forget what she's saying and doing. They are sitting around the table in a private salon at the Paradise, the most elegant restaurant in Faubourg Saint-Germain reserved for the elite of Paris society. She arrived on Général de Montriveau's arm but isn't sure she'll leave the Paradise with him. Coquetry oblige. To make him suffer. The meal was divine. They dined on glistening foie gras, red caviar, black caviar, lobster salad with a macédoine of vegetables, and a Paris-Brest. They drank vintage champagne and expensive wines. They are full, a bit tipsy, they're talking loudly and all at once. La Duchesse's melodious voice floats above the bass and baritone of Monsieur de This, Baron de That. The *crème de la crème*, idiots and luminaries, all at her feet. The general is visibly jealous of the attention she is getting and she is delighted, her strategy is working. Let him suffer a bit, he'll be all the more tender afterwards, later, when they're alone together this evening ... or tomorrow. She distributes devastating glances, laughs too loud at insignificant jokes, leans over shoulders that smell a bit of sweat and a lot of cologne. Antoinette de Navarreins, Duchesse de Langeais, a manipulative, victorious tart.

The barefoot Carmelite is still far away, the duchess has a life to live before retreating to the distant Balearic Islands where she will endlessly play the same piece of music on a wheezy organ, waiting for her lover. And she intends to make this long stretch of life before the terrible punishment, the great sacrifice, a hymn to pleasure, a poem of frivolity. The balls, the fine meals, the carriage rides, the travel, the men. The men!

The door to the private chamber opens, someone enters, seeming to glide rather than walk. La Duchesse leans over to look at his feet. He's wearing shoes equipped with wheels. Strange. He's wearing a tight camisole almost as dazzling as her cascade of diamonds. He gets up on a serving table, raises his arms while music coming from who knows where fills the room ...

Everyone freezes around the table.

Music reaches them from outside the house, low and distant, almost timid. A sad melody they all recognize.

Someone is playing the violin in the street.

Massenet's "Élégie." At least, that's what he'd told them it was called so long ago ... Back when they often requested it and he played with such obvious pleasure, his eyes closed, a smile on his lips.

Victoire puts her hand on her heart, Télesphore blanches.

"He's back! I told him if I ever saw him again, I'd kill him! He left us in peace for the past eight years!"

He throws his napkin onto his plate, stands, pushes back his chair.

"But maybe that's what he wants!"

Victoire reaches out and grabs her husband's wrist, squeezes it so hard, he bends over in pain.

"Sit down, Télesphore! Finish your turkey! If you leave this table, if you take a single step towards the door, I'll stand up, after I break your wrist – I'm strong, you know, I do a man's work – I'll pack my bags, and you'll never see me again. You hear me? Then you can try to do your goddamn janitor's job!"

Édouard is standing in front of his chair, holding a forkful of stuffing.

"Mon oncle Josaphat!"

Télesphore screams as if he'd been stabbed in the heart.

"Never say that name around here! How many times have I told you all, I never want to hear that name again!"

Victoire lets out a brief, bitter laugh.

"And don't try to take it out on your children. I'll stop you from doing that, too!"

Édouard is already halfway up the stairs to the street level.

"Édouard! Come back to the table! Immediately!"

Édouard is pulling on his boots, his coat, and his wool tuque – the one that makes him look like a fat kid that Teena forbids him to wear to work – and he's pushing open the door.

Soft, wet snow is falling on the ruelle des Fortifications. It is covering everything, tracing the outlines of the cars and the lamp posts that it crowns with a pretty cone-shaped cap, softening the points on the wrought iron fences, and giving the doorsteps a mysterious allure.

In the middle of the street, a snowman stands, his legs akimbo, his head bowed, playing a violin.

"Mon oncle Josaphat! It's been so long! Where have you been?"

The snowman doesn't raise his head to answer.

"Don't talk to me till I finish playing, my boy."

The melody ends. The last sobs of the violin land in the snow, in the middle of the millions of crystals the children in the neighbourhood call diamonds because they've never seen the gems.

"It's finished. You can talk to me."

"Where have you been, for heaven's sake?"

"Not far."

"Why haven't you come to see us?"

Josaphat raises his chin and quickly tucks his instrument under his coat to protect it from the snow.

"Because I gave your father permission to kill me if I ever showed up again."

Édouard backs away.

"Is that true?"

"Yes, it's true."

"Why?"

"That's too hard to explain. There's things that can't be explained."

"Well don't worry, he won't touch you. Ma just forbid him to leave the table. He wouldn't dare disobey her."

"Is he pissed?"

"No, hasn't had a drop all day."

"That makes him even more dangerous."

"No, you don't havta worry. He'll listen to her."

Josaphat takes a few steps towards his nephew.

"You've changed, my boy. Last time I saw you, you were still a kid."

"But you haven't changed."

"I'm too old to get old. I'm afraid I'm gonna look like this till the day I die ... Anyway, tell your mother that was my Christmas present, before leaving. Maybe for good this time."

"Why are you leaving? Stay! Go back to playing your fiddle at L.N. Messier, everyone misses you!"

"How do you know that?"

"I'm working next door. Next store over. I've got a job! I'm earning my living. Selling shoes."

"You're workin' with Mademoiselle Desrosiers?"

"Yes."

"You know she's the one who bought our house, mine and your mother's, in Duhamel, twenty years ago!"

"What? No!"

"Don't know why I told you that ... It's adult talk."

"I'm old enough to understand lots of things."

"But there's things, son, that the people they happen to don't even understand."

"Yes, I know. I have my own secrets."

"That you don't understand?"

"That I might never understand."

"Well, just don't let that prevent you from living, son."

"No, nothing's going to prevent me from living, believe me."

"Glad to hear it. I'm gonna play one last tune before I leave. Your mother's favourite."

He takes his fiddle out from under his coat, places it on his shoulder.

"When you have a chance, Édouard, tell your mother I really love her."

He lifts his bow.

"Stay, mon oncle Josaphat. Don't leave again. Don't leave, mon oncle Josaphat! Stay with us!"

"We'll see. We'll see."

The "Méditation" from *Thaïs* blends into the snowflakes, twirls with them, falls on the diamonds.

Behind the door to the apartment, her forehead pressed against the door frame, a woman is crying.

Key West
December 6, 2012, to March 16, 2013

With thanks to Louise Jobin for her
precious research on Montréal in 1930.

—M.T.

With thanks to Pierre Filion and Serge
Bergeron who know the chronology of my
characters better than I do myself.

—M.T.

A GREAT CONSOLATION

SURVIVE! SURVIVE! & MISERY'S PROGRESS

A Great Consolation, a chronicle of resilience, exposes the strenuous and disenchanted lives of the ordinary people who populate Michel Tremblay's narrative world. But it also sheds light on their fleeting moments of happiness – always too short, and almost too late. *Survive! Survive!*, set in September 1935, records glorious and tragic hours with Ti-Lou and Édouard as La Duchesse, a colourful duo whose sparkling exchanges hide indissoluble pain, despite the surrounding scent of gardenia. And there are dark, twilight hours in the company of Victoire and Télesphore as well as between Josaphat and his daughter Laura Cadieux, who has resolved at all costs to find her mother, Imelda Beausoleil. "How to survive?" these characters ask themselves as they grapple with the trials of life, the cycles of lost illusions and forgotten dreams. Victoire sums up her exasperation and despair in a terrible confession: "I'm done! Do you hear me? Done! I've had enough! Of everything! Not just of you! Of me, too! Of this damned apartment! This damn janitor job! You're just lazy, Télesphore. You're not a poet, and you're not a dreamer, you're just heartless." *Misery's Progress*, the ninth and final instalment of the Desrosiers Diaspora series, takes place in August 1941, when the families of Nana and Gabriel crowd into a new apartment on Montréal's rue Fabre. Nana, still inconsolable after the loss of both her parents to tuberculosis, must live with Victoire and Édouard, as well as with Albertine, her husband Paul, and their babies, Thérèse and Marcel. The household quickly becomes suffocating and devoid of privacy, while the war rages on and rations deprive them all of the bare necessities. But the characters of *Survive! Survive!* are oblivious to what readers of Tremblay already know: next year, in May 1942, Nana, a.k.a. the Fat Woman Next Door, seven months pregnant, will open the pages of Tremblay's fabulous Chronicles of the Plateau-Mont-Royal ...

TRANSLATED BY SHEILA FISCHMAN

ABOUT THE DESROSIERS
DIASPORA SERIES

"Wanderers. All of them. All the Desrosiers, never satisfied, always searching elsewhere for something better ..."

Renowned Québec author Michel Tremblay's Desrosiers Diaspora series spans the North American continent in the early years of the twentieth century. In nine linked books, this 1,400-page family saga provides the backstory for some of Tremblay's best-loved characters, particularly Rhéauna, known as Nana, who later becomes the eponymous character in Tremblay's award-winning first novel, *The Fat Woman Next Door Is Pregnant*, and who is based on Tremblay's own mother. The Desrosiers Diaspora follows Nana and the other remarkable Desrosiers women, including Nana's grandmother, Joséphine, and her mother and aunts, Maria, Teena, and Tittite, as they leave and return to the tiny village of Sainte-Maria-de-Saskatchewan, dispersing to Rhode Island, Montréal, Ottawa, and Duhamel in the Laurentians. In Tremblay's vivid prose, with its meticulously observed moments both large and small, the Desrosiers' tumultuous and entwined lives are revealed as occasionally happy, often cruel and impulsive.

The first seven volumes of the Desrosiers Diaspora series have been translated into English by Sheila Fischman and Linda Gaboriau and published by Talonbooks in six volumes. English translations of novels eight and nine are forthcoming in a single volume. The French originals were published by Leméac Éditeur and Actes Sud.

In the first volume, *Crossing the Continent*, we find Nana living with her two younger sisters, Béa and Alice, on her maternal grandparents' farm in Sainte-Maria-de-Saskatchewan, a francophone Catholic enclave of two hundred souls. At the age of ten, amid swaying fields of wheat under the idyllic prairie sky, Nana is suddenly called by her mother, Maria, whom she hasn't seen in five years and who now lives in Montréal, to come "home" and help take care of her new baby brother. So it is that Nana embarks alone on an epic train journey through Regina, Winnipeg, and Ottawa, on which she encounters a dizzying array of strangers and distant relatives, including Ti-Lou, the "she-wolf of Ottawa."

The story continues in *Crossing the City*, where we meet Maria as she leaves the city of Providence, Rhode Island, pregnant and alone; we also meet Nana in Montréal, two years later. Having crossed the continent from her grandparents' farm in Saskatchewan, Nana now traverses the city, alone, in an attempt to buy train tickets to reunite her family. *Crossing the City* includes vivid descriptions of Montréal's early-twentieth-century neighbourhoods, which Nana traverses as she makes her journey.

The third novel in the series, *A Crossing of Hearts*, opens during a stifling heat wave in Montréal in August 1915, as war rages in Europe. The three Desrosiers sisters – Tititte, Teena, and Maria – have been planning a vacation in the mountains, to do nothing but gossip, laugh, drink, and overeat while basking in the sun. Maria's children beg to come along. Reluctantly, Maria takes her children on the week-long trip to the Laurentians. As the reader views the journey through young Nana's eyes, we come to understand the impoverished circumstances they leave behind in Montréal, only to find poverty evermore present in the country. Yet it feels good to get out of town, and encounters with rural relatives crystallize young Nana's true feelings for her mother, as confidences and family secrets fuse day into night.

Rite of Passage finds Nana at the crossroads of the end of child-hood, facing the passing of her adolescence and the arrival of new responsibilities as her grandmother Joséphine approaches her last hours. To calm the storm, Nana reads the enthralling tales of Josaphat-le-Violon – a returning character in Tremblay's Chronicles of the Plateau-Mont-Royal. Three of Josaphat's fantastical stories contain revelations whose full influence in her own existence Nana cannot yet measure. In parallel, Nana's rebellious mother Maria languishes back in Montréal. She is torn between her desire to gather her young family around her and her deep uncertainty about being able to care for them properly.

The Grand Melee takes us to May 1922, when preparations are in full swing for the upcoming marriage of Nana and Gabriel. There's just one problem: Nana's wedding dress has yet to be bought. The mercurial Maria, torn between her desire to measure up as a mother and the inescapable constraints of poverty, wonders how to pay for the wedding. And she's not the only one battling demons – the thought of the upcoming reunion unsettles every member of the large and dispersed Desrosiers family. While the wedding invitations announce a celebration, they also stir up old memories, past desires, and big regrets.

Linda Gaboriau is an award-winning literary translator based in Montréal. Her translations of plays by Québec's most prominent playwrights have been published and produced across Canada and abroad. In her work as a literary manager and dramaturge, she has directed numerous translation residencies and international exchange projects. She was the founding director of the Banff International Literary Translation Centre. Gaboriau is a multiple Governor General's Award winner for Translation: in 1996, for Daniel Danis's *Stone and Ashes*; in 2010, for Wajdi Mouawad's *Forests*; and in 2019, for Wajdi Mouawad's *Birds of a Kind*. She was named a Member of the Order of Canada in 2015.

A major figure in Québec literature, **Michel Tremblay** has built an impressive body of work as a playwright, novelist, translator, and screenwriter. To date Tremblay's complete works include twenty-nine plays, thirty novels, six collections of autobiographical stories, a collection of tales, seven screenplays, forty-six translations and adaptations of works by foreign writers, nine plays and twelve stories printed in diverse publications, an opera libretto, a song cycle, a Symphonic Christmas Tale, and two musicals. His plays have been published and translated into forty languages and have garnered critical acclaim in Canada, the United States, and more than fifty countries around the world.